PRAISE FOR JACKIE ASHENDEN

"The sex is dirty-sweet, with a dark lick of dominance and the tantalizing potential of redemption, and an explosive ending provides the perfect closure to Gabe and Honor's story while setting up the next installment."
—*PW* (Starred Review) on *Mine To Take*

"Intriguingly dark and intensely compelling . . . explosive."
—*RT Book Reviews* on *Mine To Take*, Top Pick!

"A perfect mix of heat and humor."   —*RT Book Reviews*

"Ms. Ashenden is an incredible storyteller."
—*Harlequin Junkies*

"Sexy and fun."   —*RT Book Reviews*

"Truly a roller coaster of a ride . . . well worth it."
—*Harlequin Junkies*

"it all; engaging characters, a crazy plot, and some steamy sex."   —*Guilty Pleasures Book Reviews*

ALSO BY JACKIE ASHENDEN

NINE CIRCLES SERIES

Mine To Take

E-NOVELLA SERIES *THE BILLIONAIRE'S CLUB*

The Billion Dollar Bachelor

The Billion Dollar Bad Boy

The Billionaire Biker

AVAILABLE FROM ST. MARTIN'S PRESS

MAKE YOU MINE

JACKIE ASHENDEN

St. Martin's Paperbacks

This is a work of fiction. All of the characters, organizations, and events protrayed in this novel are either products of the author's imagination or are used fictitiously.

Copyright © 2015 by Jackie Ashenden.
Excerpt from *You Are Mine* copyright © 2015 by Jackie Ashenden.

All rights reserved.

For information address St. Martin's Press, 175 Fifth Avenue, New York, NY 10010.

ISBN: 978-1-250-05177-6

Printed in the United States of America

St. Martin's Paperbacks edition / May 2015

St. Martin's Paperbacks are published by St. Martin's Press, 175 Fifth Avenue, New York, NY 10010.

10 9 8 7 6 5 4 3 2 1

To my mother, for her absolute faith and her unconditional support. Couldn't have done it without you, Mum.

ACKNOWLEDGMENTS

Once again I'd like to thank: my editor, Monique Patterson, for helping me get the best out of Alex and Katya's story. My agent, Helen Breitweiser, for ensuring that Alex and Katya actually have a story. My dauntless critique partner and awesome friend, Maisey Yates for making sure there was an Alex and Katya to write about. My husband, the good Dr. Jax, and my two lovely girls, for supporting me while I wrote them. And lastly, to all the readers who (hopefully) will want to finally read about them!

CHAPTER ONE

Alex couldn't work out what had woken him, but something had, since his eyes were open and he was awake. The ceiling above him held no answers; neither did the two warm bodies of the women sleeping on either side of him.

It was dark, which meant it was still the middle of the night.

Fuck. This was the third night in a row he'd woken up. And unusual for him, since he had people with him. It was only when he slept alone that the nightmares came.

Yet it hadn't been a nightmare that had woken him this time—or if it had, it wasn't one he remembered.

Whatever. One thing was certain: He wasn't going to be able to go back to sleep.

He managed to extract himself from between the two women–a couple of socialites he'd picked up in the Second Circle bar a few hours earlier, both of them thrilled to be invited up to his private penthouse apartment–then bent to grab the jeans he'd left on the floor in the middle of the room. Ordinarily he wouldn't have bothered with clothes, but the past couple of weeks had left him with an odd sense of exposure and he couldn't quite feel comfortable walking around totally naked.

And of course, there was Katya to consider. Even if she didn't usually bat an eyelid. In the normal scheme of things that would have been enough for him to make it his personal mission to make her bat several eyelids, put a crack in that fearsome icy Russian façade of hers. But the past few weeks had given him more important things to think about than ruffling the feathers of his Russian bodyguard.

Things like a past he'd thought he'd left behind years ago. A casino. His sister, Honor.

A pair of silver dice.

Alex stepped out of the bedroom and made his way silently down the hallway to the lounge area. Massive windows gave a view out over New York's 2:00 A.M. skyline, the city shivering in late February snow.

He liked looking at the view when everything was dark and still–though in New York nothing could ever be said to be still. But there was a quiet to it. A peace.

Alex stood for a moment, watching the snow falling outside the window.

Because it was better to watch snow than look at the dice sitting on the table.

The dice he should have given back to Gabriel the day his best friend had given them to him.

But he hadn't. He'd kept them instead, leaving them on the low coffee table in front of the window. Burning a hole through the wood. Burning a hole in his mind.

A hole that burned straight through nineteen years of excess to a sixteen-year-old boy left bloody and traumatized on the sidewalk outside an underground casino.

His shoulder blades abruptly itched.

Alex didn't turn. "Sorry," he said unapologetically. "Did Marie wake you? It's always the quiet ones that turn out to be screamers."

"You didn't wake me," Katya Ivanova's uninflected Russian accent came from behind him.

"Don't tell me, because you haven't been to bed yet."

"No, sir."

Sir. She always called him that, no matter how many times over the past three months she'd been in his employ he'd told her not to. Not Mr. St. James or Alex. Only sir. He rather liked it.

"Why not?" He turned around.

Katya was sitting on the sectional sofa, a laptop on her knees. She was dressed as she always was, in a plain white T-shirt and black tailored pants. A shoulder holster. Her long blond hair in a tight braid. He'd asked her once why she had long hair—an obvious disadvantage to a warrior such as herself. She'd just looked at him, her green eyes full of walls and shut doors. Fair enough too. He had a few walls and doors himself.

She put the laptop down beside her. "I had to check my e-mail."

"Until two in the morning?"

"Time difference."

"Mother Russia, huh?"

She said nothing.

Usual fucking story. Alex leaned back against the window, the cold of the glass seeping into his skin, and folded his arms. "E-mails home from Mom and Dad? Brother? Sister?"

"Private e-mails." She said the words like that was the end of the conversation. "Can I do anything for you, sir?"

"Uncle? Aunt?" He paused, watching her face. She wasn't beautiful, her features too strong for something as insignificant as beauty, but there was a pleasing symmetry to them all the same. "Lover?"

And there it was, a flicker in her eyes. Easily missed if you weren't watching closely, but he always watched closely. He watched everyone closely. As a gambler, he had to.

"Lover then." He shifted against the glass. The agency he'd hired her from had an impressive list of her experience and skills—ex–Russian army special forces, a number of different martial arts, firearms specialties—but nothing at all about her private life. Which intrigued him. She was a mystery and he'd always been fascinated by mysteries. Especially if the mysteries were female.

Not good. Not good at all.

No, it really wasn't. He had very few lines in the sand. Two, if pushed. And those were: no fucking with employees and only fucking those who wanted to be fucked.

Katya Ivanova, his mysterious Russian bodyguard, was fascinating and sexy, and if she hadn't been his employee or had shown the slightest flicker of interest he'd have been on her in a heartbeat. But she was and she hadn't. Both of which rendered her untouchable.

That didn't mean he had to stop messing with her, though. It wasn't like he was going to go back to sleep in a hurry.

"You have a lover waiting for you at home, Katya mine?" he asked when she didn't speak. "A nice man waiting in St. Petersburg? Or Moscow? Or wherever the hell you're from?"

"Moscow. And you should go back to bed, sir. Get some sleep. You are tired."

Of course he was tired. He was always fucking tired. After nineteen years of running, who wouldn't be?

Restlessly Alex turned back to the view of the snow-covered city. "I can't sleep. A good orgasm is nature's sleeping pill, though, so you could get on your knees and give me a blow job. . . ."

The tease was reflexive and pointless, since she never responded with either offense or amusement. But that didn't stop him from doing it.

"No, thank you, sir," she said as if she were refusing a cup of coffee.

"So polite. Ah well, it's not like I haven't got an em-

barrassment of riches in my bed at the moment." And yet
he didn't make any move toward the bedroom. Just stood
there, staring at the snow.

"Can I get you something? A hot chocolate perhaps?"

"If you're not going to suck my cock, then perhaps you
should be the one going to bed."

Katya said nothing.

He smiled, watching the man reflected in the glass smile
with him. She took everything he threw at her, bad temper, irritation, high-handed arrogance, lazy seduction, and
swallowed it all like a black hole. Sucked it all away with
her Russian stoicism, leaving her unaffected. Strong. The
ideal employee. The ideal bodyguard.

She probably despised him secretly, and yet for all that
she had a grandstand view of his moral bankruptcy, he'd
never caught even a whiff of judgment from her. She only
stared at him with those expressionless jade green eyes of
hers.

"Alternatively I suppose I could wake up Marie and get
her to do it. What do you think?"

"You could do that, sir, of course."

He turned, glancing at her. "You're never offended by
anything I say to you. Why not?"

Her face was expressionless. "There is no value in taking offense. It's a waste of energy."

"What about my lifestyle? That doesn't offend you?"

"It isn't my place to judge anyone, sir."

"Oh, come on. Everyone judges, whether they think they
do or not. Whether they like it or not. So what makes you
exempt?" He pushed himself away from the window,
strolled up to her. "What makes you special?"

She was tall; he didn't have to tilt his head down much
to meet her gaze. And once again—reflexively—he found
himself watching her face with its proud nose and strong
jaw, watching for a hint of a blush or the flicker in her eyes

that indicated any kind of acknowledgment that he was a man and she was a woman.

There was none. He'd never been interested in people who had no interest in him–that line in the sand again. But for some reason he found himself perversely irritated at her lack of reaction, and he didn't know why.

He'd successfully managed to keep her off his radar for three months now, so what had changed?

You know what changed. . . .

"You are my employer," she said flatly. "That is all the reason there is."

"But even as your employer, you must have formed some kind of opinion about me."

"My opinion is irrelevant."

He looked down into her eyes, shadowed in the dim light of the room. "No one's opinion is irrelevant, Katya mine."

She didn't even blink. "Do you wish me to arrange transport for your friends in the morning?"

End of conversation, in other words.

He decided to let it go. There was plenty of time to bait her later. After all, he wasn't the only one who needed sleep and he'd already spotted the faint circles under her eyes, as if someone had pressed their thumbs there far too hard.

"That won't be necessary, though it's sweet of you to offer. I might keep them around another day." He wouldn't. His lovers never stuck around more than a night and that was the way he preferred it. "Go to bed. A tired bodyguard means a dead employer."

Turning, he strolled back to the windows.

The dice on the table gleamed in the light from the city outside.

"What do they mean?"

He blinked, realizing he'd stopped, his back to her. Staring at the table. "What does what mean?"

"Those dice."

A flash of something hot bolted down his spine. Shock. He didn't move, shifting his attention to the snowy view ahead of him. "Why do you think they mean anything at all?"

"You keep looking at them."

Jesus. The first time she'd asked him something that wasn't about her job and it had to be about those dice.

Conrad's dice.

Deep inside Alex, something shivered.

"Go to bed, Katya."

And this time it wasn't a request. It was a command.

Katya woke at dawn, fully alert, the way she always did, the way she'd perfected while in the army. She got herself out of bed and dressed quickly in shorts and a tank top, making her way to Alex's private gym for her usual hour workout. She carefully didn't think about the e-mail she'd gotten in the early hours of the morning. Didn't want to give in to hope. Hope had always lied to her in the past, so she was wary of it.

But still. Today she was going to have to tell Alex St. James that she wanted to be released from her contract.

Because today she'd gotten word that they'd found him. They'd found Mikhail.

And he was alive.

Back in her room after her workout–the smallest room in Alex's massive penthouse apartment because she'd insisted that she didn't need any more space than was absolutely necessary–she dressed in her usual uniform of white T-shirt and black pants, her shoulder holster and handgun. Braided her hair. Put on her black jacket. Then stepped out of her room and went down the hallway and into the lounge area.

She wasn't expecting him to be awake. Most days he didn't emerge from his bedroom until well after eleven, at least not that she'd noticed in the two weeks since he'd requested 24-7 protection.

But he wasn't in his bedroom. He was pacing in front of the window, talking to someone on his phone, still dressed as he had been the night before in jeans and nothing else.

Looked like he hadn't even been to bed.

Reflexively she checked the surroundings, but everything was in order, so she stood in the doorway and waited.

He probably wouldn't be happy with her wanting out of her contract only three months into it, but that couldn't be helped. Neither would the agency she was with be too impressed, but again, that couldn't be helped.

Mikhail was alive.

The knowledge sat inside her, a small warm glow that she tried not to think about. Emotion wasn't allowed, never had been. Not for a soldier. It was distracting and she couldn't let herself be distracted, most especially not while she was on the job. And while her contract existed, she was still on the job.

Alex St. James stopped in front of the windows, his back to her.

A tall man. Lean and muscular. Like a panther. She could see why the many women who warmed his bed liked him. But physical beauty, while pretty to look at, had never been an attractant to her.

Not that she had any feelings about him either way. He wasn't a man to her. He was a client, and that was a different thing entirely.

He turned from the windows, the light of the cold early morning falling over his face. Straight nose, aristocratic cheekbones. A long mouth women fell over themselves to get a taste of. Thick black lashes and blue eyes she'd seen smoky with seduction. And sharp as a shard of glass.

He may have been a client, but there was something

about Alex St. James that she found oddly . . . fascinating all the same.

He was the very epitome of everything she found problematic about America and Americans. Self-indulgent. Entitled. No sense of propriety or respect for boundaries. A louche, spoiled playboy. Yet there were times when she'd observed that playboy front drop, like a mask he wore, and he became something else. Something hard. Bright. Glittering.

The very opposite of Mikhail in many ways

But no, she wasn't thinking of Mikhail.

Katya frowned at the man in front of her. He looked tired, that hard, bright, glittering thing lurking in his eyes. He was staring at the dice on the table again, his mouth in a line. The kind of line that spoke of retribution.

Go to bed, Katya.

He'd been staring at those dice on the coffee table for a week now, ever since his friend Gabriel Woolf had put them there. And when Alex wasn't staring at them he was actively not staring at them, which was just as obvious.

Curiosity, which had gotten her into trouble too many times as a child and rather too often for comfort as an adult, turned over inside her, but like she did with all her emotions, she kept it locked down. Distraction could be deadly.

Apart from last night, of course, when she hadn't been able to help herself. But then the middle of the night was always a strange time and there had been something restless and wild about him that had—

Stop.

Katya ignored whatever thought had been going to occur to her. Wondering about him was not part of her remit, and besides, she would be leaving soon anyway.

Alex ended his call; his voice, devoid of its usual, lazy seductive heat, was curt.

"Fucking Gabriel," he muttered under his breath. With

a careless movement he threw the phone down onto the couch, where it bounced on the cushions before falling onto the floor. He didn't even look to see where it landed, turning once more to the windows, his hands thrust in the pockets of his jeans, the cold light falling over his naked torso.

Katya didn't know much about her client, but she did know that he never slept alone and that he spent a lot of time either in his office or in his club, not to mention hours in his gym. What he did in the gym was a mystery, but whatever it was, his body was not that of a lazy, self-indulgent playboy.

He was lean, strong. Had the body of a fighter, not a man who drank everyone else under the table and gambled away hundreds of thousands of dollars like they meant nothing. Who didn't care about anything or–seemingly–anyone.

A man of opposites. Contradictions . . .

No, she would not be curious. She would hand in her notice, then take the first plane she could get back to Moscow.

His head snapped up, his gaze like a pressure, holding her in place. "What is it?"

None of that lazy heat in his voice. None at all. The businessman underneath the playboy.

How many layers does he have? Is there yet another man under this one?

"Do you have five minutes, sir?" she asked carefully.

"What for?"

"I have to speak with you about something."

He'd gone very still, that acute blue gaze moving over her. She'd seen him do it to other people, looking at them, studying them like a mathematician working out a complex problem. He was terrifyingly perceptive.

But she wasn't scared of that look. She had nothing to hide. So she waited, knowing he would guess what she'd come for.

"You want to resign," he said flatly.

Katya folded her hands in front of her. "Yes. I have . . . unexpected business I have to attend to."

"Business? What business?" His tone was a knife, cutting through the space between them like a sword through silk.

He had been, in many ways, one of her most difficult clients. Unpredictable, mercurial, and careless she could handle. Even his occasional arrogance–she'd had many an arrogant client before, after all. But when he was like this, hard and sharp, reminding her of the General, her father, or Konstantinov, her commander, all she wanted to do was obey him.

She was a soldier. Following orders was what she did.

But sometimes, to protect a client, a bodyguard could not follow orders.

Sometimes a bodyguard had to give them.

She squared her shoulders. "Private business." Mikhail was no one's concern but hers.

"I employed you for six months. Not one. Not two and definitely not three. Six."

"Nevertheless, sir. I believe my contract allows for family emergencies." Mikhail wasn't technically family, but in every way that mattered he was.

Alex stood there, his back to the windows, hands in his pockets, his extraordinarily handsome face full of that hard, bright, glittering thing, and Katya knew she'd made a mistake. That she'd picked not only a bad time but possibly the worst time of all to tell him.

When he was like this he wasn't just difficult. He was downright dangerous.

Fortunately, she'd dealt with plenty of dangerous men in her life and she knew how to deal with them. Unfortunately, he was still her employer and she was still supposed to follow his orders.

"No," he said. "You're not leaving."

"With all due respect, sir. I am. My agency has plenty of other—"

"No," he repeated. "I don't want anyone else."

Katya said nothing. Silence could be worth more than saying any number of words; her father had taught her that well.

"Tell me about your family emergency."

He didn't like it when she was silent. Didn't like it at all. Which sometimes made her stay silent more often than was strictly necessary. Especially when he was like this.

She met his hard gaze. "That does not concern you."

"You are my employee. Everything about you concerns me."

At that moment there was a footstep behind her. Katya didn't turn; she knew who it was. Had heard the bedroom door open and the shuffling footstep of one of his pickups from the night before.

The woman–ignoring Katya as if she were a piece of furniture–sidled past her into the lounge, heading straight for him. "Alex," she said, winding her arms around his waist. "Come back to bed. It's early."

He wasn't a cruel man to his lovers–Katya had watched him pick them up with charm and flat-out sexual magnetism, then say good-bye with more of the same, and they never left angry or disappointed. Or if they were disappointed it was only because one night was all they ever got.

But when he was like this, he was cold. Untouchable. Remote.

He moved, a sinuous, graceful movement that left the woman with suddenly empty arms. Impressive. Katya hadn't known he could move like that.

"I'm up, honey," he said carelessly. "And I've got some business here. But you and Layla can stay as long as you need to."

"But I—"

He shifted, another of those quick, fluid movements, and then he was silencing her with a kiss, his hands tangled in her dark hair. Just as quickly, he let her go. "Get your pretty ass back to bed and if you're very lucky I'll join you later."

The woman was, Katya was interested to note, flushed. Seemed to always be the case with Mr. St. James and the women he kissed. And she'd seen him kiss quite a few, since he didn't appear to care whether she was there or not. Whether anyone was there or not.

The woman gave a pretty pout, glanced at Katya, frowned. But did as she was told.

As she left, Katya noticed that the atmosphere had changed and so had he. He seemed looser, relaxed almost. Another quicksilver change of mood.

"So, where were we? Oh yes. You said you wanted out of your contract for an unspecified emergency and I said no."

Katya put her hands behind her back, preparing herself with military precision. "I'm sorry, sir, but I am going to have to insist."

He smiled, one corner of that long mouth curling. But she knew by now that his smiles had nothing to do with amusement. "Katya mine. Please don't tell me you're sick of me already? I didn't think I was that much of a prick as an employer."

She'd never much liked the claim implicated in his usual endearment. Because if she was going to be anyone's, she was the General's. The army's. Mikhail's. Not the personal possession of an entitled, arrogant American billionaire.

However, Alex St. James was a very good employer. He paid her a lot of money, and she was by no means ungrateful. But with the potential of Mikhail being alive, she needed to get home. Not only needed. She *had* to. There were promises she'd made.

"You have been a very good employer," she allowed.

"But who will I have to kick my ass at Xbox? No, I'm afraid it's not going to work. I'm going to have to keep you."

"Sir—"

"My life is at stake. You realize this?"

"Like I said, the agency has plenty of—"

"You're the best. And darling, I always have the best."

Katya said nothing. She was good at being the immovable object to his irresistible force.

He frowned, a flicker of irritation passing over his face. Made a tsking sound. "No. It won't do, sweetheart. It won't do at all. Since my stepfather got shot, my life is in considerable danger. You know me. You know my routines. You know my surroundings. It'll take time for another agent to learn this stuff, and time I don't have."

He didn't appear particularly concerned about any of these things, but then he didn't appear to worry about things in general. Apart from when he got that sharp, glittering look to him, and then she guessed it wasn't worry. That, she suspected, was anger.

But he did have a point.

She was a professional and doing a good job was important to her. Leaving a client in the lurch wasn't a good look. Then again, this wasn't something random. This was about Mikhail. A fellow soldier and a man she respected. A man her father had chosen for her as a future husband— at least he had been until he'd disappeared on a mission to Chechnya two years earlier.

She'd thought he was dead–to the Russian government, he *was* dead. They couldn't afford to get involved in any rescue, couldn't afford to get involved at all. Mikhail had been told that if his unit was caught the government would deny all knowledge, and he'd taken on board the risks. That's what a special forces soldier did.

She'd tried to argue him out of the mission, but he hadn't

been able to say no. Then he'd disappeared along with his unit and no one would help her look for him. Not her father, the General. Not Konstantinov, their superior. Not any of the other military contacts she had. No one.

Going to find Mikhail alone would have been suicide. Would have been treason. So on the outside, along with everyone else, she'd mourned his loss. While on the inside she made use of some other contacts she had and tried everything she could think of to find him, even a hint that he was still alive.

And now, last night, two years later, after she'd left the army, left Russia, left everything of her old life behind, she'd gotten word that yes, he was alive.

Which meant she had to at least try to find him. Somehow. Someway.

Even if that meant leaving Alex in the lurch. Because loyalty to a fellow soldier and a friend was more important than any other kind.

"The White Knight agency is the best there is," she said, cool and calm. "Their other agents learn fast and won't let you come to any harm."

Alex just looked at her for a long moment, the crease between his brows deepening. Then he strolled toward her in that easy, fluid way he had, not stopping until he was inches away. He was smiling, his expression one of amusement, and yet his eyes burned sapphire, cold and brilliant as stars. "But like I keep telling you, sweetheart. I don't want another agent. The only agent I want is you."

Katya didn't move. Her soldier's instinct was to obey him, since he radiated authority, but she wasn't in the army now and hadn't been for at least two years. No, she was her own woman and the strange, drifting life she'd been leading since she'd come to the States was over. She had a purpose now. A mission. A goal. And like she'd been trained to do, she would attain it no matter the cost.

She met his gaze and said merely, "I'm sorry, sir."

"I'll pay you double."

"I don't need more money."

His eyes narrowed into splinters of intense blue. "Everyone needs more money, Katya mine."

"I don't."

"Then what is it you need?"

Mikhail. That's what I need.

"I need to leave, sir."

He shifted in front of her and it was strange how suddenly she noticed that he was still half-naked. That he was warm. That she could smell him, a faint, woody, earthy scent, like sandalwood, with a hint of musk. It was not unpleasant. Neither was the warmth of him. And yet . . . She didn't like it. Something about it made her uncomfortable in a way she hadn't been uncomfortable before.

She wanted to move, get a bit of space, but that would be to show weakness, and she couldn't do that. Not with him. He was a gambler, and looking for weaknesses, any sign of the kind of cards you held, was what he did. And he was good at it.

Then again, she was a soldier. And showing no weakness was part of who she was.

And she was good at it.

Katya met his gaze head-on. Giving him nothing.

At least she thought he'd given him nothing. Until he smiled the kind of smile that would have taken any conscious woman's breath away. "Oh no," he said. "Sweetheart, you aren't going anywhere."

And Katya knew that somehow, despite her best intentions, she'd given something away.

CHAPTER TWO

Secrets. The woman had secrets. Which was fine; he had
no problem with them in the normal scheme of things.
But this time he had a feeling it was those secrets that
were taking her away from him, and that was not going to
happen.

Alex said nothing as Katya got out of the limo, holding
the door open for him, her sharp gaze scanning the snowy
street for danger. Not that there was any, he suspected,
though after Tremain's shooting you could never tell.

He stepped out into the cold, his breath fogging the air.

Ahead of him was the building that was Zac's office,
the HQ of his massively successful security firm, Black
Star Security. Zac liked to keep the place, situated in a non-
descript building in the Meatpacking District, low-key, a
small metal plaque to the left of the door the only sign that
you'd come to the right place.

Zac didn't need to advertise his services. People came
to him.

Alex didn't look at Katya. "Stay with the car," he ordered, and strode up the steps toward the door. He didn't
want her coming with him, especially not when he was going to talk to Zac about her.

He'd let her have her secrets earlier that morning–if she

didn't want to tell him then she didn't have to—but he was going to find them out nevertheless.

Everyone had a price and he was going to discover hers.

He wanted to keep her, family emergency or not, because he preferred her to the hulking, muscle-bound bastards he'd had for the past year or so. She was far more attractive for a start, and for another he generally felt more comfortable around women, period. Not that he'd ever tell anyone else that.

There was also the fact that he'd spotted a spark of . . . interest–yes, definitely interest–in her eyes that morning. Interest in him.

He'd thought she was immune. Apparently not.

Alex smiled as he walked into Zac's building, because shit, he was used to being irresistible, especially to women, and knowing she wasn't as immune as she seemed gave him a certain amount of satisfaction.

The reception area of Black Star looked like any reception area for any bland business anywhere, blond receptionist behind the desk, magazines on the table, stock standard uncomfortable office furniture. There was even a potted plant, for fuck's sake.

The blonde looked up as Alex entered, smiling at him. "Mr. Rutherford is expecting you, Mr. St. James," she said pleasantly. "Please, go on through."

He blew her a kiss as he strode past toward Zac's office, not bothering to knock as he approached the closed door, just throwing it open and going right in.

Zac was sitting at his massive old-fashioned oak desk, typing something, his gaze fixed on his computer monitor. Sitting cross-legged on the end of the desk, her white-blond hair in a braid down her back, was Eva, who looked to be playing something on her phone.

It was an incongruous picture: the large, broad-shouldered mercenary in a perfectly pressed suit, at the computer, with the small, fine-boned woman in Docs, skinny jeans, and a leather jacket sitting on the desk like a child.

The two had a strange relationship. They weren't together and they never touched, but rarely did Alex see one without the other. Zac had apparently rescued Eva from a difficult situation, but what kind of situation Alex didn't know and had never asked about. Their little club—officially the Nine Circles, unofficially the "fucked-up billionaires club"—had pretty much one rule: Don't ask, don't tell.

So he didn't do either. Besides, he had too many demons of his own. He didn't need to take on anyone else's.

Eva didn't look up from the game she was playing on her phone as Alex came in, but Zac did. With perfect courtesy, he gestured to the chair opposite his desk, a deep leather armchair with a footstool. "Sit," he said with his deep, smooth, and perfectly spoken British accent. "I just have a couple of things to finish up here."

"About my lovely and mysterious bodyguard, I hope?" Alex sprawled in the chair, kicking his feet up on the footstool.

"Not only that." Zac sat and began typing again.

Interesting. Or maybe not so much interesting as worrying. At least the "not only" part was worrying. When Zac had something to tell Alex it was never going to be good, especially when he had a feeling he knew exactly what Zac was going to tell him.

He crossed his feet at the ankles and folded his hands in his lap. "Nice to see you too, Eva."

"Alex." Eva still didn't look at him.

He didn't even bother rolling his eyes. Eva was another woman apparently immune to him, and not through lack of trying. He'd persisted more as a point of honor than anything else until eventually, after she'd told him to fuck off more times than he cared to think about, he'd come to see her more as a little sister than a prospective lover. Annoying at times, useful at others, but always part of the family.

Like Honor?

Alex shifted at the thought of his real sister. The one he hadn't seen for nearly nineteen years. The one currently holed up with Gabriel Woolf, his best friend, in the guy's Colorado lodge. She'd been trying to get in touch with him but he'd ignored her texts and e-mails. Didn't answer her calls.

He wasn't ready to see her. He probably would never be ready to see her. He'd abandoned her and their mother a long time ago, and although he'd kept a watch on them from a distance, he didn't actually want to talk to them.

Fuck, what would he say? And Honor would have questions too. Like *Where did you go?* and *What happened to you?* and *Why did you never call?* Questions he wasn't going to answer, at least not in this lifetime.

Alex shifted again, pushing Honor out of his thoughts, concentrating on Zac's almost obsessively tidy office, all sleek furniture and no clutter whatsoever. The guy was so anal when it came to tidiness it made Alex want to tip over his wastebasket just to see what would happen.

"Come on, man," Alex said restlessly. "I've got shit to do."

Zac made one last movement with his mouse, then looked over at Alex, his amber eyes giving nothing away. "You wanted a report run on Katya Ivanova."

"Yeah. Did you find anything?"

"Apart from what I gave you when you first got her on contract?"

"Obviously."

Zac leaned his elbows on his desk and laced his fingers together. "What's your interest in her?"

"Oh Christ, if we're going to be having the third degree—"

"A lot of her information is classified, which makes it difficult to get hold of. And difficult to get hold of means more work for me. I just want to know whether this is idle interest so you can fuck around with her, or whether you're serious."

Alex put his hands behind his head and met the other man's gaze. "By 'fuck around' I assume you mean . . ."

"She's female. That's reason enough to ask."

Alex was aware that Eva had put down her game and was looking at him. He ignored her. He knew she had some kind of crazy protective thing going on when it came to women, and generally he was fine with that. But sometimes the assumptions she made about him pissed him off. "Jesus, can't I ask a simple question about someone without you two assuming I want to screw her?"

"No," Eva said flatly.

Resisting the temptation to be flippant, Alex looked at both of them in turn. "I never fuck around with my employees; you know this. The reason I want to know what's going on with her is that she's asked to be released from her contract."

"And you don't want to let her go?" Zac's gaze never left his.

"No. I don't. She's damn good at her job and a total professional." He allowed himself a smile. "Plus she's much better looking than any of my other bodyguards and I do like to maintain a certain image."

Eva scowled at him. "That's not the real reason."

Alex smiled back. "No, you're right; it's not. The real reason is that when I was sixteen I was raped by a guy and ever since then I don't feel super comfortable in close quarters with men."

There was a brief silence. Then Eva snorted. "Sure, use rape as a joke. That's pretty low, Alex."

They thought he was lying. Everyone always did.

He let the smile sit there. "I am pretty low, Eva. You know this about me."

"I imagine," Zac said, ignoring the sniping, "that she's returning to Russia because of a colleague of hers."

Alex gave his friend a sharp look. "What colleague?"

"His name is Mikhail Vasin. From the looks of things they were both in a special forces unit of the Russian army. He disappeared a couple of years ago in Chechnya after an anti-terrorist operation and is presumed dead. Or should I say 'was' presumed dead." Zac glanced back at his computer screen. "Apparently there's evidence he's still alive."

"So she's returning home for him?"

"They were both in the same unit for over two years." Zac looked at him. "She's ex-army, which means she'll have a very strong loyalty to her fellow soldiers. If he's been found alive, I can't imagine her sitting here on the sidelines."

No, she wouldn't. Katya had told Alex nothing of her life, but from what he'd seen of her in the past three months, she was a soldier through and through. Honorable, loyal, and upright. Pretty much the antithesis of himself, which did make it beautifully ironic that she was his bodyguard.

Man, did he love a good bit of irony.

"She told me it was a family emergency," he said to no one in particular.

"Perhaps she does consider this Vasin family. Both of their fathers were ex–KGB operatives, and are now pretty high up in the Russian military. A family business from the looks of things. If Vasin is involved in black ops activities no wonder she didn't tell you anything more."

"Not that it's any of your business," Eva added.

"It is when she wants to leave before her contract ends," Alex said without heat. "I wonder what she's planning. A rescue mission?"

"That's not the real question." Zac stared at Alex, his

gaze unnervingly direct. "The real question is what you're going to do about those dice."

Fuck. Knowing Zac and his loathing of loose ends, he should have expected the question, or at least anticipated it. Alex crossed one ankle over his knee, shifting the tension that had suddenly gripped him. "I'm going to do nothing as yet."

"Why not? Tremain is still in a coma and no one knows who's responsible. Even my sources are finding it difficult to get anything concrete." He paused. "Considering that all of this appears to be centered on your family, I would have thought you'd have shown more interest than this."

Jesus, of course Zac wasn't going to let this go. He never let anything go.

"Hey, you know me," Alex said, going for flippant. "I don't give a shit about anything."

"Sure you do." Eva folded her arms. "I think you give a shit about this."

"What makes you say that?"

"You got all tense the moment Zac mentioned it." Her gray eyes narrowed. "You know more about this than you're letting on, Alex. Why not share with the rest of us?"

Could he say it again? No, he couldn't. The truth needed to be rationed carefully; otherwise it came off sounding far more real than he could handle.

"I thought we had a don't ask, don't tell policy?" he said instead.

"When it doesn't go outside the club," Zac replied. "But in this case, it's ending up affecting rather more than just us."

"Shouldn't you be having this little chat with Gabriel instead of me in that case? He was the one who opened this fucking can of worms in the first place."

"And you're the one who was at that casino." Zac's voice held a hint of iron. "You were the one who knew your father owned it when the rest of us didn't." He paused. "Anyway, we're on this path now; we may as well continue to walk it."

Alex didn't move. Christ, he'd already given away far too much already, which for a man famous for his poker bluffs was galling in the extreme. Fucking friends. This was why he had so very few of them. He hated being read so damn easily the way Zac and Eva seemed to be able to do.

"Very Zen," Alex said. "But we don't have to walk anything if we don't want to."

Zac leaned back in his chair. "You know where the dice Tremain gave Gabriel came from, don't you?"

He willed his muscles to relax. Made himself smile. "You mean your precious sources haven't figured it out already?"

"Of course they have. They're a VIP invitation to an exclusive poker game."

"Conrad South," Alex said. He'd long been able to say the name without inflection, without even feeling anything, something he'd spent long years dedicated to. "He owns a casino in Monte Carlo. The Four Horsemen. Every year he runs what he calls the Apocalypse, a high-stakes poker game by invitation only."

"And have you ever been invited?" Eva asked.

What did he say? More truth or another evasion? "No. But that's because Conrad knows I'd wipe the floor with him."

Zac was frowning. "But why would Tremain have those dice? And why did he give them to Gabriel? What's his connection to this casino?"

Alex had an idea. But it wasn't anything that Zac wouldn't be able to find out on his own, because he certainly wasn't going to tell the other man. The conversation had already progressed way beyond what Alex was comfortable with and he didn't want to be asked yet more questions that he didn't want to answer.

You really think it still matters? Haven't the last nineteen years of your life been about making sure it doesn't?

Alex took his hands from behind his head and put them on the arms of the chair. No, it didn't matter. It really didn't. "I'll leave you to work that one out for yourself, Zac." Alex pushed himself out of the chair. "I know how you love a good mystery."

The other man's amber gaze was impassive. "They're connected, aren't they? The Four Horsemen and that casino your father owned."

Shit. The guy was far too sharp for his own good. "Don't you have a proper job to think about? Papers to file or something?"

"I have a secretary for that kind of thing," Zac said without any discernable change in inflection. "There were things about that casino I didn't like."

"What? Other than the fact you could buy just about any drug you liked there?"

"There were a great many female employees. Too many."

Alex thrust his hands in his pockets, a ripple of unease moving through him. "Surely you can never have too many female employees?"

"Don't be a prick," Eva said with some disgust. "And stop making everything into a joke. Especially this."

Alex glanced at her. There was a small silver spark burning in her gaze, a glimpse of the intensity she normally concealed under biting sarcasm. Jesus. He knew personal when he saw it and he was looking at it right now. Which made it even more imperative he leave it alone. It was either that or he got pissed off, and where that would lead was anyone's guess. Nowhere good probably.

"Angel," Zac murmured before Alex could say anything. "It's all right."

She blinked, then looked away suddenly, untucking her legs and shifting to get off the desk. "You guys stay here and argue about it all you like, but if you'll excuse me, I'm going to get some shit done."

"Eva." Zac's voice held an edge of command he very rarely used, but it stopped Eva in her tracks. "Wait."

Interesting. Whatever was going on between those two, Alex had no idea, but he was intrigued. Especially when he'd never heard Zac use that tone with her. And even more interesting, Alex had never seen Eva actually obey.

She was standing near the desk, a mutinous look on her face. "What?" she demanded, glancing back at Zac.

"Where are you going?"

Eva flicked Alex a strange glance, like they were complicit in something, though what Alex had no idea. Then she said, "Someone has to do something. And since you're too busy thinking and Alex is too busy pretending he doesn't give a fuck, it has to be me."

An unfamiliar feeling turned over inside him, a discomfort he couldn't immediately identify. "Please don't tell me you're thinking of going to Monte Carlo," he said.

"Okay, I won't tell you I'm thinking of going to Monte Carlo."

The discomfort increased. Eva only left New York if she was going to Gabriel's lodge or Zac's island in the Caribbean. And then only in Zac's company. "Eva," he said. "You can't."

"Why not? You're not doing anything and this is important."

"No." Zac had risen to his feet behind his desk. "Angel, you know you can't do this."

Color had crept into her cheeks, that strange look in her eyes pinning Alex to the spot. As if she'd recognized something in him. As if she knew. "Some people don't deserve to get away with it, Alex," she said quietly. "Some people deserve a bullet. And if you won't do it, I will."

Tension gathered in the air, thick and tight, like the tension gathering inside of him.

He knew what she was talking about. Had she heard the truth when he'd spoken? Had she experienced something similar?

He didn't want to look at her, didn't want to see the confirmation in her eyes. He'd never wanted to know her past like he'd never wanted anyone to know his. Because everything he did was about leaving that past behind. Pretending it was over and done with and didn't matter anymore. But whatever had happened to Eva still resonated for her. Still mattered. A reminder that the past was always there, a ghost that would never ever be exorcised no matter how many drugs you took or people you screwed.

But maybe it was too much for her as well, because her gaze flickered away from his at the last minute. As if she couldn't bear too much reality either.

Conscious of Zac's attention shifting from sharp to razor-like, Alex said, "You can't shoot someone without proof, Eva. And you can't get proof unless you get close to them."

"Then give me those dice and I'll get close."

"When you can't go anywhere without your faithful guard dog?"

Her color deepened. "I can—"

"More important, though, unless you can play a good hand of poker, you're not going to get anywhere near that casino."

A silence fell.

Eva's gaze shifted from him to Zac.

"No," Zac said. "I can do many things, angel, but poker isn't one of them."

Her attention returned to Alex. "Then it has to be you. You have to go to the casino and you have to get in on that game." The look in her eyes sharpened. "Then you can get that proof. Then you can put a bullet in their head."

Alex came out of the building, eyes dark as a gathering storm and the smile on his face like a tiger's. He didn't often get into tempers, but she could tell he was in one now.

"Get in the car, darling," he ordered as she straightened from where she was leaning against the side of the limo. "I have a bone to pick with you."

Katya did as she was told. She couldn't imagine what "bone" he had to pick with her—it couldn't possibly be about the job, because she knew he had nothing to complain about when it came to her professionalism—but clearly she was going to find out. Regardless, she'd be leaving soon anyway, and then it wouldn't matter.

She'd be on her way back to Moscow and Mikhail.

As the door shut behind Alex and he shifted onto the seat opposite so he was facing her, Katya folded her hands in her lap and met his stormy blue gaze. Obviously his meeting with his friends had not gone well. "What is it, sir?"

"You're ex–special forces."

That was in her résumé. Not a big secret. "Yes, sir."

"But you still feel loyalty to them?"

Interesting question. Why was he asking? "I'm sorry, sir, but how is this relevant?"

He leaned back against the seat, stretched his arms along the back of it. "You're not going back to Moscow for a family emergency. You're going back to rescue a colleague. Someone by the name of Mikhail Vasin."

Shock ran cold fingers down her spine. The information about Mikhail was classified. Extremely classified. No one should know about it, least of all a selfish billionaire playboy with a healthy disregard for his own life.

He was smiling, that casual smile that hid the sometimes terrifyingly perceptive man underneath. "I know, it's classified, right?"

She should say nothing of course, neither confirm nor deny, since she couldn't afford either when it came to Mikhail. Yet saying nothing seemed pointless. If Alex knew who Mikhail was then he knew everything.

"How did you find this information?" she asked, trying not to let her shock show.

Alex lifted a careless shoulder. "A friend."

"Mr. Rutherford."

When Alex had told her he had a meeting at Black Star that morning, she'd had no idea it would be about her, and yet that was the only explanation. She didn't know Zac Rutherford personally, but she'd had some contact in conjunction with Alex. Ex-military, that was for certain, and a mercenary too. Had spent some time in a Russian prison from the looks of his tattoos. A dangerous man, she'd always thought, and that was even more certain now, especially if he could get hold of classified information like this at a moment's notice.

"Mr. Rutherford, indeed," Alex agreed. "So there's no point in denying anything. I know it all already."

"That information is—"

"Classified. Yeah, yeah." He waved a hand. "I'm not interested in how classified is it or even how Zac got hold of it. All I'm interested in is how it pertains to our little situation here." His mouth curved. "And we do have a little situation."

Katya sat up straighter. "There is no situation."

"Sure there is. The situation is that you lied to me."

Anger stirred. She ignored it. "I do not lie."

"You told me you had a family emergency. But Mikhail Vasin is not a family member."

"No, he's not blood related. But blood ties are not all that makes someone part of your family."

An expression she didn't understand crossed Alex's features. He looked away for a second, and when he glanced back the expression was gone. "He's a friend then?"

No. He was more than that. He was a fellow soldier and the man the General had wanted for her future husband. She didn't love him, but that didn't matter. Love was a fickle emotion and played no part in her decision-making processes. Loyalty and respect carried far more weight, were far more enduring.

But then there had been that mission, the one into Chechnya to take out a potential terrorist threat. The one they both knew had to be done. And Mikhail had disappeared.

And her father had put his loyalty to his government before his loyalty to his family. Before his loyalty to her.

Katya looked into Alex St. James's mocking blue eyes. This man wouldn't understand loyalty. Or respect. Or faith. He had nothing and no one but himself. What was the point in explaining anything to him? "Yes," she said levelly. "He is a friend."

"Pretty close friend to risk your life saving."

"I risk my life for people I don't know or like every day."

"Ah, but let's not kid ourselves that's all about your altruism. You get paid very well for that."

No, of course he wouldn't understand. He didn't have that drive for purpose. For a life spent in service to the greater good. He didn't have a God. Like the many Americans she'd worked for, his only god was himself. "Money is not the only reason for living."

He gave a short, hard laugh. "No, fuck, you got that right. But you have to admit, it makes things a hell of a lot easier."

She couldn't argue with that. It did. "I do what I do for reasons other than money."

Alex tilted his head, the cold white light of winter coming through the windows glossing his black hair. "There are other reasons?" He looked mystified, but she knew he was only pretending. He did a lot of that.

"You would not understand," she said.

Another of those fleeting shadows passed through his eyes, the ones she couldn't interpret. "You're right. I don't." He shifted restlessly on the seat, lifting one ankle onto the opposite knee, the dark wool of his suit pulling tight over muscular thighs, though why she should notice that she couldn't imagine. "So tell me more about your boyfriend Mik."

Of course he would minimize it. He did that with everything. "His name is Mikhail." Misha, to her. "And he is not my boyfriend."

Alex didn't even have the grace to look embarrassed. "Whatever. I know he's a Russian special forces agent that went missing on a mission to Chechnya. A mission the Russian government denies all knowledge of. I know he's been missing for two years, which is approximately the same time you've been working as a bodyguard." He shifted again, pulling his phone out of his pocket and looking down at the screen, his thumb scrolling through what looked like a document. "In fact, not only did you leave the Russian army; you left Russia entirely a couple of weeks after he went missing."

"I'm not sure how this is relevant."

But his gaze missed nothing. "Why did you leave? You're a soldier, Katya. The same, apparently, as your father. Soldiers don't leave their families, their units, or their countries just like that."

She'd seen him do this before, focus that blue gaze on someone as if that person were the most fascinating thing he'd ever seen. As if he wanted to understand them more than he wanted his next breath. It made everyone he turned it on his slave. But she'd never been his object of fascination. And she didn't find it attractive. She found it threatening.

Mainly because she had far too many secrets.

She kept her expression neutral, the way the General had always taught her, making sure nothing showed on her face, because that's what a soldier was. A blank slate for orders to be written on. "I'm not sure what you expect with these questions."

"I expect what everyone does when they ask a question–an answer."

"In that case, I left because I wanted to travel."

There was a pause, the silence in the car becoming tense.

He'd become motionless, staring at her. Something she noticed he did at the gaming tables when he was trying to read someone.

You really have noticed an awful lot about him.

Of course she'd noticed. He was her client and knowing him and his habits was part of her job.

"No," he said slowly. "That's not it. They wouldn't rescue him. They let you down. That was your break from the church, wasn't it, darling? God didn't answer your prayers and so you lost your faith."

She kept her expression utterly blank, not letting him see how close to the bone he'd gotten. Because he was right. Her father's refusal even to consider a rescue mission had shattered her faith in both him and her country. No soldier left behind, he'd always told her. And then he'd become part of the government and politics became more important than a few soldiers' lives.

More important than you.

But no, she wouldn't think about that. Wouldn't let any hint of what she felt cross her face. Alex St. James's questions were nothing compared to Konstantinov's endurance training or what the teachers in the military school where she'd learned how to strip an AK-47 in seconds flat had done. Teaching her to remain silent and stoic even in the face of pain. "I'm sure that was not in the report Mr. Rutherford gave you."

Alex's eyes narrowed for a moment, assessing. Then he smiled again, his posture becoming more relaxed. Which was not a sign she was off the hook, as she well knew. Merely that he was trying another tactic. "You're right. It wasn't. I was merely extrapolating. Whatever your reasons for leaving, the fact remains that since Mr. Vasin is not part of your family, then your reason for breaking your contract is not acceptable. Family emergencies only work when they concern family."

Katya stiffened. She didn't need his agreement in order to end her contract of course, but it wouldn't be a good look. It was also possible he'd take legal action, again not a good look, especially for the agency that had hired her. "There is no need to make this difficult, sir," she said coldly. "I do not respond well to threats."

He laughed, in the way he always did when things got tense. "I'm not threatening you, darling. I'm flattering you. Your skills are unrivalled and I don't want to give them up."

"All good things must come to an end."

"No, they don't. They can last however long you fucking want them to. However long *I* fucking want them to." He sat forward suddenly, elbows on his knees. "Which brings me to my point. I have a proposition for you, Katya mine."

There was something about his posture that bothered her, though she couldn't put her finger on what. Almost as if he was too close and his nearness made her uneasy, like it had back in his apartment that morning.

Ignoring her unease, she frowned. Any proposition made

by Alex St. James was always to be viewed with some mistrust. "What kind of proposition?"

"The kind where you do a little something for me. And I'll do a little something for you."

"Such as?"

"I want you to work out the remainder of your contract, which now includes an extra special mission that should provide you with an outlet for those very impressive skills of yours. And in return"—his gaze met hers, sharp, piercing, which made her want to get out her gun and point it at him—"I will help you find your Mikhail."

CHAPTER THREE

Fuck. He really needed vodka.

Alex strode into his apartment, throwing his keys and wallet down onto the couch as he passed it, heading straight for the booze cabinet that held all his favorite and most expensive brands. He pulled out some Grey Goose and splashed it into a shot glass. Knocked it back.

He could feel Katya behind him, a tall, silent presence.

He hadn't wanted to explain the rest of his proposition until they were home, mainly because he was still turning it over in his head himself.

You have to be in on that game. Then you can get that proof.

Another shot. The vodka burning in his throat.

Then you can put a bullet in his head.

How many times had he thought that? How many times had he fantasized about that very thing? About taking a gun and putting it against Conrad's head and blowing him the fuck away. A hundred times. A thousand. A million. Too many times to count.

But Alex hadn't. Because killing the bastard would mean that what he'd done to Alex mattered. And it didn't matter. It had happened so long ago and he was over it. Had buried the memories under so much sex and drugs and money he could barely remember what happened.

So why are you making it matter now?

He wasn't sure. Only that something in Eva's eyes had hit him hard. Woken something up. And he didn't like the feeling in the slightest. As if someone had ripped away the wallpaper over a crack in the plaster, exposing just how deep that crack went.

All the way to his soul.

Why the hell had he decided he'd do this again? He didn't want to join Conrad's fucking game. He didn't want to investigate whatever the hell went on there.

He didn't care about that shit, not anymore.

Yet in the face of the fury he'd seen in Eva's eyes, he found he couldn't say no. He was the gambler after all, so it made sense that he be the one to go. And protesting too much would only make the whole business matter even more.

But that wasn't why he was going. He was going because Eva the recluse, the damaged, who didn't leave the city, who barely even left her apartment, had offered to go and he hadn't. And for the first time in probably a decade, he'd felt ashamed of himself.

Bad things had happened to her, things that had left their scars, and even so, she'd offered. She'd been willing to put everything on the line for something that didn't even have anything to do with her. Something that was to do with his fucked-up family. With his father.

And the thing she'd woken inside Alex was the latent sense of responsibility he'd thought had died long ago.

This was his problem to deal with. A problem he'd let slide for far too long.

Alex tightened his grip on the Grey Goose bottle and turned.

Katya stood in the middle of the room, tall in her black suit, pale blond hair tightly braided down her back, her hands behind her. She looked like a soldier on a parade ground, waiting for inspection, her expression impassive.

Except her eyes betrayed a hint of something. Hope maybe.

Who was this Mikhail to her? A friend, she'd said, but Alex didn't believe that for a minute. The lines of her face had softened briefly the moment she'd said Mikhail's name, which meant he was more to her than a mere friend. Her lover; Alex would bet anything on it.

"You said you were going to explain, sir," she said in that uninflected way of hers. "About Mikhail. About what you wanted from me."

"Ah yes, I did say that, didn't I?" He poured himself a third shot, then shoved the bottle back in the cabinet, strolling over to the couch, pulling his tie off with one hand, the shot glass held in the other. He put the vodka down on the coffee table and sprawled out onto the couch, undoing the top buttons of his white business shirt to give him some breathing room.

Katya's gaze followed him, impassive, patient. Waiting.

Jesus, sometimes he really hated that expressionless calm of hers. It irritated him intensely, especially when the unease inside himself felt so damn difficult to choke down.

"I'll help you get him out," he said, reaching languidly for his vodka and taking another sip. "I have money. I have contacts. And since I'm pretty sure the Russian government isn't going to be rushing to help you out, you'll probably need both."

"The Russian government would be very unhappy if they knew I was even considering a rescue."

"So we'll keep it quiet. You've met Zac Rutherford. He has the means to help you in a significant way without anyone finding out anything."

She was silent for a moment; nothing showing on her

face. Then she said, "You mentioned I had to do something for you."

"I did." He leaned back against the couch cushions. "There's a game I'm considering joining. In Monte Carlo. I will need your services for the duration."

"When is it?"

"In a week."

A ripple of expression crossed her features, like the movement of wind on still water. Then it was gone. "That may be too late. That may be the—"

"The only chance you have. By all means you can leave now, head off to Moscow or wherever the hell you need to get to. But what are you going to do when you get there? Do you have contacts to help you? Money?"

"I have friends back home I can call on," she responded stiffly.

Maybe she did. But he'd read the file that Zac had given him. About her life in military schools, about her father, General Ivanov, a higher-up within the Russian government. Alex was betting any contacts she'd had before she left Russia were long gone now and those who were still around wouldn't be going on any rescue mission that wasn't sanctioned by the government. Her father held too much power. No one would want to go against him.

"And these friends would no doubt love to follow you on a little jaunt to Chechnya on an unauthorized rescue mission." He took another sip of the vodka, relishing the burn. "I'm sure that would make them very popular with the government, not to mention your father."

Her posture became rigid. "This has nothing to do with my father."

"So he'd turn a blind eye to anyone stupid enough to help you?"

She didn't respond, her shoulders stiff with tension. Her

gaze shifted so she was looking out of the window behind him. "What do you want from me?"

Alex drained the shot glass and put it back on the coffee table, then settled back against the couch cushions.

As he looked at her, so tall and straight and immovable, the idea that had occurred to him in the limo now seemed ridiculous. He'd decided that if he was going to fucking Monte Carlo, he wasn't going alone. But he also didn't want his backup/protection to be obvious, because that was a weakness he wasn't ready to reveal to anyone, let alone Conrad South.

Katya hanging around in her black suit and shades, looking her usual lethal best, would betray the fact that Alex was afraid.

Katya hanging around in a dress and high heels, with his arm around her waist, now that was different. She could be a stand-in for his latest lover and no one would question it. People might recognize her as his bodyguard, it was true, but once she was wearing a gown and some flashy jewelry no one would care. They'd probably even think the whole bodyguard thing was a fake, especially if he and Katya were observed in public being physical with each other.

Of course he didn't have to take a bodyguard at all, but Zac had been insistent on Alex keeping some backup. That whoever had targeted Tremain was still out there and Alex could very well be in the line of fire. Well, he was fine with that–as long as said backup was done his way.

He tilted his head, surveying her. With her height she'd be able to carry any kind of gown off beautifully, and he was sure there were curves under that severe black suit of hers. She was fair too, which meant her skin would be pale, no perma-tan for his Russian ice princess, that was for sure. With her green eyes and blond hair she'd look amazing in a green gown. Or blue. Or white . . .

His gaze settled on her throat. Her shirt was buttoned all the way to the top, the jacket she wore over the top obscuring her shape. Not even an inch of skin beneath that collar was visible.

Abruptly he got up off the couch and prowled over to where she stood. She blinked as he came closer, a crease forming between her brows. "You haven't answered my question, sir."

"No, I know I haven't. I want to see something first." He stopped right in front of her.

"See what?"

His heart was beating rather faster than normal, which was strange. And he was aware of her scent all of a sudden. Not perfume, because she never wore perfume, but the fresh scent of something citrusy, like oranges. Her shampoo maybe or soap? Whatever it was, he liked it.

He lifted a hand and before she could move undid the buttons that held her suit jacket closed.

"Sir, I—"

"Keep still. I need to see something."

Her frown deepened as her jacket fell open, but she did as she was told, the perfect soldier.

He leaned back, running his gaze over her, and yes, he was right; there were definite curves there. The white cotton of her shirt pulled tight over full breasts, the hem tucked into her black pants revealing narrow hips. Long legs too, which made her very definitely his type. At least enough to fool the press and anyone else who happened to see them together.

"What are you doing, sir?"

"One second."

Alex quickly flicked open the first couple of buttons at her throat.

She took a startled breath, the sound sharp in the silence of the room. He glanced up at her face, and for the first time since he'd met her he read shock clear in her eyes. Shock that quickly gave way to confusion. But she didn't say anything, so he didn't stop, undoing one more button, the fabric parting to reveal smooth, white skin.

Beautiful. Perhaps this would work after all.

His heartbeat sounded even louder in his head, and though there was no reason at all to touch her, he couldn't help himself, gently laying a finger on the pulse at the base of her throat. Her skin felt warm and that pulse was beating fast. As fast as his.

She'd gone very, very still, but he felt her swallow, felt her pulse beat even faster.

The air around them had thickened, becoming dense with tension.

"Sir . . ." Her voice was soft, but he could hear a faint husky edge in it. The kind of edge a woman's voice always held when she was aroused.

Interesting. No, scratch interesting. This was downright fucking intriguing.

"Keep still a moment. I'm testing something." He moved his finger, unable to resist the temptation, stroking her and watching as goose bumps rippled over her skin in response.

Ah yes, so there was chemistry between them, and pretty damn strong chemistry. Excellent. Sexual chemistry would make everything much more convincing.

Katya moved, taking a quick step back, leaving him standing there stroking empty air. She didn't adjust her clothing, but a faint strip of color stained her high cheekbones. "I think you're mistaking me for someone else, sir," she said, her voice not quite level. "If you wanted a companion, I'm quite sure you could find another woman more suited to the job than I am."

He lowered his hand, the warmth of her still glowing on his fingertip. "There are no other women more suited to the job than you are, Katya."

"I'm not going to—"

"Let me tell you which job I mean first, before you jump to any wild conclusions."

Her mouth snapped shut, her shoulders straightening.

His own heartbeat continued to beat like a drum. Christ, he was almost on the point of getting hard, which was weird, because these days it took a lot more than the brush of a woman's skin to get him there. It must be the vodka, surely.

Alex ignored the feeling, turning away and strolling back to the couch, sprawling down on it again. "Like I said, I am going to need you at this Monte Carlo game. But this time the job will be a little different from what you're used to."

"How different?"

He met her green gaze. Held it. "I don't want people thinking you're my bodyguard, Katya mine. I want people thinking you're my lover."

At first she couldn't quite understand what he meant, because she was still finding it difficult to breathe, let alone listen to what he was saying. Her throat burned where he'd touched her; in fact, she could have sworn she'd felt the outline of his fingerprint on her skin. Each whorl and each ridge. Like a fingerprint lock keyed to a particular person.

He's unlocking you . . .

Katya blinked, trying to orient herself. She was breathing fast, like after a very hard workout, and her heart rate was up. Way up. There was also a curious tightness to her skin and an adrenaline spike that had raced through her system the moment he touched her, then settled right down low in her abdomen, a pulsing ache that her body knew even if her brain refused to process it.

Sexual desire.

She'd never had sex before, but she knew intellectually

what it was all about. And even if she hadn't, three months shadowing Alex St. James had certainly taught her more about sex and seduction than she'd ever wanted to know.

Except . . . she'd never felt desire before, at least not for a particular person. Not even Mikhail.

Her mouth was dry. She swallowed, trying to recall what it had been that they were talking about. Something along the lines of not being a bodyguard. Being his lover instead.

He was sprawled out on the couch in front of her with the kind of muscular, indolent grace reserved for lions or panthers. His shirt was open at the throat, his black hair hanging over one eye, stubble lining his strong jawline. He looked like he always did, as if he'd had one too many late nights with one too many women.

She'd always despised his utter lack of self-control and yet found it secretly fascinating at the same time. He didn't seem to care what anyone thought of him, and that held a certain curiosity for her, especially since she cared rather a lot about pleasing people.

Now, as he sat there on the couch, surely half-drunk from the vodka he'd had, something smoky and dark in his blue eyes, it wasn't contempt or derision she felt.

He's sexy.

She shut the thought down.

"And why do you want people thinking I'm your lover?" Her voice sounded like nothing was wrong, and that was good. That was very good. Her training was useful for something then.

He smiled, his mouth curving in that practiced, seductive way. "It's very simple. I don't want to look as though I need a bodyguard. It's a weakness. And I can't afford to show any kind of weakness at the gaming table. Especially not at this particular gaming table."

Her jacket wasn't buttoned the way she liked it and she was very conscious of how her own shirt was open at the throat. And of how his gaze seemed to keep dropping to that patch of skin left bare by the fabric. It was strange to be so aware of her body when she wasn't anywhere near naked, and for some reason it made her angry. "Why do you need me then?" she asked bluntly, forcing away the anger. "Do you need any protection?"

"It's not as if the threat to my life has gone away just like that, darling. And I have reason to believe that this game could be somewhat . . . hazardous."

"And what exactly does pretending to be your lover entail?"

His smile deepened. "You've seen my lovers. You know what to expect."

Oh yes, she had seen them. Hanging off his arm, leaning in to receive kisses. Touches. Caresses. He was a physical man and didn't seem to care who knew it.

She lifted her chin, struggling to compose herself. The thought shouldn't affect her. At all. "Forgive me for saying, sir, but I'm not your type."

"And what have you observed about my type?"

"You like smaller women. More . . . feminine. Pretty socialites, actresses. I am not any of those things."

"No, you're not small; I'll give you that." His gaze dropped once more down her body and she was aware of a certain kind of heat flashing through her. One she hadn't felt before because men generally didn't look at her the way he was looking at her. "But you're beautiful, Katya; never doubt it. Which makes you very much my type indeed."

That heat had begun to move through her, warming her skin. Her jaw tightened. No, men didn't look at her like that and she'd always been glad of it. Some of the girls at the military school she'd gone to had been pretty, the jewels in the crown of the Russian army, there for the recruitment posters and for the officers to gaze at. To be put in army beauty pageants and looked down on.

But she wasn't one of those women. She still remembered the day after her mother's funeral, when her father had caught her weeping in her bedroom. He'd told her that she wasn't to cry, because her mother had been weak, her suicide an act of supreme selfishness. And that from then on he would protect Katya from such things. He would make her strong. Then he'd collected up all the pretty dresses in her closet and put them in the trash, along with the dolls her mother had given her.

Femininity was a sign of weakness, of selfishness, and therefore not permitted in the Ivanov house. Katya had been okay with that. Strength and purpose were infinitely preferable to the constant ache of grief and betrayal.

"Thank you, sir," she said tonelessly. "But I'm not an actor. I'm not sure I could—"

"All you'd have to do is wear a few dresses, a couple of gowns. Look like you're madly in love with me and sit near me at the poker table. That's it." He shifted in another restless movement. "Oh, and naturally, keeping an eye out for threats to my life."

"People are aware of who I am already. They know I'm your bodyguard."

"Not outside of the States they don't. And even if they read all the crap the media spouts about me and have seen pictures of you, once they get a glimpse of you in a gown they won't be thinking bodyguard; I can guarantee you that right now. They'll probably even think the whole bodyguard thing was only a gimmick."

Despite her best intentions, a shard of anger spiked through her. Since coming to the States, she'd had to deal with this sort of thing a lot from men. Undervaluing her skills, underrating her.

"I'm not a gimmick," she said.

"No, of course you're not. But that could work to our advantage, don't you think?"

"I suppose it could," she allowed. "And then what? After this game has ended?"

"Then I'll give you whatever help you need to find your guy."

Katya didn't say anything for a long moment. It was true she would need help when it came to getting Mikhail out of wherever he was. She did have a few contacts in the army, but Alex had been uncannily correct; they probably wouldn't want to help her and risk potential discovery by the government. The General held a lot of influence and no one would willingly put themselves in his path. Even to help his daughter.

And as for the General himself, no matter that he'd been a mentor to Mikhail, his loyalty was to his government first and foremost. To his political aspirations. He'd been clear that as far as he was concerned, as far as the government was concerned, Mikhail Vasin had died on an unrelated visit to Chechnya. And that was the end to the matter.

She'd known the risks and so had Mikhail. Both of them had understood that the government couldn't afford to acknowledge the presence of a black ops unit or else risk escalating the conflict with the state. But the chance of taking out one of the major terrorist leaders had been worth taking those risks.

Except she hadn't realized how she'd feel when the worst happened. When Mikhail disappeared and the government denied all knowledge of him. When even her own father backed them instead of her.

She should have accepted the government stance as part of the job. But she hadn't.

She'd lost her faith in it and her own father instead.

"It's not brain surgery, darling," Alex said lazily. "I would have thought the decision was pretty easy. You come with me to Monte Carlo and I'll help you get your friend."

Of course it was easy. It would mean another couple of

weeks before she could start putting into motion any rescue plans, but without money or contacts, both of which Alex had told her he could get, it would take her much, much longer anyway.

So why did the thought of going with him feel . . . threatening? Because in the end it was only a job. She could wear a gown. She could hang on his arm and pretend to be his lover. It wasn't a big deal. And in return she'd take all his help and go and get Mikhail.

Why was she even hesitating?

Katya straightened her shoulders, ignored the trepidation that sat low in her gut. "Of course, sir. I'd be happy to come to Monte Carlo with you."

CHAPTER FOUR

"So, you're going then?" Gabriel's voice sounded so fucking smug, Alex wanted to throw his phone out the window.

Instead he leaned back against the limo's soft black leather seat and smiled. Though it was probably more of a grimace than a smile. "Yeah, I'm going."

"Honor's gonna be glad about that."

"I'm not doing it for her."

"Keep telling yourself that."

Alex gritted his teeth. The relationship he had with his best friend wasn't what it had been before the guy had started sleeping with Honor. The fact that Gabriel was crazy about her was a point in his favor, but that didn't make Alex any more comfortable with the idea, even though he knew he had no right to be angry about it.

You're jealous of him, that's why. That he's the one protecting her while you sit on the sidelines.

No, for fuck's sake, that wasn't it. He'd chosen to cut his ties with his family; that had been his decision. And he didn't regret it, not for a moment. Not even after his father had killed himself, even though Alex damn well knew that Honor and her mother would be hurting.

Not that he could have done anything about that anyway. He had his own guilt to bear about that little drama.

And anger and all sorts of other shit he couldn't be bothered delving into his self-conscious to sort out.

Still, that didn't mean he didn't care what happened to Honor.

"I'm curious," Alex said. "That's all it is."

"What changed your mind?"

On the seat opposite him, Katya turned her head, gazing out the window, winter sun streaking her blond hair.

Alex watched the sunshine pick up strands of tawny, gold, and caramel in her braid. "Oh, a few things," he said casually. "None of which are your fucking business."

"No problem. I'll ask Zac."

Shit. The bastard would probably tell him too. Alex willed his muscles to relax. "Do you really need to know why?"

"I'm curious," Gabriel said, his voice a conscious imitation of Alex's. Then he added in a more normal tone, "Give me all the bullshit you want. Some part of you is doing this for Honor, not just for your own selfish reasons."

Alex shifted in his seat, uncomfortable. He hadn't thought it was for Honor at the time, his head too full of Eva's confronting words, but . . . Maybe it was. After all, he did owe her a lot. Especially considering it had been the others who'd uncovered her stepfather's shady dealings. And his father's . . .

Which you already knew about and didn't tell them.

"You're a prick, you know that?" he muttered into the phone.

"Yeah," Gabriel said, unperturbed. "Oh, and Alex?"

"What?"

"Be careful, huh?"

"Always," he replied flippantly, and ended the call, sticking the phone back into his pocket.

Katya eyed him from the opposite seat. "Everything all right, sir?"

"Everything's peachy, Katya mine." Apart from his erstwhile best friend still trying to be nice to him. The friend who was screwing his sister.

He pushed the thought away. He had more interesting things to do right now. Such as this little trip to Fifth Avenue. A trip he'd organized specifically with Katya in mind. They had a few things to organize before they left for Monte Carlo, and one of them was training his bodyguard in the fine art of being his girlfriend. Which involved clothes. And not just any old clothes, but fine gowns.

And since he didn't trust her to choose them herself–he guessed she wouldn't be a couture kind of girl–he would be the one doing the choosing. After all, she had to look the part, be believable. And he had rather a lot of experience when it came to women's clothing. Especially taking it off . . .

Katya frowned. "Is there something amusing about me, sir?"

"No." Alex made himself relax. "Why do you say that?"

"You're smiling at me."

"Why shouldn't I smile at you? You're looking particularly . . . bodyguardish today."

Her brows twitched, the only sign she was aware he was playing with her. "You didn't give me a destination before we left," she said, ignoring his stupid joke. And fair enough. It *was* stupid.

Alex tapped the side of his nose. "Secret." Yeah, he was being a prick, but the conversation with Gabriel had set him on edge, making him feel restless and antsy. Like he wanted to poke someone to get a reaction. Katya, for example. Childish, maybe, but fuck, after the last few weeks he reserved the right to act like a child. It wasn't every day that your father's sketchy past as the owner of a drug-dealing high-class brothel cum gambling establishment was discovered by your closest friends.

Katya's mouth firmed. "I wish you would keep me updated about where we're going, sir. It makes my job much more difficult if I don't know the terrain."

"It's Fifth Avenue, sweetheart. Not the jungles of southern Asia."

"It's still—"

"We're going shopping. Happy?"

Her brow cleared. "I see. So we'll be going to Hart Brothers."

Hart Brothers was New York's finest and most exclusive tailor, where Alex got most of his custom-made suits. So naturally that's where she'd be expecting them to visit.

"No, alas not," Alex said. "We're going to Scott's."

"Scott's? But isn't that—"

"For women? Yes."

Not just for any woman either. Scott–she only went by one name–was one of the States' premier designers. Which meant spending lots of money. But he had no problem with that–money was made to be spent after all.

"I see." Katya gave a brisk nod and didn't ask any further questions.

No, she didn't see. She'd be expecting a meeting with one of his lovers, no doubt. Not an unfair expectation given she'd been to Scott's a number of times with him before on exactly that kind of visit. Alex liked to indulge his lovers, and buying clothes for them wasn't unusual for him.

She would definitely not be expecting to be the focus of such a trip, however.

Briefly he debated whether or not to tell her, then decided not to. He wanted to see how she'd react to surprises, since there were going to be rather a lot of them in her future as his pretend girlfriend. She'd need to know how to handle herself. Probably with aplomb, but then it was good to test these things out first beforehand. A rehearsal as it were.

Oh sure. You just like keeping her off balance because you're fascinated by her.

Well, that was true. He couldn't deny he was intrigued by her and had been from the day she'd started working for him. He'd never met a woman like her, and new and different always captivated him.

"Mr. St. James?" David, his driver, spoke from the front of the limo. "Pull up outside okay?"

"Yeah, that's fine." Alex smiled at the woman opposite him as the limo came to a stop. "After you."

She didn't bother with a reply, since one wasn't necessary; she was always first out of the car.

Katya did her usual check up and down the crowded street, then pulled the door open for him.

"Would you like me to stay here?" she asked as he got out, pulling his cashmere overcoat tighter around him against the chill.

"Not today. I need your beautiful presence with me, my sweet."

"Certainly, sir."

The store entrance was discreet, just a black door with the name Scott on a plaque beside it. There was a buzzer, which Alex pushed, the door swinging open silently after a couple of seconds, allowing him entrance. He stepped inside, Katya following at his heels.

Going into Scott's was like walking into a cloud. White walls. Thick, soft white carpet. A massive sectional sofa in white leather right in the middle of it. Huge gilt mirrors were propped up against the walls, put there for clients to look at themselves while trying on clothes.

Scott herself stood near the couch, a petite, black-clad stunningly beautiful African-American woman in her late sixties.

"Alex darling," Scott said in her lilting southern drawl, approaching him as he and Katya entered, enveloping him in a light, insubstantial hug fragrant with hints of magnolia, her signature scent. "How lovely to see you. It's been too long, my dear."

"Far too long," he agreed. "Were you this beautiful last time I saw you? I swear you get lovelier every visit."

She laughed at his outrageous flattery, a delicate, musical sound. "Oh, honey, you should see the picture in the attic. Now, I hear you're bringing me a very special client?"

He smiled and stepped aside, sweeping his hand around to indicate the tall Russian bodyguard standing silently behind him. "I am. And here she is."

Katya turned her head, looking behind her in turn.

But Scott knew immediately. She shot him a look. "You're serious? Not your usual type, I have to say."

Katya was turning back around, another of those quizzical frowns creasing her forehead. A frown that deepened when she found them both staring at her.

"No," he said, meeting her green eyes, watching as the moment of realization hit her. "She isn't. At least not yet."

"Me?" Katya's voice was careful. "You're talking about me?"

"Well, of course. Do you see anyone else behind you?"

Open shock crossed her features followed by the briefest flash of irritation, both of which were then swiftly repressed. "Of course," she said with equanimity, putting her hands behind her back and settling into an "at ease" position.

Giving him nothing.

He almost smiled, a spear of hot anticipation shooting through him. The same feeling he got when he suspected an opponent had a shitty hand and yet kept bluffing. Making him want to push and keep pushing, to break that bluff wide open, expose their weakness

He could do that with Katya. Break her open. Test his icy Russian bodyguard for weaknesses. Hell, he already knew she had one–her Mikhail. How many more did she have?

Why the fuck do you want to know? She's not an opponent you're psyching out—

No, but that didn't stop him from wanting to do it. Jesus, he had to have something to keep his mind off venturing into Conrad South's lair again, and since he'd given up coke it would have to be playing with Katya. It wasn't as if she couldn't take it.

Another ripple of interest chased through him. Yeah, she wouldn't be a pushover; that was for sure. She was strong. A match for him . . .

Weren't you not *supposed to screw with employees?*

Well, that voice in his head could shut the hell up. No, he wasn't supposed to. But in this instance, he just couldn't seem to help himself. And resisting temptation had never been his thing.

"Hmm," Scott said. "You'd better explain yourself, Alex dear."

He glanced at her. "Nothing of what happens here is to leave this room, understood?"

"You're questioning my discretion?" Her silky drawl was lazy, yet he didn't miss the pointed edge in the designer's tone.

"Of course not. Just making sure we're all on the same page."

"Honey, forget about the page. I wrote the whole damn book."

He laughed. "In that case, Scott, meet my bodyguard, Katya Ivanova. She's going undercover as my lover. And your mission, should you choose to accept it, is to make her look the part well enough that no one would even think the word 'bodyguard' could ever be applied to her."

Scott didn't even blink, gazing at Katya with a critical eye. "You sure don't give me the easy jobs, do you?"

His bodyguard didn't move or relax her posture, her gaze as impassive as usual. She was looking at some spot on the wall behind him, giving no sign she was even aware they were talking about her.

But he knew she was. He would bet on it.

"If anyone can help, it's you," he said, giving the designer a dazzling smile. "I want a full wardrobe for her, from lingerie to gowns and everything in between. We're going to be spending most of our time in Monaco, so the labels are going to matter."

"Naturally," Scott said. "Okay, give me a minute while I get my tape measure." She flicked a glance at Katya's motionless figure. "Why don't you go get out of that hideous uniform, honey? I'm going to need to get some measurements off of you."

As the designer left the room, Katya's gaze met his. There was temper lurking in her eyes, tiny sparks of gold amidst the green, and goddamn him but he liked that.

Crossing over to the couch, Alex shrugged out of his overcoat, laying it over the white leather, then sat down on the couch, making a little waving motion with his hand. "Well, go on now. Do as the nice lady said."

Katya didn't move. "Lingerie isn't necessary. I have plenty of my own."

"Of course it's necessary. You're playing a part. And it's much easier to get into character if you're wearing a costume."

"I'm sure actors don't have special underwear made for them as well as costumes."

"How would you know? Have you done any kind of amateur dramatics?"

Her expression didn't alter, but he could see lines of tension around her mouth. How fucking satisfying. "No, sir," she said flatly. "I have not."

Alex tipped his head back against the white leather of

the couch. Perhaps he didn't need to be quite such a prick. "The lingerie matters depending on the gown. But if you'd rather you didn't get some free underwear, that's up to you."

She looked like she might say something else to that but must have thought better of it, because her mouth firmed and she went over to the changing area instead, drawing the curtains closed with a sharp movement.

Oh yeah, he was going to hell for this, for sure. Then again, he'd been on the road to hell for years, and quite frankly, it was nice to have some scenery for a change.

A minute later, Scott reappeared with her tape measure, disappearing again behind the curtains where Katya was.

Alex took out his phone while he waited, scrolling through his e-mail. There was nothing much of interest, just the usual club shit to deal with, plus a confirmation e-mail from the manager of the Fourth Circle, Alex's club in Monte Carlo, confirming his arrival date.

As he was replying, a text from Zac came through. It was, in his usual terse style, short and to the point: *You still committed?*

Alex grimaced and texted a reply: *Of course. I told you I was. Did you think I would change my mind?*

Zac's response came through a second later: *Yes.*

Oh, for fuck's sake. *Well, I'm not. What's all this about anyway?*

There was a pause. *My sources have officially come to a dead end. Whoever they are, they've hidden themselves well. With Tremain still in a coma, this game is our only lead.*

Alex scowled at the screen and texted back: *Why are you so invested in this?*

Because it matters to Eva. That's reason enough for me.

Jesus, those two. He didn't understand it. Then again, he was a selfish bastard, so of course he wouldn't.

Alex put the phone back in his pocket, temper sitting

like acid in his gut. Sure, he may have agreed to this little mission, but that didn't mean he had to like it. Or want to go. The thought of seeing Conrad again made him feel—

No. He felt nothing about Conrad. Nothing at all. Because, Jesus Christ, it had been nineteen years since it had happened. It had no power over him anymore.

The sound of Scott's heels made him look up as she exited the changing area, heading once more toward the back of the shop. "I'm going to bring a selection of items for her to try. This may take some time." She paused and glanced back at him. "You might want to go do business or something."

Alex shook his head. That hadn't been in his plan. "I want to choose what she'll be wearing."

Scott gave him an exasperated look. "You don't trust my taste, darling?"

"Of course I trust your taste. But she's going to be my girlfriend, which means I get final say." If she was going to be playing the part, he wanted it to be utterly convincing. Which meant he got to choose the clothes.

You can't wait to see her in something other than that fucking suit; don't deny it.

Yeah, well, that too, and why not? He could certainly use the distraction right now.

Scott rolled her eyes as she resumed walking toward her workroom door. "Dear God, save me from bossy men."

Katya stood in the changing area, ignoring the luxurious carpet beneath her feet and the elegant chaise lounge up against the wall to her left, staring a hole through the heavy, thick white brocade curtains that shielded her from the man outside.

She'd endured the ignominy of being measured by the elegant designer, removing her jacket but steadfastly refusing to take off any more of her clothes.

Irritation snapped and crackled inside her like boiling oil in a hot frying pan.

How dare he keep her in the dark about this ridiculous shopping trip. Surprises were anathema to her job, and the fact that he hadn't told her either where they were going or what the purpose of the trip was infuriated her.

That it was her own fault didn't make things any easier. She hadn't pressed him when he'd waved away her enquiries about where they were going, too caught up in thinking about the intel she'd received from the contacts who'd found Mikhail. More information about where he was being held and by whom. She'd been strategizing in her head the whole day and hadn't been paying attention. A cardinal error.

Now she had a shopping trip sprung upon her and the worst part was she couldn't argue with it. Alex was right. She *did* need appropriate clothing for this mission. It wasn't like she had any herself, especially since the pretty, frilly little bits of nothing Alex's lovers usually wore would only get in the way of her being able to do her job. Tight dresses were restrictive, and exposing lots of skin meant having nowhere to hide her weapon.

Being sexy, looking pretty, wasn't important anyway. It was vanity of the kind her father had always despised.

She cursed in Russian under her breath, the whisper of her mother tongue grounding her.

If Alex had genuinely forgotten to inform her about this trip, she would have forgiven it. But he hadn't. He'd not told her very deliberately. And then when he'd sprung it on her, he'd stood there watching her, gauging her reactions. Waiting to see what she'd do.

She'd seen him do this to other people. His gaze would sharpen, become watchful, a slow, lazy smile turning his mouth. Then he'd prowl around the edges of their defenses like a panther, testing for weaknesses, looking for a way in. It was unnerving, not to mention irritating.

With an effort, she forced away her annoyance. Getting emotional wasn't useful in any case. It clouded the mind and adversely affected judgment. "Think with your brain, Katya," the General had always told her. "Not with your heart." *Don't be like your mother,* in other words. Good advice, not that Katya had any intention of being like her mother. She was stronger than that.

The curtain pulled back and Scott, the designer who didn't seem to have another name, returned, a length of shimmering green fabric over one arm. "Child," she said in a tone that brooked no nonsense. "You're not trying on this dress while wearing a gun."

Katya straightened and put her hands behind her back. "I'm sorry, ma'am, but I can't do that." Giving up her weapon was not happening. She'd already been distracted today and made an error in not pressing Alex for a destination. She wasn't going to make another one.

The older woman gave her a shrewd look. "You're angry at him for not telling you about this."

Katya blinked, forcing away her surprise. "I'm not angry."

"Of course not. You want revenge, honey? Put on that green dress and he won't know what hit him."

She found herself blinking again, but this time it wasn't with surprise. "I . . . don't know what you mean."

Scott only smiled. "You've got your hands full with that one, let me tell you. Give him an inch and he'll take a mile. But I think you know that already. Want my advice?"

"No, thank—"

"He's hooked, believe me. So hold out as long as you can. That's going to keep him on the end of the line. Then all you have to do is reel him in."

It took a moment for the words to sink in, for the meaning to become clear. And by the time she'd formulated an answer, the designer had given her a wink, then turned around and vanished through the curtains.

Katya cursed a second time. Clearly the woman assumed she was interested in Alex, a natural assumption, since nearly every woman she'd come into contact with over the course of the last three months had been. It wasn't the first time she'd had that implication leveled at her either. But it was the first time she'd heard it implied that *he* was interested in *her*.

It made her extremely uncomfortable. Men tended to see her as competition, and those who didn't dismissed her entirely. Not many showed sexual interest–she was too tall, too strong, too honest, for their liking. She didn't care. She had no interest in embarking on an affair with a fellow soldier that could potentially undermine the integrity of the unit.

She had even less interest in embarking on an affair with a client. That crossed all kinds of boundaries and she wasn't prepared to put her reputation at risk like that.

Abruptly the curtain was shoved back and this time it wasn't Scott, but Alex himself. And as soon as he stepped into the small changing area, the curtain falling shut behind him, enclosing them in the tiny space, the discomfort inside her doubled.

She had the strangest feeling that she couldn't breathe. His presence felt too large for the space, the subtle spice of his scent disturbing her on a level she wasn't prepared to acknowledge.

She fought the urge to shift away from him. Thank God she hadn't undressed like the designer had asked her to; otherwise she'd be standing here in her underwear. The thought sent a prickle of unfamiliar heat through her for some reason.

"Can I help you, sir?" she asked, keeping her voice level.

His barbed blue gaze swept over her. "Give me your gun."

"With all due respect—"

"The gun." He held out his hand. "Please."

She took a silent breath. "And if an attempt on your life were to happen while I was in here without my weapon?"

"Your dedication to your job is commendable, darling, but since your weapon would be with me, I would be able to protect myself."

"I'm sorry, but you do even know how to use it?"

"As your employer I am authorized to disarm you if I see fit. I see fit now." He curled his fingers in a beckoning gesture. "Do as you're told, like a good soldier."

She didn't want to, but now she had no choice.

You're making this into a far bigger deal than it needs to be.

Yes, she was. And she needed to stop it. The mission to Monte Carlo would go far easier if she just accepted whatever happened. Then she could get on with the more important problem of rescuing Mikhail.

Reaching into her shoulder holster, she withdrew her Springfield 9mm without a word and placed it in Alex's palm.

Alex glanced down at it a second. Then he gripped it, checked the magazine, the safety, and raised the weapon smoothly and pointed it at the wall above her head. His hand was rock steady, his movements totally confident. He held the gun pointed there for another couple of seconds; then he lowered it, his mouth curving in an odd smile. "Thank you," he said. "And yes, if you're wondering, I do know how to use a gun." He slipped the weapon into the pocket of his suit jacket. "Now, put on the dress, there's a good girl."

Then he turned and left, letting the curtain fall back behind him.

A third curse was tempting, but that would be an indulgence. She'd put on that damn dress instead and get this ridiculous shopping trip over and done with.

Shrugging off her shoulder holster, she began undoing her shirt, taking it off and laying it on the chaise before doing the same with her pants. Standing in the changing area in her underwear, separated from the rest of the space by only a curtain, made her feel vulnerable. It wasn't a feeling she was familiar with and she didn't like it. She could kill a man with her bare hands, and yet standing there in panties and a bra, knowing Alex St. James was on the other side of that curtain, was . . . exposing.

She reached for the green dress. It had very thin straps and appeared to be made out of some kind of fine, silky fabric that looked like it would tear under the slightest pressure. Gingerly she stepped into it and pulled it on. God, it was tight.

The curtain twitched and Scott was suddenly behind her. "Here, let me zip you up."

Katya inhaled as the other woman tugged up the zipper and the dress fastened around her like a straitjacket.

"Oh, that's perfect," Scott said, putting firm hands on Katya's hips and turning her around like she was positioning a doll. "Absolutely perfect."

It didn't feel perfect, though. It felt like she was trapped. "It's tight," she said stiffly.

"No, it's not." Scott reached out and began pulling the fabric here and there. "That bra is dreadful, though. You won't be able to wear that."

"But I—"

"Come on, child. Better go show your sugar daddy."

Before she knew quite what was happening, Katya found the curtain being hauled back and Scott was propelling her out of the changing area and into the rest of the store.

Alex was sitting on the couch, doing something with his

phone, and at the sound of the curtain being pushed back he looked up.

An expression she didn't recognize flared in his eyes, a flash of intense blue. Then he put his phone away and got up off the couch, stalking toward her.

There was something predatory about the way he moved. A sleek, fluid motion that set off all kinds of alarm bells ringing in her head. She tensed as he came closer, her instincts going into fight mode, one hand already moving toward where her gun should be.

He's not a threat. He's your employer. Stand down.

God in heaven. What was she doing?

Katya fought down the urge to move into a defensive posture, clenching the hand that had gone for the gun instead. It left her arm at an awkward angle, but then that was okay, since everything about this was awkward in the extreme.

If he'd noticed her going for her weapon, he gave no sign, coming to a stop in front of her, giving her figure a long, slow scan.

She stood there, her awkwardness increasing, not knowing what to do with herself. Being the center of attention felt wrong on every level, since protection was all about remaining out of the spotlight.

Finally, Alex's gaze lifted to hers. "You don't like it." It wasn't a question.

Well, her discomfort was probably quite obvious. "No. The dress is too tight. I won't be able to run in this or fight."

He smiled and it looked like–for once–a smile of genuine amusement. "Running and fighting isn't generally a prerequisite for being my girlfriend, Katya."

"I'm still your bodyguard, sir. That fact remains no matter who I'm pretending to be."

His gaze dropped again, to the bodice of the dress. And he frowned. "You're a soldier. Aren't you supposed to be able to adapt to difficult terrain? I'm sure you can figure out how to run and fight adequately in a dress. But first of all, that god-awful bra has to go."

A prickle of irritation chased through her. She was wearing her usual—a black, utilitarian sports bra—and no, of course it didn't go with the dress. But it gave good support and that was all she required from her bras.

"My sports bra is not 'god-awful,'" she said. "It's excellent under Kevlar."

"Kevlar? Jesus. Since when do my girlfriends wear Kevlar?" He made a motion toward the huge gilt mirrors. "Go on. Go and see for yourself what I'm talking about."

A strange reluctance gripped her. She hadn't worn a dress since the last winter ball at the exclusive military school she'd attended. Wearing those frilly, frothy gowns that all the other girls had gotten so excited over had felt wrong to Katya. Made her feel like that little girl her mother used to take to the GUM department store in Red Square and spoil with pretty dresses. Or to the Moscow Botanical Garden to see the roses.

An indulged, weak little girl who'd fallen apart when her mother had died.

Katya wasn't that girl now, though, her father had made sure of it, and it wasn't as if wearing a dress would change the years of training that had gone into making her who she was.

Dismissing the reluctance, Katya went to stand in front of one of the mirrors, staring fixedly at her reflection. The green silk hugged her curves, her legs left bare by the mid-thigh-length hem, making her look . . . not like herself. Like someone softer, more feminine, vulnerable, *weaker* . . .

Katya decided to ignore the woman in the mirror, concentrating her attention instead on the bodice of the dress where the edges of her sports bra showed, the thick black straps over her shoulders spoiling the look.

"See what I mean about the lingerie?" Alex wandered over to stand beside her, meeting her gaze in the mirror.

"I don't have to wear this," she said. "I can—"

"You'll wear what I tell you to wear," he cut her off, a thin edge of iron running through his voice. "This isn't about you and your comfort zone. This is about the job I'm employing you to do."

More irritation crackled inside her, but she dismissed it the way she'd dismissed her reflection. He was right. This wasn't about her. This was about the job he'd employed her to do and one he was going to pay her very well for. Getting annoyed about the clothes she had to wear was personal and not at all professional.

Still, there were some aspects about this particular mission that he hadn't briefed her on and that was definitely something she needed to remedy. Information was important to any protection job and she needed more.

"A job I've yet to be briefed properly on," she reminded him. "I hope you were planning to do that before we leave?" She didn't bother hiding the pointed tone of her question. If he could make snide remarks about her undergarments, she could do the same about his lack of planning.

Unexpectedly she caught a glimpse of something in his eyes, a hesitation almost. "All in good time," he said, turning away. "Go try on the next dress. And ditch the bra."

The next dress was on a clothes rack that Scott had wheeled over, a number of other dresses hanging there that all looked either frighteningly brief, tight, or otherwise impractical. But as Scott disappeared into her workroom again, Katya kept her mouth shut on her protests.

Mikhail depended on the success of her mission for Alex St. James, which made doing a good job of it imperative.

She tried to keep hold of that thought as she contorted herself into various different outfits, all of which were uncomfortable and constricted her in some way. They were all pretty much impossible to wear with a holster, and Kevlar was going to be out of the question.

As she shuffled out of the changing area for the tenth time, the gown this time floor-length, strapless, and made out of some kind of fabric that looked like liquid gold poured all over her, she said, "You're going to have to get a few things made for me if I can't wear my holster."

Alex looked up from the rack of clothes he was leafing through. He didn't say anything for a moment, staring at her intensely. Then he came toward her in that long, loping, dangerous prowl.

"What things?" He swept his gaze over her, blue eyes glittering. Like he was . . . hungry.

Disturbed, she turned to face the mirror, since no matter how uncomfortable she found her reflection, it was still better than looking at him with that hungry expression in his eyes. "I can't wear my weapon if I'm in these dresses. I need an alternative to my holsters."

He moved behind her, his footsteps muffled by the thick white carpet, standing much closer than she was comfortable with. In the mirror she could see him, nearly a head taller than she was, his gaze following the line of the gown over her hips, stomach, and thighs, all the way to the floor.

A tight, restless feeling turned over inside her, making her uneasy. She didn't like these dresses, didn't like the way they made her look. Made her feel. As if she wasn't totally in command of herself anymore. As if she were someone else.

Katya focused on a point over her shoulder, away from him and the disturbing reflection in front of her.

"What kind of alternative?" His breath feathered the

back of her neck and over her shoulders, left bare by the gown.

God, were those goose bumps? She didn't look to check, because if they were she didn't want to know.

"I'll need purses with a weapons compartment. Makes drawing easier. Though for some of these dresses a thigh holster will work."

"That can be arranged." His straight dark brows twitched, his gaze switching from the dress to something at the back of her head. "Hmmm. This gown is perfect. But . . . hang on. . . ."

She didn't know quite what he was doing until she felt his fingers in her hair. Her spine stiffened. "Sir?"

He didn't respond, but she could feel him pulling gently on her braid and then warmth down her back as he completely unraveled it.

Her breath caught as he combed through her hair, spreading it out over her shoulders, and when the tips of his fingers brushed her bare skin a small sound nearly escaped her.

"Better," he murmured. "Oh yes, much better. See? Look at yourself, sweetheart, and tell me what you think."

Katya lifted her gaze to the mirror, but this time it was different. This time the past came rushing down on her like an avalanche, swallowing her whole.

There was a woman in the mirror. A woman in a golden gown that clung to every curve, with her hair spread out over pale shoulders, cheeks lightly tinged with color, green eyes flecked with gold like summer leaves turning in the autumn.

Mama—

Katya blinked. Hard. No, she didn't look like her mother in the slightest. Anna Ivanova had been shorter, curvier. Prone to crying at the drop of a hat or laughing just as easily. Over-emotional. Vain.

Her mother going to the Bolshoi with Katya's father. In a golden gown, her hair down, Katya had thought she looked like an angel from one of the beautiful icons in St. Basil's Cathedral. Katya had clung to that gown, begging her not to go out, not to leave.

"I'll never leave you, little cat," her mother had murmured, catching her up in her arms. "Never in a million years."

But she had left Katya. In the end, Anna had left everyone.

"Beautiful," Alex said in Katya's ear. "Don't you agree?"

The images of the past wavered, insubstantial as smoke. Ridiculous to be remembering these things now. Anna Ivanova was seventeen years dead and her daughter was a soldier, not a clingy, desperate child.

Katya forced away the memories, studying herself with an objective eye. "I look the part."

"You most certainly do." His hands came to rest on her hips, a featherlight touch. "Though I'm afraid, darling, you'll have to lose the underwear."

She held herself motionless, aware of the way his fingertips were resting on her. As if the material of the dress weren't even there and he was touching her bare skin.

"Why the underwear?" She kept her voice cold and flat.

"Shows through the dress, see?" Gently he ran the tip of one finger along the slight line that marked the waistband of her panties. "My lovers tend to be very conscious of that kind of thing."

She met his gaze in the mirror. There was a challenge there. A dare. He was pushing her, wanting to shock her, no doubt. Because that's what he did.

He was probably telling the truth about the underwear–his women did tend to be very fussy with their appearance–but if he was expecting her to blush and refuse he was going to be sadly disappointed.

She wasn't one of his lovers. She was a special forces soldier from a highly specialized unit. She'd killed men before, and if she wanted to she could probably kill him.

She would not be unsettled by a few silly dresses and the touch of his hand.

Katya stepped away from him. With a certain brisk efficiency she reached up under the gown and pulled down the plain, black cotton panties she wore, stepping out of them and balling the cotton up in one hand. Then she smoothed the wrinkles out of the gold material and shot him a cool glance. "Better?"

His eyes had widened and she was very satisfied to see surprise lingering there. "Well, that was unexpected." He raised a brow. "Are you sure you don't want me to hold them for you while you check in the mirror?"

Of course. He had to keep pushing, didn't he?

"No, thank you," Katya said. "Are we done here, sir? I'd really prefer that we get on to that briefing session you mentioned. I need to draw up some security plans, and for that to happen I'll also need more information about where we're going and why."

Alex didn't reply, only giving her a long, measuring look, an odd smile playing around his beautifully shaped mouth.

That wasn't the best move you could have made.

No, perhaps it hadn't been. Because she had the sense that she'd woken a sleeping tiger. And he was hungry.

"Yes," he said slowly. "I think we're done here." Then he turned. "Scott? We'll take the whole fucking lot."

CHAPTER FIVE

As the car came to a stop, Katya was already leaning forward, her hand on the door handle, all ready to get out first.

"No," Alex said flatly. "Remember who you are now." And he could almost see the mental readjustment it took for her to sit back down in her seat.

Jesus Christ. They hadn't even left the country and she was already forgetting who she was supposed to be.

"I'm sorry," she said, her mouth a hard line. "It won't happen again."

Yes, it would. It was inevitable. He'd bet a million bucks on the fact that Katya hadn't ever played this kind of part before, and it seemed obvious that she wasn't going to slip into it easily.

Had he made the wrong decision in wanting her with him? Perhaps he should have gone alone after all.

Then again, Zac had been clear he shouldn't turn up for the Apocalypse poker game without some kind of backup. Especially when Conrad would be expecting Tremain to turn up, not Alex. Though probably by now the guy would know Tremain was in the hospital and would have written him off the list of players.

Which was fine. That would give Alex a massive advantage in terms of the element of surprise, because nothing put opponents off more than shocking the hell out of them.

And he was going to need that advantage.

This game was going to fuck with his head in a big way simply because of who Conrad was, and if Alex wasn't totally confident that was going to get to him. Normally he had no problem with out-psyching people. But this . . . This was different.

You're afraid.

No. Fuck, no. He wasn't afraid. The past was over and done with, and it couldn't touch him now. He was going to arrive in Monaco with a beautiful woman on his arm, confident, powerful. In-fucking-vincible.

Alex glanced out of the window of the limo to where his Gulfstream stood waiting on the airport tarmac while the last of their luggage was loaded. "Don't make promises you can't keep, sweetheart," he muttered.

"I don't," Katya said in the same flat tone. "Neither do I make the same mistake twice."

He looked at her and wanted to smile. Because she sounded exactly like her usual stoical Russian bodyguard self and yet the woman sitting opposite him now didn't look even remotely like a bodyguard.

In one of Scott's exquisite suits, she was tall, elegant, and although she'd never be conventionally beautiful, the potential he'd already glimpsed, had been fully realized now.

The skirt she wore was high waisted and slim fitting, ending just above her knee, outlining the swell of her hips and the long, lean length of her legs. The matching jacket was buttoned and belted, the plain white blouse she wore underneath setting off the soft green of the fabric. On her feet were a pair of sexy little black ankle boots, another purchase from Scott's. Her hair he'd decided she could leave loose, since the color of it was beautiful and he liked it over her shoulders.

A stunning woman. A woman worthy of being on his arm.

It made something hungry come to life inside him.

He settled back in his seat and folded his arms. "That sounds suspiciously like a challenge. And you should know better than to offer challenges like that to gamblers like me."

A crease deepened between her fair brows. "It's not a challenge. Merely a statement of fact."

Which naturally roused all his competitive instincts like blood in the water roused the appetite of a shark.

This time he did smile. "Would you care to place a small wager on that?"

"Excuse me?"

"A bet, Katya darling. You said you don't make the same mistake twice. I bet you will."

"This isn't a game," she said repressively. "It's a matter of professional pride."

"Ah, but life's a game, isn't it? So why not play?" He stared at her because it was easier to stare at her, to push her, than think of their destination, no matter how many silent pep talks he gave himself. "Let's try this. If you make another slip, I claim a forfeit and whatever the forfeit is, you have to pay it."

Her gaze narrowed as if he'd spoken in some kind of ancient language she couldn't translate. "Why?"

"Why what?"

"Why would I want to do that?"

"Because it's fun? Because it adds spice to a boring trip? Because I'm your fucking employer and you need to do as you're told?"

As always, she didn't rise to the bait. "I'm sorry, but this concerns my ability to do my job and I take it very seriously. It should not be reduced to a game of chance."

"Jesus. You really know how to suck the fun out of everything."

Katya glanced out the window at the jet. "Sir, if I'm not much mistaken, we're going to be late taking off if we don't start boarding."

So she was going to ignore him, was she? Blow him off the way she always did?

Fuck that.

Excitement coiled tight inside him. The thrill of the hunt, of a challenge to be met. It had been a long time since he'd felt that spark, too damn long. Once it had been the game that did it, the cards in his hands, the roll of the dice, chance his plaything. Or booze, or drugs, or sex, or money. Yet those things inevitably palled, their pleasures brief.

This, though . . . This was different.

Because of her. Because she's different.

Yeah, well, maybe she was. And messing with her crossed the line. But he'd never been one to give up a thrill for however long it lasted and he wasn't about to start now.

Not with Conrad South only a few hours away.

"By all means, let us board." He leaned forward and lowered his voice. "But as soon as we're on that fucking plane, you're going to make me that bet, Katya Ivanova. And if you don't like it, you can stay here."

Her eyes widened fractionally, but she didn't say anything.

Alex smiled. "Now," he continued in a more normal tone. "I'm going to get out of this car and then I'm going to offer you my hand. You'll take it and walk with me to the jet. And you're going to smile like this is the best thing that's ever happened to you, are we clear?"

"Yes, sir," Katya replied, expressionless.

"And that's another thing. No 'sir.' Unless you're naked and I'm holding a whip."

Wretched woman didn't even bat an eyelid. "I will call you 'sir' in private, as per our relationship as employee and employer. In public I will call you Alex."

He didn't know he'd been waiting to hear his name on her lips until she'd said it, her faint Russian accent making the long *A* sound incredibly sensual.

Dear God, he was going to have to be careful here. Otherwise she could turn out to be a toy he enjoyed playing with rather more than he should.

He got out of the car, the cold already beginning to bite, and turned, extending his hand to help Katya out. She hesitated only briefly, reaching for him. He closed his fingers around hers as she slid out of the car, gingerly maneuvering herself. Her skin was cool to the touch, gradually warming as she straightened. For some insane reason he didn't want to let her go, so he didn't, lacing his fingers through hers.

She resisted a second and then her hand relaxed. A smile turned her mouth. It was fairly wooden, but only he would know that.

"Excellent," he murmured as they turned toward the plane. "Oscar worthy even."

"Thank you," she replied, still smiling that wooden smile.

What would a natural smile look like?

The idle thought crossed his mind and stuck there like a fishhook catching on a rock. Had he even seen Katya smile? Properly? No, he didn't think he had. In fact, he'd never seen her angry either, or in any other way emotional.

You could make her emotional.

The thrill lurking deep inside him was electric as they boarded. Oh, that was bad, very bad. But shit, he'd never been a good boy, had he? And getting an unguarded emotional reaction out of his Russian bodyguard was a challenge he couldn't refuse.

Katya was expressionless as the stewardess showed her to one of the seats and helped her stow the Prada purse that was the only hand luggage she'd bought with her. Yet Alex didn't miss the way her gaze scanned the jet's interior, measuring, assessing.

Goddamn bodyguard.

He sat down in the chair beside her, buckling up his seat belt, conscious that the unease he'd been feeling all day had gradually begun to ease now he was in the jet.

It was one of Alex's favorite places to be in all the world, its interior the place he spent more time in than any of his personal apartments in the Nine Circles clubs—all saving the New York apartment. He liked the sense of freedom that came from being thousands of meters above the earth, unconnected to anything or anyone, untethered and soaring.

Sometimes he'd just sit in the luxurious white leather seat and stare out the window at the clouds passing below, not thinking of anything at all. It was the closest he'd ever gotten to true peace.

He reached over and put his hand over Katya's where it rested on the arm of the seat.

She glanced at him, eyes narrowing, but didn't pull away.

"Take my hand, darling," he murmured. "And lean in while we take off. Pretend you're scared and you like being close to me."

A flash of what looked like irritation crossed her features; then it was gone and that wooden smile was back. "Certainly, s—I mean, Alex." Her hand turned over, fingers curling around his, and she edged closer to him.

A thread of her scent caught him, and not the expensive perfume he'd ordered for her, the kind one of his lovers would normally wear, but the sharp, simple smell of oranges. Katya's true scent.

And for some completely inexplicable reason, the tension in his gut that had been sitting there for the past two weeks eased even further. As if the smell of her and the warmth of her fingers around his made some kind of difference.

Insanity.

Yet he didn't move away as the plane took off, nor did he let her go.

Katya's muscles had locked up. Ridiculous. All he was doing was holding her hand and yet it felt like she had a hot coal resting in her palm. She didn't like the sensation any more than she'd liked any of the other uneasy feelings being close to Alex St. James seemed to generate.

Feelings? It's sexual attraction; don't deny it.

As soon as the plane leveled off, Katya pulled her hand away from him, ignoring the snide voice in her head. It couldn't be sexual attraction. She hadn't experienced any of the same physical symptoms when she'd been close to Mikhail, and if there was one man she should feel them for it was him. Not for some self-indulgent, selfish American playboy.

Well, whatever they were, she had to ignore them. They were distracting and that could be dangerous. That could end up being fatal for either her or her client.

She had to be on her guard.

The stewardess approached, tall and blond and willowy, smiling at both of them, not only Alex. It was strange to be on the receiving end of such attention. Bodyguards were supposed to fade into the woodwork, not be noticed. Yet another damn thing about this mission that made Katya uncomfortable.

Alex ordered drinks before she had a chance to refuse, undoing his seat belt and grabbing one of the gossip magazines on the table in front of him.

"I shouldn't have anything to drink," Katya said. "Not while I'm on the job."

He dropped the magazine in her lap. "You'll have to. Not unless you want pregnancy rumors happening, since that's the only reason one of my lovers wouldn't have at least one glass of champagne."

Apparently nothing about this was going to be easy.

Frowning, Katya looked down at the magazine in her lap. "What's this?"

"Research. I don't know how much celebrity gossip you're aware of, but if you're with me you'll need to be up with who's who."

She wasn't interested in the slightest about the lifestyles of the rich and famous. Hadn't she seen all she needed to in the past three months with him anyway?

"Will we be encountering any of these people?" She gestured at the magazine.

"Maybe. That's the wonderful thing about Monaco. You never know who's going to turn up." There was an undercurrent in his voice that made her think he meant something by the words, though what she had no idea.

Yet another reminder of the glaring gap in her knowledge: the reason for this visit in the first place. He'd been very good at avoiding the subject whenever she tried to bring it up over the past few days and she was starting to think that he didn't want to tell her, though she couldn't imagine why. Didn't he want to keep her up-to-date? Make her as effective as possible in protecting him?

God, how she hated not knowing things. She didn't feel like she'd had enough intel about what they were heading into in Monaco, and that could turn out to be a problem if they weren't careful.

She'd spent some time researching Monaco, the layout of the Fourth Circle, one of his Nine Circles clubs where they'd be staying, as well as the Four Horsemen casino this poker game was supposed to be held in. However, she had nothing to go on about the Apocalypse poker game itself, since there appeared to be no info available about it. A fact that did not make her feel any better about this whole mission.

She'd even done a quick search for information about the owner of the casino where the game was supposed to take place. One Conrad South. But she hadn't been able to turn up much about him either. At least nothing she didn't already know. He was the rich and apparently very private owner of the Four Horsemen, one of Monaco's most exclusive casinos. And that was it.

All in all very disappointing.

The stewardess brought over the champagne, placing two glasses on the table in front of them.

Alex leaned forward and picked up his glass, raising it. "A toast, darling. To a wonderful week in Monte Carlo." That look was back in his eyes, the one he'd given her in the limo before they'd gotten onto the plane. When he'd demanded she accept that bet. A dare. A challenge.

Well, she hadn't appreciated it then and she didn't appreciate it now. Especially not with her mile-wide competitive streak, the same one that had driven her to graduate at the top of her class at military school. That had driven her to prove herself to her father, to be the strong soldier he'd wanted her to be.

To prove you're not weak like your mother.

Ah, but that was one thing she didn't have to prove, not anymore.

Katya picked up her glass, pasted what she hoped was a dazzling smile on her face, and knocked her glass against his. "To Monte Carlo."

His mouth curved as he took a sip of the wine, sprawling back in the chair next to her. "Very good. But it's going to take more than a smile and champagne to convince people you're my latest acquisition." He glanced at the heavy and no doubt horrifically expensive Rolex on his wrist. "We have about nine hours before we reach Monaco, so I'm thinking we could get in some practice with a few things."

She allowed herself one sip of wine before putting it back on the table. It was dry and quite a bit more delicious than she expected, but she didn't normally drink and didn't want to start now, no matter what he said about pregnancy rumors.

"Yes," she said. "Excellent idea. I have some questions." Now perhaps she could finally pin him down about the real reason they were attending this poker game.

He gazed at her over the rim of his wineglass. "I wasn't thinking about questions, sweetheart."

Katya shifted surreptitiously in her seat, trying to loosen the fabric of her skirt. It was annoyingly tight and she didn't like it. In fact, she didn't like anything about the restrictive outfit Alex had chosen for her today. Then again, she was probably going to have to get used to that, since most of the outfits she'd be wearing would be restrictive.

Just as she was going to have to get used to not having her weapon on her.

She'd tried to tell herself that was a good thing, since becoming too reliant on your gun was a mistake. Besides, if she wanted a deadly weapon, the heels of the stilettos she'd been forced to wear and couldn't walk in would do nicely.

"What do you mean then?" She shifted again, her feet aching. "I'm still expecting a briefing on the situation we'll be walking into when we get to Monaco."

Alex waved his glass negligently. "It's a poker game. What more do you need to know?"

"You've never been worried about being seen with a bodyguard at any of your other poker games. Why is this one different?"

"I'm not sure that information is relevant to the mission."

"Forgive me, sir, but everything is relevant to the mission. As I think I've explained to you, the more I know, the better I can protect you."

There was a gleam she didn't trust in his eyes. "And you just made another mistake."

Oh dammit. Alex. His name was Alex. Why did she find it so difficult to say?

He put his glass down. "Make me that bet, Katya. It'll help keep you on track if nothing else."

She didn't make mistakes, at least not usually. And she certainly didn't want to turn her job into a game. "You've left it too late. We're in the air now. I can refuse."

"I can also not help you find your boyfriend." He smiled. "See? We're even."

Katya had a sudden vision of herself flinging the wine in his face, then following it up with a swift punch to the throat. It was a very satisfying vision. Unfortunately, though, violence wasn't exactly the most intelligent way to deal with difficult clients.

She needed to be subtler than that, especially with him. "Very well," she said, trying and failing to keep the curt sound out of her voice. "I'll make you your bet."

His smile widened. "Excellent. So, another mistake and you owe me the forfeit of my choice. A mistake being anything that will betray the fact that you're not actually my lover."

"And if I don't make any more mistakes?"

"Fair's fair. When we return to New York, I'll be the one to pay the forfeit of your choice."

"Very well." She made her tone expressionless. "I agree."

He extended his hand, a wicked glint in his eyes. "Shake on it."

Katya didn't hesitate. She reached out and took his hand, delivering the firm handshake she normally used with clients.

Except he didn't let go, and she found her muscles locking up again, that familiar prickling heat creeping over her skin. She met his intense blue stare and her breath caught.

That look . . . She'd seen him look at plenty of other women like that, but never had it turned on her. As if she were something delicious he wanted to eat.

No wonder other women melted under that gaze. No wonder they fluttered and swooned like butterflies around him.

Pity she wasn't one of those women.

The General had once given her a lecture on the temptations of the opposite sex and how she had to keep herself pure. That her strength lay in being untouchable. That her loyalty to her commander and her country couldn't be compromised by a man. Unless that man was Mikhail of course.

She'd stayed true to that advice even after she'd left Russia and she certainly didn't want to compromise her position now.

Are you sure about that?

Oh yes. She was sure.

Katya fought down the heat and the tremble that gripped her, and raised an eyebrow instead. "What now?"

"My original thought on how we could spend the next nine hours, darling. There's a few things we need to work on, such as physical closeness. It's not going to be very believable with you flinching every time I touch you." He turned her hand over in his, rubbed his thumb over her palm in a gentle caress. Sparks shot up her arm and it was only sheer force of will that held her still, determined not to move a muscle.

"I do not flinch," she said coolly, willing her arm to relax and ease the tension out of her fingers.

"Au contraire. You're as stiff as a fucking board right

now and I'm only holding your hand. What are you going to be like when I kiss you?"

Kiss her? He was going to kiss her?

Of course he's going to kiss you. You're supposed to be his lover.

An image flashed in her mind, of the woman in his apartment a few weeks ago, when she'd asked him about the dice. Of how he'd looked as he'd kissed her. His dark head bent, intent and sure and ruthless. And the way the woman's body had melted against his . . .

Katya set her jaw, deliberately erasing the provocative image from her head. "I'm sure I can manage," she answered, keeping her voice flat and expressionless.

"I'm not convinced." He cocked his head, light from the windows sheening the inky black of his hair. "And if I'm not convinced then no one else will be."

Again, he was right. But she didn't like it. Didn't like it at all.

Why not? He's just a man and this is only a job.

That was true. And she'd had three months of close observation of Alex's many and varied lovers, of their behavior around him. She could do that. She wasn't an actress, but she could pretend.

"Very well," she said, keeping a tight leash on her reactions as he idly brushed his thumb over her palm again, sending more prickles of that odd heat washing over her skin. "What did you have in mind?"

He searched her face and she knew he was looking for some kind of reaction from her, perhaps even hoping for it. But she only looked coolly back, betraying nothing.

A mistake. Because a glint of deep, intense blue suddenly lit in his eyes and she knew she'd woken something in him. Something that should have stayed asleep.

He released her hand and rose to his feet. "What do I have in mind?" he echoed, crossing over to the white leather couch opposite them and sitting down on it so he was facing her. "I'm thinking a demonstration. I want you to convince me that you're desperate for me. That you can't get enough of me. That all you want is for me to take you to bed." He clasped his hands between his knees. "I like my lovers to be frank and uninhibited about what they want. I'm sure you know what I'm talking about."

Oh yes, she did. His lovers generally were *very* frank.

Adrenaline had begun to buzz in her veins. Like the rush she got on an intensely physical mission. Where there was nothing but the end goal in mind, only your orders to obey. Where everything was simple and there was no politics or murky loyalties, or unexpected betrayals. A dangerous thing to think when nothing that concerned Alex St. James would ever be that simple.

But this was her mission and she was going to accept it.

"Certainly," she said. "I can do that."

Katya pushed herself out of the chair, taking a moment to get her balance on the unfamiliar shoes and to smooth down the wrinkles in her skirt.

Alex had leaned back on the couch, stretching his legs out in front of him, his arms folded. Watching her as if ready for some kind of performance.

She'd never done this before, but it wasn't as if she'd been blind these past three months.

The woman in his apartment was clear in her mind. The one who'd wrapped her arms around him and asked him to come back to bed, all warmth and sleepy sensuality. She could do that, oh yes, she could.

Katya let a smile turn her mouth and dropped her lashes halfway. Then she walked slowly across the jet's soft white carpeting, the unnaturally high heels guiding the movement of her hips. She kept her gaze on his as she walked, not breaking eye contact.

He waited and she was very conscious of a gathering

tension. One that hadn't been there before and shouldn't be there now. But it was too late to pull back, too late to stop. She just had to ignore it, pretend it wasn't there.

She came to a stop in front of him, standing with legs apart on either side of his. Then bent, putting one hand on the arm of the couch and the other on the back of it, leaning over him, looking down into the deep, intense blue of his eyes. They widened slightly and she had the feeling she'd surprised him.

About damn time.

She kept her smile where it was, lifting her hand from the arm of the chair and running a finger along the warm skin of his hard jaw, feeling the brush of stubble. "Alex, darling," she murmured, her voice low and husky. "Why don't you come to bed? I'm so lonely there all by myself."

He didn't say a word, only held her gaze. But she felt the muscle in the side of his jaw clench, saw the faint rise of color on his perfect cheekbones.

Interesting. Was this little performance doing something to him?

An unfamiliar sense of satisfaction gripped her, a feeling of power she'd never experienced before. Pushing her advantage for reasons she couldn't have explained, Katya lowered her head a bit more and let her trailing finger move along the line of his lower lip, tracing the full curve of it. The contrast of the roughness of his jaw to the softness of his mouth was . . . intriguing.

He remained motionless as she touched him, no expression whatsoever on his face. And yet there was a flame in his eyes. And it burned hot.

Stop, you fool.

He smelled good, a subtle, expensive aftershave that had hints of sandalwood and musk in it. But beneath it another scent, hotter. Raw. The scent of the man beneath the custom-made suit and the lazy smile. A different man.

Finish this.

But she couldn't seem to pull away or stop touching his mouth, and for some reason she was achingly aware of the stretch of his long, lean body beneath her. She lowered her head even farther, so their lips were inches apart, feeling the absurd need to test his boundaries as much as he was testing hers.

"Alex . . ." she whispered, caressing his name.

His body tensed and she recognized it with the instinct of a fighter. Saw his hand begin to reach for her.

Katya pushed herself away with a sharp movement, straightening and wiping the smile off her face. Looking coolly at him as if his nearness had had no effect on her whatsoever. And of course it hadn't. This was a test for herself as much as for him, and one she'd passed with flying colors.

She put her hands behind her back so he wouldn't see them shake and raised an eyebrow. "Convincing enough for you?"

CHAPTER SIX

"Good to have you back, Mr. St. James."

Alex gave Marc, the manager of the Fourth Circle, a short nod. "Are my apartments ready?"

"Yes. Everything has been arranged for you and Miss Ivanova."

He seemed to be exquisitely conscious of Katya standing next to him, of the warmth of her hip beneath his palm. Of that maddeningly simple, innocent scent of oranges.

He'd never been so aware of another person and it pissed him off.

He should have done something on the plane, when she'd leaned over him, touching him, her lips millimeters from his. He should have grabbed her. Kissed her. Shocked her in some way. Punished her for making him hard with a mere touch. For making him want what he knew he shouldn't have.

And most of all for getting under his guard.

Convincing enough for you?

Oh yeah, she'd been convincing. Too fucking convincing. And for the first time in his life, he hadn't known what to do or what to say. He'd muttered something, he couldn't remember what, then had gotten out of the chair and found himself some work to carry on with, anything to distract him from the desire coiling in his gut. From the hard-on in his pants.

He wasn't used to self-restraint and that didn't do anything for his mood either. But he didn't want her to know how she'd affected him. Jesus, one touch. On his fucking mouth. Sure, they had chemistry, but he'd had chemistry with other women before and none of them had managed to get him so hard so quickly.

Dangerous . . . .

Dangerous? Where the fuck had that come from?

Alex shrugged off the thought. No, chemistry wasn't dangerous and his unease was only due to Conrad's damn poker game. Nothing to do with Katya herself. God, what he should have done was taken her when he'd had the chance. Indulged himself like he did with anything he wanted, rules be damned.

Because he certainly couldn't have her now. That would be tantamount to dropping his guard and giving her the control, admitting she was a weakness. And he sure as shit wasn't going to do that. He could control himself. People thought he had no restraint at all, but that wasn't true. Just because he didn't exercise it didn't mean he didn't have it.

Whatever, Katya was going to have to stay firmly in the employee zone for the next week.

Doesn't mean you can't play with her, though. . . .

Alex splayed his hand on her hip, testing her. She didn't tense, her body relaxed next to his. No, this wasn't going to happen. He was *not* going to be the one this was difficult for, no way in fucking hell.

He leaned in, his mouth near her ear. "Why don't you go upstairs, darling? Freshen up. Have a nap. We've got a couple of hours before dinner."

She turned her head, pulling subtly away. "What about you?"

The front doors of the club slammed as the last of their luggage was brought in. Marc had already gotten the Fourth Circle staff working with luggage carts to maneuver the suitcases into the elevators.

"I'm going to do a small tour of the club," Alex said. "Make sure everything is set up for tonight."

Katya gave him a narrow look. "There are no events planned for this evening."

He smiled. This was going to piss her off, but turnabout was fair play, wasn't it? "There is now."

Her brows twitched together. "But according to the schedule—"

"Fuck the schedule. There's always a party when I arrive at the Fourth Circle."

Her mouth thinned in irritation. "You should have—"

Alex let his hand move from her hip down across the curve of her butt and squeezed. Her eyes went wide, that delicious mouth clamping shut. And along with the usual satisfaction, more disturbingly, came the prick of guilt.

"Prick" being the operative word. . . .

Yeah, the butt squeeze was a dick move, but he loathed being on the back foot. Hated feeling out of control. Most especially when he was the one who was supposed to have the advantage. Most especially when he fucking *needed* the advantage.

Monaco was Conrad's territory, and if Alex wanted this mission to go the way he wanted it to he was going to need *all* the advantage he could get. And if that meant reminding one bodyguard of her place, then that's what he'd do.

"I can do whatever the fuck I want," he murmured, still smiling at her, not bothering to keep the harsh note of anger from his voice. "This is my club, sweetheart, and I don't have to answer to you. So how about you get upstairs and leave me to do what I normally do."

A glint shone bright in her gaze for a second before her expression wiped clean. "Of course. I will assume you are safe here then." Then she turned fully to him and put her hands on his shoulders, rising up on her toes to brush her mouth against his cheek. "I'll see you upstairs," she said in a louder tone. "Don't keep me waiting." Stepping back and away from him, she turned and walked over toward the elevator, her hips swaying, her walk more confident than it had been in the plane and yet just as sexy.

Fuck. Every time he thought he'd one-upped her, she matched him with something unexpected.

He tried to forget about her, sequestering himself in the office with Marc for an hour or so to go over the club's figures.

It was performing well, the latest overhaul and redesign having done wonders for patron numbers. Alex had had the whole club redecorated about six months earlier, giving the place a Victorian brothel/opium den feel that involved lots of dim lights and wall sconces, rich, dark wallpaper, and gauzy hangings. The seating, couches and armchairs, recovered in deep red velvet while the low tables, in a dark wood, were slightly more Eastern in influence.

The new look had been a hit according to Marc and certainly the numbers reflected that.

Normally studying successful figures and working out how he could make them even more successful was something Alex enjoyed, but he couldn't seem to concentrate on them right now, that deep unease he couldn't seem to shake settling down into his bones.

Perhaps it was the jet lag—he didn't recover from it as well as he used to.

It's not the jet lag and you know it.

The Fourth Circle's office had nice views over Monte Carlo Bay from its position overlooking Port Hercule, and it was a beautiful winter day, the glittering blue of the Med in contrast to the white sails of the moored superyachts. A nice change from New York's icy gray streets.

But he didn't see the view, because of course it wasn't the jet lag that was making him feel that way. He'd been in Monaco before and hadn't felt this uneasy.

Admittedly, he'd never gone out of his way to confront Conrad before, at least not the way he was intent on doing now. And naturally enough, delving into all that old shit again, turning up all those old memories, was always going to be difficult. But he could cope, right? It didn't matter anymore, after all.

He hadn't been kidding when he'd told Katya about the Fourth Circle party. An impromptu party was just the thing to announce his arrival, a show of strength and confidence. Plus it had the added advantage of screwing with Conrad, who wouldn't be expecting him. It would keep the guy guessing as to why Alex was in Monte Carlo and what his intentions were.

Unless Conrad didn't give a shit. But Alex was betting he did. And he certainly would once he found out that Alex was a player in his precious game.

"Marc," Alex said, turning from the window. "I'm feeling in a party mood. Get the word out I'm throwing a welcome back to Monte Carlo party, but make it an open secret so we have lots of hopefuls turning up at the doors. I want free glasses of champagne to welcome everyone and free cocktails to those most outrageously dressed. Staff need to be fully costumed up and I want Katie-Lee to do her show tonight. You know, the one with the ribbons."

Restlessly he moved from the window over to the opposite side of the office. The whole wall was privacy glass, giving him a prime view of the interior of the main bar.

"Sure." Marc made a few notes on the tablet computer he held in his hand. "Anything else?"

Alex gazed moodily out through the glass. Several bar staff were already out there, getting things ready for the evening. He imagined the place full of people talking and laughing, drinking and having fun. Katie doing her burlesque act. Music filling any spare spaces in the silence. He'd sit in the VIP area—a series of couches on a stage set above the rest of the bar—greeting people he knew, making sure everyone was aware he was back in town. Katya would sit with him and he'd make a big thing of her as his new lover.

And then, once the show was over and done with, he'd go off and find himself something to dull the unease, make him feel in control again. A woman, maybe. He'd have to keep it on the down-low since Katya was supposed to be his lover, but sex usually did the trick and didn't leave him with as bad a hangover as booze. He wasn't as young as he used to be after all.

"No," he said, staring into the empty bar. "I think that's it for now."

As Marc went out of the room to get the organization started, Alex's phone buzzed. Getting it out of his pocket, he glanced at the screen. Another damn text from Zac.

Any new information?

Christ, he'd only just gotten here; what did the guy expect?

No, Alex texted back. *I've only just arrived so I decided to throw a party.*

Which would wind Zac up no end. Then again, the guy was so anal, he practically deserved it.

Almost instantly Alex's phone rang with a call. But not from Zac.

Alex pressed the button, answering it. "This is about the party isn't it?"

"You've got to be kidding me." Eva sounded incensed. "Your stepfather is in the hospital, in a coma. Gabriel and

Honor are in hiding in case some bastard comes gunning for Honor. And you're throwing a fucking party?"

Anger rose inside him, but he fought it down because Eva had no idea what he was dealing with here, the demons he had to wrestle. The fact that in two days' time he was going to have to face the man who'd hurt him. Who'd held his head down over a shitty bathroom vanity and jerked his jeans and underwear down. Who'd forced himself inside Alex while he'd cried at the pain. At the humiliation. Wept fucking tears that had been still on his cheeks when the prick had finished, evidence of his weakness.

And afterwards kept quiet so the father he'd adored would never know what a victim his son had turned out to be. So *no one* ever knew.

Including Eva King.

"Relax," he said, his voice soothing while inside he felt anything but. "There's a private cocktail party in a couple of days for Apocalypse players to meet each other and to scope out the venue. I could go check it out tonight, but visiting any earlier would look strange and possibly indicate a lack of confidence. This is all about power plays, Eva, and those I'm very good at indeed."

There was a grumpy silence down the other end of the line. Then she said, "This is important, Alex. It's important to me."

He almost said it, almost asked why. But he didn't. Because maybe it would confirm what he suspected, that he and Eva shared a common experience. And he didn't want to know that if so, especially when it wasn't the kind of experience you wanted to share with anyone at all, let alone a friend.

So all he said was, "Trust me, Eva."

There was more silence. A difficult one this time, and he found himself tensing, preparing for confidences he didn't want to hear.

But like he hadn't asked the question, she didn't offer anything more other than, "Wonderful. I guess I have no choice." Then she ended the call without another word.

Katya woke with a start and lay there blinking up at a very red-looking ceiling, taking a couple of seconds to orient herself. Which was a couple of seconds more than normal.

Damn jetlag.

Slowly, she sat up, then swung her legs off the bed and onto the floor, allowing herself another look around the room to make sure everything was as she'd left it.

The décor was so overblown she hadn't at first known what to make of it. The walls were papered with some kind of Chinese-style pattern in red and gold, the floorboards polished wood and scattered with brightly colored silk Persian rugs. And taking up center stage in the middle of the room was a massive, intricately carved four-poster bed hung with red silk curtains. The quilt on the bed was almost the same color, patterned with gold, the sheets beneath black silk.

It was clearly a room designed for seduction. And that wasn't even taking into account the bathroom, with its huge circular sunken copper bath, big enough for at least five people, and shower obviously designed for a football team.

This was supposed to be Alex's personal apartment and the contrast between this and his penthouse in New York couldn't be more pronounced. In New York there were massive windows, light, and clean lines. Here was sensual opulence, self-indulgence, and excess.

She didn't like it, preferring simplicity and practicality. But then that was Alex St. James's creed: everything in moderation except moderation.

The General, brought up in Soviet Russia, would have been appalled.

Sliding off the bed, Katya glanced down at her watch.

Looked like her short nap to catch up on missed sleep had lasted for much longer than she'd intended–she'd slept a whole three hours.

The sound of the shower came from the bathroom and for a second every sense she possessed went still, listening. Poised to deal with any unexpected intruders.

And then her brain caught up.

Alex must have come back to the apartment. Which meant he'd returned while she'd been asleep.

Unease shifted inside her. She didn't normally sleep so heavily and had trained herself to wake up at the slightest sound. Yet he'd come in and gone through into the bathroom without waking her.

She took a breath, forcing aside the feeling. She had more practical things to think about anyway, such as getting a proper briefing from her more irritating by the moment boss.

He'd steadfastly refused to talk to her the rest of the flight from New York, involving himself with paperwork that he ostentatiously spread all over the table. She didn't know why that was, only that it must have had something to do with her little power play and that he wasn't happy about it. Strange when her proving she could play the part he'd asked her to was supposed to be the whole point.

And then there'd been that instance downstairs as they'd arrived, when he'd been quite clearly angry with her for questioning his schedule.

She couldn't work *that* out either. The squeeze to her buttock had been unexpected and unwarranted. But she'd seen the glint in his eyes as he'd delivered it. He was putting her in her place, no question.

Because you got to him.

Katya looked toward the bathroom. The sound of the shower had ceased.

Had she? And, if so, in what way?

She frowned, disturbed by how satisfying she found that thought. And by how much she wanted to do it again. Which was complete madness. This wasn't about her. This was about the mission.

The door to the bathroom opened abruptly and Alex strode out, his black hair still wet, curls of it sticking to his neck. All he wore was a towel.

Katya felt something inside her sit up and take notice, wanting to watch him. Odd. She'd seen him shirtless many times before. Yet . . . she couldn't seem to stop herself from noting the hard-cut muscle of his torso and the way the water drops on his skin only seemed to highlight the intriguing dips and hollows of his chest and abs.

Her fingers itched, as she remembered the softness of his mouth and roughness of stubble. . . .

No. He was an impressive physical specimen, it was true, but that was all.

He didn't say a word to her, stopping in front of the closet where the Fourth Circle staff had put away all her and Alex's clothing earlier in a flurry of activity. The doors of the closet were the same red and gold Chinese silk as the walls, and when he pulled them open she saw the insides of the doors were mirrored.

Had he even seen her? Did he know she was awake?

She opened her mouth to speak only to have the words die in her throat as he dropped his towel.

"Good morning," he said casually, not turning around. "Or should I say good evening. Did you have a good nap? By the way, you have the cutest little snores when you're asleep."

Katya frowned. She'd seen plenty of naked men before, both during her training and afterwards. The sight had never affected her in any way and didn't do so now. So what was with the towel drop? He was always calculating in his actions, which meant he was trying to do something. Prove a point. But what was it? Was he trying to embarrass her perhaps?

Folding her arms, Katya let her gaze drift down his bare back, watching the graceful play of his deltoids as he reached for a drawer inside the closet, taking out a pair of black boxers. Letting herself look lower still, over his narrow hips and muscular buttocks, long, lean thighs—

Are you sure it doesn't affect you?

"Something I can help you with?"

Her head came up with a jerk, his intense blue gaze meeting hers in the mirror.

And, oh God, she could feel heat rising to her skin. A blush. How . . . . strange. And, even stranger, the fact that he'd caught her watching him made her want to look away. She didn't, though. To do so would betray the fact that his nakedness had affected her, and it hadn't.

One corner of his mouth lifted. Yes, as she thought. This was another of his games.

"No, sir," she said coolly. "I'm merely observing the fact that your exercise regime must be fairly intense."

"Yes, it is." He made no effort to put on his underwear, merely standing there, studying her in the mirror. "You're a little flushed, darling. What's the matter?"

"Nothing's the matter." She lifted her chin. "I was hoping for that briefing."

"Ah yes, that." Without any hurry at all, he stepped into his boxers and pulled them up, then reached for a hanger that held a tuxedo jacket and a pair of black pants. "It'll have to wait until after this party tonight."

Frustration edged out the heat in her cheeks and the itch in her fingers. "I'm going to have to insist. How can I be expected to perform my duties adequately without the proper information?"

"Oh, *you're* going to have to insist, are you?" He pulled on the pants, tugging up the zipper and buttoning them, then reaching to pull a plain white shirt off another hanger. Turning, he faced her, shrugging on the shirt but not doing it up, his chest bare. "Perhaps you've forgotten you're employed by me? Perhaps you need a reminder?"

She could hear the edge in his voice. So he was angry. Still. "Have I done something to offend you?" she asked bluntly.

"What makes you say that?"

"You seem . . . angry. And you're standing around . . ."— she gestured at him—". . . naked–at least more naked than usual. Also, downstairs earlier you pinched me."

"I'm not angry. I'm merely standing around naked because we need to be comfortable in each other's presence. And I pinched you earlier because we were in the foyer of my club and you were arguing with me about schedules. I had to do something to remind you of your place. In fact, you're damn lucky I didn't call that a mistake and demand my forfeit." His voice was smooth, the edge gone.

"I was careful. No one heard me ask."

"Nevertheless. My lovers don't concern themselves with my schedule, so don't mention it in public again. Now." He turned back to the closet. "My party will be well under way soon and we need to make an entrance. So why don't you go change into something a little less comfortable."

So, not even an hour into this and she'd made yet another mistake. God, who knew that acting a part that appeared to be so simple, would turn out to be so difficult? For the success of this mission, she was going to have to do better.

"Indeed," she said. "Did you have something specific in mind?"

He was leafing through the hangers, examining the quite frankly excessive collection of dresses and gowns he'd brought along for her. "I think perhaps . . . this."

It was not, much to her relief, the shimmering golden

gown, but the green silk cocktail dress with the whisper-thin straps. Which meant no bra and, because the skirt was short, no thigh holster either.

"Of course," she said levelly. "If you'll give me five minutes, I'll put it on."

He came over and laid the dress on the bed, then turned, the look in his eyes glinting. "I would do it now if I were you. We don't want to be late."

"Certainly." She paused, waiting for him to leave the room. But he didn't move and a slow realization began to dawn inside of her.

God in heaven. He wanted her to get dressed in front of him.

Her shock must have been obvious, because he said smoothly, "Like I said, we need to be comfortable with each other, Katya mine, and a little mutual nakedness definitely helps that along."

She'd undressed in front of people all the time in the army. There was no privacy in an army barracks after all. Yes, it had only been in front of women, but that didn't matter. Her body was a well-maintained, well-oiled machine and she'd never been self-conscious or embarrassed about it. But this was different. Alex wasn't a fellow soldier; he was a client, her employer.

A man . . .

His gaze was bright edged, a shard of blue glass. And she knew that despite what he'd said, he *was* angry. And that he was punishing her for the slip down in the foyer.

By rights she should be offended and outraged at his suggestion. Yet it wasn't either of those emotions that gripped her but something else. A strange thrill. A sense of her own power like the one she'd had on the plane. Almost as if she wanted to be naked in front of him just to see what his response would be. A challenge . . .

He was so arrogant. So insolent. Well, if he was expecting some kind of protest from her, he was out of luck. She wasn't going to give him one.

"Of course, sir," she said calmly.

Katya stepped back from him, and keeping her eyes on a point somewhere in the middle of the tanned skin of his chest, she began to unbutton the tight white blouse she wore in brisk, economical movements. Taking it off, then folding it neatly on the bed. She'd gotten rid of her shoes before her nap, so she proceeded straight on to unzipping her skirt and pushing it down, folding that neatly too and putting it on top of the blouse.

She could feel his surprise like a pulse in the air and a deep pleasure twisted inside her. Being able to surprise him shouldn't matter to her, but for some reason it did. It made her feel strong in a way that had nothing to do with physical strength or with following orders. With being a perfect soldier. Perhaps she should have questioned it, yet she didn't. It made her want to push even more.

Ignoring him, she reached behind herself to unhook her bra, slipping the straps off her shoulders, dropping the bra on top of her skirt.

Alex said nothing. But she could feel him watching her, could sense his surprise deepening into shock. It made her feel even more powerful.

Katya put her hands on her hips and pushed down her plain black underwear without hesitation. She stepped out of it, folding it as neatly as she'd folded everything else and putting it on top of the skirt. Then she turned to face him, completely naked, and looked him in the eye.

He stood there very still, the expression on his face taut. That angry glitter had faded completely from his eyes and she had the sense that he was struggling to keep himself composed and his gaze on hers, to not look down the length of her body.

That he was even trying not to was a victory she hadn't

anticipated. That feeling of power spread through her, un-familiar and unexpected. How was it that she could stand naked in front of a fully clothed man and yet be the one with the advantage? How could she be the one holding all the cards?

However that worked, she would take it.

"Do you mind if I have a shower first, sir?" she asked coolly. "I'd appreciate it if so."

"Go." The word was brusque and rough. "Have your shower. I'll be waiting in the lounge."

And this time it was he who turned away.

He who left the room without a word.

CHAPTER SEVEN

Shame and lust sat in Alex's gut. An uncomfortable, volatile mix. Years ago he'd sworn he'd never let himself feel it again, not after what had happened in his father's casino. Alex had almost drowned in humiliation back then, the shame of the rape a piece of sharp glass that kept cutting him to shreds even after he'd escaped to Gabriel's scummy apartment.

His only comfort then had been the fact that no one knew about it. But then he'd gotten the news of his father's suicide and he'd wondered if somehow Conrad had told him. And he had . . .

But no. Daniel St. James couldn't have known. Because surely Conrad wouldn't have been so brazen. Whatever, it didn't stop the guilt from eating away at Alex for that too. For the way he'd run, escaping without a word. Leaving behind the father he'd loved and who'd needed him.

From then on he'd decided that if he wanted to survive the guilt and the shame, if he wanted to leave it behind forever, he'd have to end his own existence too. Not suicide, since he couldn't quite bring himself to do that, but nevertheless finding an end somehow. A way to stop being Alexander St. James, the good son, a credit to his beloved father and light of his proud mother's life. Adored older brother to his little sister.

So he had. He'd become someone else entirely. Strong and confident. Someone who did whatever the hell he wanted and didn't give a shit about anything or anyone, still less be ashamed of who he was.

Yet for the first time in years, as he sat with Katya in the palatial VIP area of the Fourth Circle, he felt that shame again like a hot coal in his gut.

The party had gotten to the raucous stage, packed with the rich and famous of Monaco who'd turned out for Alex's secret party in droves. The dim lighting of wall sconces and Eastern lampshades of colored glass cast glittering reflections off gowns and luminous bare skin, jeweled cuff links and expensive watches. People lounged on red velvet couches or sprawled in large armchairs if they were lucky to find seating. If they weren't they leaned against the opulent red silk walls or stood in groups if they could find a clear space.

Above the crowd, hanging from silken ribbons attached to the ceiling, Katie-Lee, dressed in nothing but a see-through sequined red bikini, did her burlesque act, the ribbons wrapping around her long legs as she spun and stretched like a trapeze artist.

On the red velvet couch beside him, Katya sat with her legs elegantly crossed, encased in the green silk cocktail dress that left most of her shoulders and a long expanse of thigh exposed. Her hands were folded in her lap, resting on her matching green silk clutch. He had an arm around her waist and he could feel the warmth of her beneath his palm.

Her muscles were relaxed, but that didn't mean she would be. He knew that sharp gaze would be scanning the room, looking for threats. And the reason her long fingers rested on her clutch was because her weapon was inside it, within reach.

Since they'd come down to the party, she hadn't put a foot wrong, acting the part of his girlfriend to perfection. Before they'd even gotten to Monaco, Alex had worked out a small fiction about where they'd met, at a Second Circle party, and what she did for a living—a model for *Russian Vogue* visiting the States. No one would enquire closer. No one would be interested in yet another of his girlfriends.

The VIP area was full of people lounging around on the other couches. Acquaintances of his, and others he'd admitted for political reasons. A famous actress. A singer. A media magnate and his entourage.

Alex had been subtly trying to get information about Conrad and the upcoming Apocalypse game from various different people, but he hadn't learned anything useful. At least nothing he wouldn't be able to find out at the upcoming reception in any case.

A glass of vodka sat on the table in front of him, and even though he was on to his third it still wasn't enough to douse the ember of shame that refused to burn out.

The one that told him he'd gone too far with Katya up in the bedroom. That he'd crossed a line.

He turned his head, looking out over the crowds of people, very conscious of the woman who sat beside him, as simple and elegant in her green cocktail dress as a stalk of fresh grass in a field of overblown hibiscus flowers.

He knew now what lay beneath all that green silk: Long, lean muscles. Smooth, pale skin. Small, perfectly round breasts. A thatch of silky blond curls.

She'd stood there naked and proud, with her chin raised, steadily meeting his gaze. Her cheeks had been flushed, but she hadn't been embarrassed in the slightest. In her eyes had only been courage and determination, a strength of will he'd sensed yet not fully understood until then.

That had been the moment he'd felt the shame creep over

him. Shame at himself for what he'd made her do, for punishing her when it was his own unease about Conrad he was taking out on her.

And along with that shame, a spear of complete and absolute lust.

Because she was beautiful, all sleek muscle and a honed strength that only seemed to emphasize her femininity. Christ, he'd wanted her. In a way he hadn't wanted anyone else in years, and that was one hell of a fucking problem.

The balance of power had shifted between them and he'd felt it the moment she'd taken her clothes off, without protest. Without embarrassment. That had been the moment he'd lost the game. The moment she'd won.

And that rendered her completely untouchable. When it came to lovers, he *had* to be the one in charge, the one who held all the power. There was no negotiation, no compromise. If he wasn't calling the shots, then he didn't get laid. Simple as that.

Katya shifted beside him and he felt the muscles of her thigh bunch, then relax beneath his palm. Strong, sleek. A beautiful female animal. Trained to fight. To kill. To protect . . .

An ache clenched hard inside him and he couldn't breathe. How long had it been since he'd wanted something he couldn't let himself have? Too long. Perhaps he'd never done so. But however long it had been, he couldn't have her. Completely apart from the fact that she was his employee, she would never surrender willingly to him. And he couldn't have it any other way.

Alex let his hand drop away from her, moving to put some space between them, leaning forward to get his vodka and take a sip. He was aware of her glancing at him, that familiar crease between her fair brows. Probably puzzling about him again.

Christ, he was a prick. He shouldn't have even started this game with her. She wasn't a player like he was. She had far too much integrity for the kind of shit he liked to pull. Far too much honor.

Beneath the scent of expensive aftershave and perfume, spilled alcohol and the sweat of too many people, he could smell the sharp, faint scent of oranges—

Disturbed by the combination of shame and lust, by the way it reminded him of too many things he'd spent too many years trying to forget, he abruptly got to his feet.

"Alex?" She spoke quietly and yet he still heard her through the noise around him, her accent caressing his name like a prayer. "Where are you going?"

"To get another drink," he muttered. "I'll be back."

With his staff circulating around the place, he didn't actually need to move to get a drink, but he couldn't sit there with her any longer, not with that fucking mess of emotions sitting inside him like a lead weight.

Going down the stairs of the stage that set the VIP area apart from the masses, he began to thread his way through the crowd, moving toward the bar. People greeted him as he went and he stopped to chat every so often, smiling, acting the gracious host, pretending, like he always did, that he was having the time of his life.

When he got to the polished black wood of the bar, he turned and leaned against it, staring out over the crowd, his heart beating fast. He didn't look toward the VIP area and Katya, keeping his gaze on the shifting mass of people.

He felt overwhelmed all of a sudden. As if he couldn't stand the noise, couldn't stand the crowds. As if he wanted to be somewhere quiet and dark and silent. Alone.

"Mr. St. James?"

He turned sharply. Beside him a beautiful blonde stood leaning against the bar. She wore a red sequined dress with a plunging neckline that displayed the curves of her generous breasts to perfection. Her pouty mouth was the same color as her dress and was turned up in a seductive smile.

And he felt relieved because this was familiar. This kind of game he'd played many times before, and she was clearly a woman who knew all the rules.

He leaned his hip against the bar. "What can I do for you, sweetheart?"

Her eyelashes fell halfway, the deep blue of her eyes glinting up at him. "Oh, I just wanted to say thanks for the great party. This place is fantastic." Her accent was British, London from the sounds of it.

Not as sexy as Katya's.

Alex pushed thoughts of Katya from his head. Perhaps this was what he needed to get rid of all these unwanted emotions. A woman, rather than vodka. Sex, his other drug of choice.

"Glad you think so. Can I get you a drink? Champagne maybe? On the house of course."

Her smile deepened and it was as fake as her breasts, but he didn't care. He wasn't after sincerity. Or integrity. Or honor. Or pride. He didn't even particularly want her. Sometimes all he really craved was oblivion.

"How did you know?" She moved closer, put a hand on the bar next to his, her fingers almost brushing the tips of his own. "I'd love a glass of—"

"Alex," a smoky Russian voice said. "There you are. I wondered where you'd got to."

A tall, slender body moved in between him and the woman in the red dress, an arm winding around his waist in a proprietary fashion. Green eyes met his, a spark of what looked like anger glinting in the depths. "You should not leave me like that, darling," Katya purred. "I was all alone."

He didn't move, a shock of desire swamping him. A de-

sire that hadn't been there until she'd shown up. Behind
Katya, the woman in the red dress was frowning, a dis-
tinctly pissed-off look on her face.

Jesus. Though he never committed himself to any
single lover, he didn't usually go off and start flirting with
someone else while the woman he was sleeping with was
in the vicinity. But of course he wasn't sleeping with Katya,
and he'd forgotten for an instant who she was supposed
to be. This time it was his fault. He was the one who'd
slipped up.

Meeting Katya's gaze, he held himself still, trying to
ignore the way every sense he had seemed to be attuned
to her arm around his waist and the nearness of her body
to his. "My apologies, sweetheart," he drawled. "I was just
getting a drink. As you can see."

She put a hand to his chest, letting it rest there. "I'm not
sure it's a drink you're after." Turning her head slightly to
include the woman standing behind her, she said, "Sorry,
but I'm going to have to steal my boyfriend away. We have
some business to attend to."

A flash of anger crossed the blonde's face, anger that
was out of proportion to a simple thwarted seduction, but
Alex didn't have time to work out why that was because
Katya had stepped back, was lacing her hand in his and
starting to lead him away.

He didn't protest, allowing her to pull him through the
crowd a little way before he stopped dead, pulling her up
short. "Nice show of possessiveness, Katya mine. You do
the jealous girlfriend very well. Did you practice that in
the shower?"

She turned on him, the lines of her face set, a fierce look
in her eyes. "You need to come with me," she said quietly,
forcefully, ignoring his tone. "I have to talk to you."

A petulant, childish anger flared into life, but he fought
it down, determined not to give in to the emotions she

seemed to draw from him so easily. Raising a brow, he said, "And since when do you get to issue the orders?"

She stepped closer, specks of angry gold glinting in her eyes. "Since I've been given the job of protecting your life. And since you don't seem to take that very seriously, I have to."

"But my life isn't in any—"

"We need to have a discussion, Alex," she said fiercely, enunciating his name very clearly. "And we need to have it now."

What the hell? What had brought this on?

A petty thought occurred to him. Perhaps she really was jealous.

Why the fuck would you think that? For her to be jealous she'd have to feel something for you, and she doesn't.

Jesus, this situation really was starting to slip out of his control if he found that disappointing. Time to claim some of the power back.

"Sure," he said easily. "We can go to my office. It's near the bar."

Without waiting to see if she would follow, he turned and headed through the crowds of people, going around the bar and toward the expanse of mirrored privacy glass, partially obscured by velvet curtains.

He pulled aside the curtain to find the door handle, keying in his personal code to unlock the door. Then he held it open and stood aside, waiting as Katya went past him into the dim office beyond.

Pulling the door closed after him, the sound of the club instantly muting, he hit the light switch, hidden lights in the ceiling casting a wash of soft illumination over the room.

"Okay," he said, "so I fucked up with that woman. I'm sorry; that was my mistake."

Katya put her hands behind her back, falling into her "at ease" stance, giving no sign she was satisfied or otherwise with his apology. "You said your life wasn't in any danger, but quite frankly, sir, you have no idea. That woman you were speaking with? I overheard her in the ladies' bathroom talking to someone on the phone. She said she was going to 'get closer' to you."

Shock moved through him, slow and thick. He took a breath, struggling to get his head together. "What? When was this?"

"Earlier in the evening. Just after we came down. I've been watching her all evening. She tried to get into the VIP area but was denied."

Holy shit, he hadn't even noticed. "Why didn't you tell me sooner?"

"You were in no immediate danger and I had the threat under control."

Fucking hell. "Did you get any hint of a name?" he demanded. "Any clue as to who she was talking to?"

"No, sir," Katya answered crisply, fully in soldier mode now. "I only heard her as she was leaving the bathroom. By the time I followed, she'd already ended the call."

Alex turned, stalking toward his desk and running a hand through his hair, needing to move. Needing to think. His thoughts felt sluggish, the alcohol sitting like acid in his stomach.

So, clearly that woman had not been after a random hookup. She'd targeted him for a reason. But why? And who had sent her? What did they want? No one had known he was even in Monaco until this evening, so whoever had sent her had to be someone in Monte Carlo—

Fucking Conrad South. It had to be.

Alex's heartbeat accelerated, his mouth drying. He put his hands on the edge of the desk and leaned against it, trying to hold on to something because, Jesus, it was clear he didn't have a good grasp on anything else at the moment.

You fucking idiot. You weren't paying attention, were you? You were too busy playing with her . . .

Behind him Katya said, "I'm here to protect you, sir. But I can't protect you if I don't know the direction the bullet might come from. Which means I need that briefing. I need to know why we're here and I need to know now."

Katya stared at Alex as he leaned over the desk, his shoulders hunched, his arms rigid. This was about more than a poker game; she was sure of it. Because if she didn't know any better, she'd have said that Alex St. James was afraid. He'd never appeared afraid of a game before, which meant there was something about *this* game that was getting to him. This was personal in some way.

He didn't say anything, his posture so full of tension he was practically vibrating with it.

Outside the office the bass thump of the music was so deep she could feel it in her chest. But the room must have had some kind of heavy-duty noise dampening going on, because that was the only sound. It was strange to be in here in the quiet while outside a party was going on.

The office was as opulent and excessive as the rest of the club, lots of wood paneling and deep red velvet curtains over the windows. Tall bookshelves and a claw-foot armchair near the desk, the décor reminiscent of a Victorian gentleman's study.

Alex didn't say anything and she thought for a moment that she wasn't going to get her explanation. Then he said, "We are here for a poker game. But . . ." He paused.

She waited, watching him, the light glancing off his inky hair.

He'd been silent with her ever since he'd walked out of

the bedroom. Even when they'd gone downstairs and he'd introduced her to people as they'd sat on that overblown red velvet couch, his arm around her in a possessive show. But he hadn't spoken to her directly or made one of his subtle digs. He hadn't even looked at her.

It was clear her victory up in the bedroom had changed things between them, and she could take a guess as to why: Alex St. James didn't like to lose. So now he was putting distance between them, as if he'd decided he didn't want to continue the game they were playing. And that was disappointing. Because for some insane reason, she wanted to keep playing it.

The silence was so loud. Deep as the bass of the music.

"The organizer of the game is a man called Conrad South," Alex said finally. "He owns the Four Horsemen casino. He's . . . an old enemy of mine."

That she knew already due to her research, but not the personal connection. An enemy. Interesting.

Katya frowned at Alex's strong back. "You don't want to play." It came out more as a statement than a question, since it was obvious to her that he didn't want to.

"No." His voice was soft. "I don't."

"So why are you?"

"It's a long story."

"I would like to hear it."

He didn't turn, but she could hear the soft outrush of his breath. "We think there's something more than gambling going on in Conrad's casino. I'm taking part in the game as a bit of reconnaissance, since no one else can play poker as well as I can."

"We?"

"My friends . . . Zac, Eva, and Gabriel."

Katya studied the rise of Alex's broad shoulders, his bent head. "How do you know there's something more going on?"

Slowly, he shifted, turning around to lean back against the desk, his long fingers curling over the edge of the wood. His jacket was open, his shirt unbuttoned at the throat. The light from above shadowed the flawless bone structure of his face, leaving his eyes in darkness. He wasn't smiling now and she had the impression that she was seeing yet another layer of him. Perhaps the man he truly was, not the debauched playboy he showed to the world.

A deeper, more thoughtful kind of man.

Curiosity twisted inside her. As if he were a jeweled box she wanted to open to find out what was inside.

"Like I said, it's a long story. Around a month or so ago, Gabriel got involved with my sister and found out a few of my family's nasty secrets. Like the fact my father and some friends of his were involved in an underground casino years ago. Not just gambling, but drugs and prostitution too, all kinds of shit. Dad owned the casino, ran up a lot of debt. He . . . committed suicide after it all got out of hand." Alex's voice was weirdly flat, toneless. Like he was reciting a story. "One of his friends stepped in to cover up his links to the casino and ended up marrying my mother. Gabe discovered this guy–my damn stepfather–was still laundering money for this fucking casino. We were hoping to discover more about it, but my stepfather had the bad manners to get himself shot before he could give Gabe any information."

It took a moment to process. Alex's stepfather shot. Drugs. Prostitution. She hadn't known what to expect as an explanation, but it wasn't that.

His father dead by his own hand . . . *Like Mama* . . .

"Sir, I . . ." she began, then stopped. What could she say? She had nothing to add and certainly didn't want to get into comparing their losses. From the sounds of it his father had been weak like her mother, and there was nothing Katya could say to that.

Yet she was aware of a dull, sympathetic anger inside her.

He was betrayed too. . . .

"You don't know what to say?" Alex finished for her. "Well, you don't have to say anything. And you don't have to be sorry. My father's life was complicated and . . ." Another hesitation. "I guess you could say he chose the easy way out. Anyway, that's got nothing to do with what's going on with this poker game." The words were level, but she could hear the undercurrent of anger beneath them. It was obvious Alex's father's death had hurt him.

Like your mother's death hurt you.

Katya's jaw firmed. No. She was not hurt and she did not grieve. Not anymore. "I understand," she said.

"I don't think you do. But it doesn't matter. My father's long gone and I barely knew my stepfather. In fact, I haven't seen my family for nineteen years."

"I haven't seen mine for five." The words came out before she could stop them, and the look on his face sharpened.

"Why not?" he asked.

She wasn't prepared for the shift in focus, though she should have expected it. But it was too late to avoid the question now, especially when he got that searching look in his eyes. Except . . . it didn't look like he was hunting for a weakness this time, only being curious.

"My father is a soldier and a government man," she said, reluctant. "And he refused to help me find Mikhail, even when I begged him to. He told me that the needs of our country outweighed the life of one man and I should forget him."

She still remembered the iron in her father's voice, the stony expression in his brown eyes.

He'd always taught her that loyalty was more important than anything else. More important than love or hate.

Yet he'd been prepared to put politics ahead of the lives of his countrymen, his ambition ahead of loyalty. That knowledge had been the first crack in the bedrock of her unthinking obedience to him.

"Outweighed the needs of his daughter too," Alex said quietly. And it wasn't a question.

Katya ignored the unease that bit deep at the softly worded statement. "No, my needs were not relevant. He was supposed to be loyal to his fellow soldiers. And he wasn't. He put his own political ambitions ahead of lives."

"Is that why you left Russia?"

The dull anger in her chest sharpened. "Yes. If he wasn't going to help Mikhail, I would find someone who would."

"And Mikhail is *that* important to you?"

"Loyalty is important to me. But what has this got to do with the poker game?" The change of topic was graceless, but she didn't care. Exchanging the truths of their lives with Alex was even more uncomfortable than the games he played with her.

If he was disappointed with her change of subject, he gave no sign. "Tremain–that's my stepfather–shoved a pair of silver dice into Gabe's hand after he got shot."

"Silver dice?" She stopped. "Oh, the ones on your table?"

"Yes."

She studied his face. There was no expression at all on it. "What is their significance?"

"The Apocalypse game is by invitation only. And those dice are the invitation."

"And why is this game important? What do you hope to find?"

"Conrad South is one of my father's old college buddies. He has links to the casino my father used to own. Links with my stepfather. Something's going on with them and whatever it is has hurt my friends." He paused. "Has hurt my sister."

The woman Gabriel Woolf was involved with. The woman Alex hadn't seen in nineteen years if what he'd said was true. "But I thought you didn't . . ." Katya stopped, knowing what she was about to say was harsh.

His expression was impenetrable. "I didn't what? Say it, Katya."

"Forgive me, but why should you care? I thought you didn't have any loyalties to anyone."

Unexpectedly he looked away. "Yeah, well, I thought I didn't either. Turns out I do after all." He let out a breath. "But don't worry. Playing in Conrad's fucking game is for my own selfish needs too. I wouldn't want you to start thinking I actually gave a shit."

She frowned at him. That was a lie; she was sure of it. "And what are your needs?"

"That's my business." There was no room for argument in his voice. "All you need to know is that Conrad probably isn't after my blood, so I doubt that woman was going to kill me. I suspect what she wanted was information."

Katya didn't argue. The conversation she'd overheard the woman having in the ladies' room had been enough to prompt Katya into action to protect her employer. But the woman herself hadn't seemed dangerous. Then again, sometimes it paid to be over-cautious, especially if you were unsure of the situation. "So if Mr. South isn't after your blood, why do you need me?"

"Because someone connected to him might be. Especially when I turn up at this game and they figure I'm after some answers. They took a gun to my stepfather in order to protect their secrets; I don't imagine they'll think twice about doing the same to me."

She turned the information over in her head. It all seemed very vague. "And what answers do you hope to find at this poker game? You didn't answer me."

Alex lifted one shoulder in a simple, elegant movement.

"That's because I don't know yet. We have this reception in two days to meet the other players. Perhaps we'll find out more then. At the very least we'll find out what kind of situation we're walking into."

"We, sir?"

His gaze settled on her. "Yes. We. You'll be attending."

Someone fumbled with the door handle to the office all of a sudden and Alex tensed. "Come here, Katya," he ordered curtly.

She was already moving, responding to the order automatically, coming over to where he stood near the desk.

"I'm sorry," he said. "But there's only one reason I bring a woman into this office and it isn't to talk."

Before she could respond, he reached for her, jerking the hem of her dress up to her hips. Then he gripped her, turning her so the edge of the desk pressed against her thighs, and pushed her down over it, pulling her leg up around his lean waist.

She had no time to prepare. No time to protest. One moment they were talking about the poker game; the next she was on her back over the desk, the wool of his tuxedo pants brushing against her inner thighs, his arms braced on either side of her head, his eyes dark as he looked down at her.

The door opened, the sounds of the party going on outside rushing in. And then a startled, "Oh, I'm sorry, Mr. St. James, I—"

"Fuck's sake, Marc," Alex said. "Can't you see I'm busy?"

"Yes, of course," came the other man's voice. Then the sound of the door shutting, the noise of the party once again muted.

Alex didn't move. Staying exactly where he was, his hips pressing between her thighs, his hands braced beside her head, staring down at her, a strangely intense expression on his face.

And for some reason she didn't move either. Because it felt like she was drowning in a flood of sensation. The press of his body between her legs. The brush of the prickly wool of his pants. The hard wood of the desktop beneath her. And heat. So much heat.

Her breath was starting to get short, coming faster, her mouth drying, her heartbeat accelerating wildly. And she was beginning to ache. Down between her thighs, in her sex. A pressure slowly building. It was . . . God . . . unfamiliar, overwhelming. Too much.

All she needed to do would be to lift her hips, flex them a little, and that would bring her into contact with his zipper. She could press herself against him, relieve that ache.

His breath caught as if he'd read her exact thought, his gaze shadowed as he looked down into her eyes.

The tension between them became dense, like they were fathoms deep underwater.

She didn't speak and neither did he. They stared at each other.

He was getting hard; she could feel it, the heat of him like a furnace she wanted to get closer to. Burn herself on. And God, she wanted to move. Tilt her hips just so and her clitoris would be pressing against all that hardness. All that heat.

Her thighs began to tremble, her breathing coming faster, sharper.

Get up. Move away. Stop this now before it's too late.

But she didn't do any of those things. She lay still instead, caught on the edge of something intense. Something that would change her if she moved, if she did what her body was desperately urging her to do.

She couldn't do that, though, couldn't cross that line. And yet . . . she couldn't move away either. Because this feeling, this exquisite, unbearable ache, was unlike anything she'd ever experienced and she just couldn't bring herself to end it.

He knows you want him now.

Of course he knew. Perhaps he'd even known before this. It didn't matter now, though, because now there was no hiding it. The fact that she hadn't protested or made a move to stop him had announced it as clearly as if she'd said it out loud.

But she wasn't alone. He felt it too.

His eyes glittered a deep, intense blue, red staining his perfect cheekbones, and he was looking at her like a starving wolf looks at prey. Hungry. Almost . . . desperate.

She'd never seen him look at any woman that way before.

And still he didn't move. As if he couldn't bear to tear himself away from her and the heat that was building between them.

This was power. This was strength. She could feel it inside her, growing. And she knew that if she wanted to take it, she could have it. And that she could use it over him.

"Alexei . . ." His name in Russian, half a prayer, half a plea.

Abruptly he cursed, a vicious sound in the silence of the room, and shoved himself away from her, taking a few steps, then turning so his back was to her. The tension poured off him in waves, his shoulders tight. "I'm sorry," he said in a rough voice that didn't sound like his. "I'm sorry about what happened up in the bedroom. And I'm sorry about now."

Katya pushed herself up on the desk, her arms trembling, her thighs aching. Dizzy at the sudden break in the atmosphere. "I don't—" she began thickly.

"You go up to bed if you want," he interrupted, his hands moving as he adjusted himself. God, he *had* been hard for her. "I'm going to stay down here for the party. Don't wait up for me."

Then he strode to the door, pulled it open, and went out.

She sat on the desk after he'd gone, waiting until the weakness in her arms, in her legs, had faded. Until the painful ache between her thighs had subsided and her breathing had normalized. It took a lot longer than she'd expected.

Afterwards she let herself out of the office and back into the club.

It was noisy and even more packed than it had been before. And she knew she should stay, that it was her job to do so. But for the first time in two years, she couldn't face being with her client. Sitting in close proximity to him for another few hours, her body gripped by this strange hunger.

It was better to put some distance between them. Give her some time to remember her place. Remember who she was and what she was supposed to be doing.

Being his bodyguard, not his lover.

No matter how much the thought of that intrigues you.

Katya did not let herself think about that. Instead she threaded her way through the crowd and out of the packed bar, returning to Alex's private apartment.

She made herself up a bed on the long black velvet couch in the lounge area, changing out of her green dress and into a tank top and shorts to sleep in.

But even after she'd turned the lights off and settled down to sleep, she couldn't seem to relax.

Because regardless of how many times she told herself she wasn't interested, that her job was more important, that he was a client, her body had woken up and it was hungry.

It wanted Alex.

CHAPTER EIGHT

The Four Horsemen was in an old, historic building near Monte Carlo's famous casino. There was a piazza out front full of expensive sports cars, glossy limousines, and parking valets ready to do their jobs.

The car Marc had organized for them drew up to the wide, sweeping steps of the building. On the lintel overhead, the stone figures of War, Pestilence, Famine, and Death rode into battle, swords held aloft.

Alex didn't look up, but he felt like one of them all the same. Except he didn't have a sword. Or a horse. His only armor his confidence. His success. And the strength he made sure he projected.

It was all a sham, every single iota of it. But that had never stopped him before and it didn't stop him now.

He hadn't seen Conrad South in nineteen years, yet Alex wasn't sixteen anymore. The kid who'd been brought into the casino by his father to watch for card counters had been fourteen, in his first year at high school, his head full of the bright future that lay ahead of him. Whether to be a lawyer like his dad or to follow his true passion and study math.

And then his father had told him about his other life. About a mysterious place where people played games of chance, where fortunes were lost and won. Where people cheated and where Alex's brilliant memory and affinity with numbers were needed to stop it.

He'd been so thrilled to be asked. To be trusted with his father's big secret. To be drawn into this fascinating other world. It had been like being sworn into a special club, and Alex would have done anything to stay a part of it. To prove to his dad that the trust he'd given his son wasn't misplaced.

And as it turned out, you did do anything.

Yeah, he had, his body payment for the debts his father had incurred while running his fabulous casino. Debts Conrad had paid out of his own money and subsequently demanded recompense for.

"Your father won't know," Conrad had whispered to Alex in that cold, echoing bathroom. *"It'll be our little secret. You're doing a good thing, son. You're helping him. Remember that."*

Oh, Alex had remembered it all right. That had been what he'd clung to in the aftermath.

Until his father had killed himself and Alex had had nothing to cling to anymore.

But no, he wasn't thinking about that now. Those minutes in the men's bathrooms of the Lucky Seven casino were only a dim memory. A memory that had no meaning. That didn't touch him.

The car door slammed and he turned on the step, his breath fogging in the cold night air. Katya was coming toward him, a shimmering vision in the golden gown he'd insisted she wear tonight.

And he realized he was wrong. He did have a sword. And she was it. Tall, straight, and gleaming in the dark. Deadly and beautiful, her edges hidden by the scabbard– that gown.

He'd made her wear her hair loose and it hung in a golden fall over her shoulders and down her back, bright as a newly minted coin. She wore a wrap around her shoulders, but he knew they were bare beneath it, the gown clinging to her figure like a slick of molten gold. She wore no jewelry; she didn't need to. With her pale skin, glossy hair, and green eyes, she didn't need gems to sparkle.

He watched her as she came toward him and he felt his cock get hard at the sight.

Two days since that moment in his office, when he'd turned her in his arms and yanked her dress up, pushed her back on the desk. He should never have done it, but it was true that he didn't bring a woman into his office to talk. And if he'd been spotted merely talking to Katya then the gossip would have been rife. Better not to draw attention to her by implying that she was special in some way.

At least that was his story and he was sticking to it.

Yet as she'd lain on her back on the desk, her eyes wide, the wet heat of her pussy pressed against his dick, he'd gotten so hard so quickly that he'd forgotten how to breathe.

He'd never felt a desire like it, not even when she'd stood before him naked upstairs in their bedroom. Pure as a gas flame and twice as hot, it had become even more intense when he'd seen it reflected back at him from the depths of her eyes.

She'd wanted him too.

But, struggling against every instinct he had, he'd held back. There were his ostensible reasons—the "she is my employee and I can't cross the line" bullshit. But there were also deeper, more personal reasons.

What was between them felt too raw, too wild. Too intense. He wanted her too much, an unfamiliar and uncomfortable sensation. One that felt like a weakness he shouldn't have. And though she might eventually have surrendered the control to him in the way he required from his partners, raw passion was not what he wanted. He preferred easy and manageable. Even forgettable. In fact, forgettable sex was the best kind there was because it demanded nothing of him and took nothing in return.

It would not be forgettable with Kaya. So he'd pushed himself away from her and for the past two days he'd busied himself with the day-to-day running of the Nine Circles chain, filling his head up with what he did best: numbers, sales figures, and percentages. And a few online poker games to get his head into the right space.

There had been e-mails from Zac, a few texts from Eva. A phone call from Gabriel and a single text from Honor. But Alex had ignored all of them.

They were all distractions and distractions were the last thing he could afford.

Alex held out his arm and Katya linked hers through his. The scent of oranges wound around him, cutting through the bite of snow in the air.

No, he wasn't going to look to see if she was wearing underwear beneath that gown. Or ask her what she'd been doing with herself the past couple of days he'd been ensconced in his office.

She was only his employee and he didn't need to know those things. What he needed was to stick to the line he'd always drawn and not cross it.

As they walked up the steps, he could feel her gaze on him, studying him.

In his office he'd given her a glimpse as to what they were walking into, the barest of bare bones. But he hadn't been able to tell her the whole of it. And he wouldn't. That kind of truth was one he doled out rarely and only when no one was likely to notice.

Fuck, he'd already given it to Eva not a week earlier. He couldn't bring himself to do it again and certainly not to Katya. All she needed to understand was that Conrad was the enemy. That was it.

As she and Alex approached the entrance, he found he'd

tugged her close, as if he could absorb some of her strength the way he was absorbing the scent of her skin and hair. He should have put some distance between them, but he couldn't quite bring himself to do so.

A man in a black uniform stood by the door, opening it as Alex and Katya approached, ushering them into the casino foyer. It was floored with white marble, the soaring ceiling supporting a massive chandelier that cast glittering light everywhere. A wide, sweeping staircase with a scrolling banister led to the upper floors while ahead of them was a big set of gilded double doors.

Another man waited beside the doors, not Conrad, thank Christ. He was dressed in the black uniform of the casino and he was smiling as they came closer. A smile that faded as he took in Alex.

Good. Although Conrad must know he was in Monaco, he certainly wouldn't be expecting to see Alex walking in through the front doors of his casino, still less as a player in his precious game, and that meant the element of surprise was still on Alex's side.

"Mr. St. James," the man said, inclining his head. "It's an honor to see you here, but this is a private—"

"I know it's a private game. Nevertheless, I believe I'll be playing." Alex took the dice out of his pocket and held them out.

The man looked down, his expression wiping clean at the sight of the silver dice sitting in Alex's palm.

The Apocalypse game was legendary in poker circles. Seven players only and only the best players at that. It had always been a given that Conrad, as the host, chose the players, but Alex was starting to suspect that wasn't true. That all was not quite as it seemed. After all, Guy Tremain wasn't a poker player. And that made it puzzling that he'd had a pair of Apocalypse dice in his possession.

Unless it wasn't Conrad who chose the players and sent out those dice.

Alex studied the man's face, but clearly Conrad had employed him for a reason, because Alex couldn't tell what he was thinking as he glanced down at Alex's palm. "Of course," the man said expressionlessly. "Please, go on through. Mr. South will be there shortly."

He stepped forward and opened the double doors, ushering Katya and Alex through into another room.

"He didn't expect you," Katya said quietly in Alex's ear. "And neither does Mr. South, correct?"

"No." Alex scanned around the room as the doors shut behind them. "Conrad would never have invited me, which means he doesn't know I'm coming."

The room looked like a reception room in a French palace. Polished parquet flooring gleamed, Persian silk rugs adding warmth. Delicate gilt couches and armchairs were arranged at intervals, with low tables between them. A massive fireplace was set in one wall, a fire burning in the grate, filling the room with warmth and a welcoming glow. Thick gold brocade curtains covered the windows, adding to the drama and richness of the décor.

A large number of other people were sitting on the various chairs or talking in groups. The men were in tuxedos, the women in glittering gowns. Waitstaff with trays moved between the groups, dispensing drinks and canapés. Music played, classical and refined.

Jesus, what pretentious bullshit all of this was.

Several people turned toward them as they moved into the room, and he could feel their gaze weighing him, sizing him up. Pricing him. He knew some of them–big players in the poker world–but not the others. Perhaps they were hangers-on or part of the players' entourages.

Conrad wasn't among them.

A deep, cold unease gripped Alex and he had to take a slow breath to fight it back down again. Disengaging his arm from Katya's, he slid it around her waist instead, urging her closer, making it clear to the rest of the players in the room who she belonged to and what she was doing here.

As his fingers rested on her hip, he felt the smooth fabric of her gown. No fucking underwear.

And just like that his focus changed, shifted. From the sense of threat and challenge in the room, of other players measuring him, judging him, the way most games started, to the warmth of the woman next to him. To the feel of the firm muscle of her thigh and the knowledge that she was completely bare underneath all that molten gold fabric.

Holy fuck. When the game actually started he was going to have to get her to wear something else; otherwise he'd never be able to concentrate properly.

A waiter approached them with a tray full of champagne flutes. Alex waited until Katya had taken one, then took another for himself.

"Is Mr. South here?" she murmured as she took a sip.

"No. He'll wait until everyone's arrived and then he'll come and greet us all in person."

"How do you know?"

"I've heard people talk about it. The Apocalypse is moderately famous in poker circles. Only the elite are invited."

Down one end of the room was a bar, the light glittering off the mirrored glass wall behind it where all the bottles were stacked on shelves. Nearby a small nook had been created, partially shielded from the rest of the room by antique painted screens.

Liking the idea of a bit of privacy, Alex headed in that direction and was satisfied to discover that one of the armchairs faced the rest of the room, giving whoever was sitting in it a good view while at the same time remaining screened from curious glances.

"Who are all these people?" Katya asked as she sat down in the armchair next to him, placing her wine on the table while keeping a tight hold on the little gold clutch that he knew held her weapon. "Are they players too?"

"Some will be. There are only seven players in the Apocalypse. The other people here are either part of the players' entourages or they're friends of Conrad's. The Apocalypse reception is quite a big deal in Monte Carlo and getting an invite is problematic."

Katya lifted her wineglass, but he could see she wasn't actually drinking, her sharp, green gaze scanning around the room. "That man over there by the fire is a mercenary," she murmured. "Or at least, he was. And I suspect he is also carrying a weapon."

Alex glanced over in the direction she'd indicated. A tall, massively built man stood alone by the fireplace, a small tumbler full of amber liquid in one hand. With his dark hair shorn close to his skull, a nose that had clearly been broken a number of times, and a scar twisting his mouth, he looked out of place. Like a convict escaped from prison rather than a wealthy poker player. He should have been in camo gear with ammunition belts slung over his shoulders and toting a machine gun rather than dressed in a tuxedo, sipping from a delicately cut crystal tumbler.

Alex leaned back in his armchair. "How do you know? He looks like one, I'll give you that."

"The tattoos on his hand."

Alex narrowed his gaze, spotting black ink covering the man's fingers. "And the weapon?"

"The line of his jacket gives it away." She leaned back in her chair too, but Alex knew it wasn't because she was relaxed. "Why would there be a mercenary here and why is he armed?"

Christ, he didn't know. But he didn't like it; that was for sure. He hadn't heard of armed mercenaries at any of Conrad's receptions. "Anyone else with weapons?"

Katya swept another slow glance over the room. "The waiter who served us had one. As to the rest . . . I'm not sure." A familiar crease appeared between her brows. "I don't like this."

Alex didn't much like it either, but there was little they could do about it short of leaving. And he couldn't do that, at least not yet. "I haven't heard of anyone getting shot at in an Apocalypse game," he said lightly. "I hardly think I'll be the first."

She looked at him. "I can't make that assumption. Assuming anything can end up being fatal."

He raised a brow at her. "So what do you suggest we do?"

"We can leave."

"I can't. Displaying anything less than total confidence will undermine my position. That guy is probably there to psych people out anyway. Poker games are one big mind fuck, Katya mine; never forget that."

Her mouth tightened, but she said nothing, her gaze once more going to the big man beside the fire. "I should have worn something else. I won't be able to move as fast in this gown if something happens."

At that moment a group of people down the other end of the room shifted, a man's deep laugh drawing Alex's attention.

Because he knew that laugh. Had heard it before.

The cold inside him settled, heavy as lead, dense as the space inside a black hole.

A woman in a pink gown moved and behind her he could see a man in a white dinner jacket. A familiar man.

It had been years since he'd seen Conrad South, but Alex would have known him anywhere. He'd aged but not badly, the only white in his black hair at his temples. He'd gotten a little more jowly and there were bags under his hazel eyes, but he was still handsome.

It didn't seem fair. The fucker must be in his sixties now and yet he looked at least a decade younger. Perhaps he had a painting in the attic that showed his true age, his true nature. Or maybe the innocence he'd taken from his victims kept him young. Because there had to be other victims surely? One sixteen-year-old boy would hardly be enough for a man like Conrad.

"Sir?"

Katya's voice nearby, the question soft. And he realized that he had his champagne flute in a death grip and every single muscle in his body was coiled tight with instinctive loathing. With wild, helpless fury.

It's not over. Even now.

His jaw felt brittle, his bones like they were made out of glass. As if one move would shatter him.

"Alex?"

The sound of his name in her soft, accented voice pulled him out of it. Tearing his attention from the man at the other end of the room, Alex met Katya's steady gaze.

"It's him isn't it?" she asked. Because of course it was obvious by now what had made Alex freeze like that. What had brought his weakness bubbling back to the surface. "What did he do to you?"

The effort of will it took to pick up his glass, to sip at the liquid in it, was almost too much for him, but he forced himself to do it. To relax his tight muscles. To push away the memories of hard, white porcelain against his cheek. Of pain. Of blood in his mouth where he'd bitten his tongue to keep from screaming.

"That's none of your business," he said, not caring how it sounded. "Like I told you earlier, all you need to know is that he's an enemy."

She didn't look away, continuing to study Alex. "If I knew what he did, I could protect you—"

"But you are never going to know that, Katya. So why don't you be a good girl and shut the fuck up?"

The words were hard and cold, but he couldn't seem to moderate his tone. Helpless fury burned in his veins, slowly rising, slowly building.

It still hurts. It still matters. You haven't escaped what he did to you. You will never *escape . . .*

No. Fuck, no. He *had* escaped it. He'd buried that fifteen minutes where the stupid, innocent boy he'd once been was destroyed, suffocated it under so many other experiences he couldn't even remember what had happened, still less feel it.

It didn't affect him anymore. It didn't matter. It just didn't fucking matter.

He was thirty-five now, not sixteen. The owner of an incredibly successful chain of clubs. Rich and powerful in his own right. Conrad had no power over him, none at all.

Katya said nothing, her face smoothing over, becoming expressionless. He'd hurt her probably, but that was too bad. What could he say anyway? *I was raped by that fucker over there when I was sixteen.* Or no, he couldn't even say *raped.* Not when he'd given his consent, hoping like hell Conrad would leave his father alone afterwards. That Conrad wouldn't follow up on the threats to tell Alex's mother and sister about Daniel St. James's secret life.

Yet in the end it had been for nothing.

Alex had let his father's friend have him and his father had died anyway, his mother and sister left struggling. And he, unable to bear the shame, had run away.

Yeah, sure. He could tell Katya all that. He'd done it before after all, the truth masquerading as a lie. But she'd see through him and he couldn't bear that. He didn't want this strong, courageous woman to know what a fucking coward he was.

"Of course," she said, her voice devoid of expression. "Forgive me. I should not have asked."

Across the room, Conrad was now moving on to another group of people, doing his rounds of the players. No doubt one of his minions had informed him of Alex's presence, but Conrad didn't look in Alex's direction. At least not yet.

Perhaps the guy didn't care. Perhaps the guy didn't even remember.

Alex's hand holding the wineglass had begun to shake, so he put it down, curling his fingers into a fist.

Christ, he needed to pull himself together, because Conrad was going to speak to him, no doubt about it, and if he couldn't handle that he was never going to survive a whole fucking game. He couldn't afford to show he was rattled because any chink in his armor would be a weakness that another player might exploit.

Alex's confidence and his ability to remain cool under pressure, to remain in control, not to mention his card-counting ability, were his most important weapons when it came to poker and he needed to make sure all of those abilities were rock solid.

Conrad had stopped to talk to the man near the fire, but not for long. The man's stony expression didn't change as Conrad said something to him, then turned away, beginning to come down toward Alex's end of the room.

In the armchair beside him, Katya shifted. And then her hand covered his on the table.

He wasn't expecting it, a shock of heat holding him still for a long moment. And when he turned his head, he found her looking steadily back, an expression he couldn't read in her eyes.

"I will protect you, sir," she said quietly, seriously. "Have no fear."

* * *

Anger flared, hot and blue in his eyes. But she was ready for it. He was a man who hid his emotions well and he wouldn't like knowing she'd spotted his fear. No man did, especially when a woman was the one who'd noticed it.

But then how could she not? Alex was only meters away from his enemy and drawn as tight as a bow, his long, lean body almost vibrating with tension. And she knew fear; she'd experienced it herself many times on the missions she'd undertaken with her unit.

But as the General had taught her, fear could be harnessed, could be a valuable tool as long as you didn't let it get the better of you. It could get your heart pumping and your mind thinking coldly, cleanly.

However, in order to harness it, you first had to admit you were afraid.

She didn't look away from Alex's hot blue gaze. She knew how galling it was for men to have a woman protect them. But she also knew that when danger threatened, when their lives were at stake, most didn't care who stopped the bullet as long as it was stopped.

"I'm not afraid," he said in a hard voice. "Remember who the fuck you are, Katya Ivanova."

"I remember," she responded levelly. "Regardless of who I'm pretending to be, I'm your bodyguard. My job is to protect you. And I will."

His mouth twisted. "Look around, sweetheart. There are no bullets here."

Katya ignored the bitter sarcasm in his tone. He was trying to hide the fact that he was afraid; that was obvious to her. And no wonder, with his enemy making his way across the room toward them.

It would be better not to argue, not now. It would only make things worse and she didn't want that. Her job was to help him, not further expose him.

You care too much, Katya. That has always been your weakness. . . .

Her father's voice echoed in her head, but she ignored it. This was not about caring. This was about doing her job. That was all.

As she remembered how Alex's fingers had tightened on her arm as they'd entered the casino, pulling her close, an idea came to her.

"But not all fatal shots come from guns," she murmured. "Stay in your seat." Before he could respond, she rose from her chair and sidled around the table to him. He leaned back, his gaze on her, still as a hunting cat. She smiled at him, just in case anyone happened to see past the screens surrounding their little seating area; then without hesitation she turned and sat directly in his lap.

At first all she felt was heat pressing against her thighs and buttocks, up along her spine. Then, slowly, the tight coil of his muscles beneath her. She hadn't imagined his tension; she could feel it like an electrical current singing through him.

She leaned back against his chest, willing him to play along. No, there were no bullets here, but that didn't mean he wasn't in danger. And her job was to put herself between him and that danger, even physically if she had to.

Are you sure that isn't an excuse to get close to him?

No, of course it wasn't. She'd had two whole days to beat this inconvenient sexual awakening into submission and in the privacy of his personal gym she'd had a good stab at it, working out until she was physically exhausted. Until the ache inside her had vanished.

The problem was that it hadn't stayed gone, reappearing every time she got near him.

Luckily, since he'd remained working in his office for the past two days, she hadn't had the opportunity. She'd spent the time she wasn't in the gym trying to find more information about the Four Horsemen and the Apocalypse game. But as she'd discovered even before she'd left New York, there wasn't much. The game itself, apart from the fact that it was one of poker's most elite tournaments, had a great deal of secrecy surrounding it–there were rumors that it didn't even have a prize pool; the notoriety gained from being the Apocalypse winner was apparently reward enough.

Except that information didn't help her now as she sat in Alex's lap, the heat of him pressing everywhere, waking the ache she'd hoped to get rid of.

He didn't say anything, remaining silent and still beneath her. And she wondered if she'd made a mistake. That perhaps this was too far even for one of his girlfriends. Then one arm slid around her waist, pulling her tight against him, his palm on her stomach, his fingers splayed out in a strong possessive hold. Her heartbeat began to speed up as his breath whispered over her bare shoulders, as he shifted, settling her more firmly in his lap.

No, she hadn't made a mistake. The tension in his muscles had begun to loosen, his breathing becoming more regular.

"What are you doing, sweetheart?" he murmured in her ear, making a strange shiver sweep over her skin. "Is this some kind of new bodyguard move I wasn't aware of?"

"You want to appear strong and confident," she murmured back. "What is stronger and more confident than you being intimate with your lover in front of everyone?"

"Jesus." He gave a soft laugh. "I think you're enjoying this role way too much."

But she ignored that because Conrad South was making his way toward them, an insincere smile on his handsome face.

"Alex," the older man said, approaching the table. "They told me you were here, hiding down the back. Good to see you again. It's been a long time." He held out a hand.

Beneath her, Katya felt the flex and release of Alex's muscles, tension coiling, then loosening. "Hasn't it? You'll forgive me if I don't get up," he said carelessly, his voice smooth and regular. "As you can see, I have my hands full at the moment."

South's hazel eyes met Katya's for a second. He smiled at her. It was probably meant to be friendly, but there was also something greedy in it. As if she were a jewel in a shop window he wanted to buy but couldn't afford. "I can see and I approve." He sat in Katya's abandoned chair, running a hand through his perfectly coiffed black hair. He was going gray at the temples and he looked as if his flesh sat more heavily on him than it should. Yet he had a handsome man's confidence and projected a powerful man's authority, the two combining in an undeniable charisma.

Katya had met men like him before, at the private functions her father had hosted for his political friends.

She distrusted South instantly.

"Conrad," Alex said, "Meet my newest acquisition. Katya Ivanova."

South leaned back in his chair, his gaze heavy lidded and sleepy. Yet the gaze beneath those lids was sharp as a blade. "Pleased to meet you, Miss Ivanova. I hope this bastard is treating you well."

"Yes, thank you," she replied, settling her head back on Alex's shoulder. She could hear his heartbeat. It was racing.

"So polite." That edged hazel gaze shifted from her to Alex. "Where do you find them? I didn't think you liked blondes." South was still smiling and yet there was something unfriendly under those words. A meaning she didn't understand.

"Oh, I've discovered I prefer them," Alex answered. "After all, isn't that what gentlemen do?"

"I wouldn't know, not being a gentleman." The older man tilted his head. "I'm supposed to welcome you to the game. Tell you what an honor it is to have you at the table. Except . . ."

"Except you didn't invite me."

"No." The word was said on a long breath. "I didn't. Which begs the question as to who did."

Alex shifted again, his body moving under hers as he got something out of his pocket and leaned forward, putting it on the table in front of them. His arm tightened around her as he did so, keeping her exactly where she was. When he took his hand away she saw the two silver dice sitting on the polished wooden surface.

Conrad's gaze dropped and he looked at them for a long moment. Then he reached for one, picking it up and studying it a second before placing it back on the table.

"They're not fakes," Alex said.

"No, I can see that. How did you get them?"

"UPS delivered them straight to my door."

The older man gave a short, hard laugh. "Stop fucking with me, boy."

"Oh, been there, done that." Alex's voice was lazy. "I've got no desire to do it again."

An expression Katya couldn't read crossed the other man's face, the smile slowly fading. "Tell me where you got them or else you don't play."

"It doesn't matter how I got them. All that matters is that I have them. That's all I need to play, Conrad." Alex said the name like it tasted bitter in his mouth. Like a curse.

"I can prevent you from playing."

"No, you can't. In fact, you have only one rule: If you have the invite, you can play." Alex paused. "At least, from what I hear."

South's features had settled into complete and utter neutrality, blank as a wall. "Yes, and they are my rules. To make or break as I see fit."

"So you really want to draw attention to yourself by

forbidding me to play, hmmm?" Alex sounded almost amused. "That's not like you. Anyone would think you were afraid."

The other man didn't move. "Those are Tremain's dice, aren't they?"

Katya felt Alex's muscles tense again. Except when he spoke he sounded bored. "Are they? Do you all have a pair then?" He laughed. "No, on second thought, I don't think you do. None of you do, you fucking ball-less cowards."

Conrad smiled. "You sound angry, son. Perhaps you need more than that fine piece of pussy sitting on your lap. Perhaps you need something a little harder, rougher."

The arm around Katya's waist was like a steel band, rigid with tension. She let out a breath, relaxing against him, her muscles going loose, hoping to ease whatever it was that held him tight.

Then suddenly she felt his fingers in her hair, turning her head on his shoulder so she looked up into his burning, blue eyes. A scorching glance that held fury and determination and something else she didn't understand.

That was the only warning she got.

His fingers curled tight and he bent his head, covering her mouth with his.

Her mind blanked in shock, searing heat bursting inside her, that ache she'd been trying to ignore for the past two days springing back to life, hungry and wanting.

She'd never been kissed before, and in the few vague fantasies she'd allowed herself she'd imagined kisses to be soft and dry and, she hoped, pleasant.

But this kiss was none of those things.

It was gentle, with a deep, insistent sensuality that had her mouth opening in response before she could even think straight.

Alex's tongue traced the line of her lower lip, then slipped inside her mouth, exploring her. She tasted the wine he'd been drinking and something else, a delicious, spicy edge that made her want to explore him in return.

His fingers tightened in her hair, holding her as he stroked his tongue deeper still, the sensuality of the kiss turning hotter, blatantly sexual.

The world began to dim around the edges and she couldn't remember what she was doing or why she was here. There was only this moment, this contact. The heat of his mouth on hers and the driving ache that she knew no amount of working out was ever going to get rid of.

She wanted to respond to him, to kiss him back, but she didn't really know how. And then, suddenly, way before she was ready, he lifted his head. For a second he only looked at her and she was lost in the fierce blue glitter of his eyes, in the raw heat and hunger she saw in them. Then he turned his head, that seductive mouth of his turning up into a satisfied smile. "There's nothing wrong with this fine piece of pussy, believe me," he drawled, his voice holding a sensual note to it. "Why the fuck would I want rough when I have warm, wet, and willing?"

Another shock went through her. She'd forgotten about the man sitting opposite them. Forgotten completely. And the kiss had apparently been for his benefit.

Katya struggled to get her breathing under control, for the strange shaking that had taken hold of her to ease. She let her head tilt against Alex's shoulder so she could see the other man's face.

If their little display had affected him, he gave no sign, merely lifting a shoulder. "Then why are you here?"

"I'm here same as the rest of the players. Because I got an invite. Because I want a good game and a decent opponent." Alex paused. "And because I'm hoping that this is the year you decide to play."

South's smile deepened into one of genuine amusement. "I don't play, son. I never do."

"Oh, I think that perhaps this year you'll make an exception."

"And why the hell would I want to do that?"

"Because if you do . . ." Alex paused again and she could hear his heart beat faster, feel his lean body beneath her become tense again. His fingers moved in her hair, a gentle, absent caress. "You might get the chance to, uh, revisit happy memories, shall we say."

Something sparked in the other man's gaze, a brief flare, and then it was gone. "I don't know what you're talking about."

This time it was Alex's turn to laugh and she couldn't help shivering at the sensuality implicit in the sound. "Don't be coy, Conrad; of course you do. Or is rough not so much what you're into these days?"

Her mouth burned, her thinking sluggish, her heartbeat still out of control. The undercurrent of the conversation had entered territory she didn't understand and everything felt extremely dangerous. Like a match in a gas-filled room, one spark could make everything explode.

Dear God, no wonder the General had told her that sex was a distraction. That it diluted the blood and clouded the mind. He was right it did. She had to concentrate. Be cold, sharp, and clear.

Shifting in Alex's lap, she put one hand on his thigh and squeezed once, a silent warning to him of her concern. Then she gave the room a quick scan, watching for any other danger. But the only person looking at them was the tall, scarred merc standing next to the fire, his black gaze full of an emptiness that was horribly familiar to her. She'd recognized it in soldiers who'd seen and done traumatic things. Men who'd lost their souls.

Cold began to steal through her. What was going on here?

The mercenary was dangerous, yes, but she got the sense

that the real danger was coming from the man sitting opposite Alex. And the strange tension between the two of them. A tension that seemed almost . . . sexual. Which couldn't be right, surely? She didn't think Alex was into men; at least she'd never seen him with any nor had he ever displayed the slightest sign of interest.

His hand settled over hers where it rested on his thigh and pressed down, holding it there, the warmth of the contact stopping her breath. Making her forget the mercenary beside the fire, making her forget why she was even here in the first place.

All she could think about was the searing heat of Alex's mouth, the softness of it as it moved on hers, the rich taste of him—

Remember who you are. And what you're supposed to be doing.

"You wouldn't know what I'm into, son," Conrad was saying thoughtfully. "It's men's business and I don't see any men sitting here."

"Petty," Alex murmured. "Very petty. I thought you were better than that." Amusement entered his tone again. "Just think of all the satisfaction you'd get out of beating me and reminding yourself of the good old days. It's a great deal, wouldn't you say? How can you lose?"

The good old days . . . What did that mean? And why was Alex goading him into participating in the game?

The other man didn't say anything for a long time, merely sitting there, studying Alex. "And what would you get out of it?" Conrad asked eventually.

"Me? I'd get nothing out of it." Alex's voice got softer, deeper. "Nothing except the satisfaction of beating you and taking you for everything you own, motherfucker."

Conrad's smile was a wolf's, full of teeth and hunger. "You'd really think I'd put myself in that position?"

"Yeah, I think so. I think you can't resist another go. I

mean, I haven't exactly led the life of a priest, have I? Think of all the things I've learned since then." His voice held an almost sensual roughness to it, like a man promising seduction, and Katya was conscious again of that weird tension. Of that hungry look in Conrad's eyes, in his smile.

This seemed . . . not right. She had the sense that something had happened between them. Had it been sexual?

"Plus, if you're really lucky," Alex went on, "I might throw the Circles clubs into the pot too, just for kicks."

Katya's breath caught. Staking the clubs? He could not be serious. What the hell was happening between these two men?

South stared at Alex and another long, tense moment passed. Then he levered himself out of the chair, his smile completely impersonal. "I'll think about it," he said. "Do enjoy the rest of the evening."

CHAPTER NINE

Alex's heart was thumping, the blood racing through his veins. He felt like he'd just bluffed a win from a nine and a five.

Conrad hadn't agreed, but Alex had seen a flash of interest in the other man's eyes. Even after all these years, the prick still wanted him. Which meant he had discovered a weakness. A weakness that could be exploited.

And fuck, he was going to exploit the hell out of that one. Because he hadn't known until that bastard had sat down and started with the implications how deeply, terribly angry he was. The rage was a fire in his blood and he wanted Conrad South to burn. Wanted him at his mercy. Begging. Maybe even begging for his life the way Conrad had made him beg once.

"Sir?" Katya's voice was soft, but when he looked down into her eyes he could see the concern in them. "You staked your clubs?"

The anger inside him turned, morphing into something else, fire of a different sort.

He shouldn't have kissed her like that, but, shit, when Conrad had brought up the past he'd had to get the upper hand back. Refuting the other man's claim on him with a public display of his sexuality.

Yet that kiss . . .

He stared at Katya, at the full softness of her mouth. She'd tasted like summer, all sweetness and heat, and he'd almost forgotten about the man sitting across from him. Almost forgotten his reasons for kissing her in the first place.

And you want to do it again.

Yeah, he did. It was all kinds of bad and all kinds of wrong; it crossed the lines he'd drawn and then some. But he couldn't leave now and he had to master this anger somehow. And the best way he knew of to do that was to master someone else.

Master her.

Fury raged under the surface of his skin, slipping out of his control, adrenaline pouring through him like the rush that comes from a needle and the very purest heroin.

His fingers were still twisted in her hair, the strands silky and soft against his skin. He curled them tighter, drawing her head back against his shoulder. "Here's the deal," he murmured roughly in her ear. "We can't leave yet. Conrad would see it as a weakness and there's no way I'm giving him that kind of ammunition. But that leaves me with two choices. Either I get your gun from your purse and put a bullet in him. Or I show him I don't give a fuck in some other way, just in case he comes back."

Her body tensed against his. "What way?"

"I think you know."

She tensed even more, staying silent a long moment. Then she said quietly, ignoring him, "There is something between you two. I can sense it. He's more than merely an enemy, isn't he?"

Of course she would have picked up on the tension between him and Conrad. She was too sharp, too perceptive, not to. She'd probably even figured out the nature of it, which meant he had to shut down this conversation before she started asking questions. Questions there was no way in hell he was going to answer.

"That's none of your fucking business. You said you would protect me. So now it's goddamn time to protect me."

She gave him a wordless, measuring look. Like she could see past his anger to what was underneath. "That is not what I meant."

His hand had started to shake where it was knotted in her hair and across the room he could see Conrad talking to a group of people. The other man's gaze kept returning to where Alex and Katya sat, watching them. . . .

He'd only begged once before in his life and he'd sworn he'd never do it again.

But he did.

"Please, Katya," Alex whispered hoarsely. "Because I am drowning and I need you to save me."

Beneath the chatter of conversation he heard the rush of her indrawn breath. Felt her body go rigid. And he couldn't think why he'd said something like that. Not when it admitted to a weakness he couldn't afford.

Katya twisted her head, looking up at him, the light shimmering over the gown where it pulled tight over her breasts, the gold sparkling in time with her breathing. He didn't want to meet that searching gaze of hers, but he made himself do it. Made himself hold it.

There was an expression he didn't understand in her eyes, but he felt the moment the tension left her body. When she relaxed against him. "Tell me what you want," she said.

He ignored the relief, since he had no room in him for anything other than need and rage. Shifting, he angled his body so she was tucked more closely against the side of the chair, then looked down at her. "I want control. Your complete obedience. I want you to do exactly what I say,

when I say it. No questions. No arguments. No protests."
He paused, letting her see exactly how serious he was about
this. "And I want your consent."

Her gaze flickered, the smallest of hesitations. "You
have it."

Just like that? Without even knowing what he was going to do or what her complete obedience would entail?
"Katya. Are you sure?" Because he had to be.

"I am a soldier, sir. Following orders isn't anything new."

Christ. Of course she was a soldier. A courageous one.
"I won't do anything to hurt you or embarrass you." The
storm inside him relented a little. "And I promise that what
you'll get in return is pleasure."

She looked away abruptly at that and he could feel a different sort of tension creep through her body. "I am not
doing this for me. I am doing this for you."

No, that's not how it worked. That's not how *he* wanted
it to work. He shifted again, reaching out and gripping her
chin, turning her back to face him. "I don't just want your
consent, Katya. I want your desire too." Because he'd never
touched anyone who didn't want him and he wasn't about
to start.

A flash of uncertainty crossed her features, that blank,
Russian stoicism dropping for a moment to reveal an unexpected vulnerability. It made his chest tighten for reasons he didn't understand.

Her jaw tensed under his fingertips. "You know you have
that already."

"I want to hear you say it. I *need* to hear you say it."

She let out a breath but didn't look away this time. "I
want . . . you, sir."

The desire that gripped him in response was almost
shocking in its intensity.

This was supposed to be a bad idea, remember?

Perhaps it was. Then again, if he could manage the

intensity of this he'd be able to manage anything Conrad threw at him. Hell, it would even be a good test.

"Sir," he echoed. "That's the third time you've said it in public. Which means I win our little bet and you owe me a forfeit."

A fleeting, puzzled look crossed her face. "What forfeit?"

"This," he murmured. And because she'd given him her consent and had surrendered to him the control, he used it.

Alex bent his head and took her mouth.

Softness and heat engulfed him, such a heady contrast to that cold, expressionless front she liked to put up. The taste of her went straight to his head like the very finest champagne. Like a straight flush in his hand and millions on the table.

She stiffened against him a second, then relaxed, her lips parting as if she'd been waiting for him to kiss her all this time. Jesus, she was delicious.

He swept his tongue deep into her mouth, spreading his fingers in her hair, cradling the back of her head and tilting her so he could kiss her deeper, explore her more completely.

Now he had the control, the rage inside him began to fade, melting away in the heat of the kiss, allowing him to take his time, subsume himself totally in the taste of her.

Katya gave a little sigh and he felt her respond, her tongue tentative as it touched his, as if she hadn't done this before and wasn't sure of what to do. Her hesitancy was seductive, so he demanded more, intensifying the kiss, craving her submission to the desire that had taunted him from that moment on the plane when she'd bent over him, teased him.

He let it burn for a while longer, then lifted his head, staring down into her face.

A deep flush colored her cheeks, the green of her eyes stained with small gold flecks, vivid against her pink skin. Her stoic Russian front had gone, leaving in its place a deep well of sensuality he'd never guessed at. He could see it in her eyes, in the shortness of her breath, and in the way she said nothing at all, merely staring at him as if she wanted him to kiss her again.

Christ, how satisfying was that? It made him feel good that he could do this to her. That he could get under her guard and under her skin.

He flexed his fingers in the gold silk against his palm. "Why do you have long hair?" he asked, giving in to idle curiosity. "I've been wondering for a while."

"I'm not sure that's relevant to—"

"No protests. No arguments. And complete obedience," he reminded her, his fingers curling tight.

Her gaze wavered and he could see realization begin to dawn in her about what she'd agreed to. And that this was clearly a painful topic. But shit, she'd seen what Conrad had done to him. She'd heard him beg her to save him. Why couldn't he demand a little something in return?

"It's neat and easy to braid," she answered eventually.

"Liar." He could always tell. "The real reason, Katya."

Dark, gold-shot lashes lowered, her attention focused on his throat. "My mother used to brush my hair when I was little. It's the only thing I have left of her."

The words hit him like the glancing of a badly aimed punch, the raw note in them unexpectedly painful. "Your mother?"

"She died when I was young. A long time ago." This time her voice was flat, indicating that this was a closed subject.

So . . . she'd lost a parent too. Sympathy clenched like a fist in his chest, catching him unprepared.

He shifted the hand behind her head so his thumb was

free, running it along her cheekbone, touching the smooth skin gently. "I'm sorry. That must have been tough."

But the tension in her jaw didn't relax, and when her lashes rose the look in her eyes was like a door shutting in his face. "It was a long time ago," she repeated. "I have forgotten her."

Another lie. If she'd forgotten why was her hair still long?

He wanted to push, wanted to find out more. But this wasn't the time or the place for confidences. And he hadn't set out to discover the secrets of her soul, only to master her physically for a few brief moments.

Shifting his free hand to her waist, Alex moved it higher, gently cupping one breast. Her mouth opened in a soundless gasp, the gold in her eyes flaring. "Then let me make sure she stays forgotten," he said softly. "In fact, I can make sure *everything* stays forgotten."

Katya was so warm, her nipple hard beneath the clinging fabric of her gown.

"There are two things I should tell you first," Katya said, her voice thick as mink fur.

He paused but didn't remove his hand. "What?"

"I have made a promise to someone." She took a short, hard breath. "A promise to a man."

The oddest sensation twisted inside him. Almost like . . . jealousy. Which was weird because he'd never been jealous of anyone before. You had to care in order to be envious and he'd never cared. But for reasons he didn't understand, he found himself caring now. "Mikhail?"

"Yes."

Mikhail Vasin. Who wasn't here.

Alex kept his hand right where it was. "And the second thing?"

Katya didn't look away. "I am a virgin."

* * *

Alex's eyes widened and no wonder. He probably didn't meet very many virgins. Perhaps she shouldn't have said anything. Then again, she wasn't ashamed of it and if he was going to touch her it was better that he knew she was a novice at this kind of thing in case her reactions were off.

She was still angry at him for forcing her to reveal the truth about her hair. About why she'd kept it long. The realization had been painful because she'd never examined her own reasons for it too closely, and yet he'd managed to get it out of her with ease. All it had taken had been the command in his voice and she'd obeyed like the soldier she was.

Maybe that was why she'd told him about her virginity. To get back at him.

"You're a virgin," he repeated flatly.

She was very conscious of how tense his body had gotten beneath hers, a frown appearing between his straight, dark brows. His hand didn't move away, but neither did it stroke her. It was maddening.

Her skin burned, her gown feeling even tighter than it was already. She'd never been touched like that before, never dreamed it could make her feel so much and with such intensity. Sometimes, on nights when she'd been unable to sleep, she'd given herself a brief, pleasant orgasm. A simple release, nothing more. But the feeling of Alex's hand on her body was nothing like her own. She couldn't control it, for a start, and that fact alone had turned out to be far more erotic than it had any right to be.

"Yes," she said. "I hope that isn't a problem."

"Fuck, you really have to ask?" Alex's voice was hard. "Of course it's a problem. Why the hell didn't you tell me this earlier?"

"Because it wasn't any of your business."

"Jesus, Katya." He began to take his hand away.

I am drowning and I need you to save me . . .

A heavy weight shifted in her chest and she found she was reaching for his hand, her fingers closing hard around his wrist, holding it exactly where it was. The feelings his touch had generated inside her were confusing, yet she didn't want him to stop.

There had been something very satisfying in knowing he had the command. And that she was to obey him. It calmed her.

Well, of course. You're a soldier. You're born to obey.

No, it was more than that. A commanding officer gave the orders and the soldiers obeyed, but there was no give-and-take. With Alex it was different. She could see how her surrender to him had instantly made him relax. Made that terrible, burning rage in his eyes fade, leaving behind open hunger. For her.

Giving up control should have undermined her strength and yet it didn't. For some reason it only made her feel more powerful.

She didn't understand it, but one thing she was sure of; she wanted more.

"What are you doing?" he demanded, blue eyes glinting. "We can't go on; you realize that, don't you?"

"No, I don't." She could feel the tension in his arm, his muscles tight and hard. He was strong, and if she was to fight him he wouldn't go down easy. "I don't want you to stop."

"If you want me to be the one to introduce you to the gentle delights of sex, you've got the wrong man, darling." His voice held a bitter edge to it. "I don't do virgins."

"You said you were drowning. That you wanted me to save you. So let me save you."

There was anger again in his eyes and she didn't understand it. "Let go of my hand, Katya." The words were quiet, but she heard the steel in them.

She ignored him. "Do you really think that merely be-

cause I haven't had sex, I know nothing about it? That I'm some kind of innocent girl?" She tightened her fingers around his wrist, letting him feel her strength. "I wasn't in the army to look pretty and be on the recruitment posters. I was a soldier. I was in the army to protect my country. I've taken lives and I probably will again. So don't make the mistake of thinking I'm an innocent just because I haven't been with a man."

A muscle ticked in his jaw. "You think innocence is entirely about sex? It's not. When you've had your soul ripped to shreds in front of you, then you can talk to me about innocence."

She stared at him, caught suddenly by the glitter of what looked like pain in his eyes. That heavy weight in her chest shifted again. "Your soul? How?"

"I'm not answering that question now, sweetheart." He twisted his wrist, breaking her hold. "We're done here."

No, oh no, they weren't. She'd heard the roughness in his voice when he'd begged her to save him, felt the strain in his muscles and seen the shake of his hand. He'd been desperate. Well, so was she.

She wanted this. Wanted the intoxicating, heady rush that filled her when he touched her. Wanted to know what would happen if he kept doing it.

But more than any of that, she wanted to save him.

"You asked for my obedience. You asked for control. And I gave both to you." She made no effort to shift and allow him room to get out of the chair. "Do you think I gave you those things for nothing?"

His gaze was shadowed, his expression impenetrable. "And what about that promise you mentioned? The one to Mikhail? Were you saving yourself for him?"

A thin thread of guilt wound through her. Yes, she had made a promise to Mikhail. She'd promised to accede to her father's wishes and marry him once he'd returned from

the last mission. Loyalty was the bedrock of her existence and part of that was a certain physical loyalty.

But you're not in love with him and he's not with you . . .

"I don't love him." She said the words aloud, making them true. "And he's not with me. I'm not saving myself for anyone."

"So why haven't you had sex yet?"

"Because I haven't found anyone I've wanted to have it with. That doesn't mean I don't want it."

Alex gave a soft laugh. "You don't know what you're asking for, Katya mine."

"So show me."

He was silent a long moment, his gaze razor sharp as he searched her face. "I will do whatever I want," he said softly. "Are you prepared for that? In public? In a room full of people?"

He was trying to intimidate her. Make her change her mind, no doubt about it. "There are screens. No one can see us. You also said you wouldn't hurt me or embarrass me, remember?"

"Fuck, darling. You trust me that much?"

On the surface Alex St. James was the least trustworthy man she'd ever met. But the night before last, she'd seen behind the playboy mask. She knew that whatever he was doing here with Conrad South, it was costing Alex and, though he'd told her he had his own reasons, he wasn't doing it entirely for himself. He was here for his friends. For his sister.

"Yes," she said unhesitatingly. "And now it's your turn to trust me."

His eyes darkened, and for another long moment he didn't move.

Then suddenly he shifted, easing her body farther to the side, into the crook of the armchair, twisting until the wide expanse of his shoulders added another layer of privacy to

the screens already shielding their little nook from the rest of the room.

He lifted his hand again, running his fingers along her jaw, before sliding them down her neck, his thumb resting in the hollow of her throat. A shiver swept over her, as if his touch had just sensitized every inch of skin.

"Keep still," he murmured. "I'm going to touch you. And while I'm touching you, I want you to talk. Tell me about Russia. Tell me about Moscow."

His fingers moved to trace the line of her collarbone and her mouth went completely dry, goose bumps rising on her skin. "W-why?"

"Because I asked you to. No questions, no protests, Katya mine."

Katya licked her lips, trying to get her mouth working. "Moscow is . . . beautiful. In winter you can skate in Gorky Park." His fingers trailed further across the swell of her breasts as they pressed against the fabric of her gown. "And the snow on St. Basil's Cathedral . . . It's so perfect it doesn't look real." And down again, stroking the curve of one breast, pausing to circle lightly around her nipple.

She shivered, fire rippling through her, sweet and unfamiliar, an insistent ache between her thighs gathering tighter. Her nipple was hard and sensitive, her breathing uneven.

"Go on," he said quietly. "Tell me more."

"In summer, the roses at the botanical garden smell so good." His fingers now spanned her breast, his palm cupping the weight of it. "A-and there is the Bolshoi Theatre. . . . The dancers are . . . so graceful."

Alex's fingers circled her nipple, tracing the hard outline gently over the fabric of her gown. Her breath hissed at the sharp edge of pleasure that slid through her and she had to fight to remember what she was saying.

"Keep talking."

She swallowed. "There's art down the Arbat . . . a shopping street." Her voice sounded thick, husky, his gaze on hers as his fingers moved, lazily toying with her nipple, squeezing her breast gently as if measuring it. "You can get your p-portrait painted. . . ."

The flame in his eyes burned and she wanted desperately to keep talking, to keep doing exactly what he told her to. Because she could see how affected he was by this. By her.

The rest of the room faded away, dimming at the edges of her sight. All she could see was his face, the deep, hot blue of his eyes, the red stain on his cheekbones. The desire he didn't hide.

"Do you like art, Katya?" His voice was insistent, his fingers circling around and around the hard point of her nipple. Then he pinched her. "Or did you prefer dance?"

She barely heard him as the arrow of sensation pierced her, a soft, needy sound escaping her throat, and she shifted, unable to keep still. The movement arched her back, pressing her breast even more firmly into his palm, the heat of it burning through her dress.

"Answer my question," he ordered roughly, the sound of his voice as much a caress as his touch. "And keep still."

"D-dance," she managed to say, hoarse as his fingers continued to tease her. "I . . . w-wanted to be a dancer when I was little." The words were spilling out and she couldn't seem to stop them. "But my f-father wouldn't . . . let me."

"Why not?" There was an intensity in Alex's expression: the gambler studying an opponent. Which was odd, since she wasn't his opponent. Yet she didn't feel threatened by it. No, more like the opposite. Being the center of his attention was profoundly erotic.

"Answer me," he whispered, that searching, fierce expression consuming her. The hand on her breast slid lower, over her stomach, out toward her hip, then back again, the heel of his palm coming to rest lightly over the most sensitive part of her, his fingers facing down and spread like he was guarding her sex. "Or I'll stop touching you."

"My mother d-died. And he thought dancing was . . . weak." The pressure of Alex's hand on her clitoris increased, then began to move in tiny, precise circles, and she forgot entirely what she'd been saying. The sensation was electric, a shock of pleasure filling her up. Her hips lifted helplessly, her body quivering, her breathing becoming ragged. "Oh . . . God. . . ."

"Dancers are strong, Katya," Alex murmured. "There's nothing weak about them."

No, he was wrong, but she couldn't think why because the subtle movement of his hand was building the pressure slowly, inexorably, until she wanted to scream. She felt like she was going to break open and everything she was would come spilling out. And he would see it. He would see her exposed and raw and vulnerable.

Weak. Breakable.

"You're wrong," she said raggedly, desperately. And she fumbled for his wrist, trying to pull him away. "I can't . . . you have to stop."

His movements paused, but his hand remained exactly where it was. He leaned over her and the look on his face . . . it was like he knew exactly what she was feeling. Like he could see her fear.

Her heartbeat thudded loudly in her ears and she couldn't breathe. Where had this fear come from? She didn't understand it.

"Katya." There was a gentle yet inflexible note in his voice. "Take your hand away. That's an order."

Yes, an order. That was familiar. That was something she could do. Her fingers loosened and fell away.

"Now close your eyes."

And she did, letting the darkness protect her.

Then the heel of his hand began to rock against her again, his fingers pressing lightly. "You said you trusted me," he whispered in her ear, his breath feathering over her skin. "So do it. It's my turn to keep you safe."

The words touched something inside her. Something deep. No one had ever protected her, at least no one who wasn't a fellow soldier. She'd always been expected to protect herself. But this was unfamiliar territory and she needed someone at her back.

She needed Alex.

Katya shuddered as the pressure built once more. "Alexei . . ." His name in Russian, a mere breath. *"Pozhaluysta . . ."* Please.

And he answered, his mouth covering hers as the movement of his hand brought the pleasure to an intense, aching point. And she let him take the moan that broke from her as the point exploded, the orgasm detonating, a shock wave moving through her body as intense as a nuclear blast.

There were lights behind her eyes, a bright spray of color like the flash of fireworks at a parade. Holy God. . . .

She couldn't stop shaking, but he kept his mouth on hers, kissing her, silencing her sharp gasps until the intensity began to lessen, the heat fading into gentleness. Until the quivers vanished and she lay still in the crook of the armchair, her breathing returning to normal.

Eventually his mouth moved away, but she didn't open her eyes.

Strangely, she kept thinking of that woman she'd seen kissing Alex back in New York. And how flushed the woman had been and how she hadn't understood why.

Well, now she did.

"Katya." His voice was soft, murmuring near her ear.

She didn't want to open her eyes, but eventually she cracked her lids open to find his gaze on hers. Steady.

Watchful. The spark of desire glowed steadily there too, but if he was impatient for anything he gave no sign.

"Are you okay?"

"Yes." It came out more as a croak, but she didn't care. "Are you?"

A smile flickered around his mouth. "Not really. I'm going to have to wait awhile before we can move."

"Why?"

Alex took her hand and moved it surreptitiously down over his groin. "That's why."

Beneath the wool of his pants she could feel the long, thick length of his erection, the look in his eyes glinting as she touched him. "Do you want me to—" She stopped, suddenly unsure about what to offer him.

But he only lifted a shoulder. "No. It's going to be a little difficult right here and now anyway." He eased himself away from her, giving her a bit of space, bracing himself on the arms of the chair to keep her further hidden from view.

"What about you?" She had to ask. It felt wrong to take all that pleasure for herself and offer nothing in return.

"I don't need anything."

She frowned. "But . . . You're hard."

"I just watched you come. That would make any man hard."

"I don't want to just take, Alex. I want to give too."

"No." The word was final. "Oh, I got what I needed, sweetheart, believe me. But anything more will make things unnecessarily complicated and it's a distraction neither of us can afford."

Disappointment gathered in a small, hard knot, which was strange. Because he was right. And she'd never expected this to happen anyway. Yet for some reason that didn't make her any less disappointed.

She glanced away so he wouldn't see it, trying to find

and put in place her armor, her professionalism. "Yes. I understand."

But perhaps for the first time, even though she did understand she didn't agree.

Because for the first time, she knew what she'd been missing out on for the past ten years of her life. And now that desire was out of the box she'd locked it in, out of the cage she'd designed for it, she wasn't at all sure she wanted to put it back in again.

She wasn't even sure if she'd be able to.

CHAPTER TEN

Alex lounged back on the red velvet couch and kicked his feet up on the desk. The Fourth Circle bar was gearing itself up for another night, staff moving here and there, stocking the bar, adjusting the lighting on the dance floor, shifting around some of the furniture, or doing various other tasks.

He frowned as one of the bartenders passed him wearing the skin-tight black trousers, loose white shirt, and red brocade waistcoat that were part of the men's uniforms. It was supposed to be reminiscent of a Victorian gentleman's outfit, except a bit rakish and disheveled. Like they'd just come half-dressed from their mistresses' beds. But Alex wasn't so sure about it now. It seemed a bit . . . obvious.

Maybe it won't be your problem too much longer.

Alex scowled as the thought insinuated itself into his brain, making the spreadsheets he'd brought up on the laptop on the table in front of him blur.

A couple of days since Conrad's reception and Alex still hadn't had any word about whether the guy had accepted his bet and was going to play or not. The anger since that night remained inside him, a hot coal of rage that wouldn't go out.

For the past nineteen years he'd been fooling himself. Letting himself believe the lie that what Conrad had done to him didn't matter. Because it was easier and less painful than to accept that it did.

But as it turned out, it wasn't either easier or less painful.

Fuck, he wanted that prick sitting across the gaming table from him. Wanted to reduce him until he wasn't a man, only a begging, weeping, humiliated mess. Hurt him the way he'd been hurt.

The need was so intense he could almost taste it. Was this what it had been like for Gabriel when he'd been trying to destroy his father? This anger? This desire for blood? It had never touched Alex before because he'd never let anything or anyone get close enough to him to matter. But now . . .

On the dark wood of the table, his phone went off.

Alex glanced down at the screen as he reached for the vodka he'd poured himself.

Speak of the fucking devil. Gabriel.

Alex reached for the phone and hit the button. "What?" he demanded without preamble. He'd already called Zac about what had happened at the reception, naturally leaving out a few of the more personal things, but passing on the names of the other players there. Any information was good at this point and Zac had wanted to follow up on the other people participating in the game.

Not that there was much in the way of information. Alex and Katya had stayed for another hour and a half after Conrad had left them, but they'd learned nothing of any interest. Katya had wanted to speak to the mercenary who had been standing beside the fire, but he'd gone by the time she and Alex were ready to mingle with the other people.

Don't think about that. Don't think about the softness of her breast beneath your hand or the heat between her legs. The heat you could feel through the fabric of that golden gown.

Don't think about the fact she's a virgin and no matter how badly you want to fuck her, you won't.

And most important of all, don't think about the way she trusted you at the end.

Of course he wouldn't think about it. Not thinking was what he did best, after all.

"I told Zac everything," he continued. "So don't even start asking me."

"Yeah, I'm not calling about what you told Zac."

Alex leaned back and took a sip of his vodka, relishing the burn of the alcohol in his throat. "Then what for?"

There was a silence down the other end of the line. "Conrad South," Gabriel said eventually. "I want to know about him."

"Why? He's probably not your father, if that's what you're worrying about." It was a stupid thing to say, since Alex really had no idea. Anything was possible.

"I don't give a shit about whether he's my father or not," Gabriel said. "Zac's done some investigation into the Seven Devils, your father's little group of buddies. Eva got him the names. Conrad South was one of them."

Alex tried to relax his tight muscles. The others were bound to find out at some point and in many ways it was a surprise that they'd taken this long. "And?"

"You knew."

He idly shook the ice cubes in his glass. "Yeah, I knew."

Another long silence.

"Jesus fucking Christ, Alex. You didn't think that this might be something you'd want to pass on maybe?" Gabriel sounded pissed, which was kind of understandable.

Alex should have told them that back in New York, but at that stage he'd been in avoidance mode. And that included all those bad memories. Not speaking about what went on in the casino, keeping everything secret, was an old habit anyway. A habit that died hard.

"I had my reasons." Alex tipped back his glass and drained it in one go.

"Which you're *still* not going to share."

The vodka warmed his gut, easing the tension. "Don't ask, don't tell, brother. I assume that's still good enough for you?"

Gabriel said nothing, not that there was an answer to that, as Alex well knew. The club rules were the club rules. Eventually his friend asked, "Got anything you *do* want to share?"

"What can I say? South was one of Dad's cronies and yeah, he's done very well for himself with the Four Horsemen."

"Too well, judging from the financial reports Zac managed to find. The bastard's raking it in."

Alex lifted a shoulder. "He's a big player. He knows how to make money. So what?"

"Zac thinks it's more than gambling going on there."

"What? Another setup like the Lucky Seven?" Alex thought back to the Four Horsemen's bar, where the Apocalypse reception had been. There hadn't been anything sketchy that either he or Katya had noticed, apart from the merc hanging around. Just another expensive bar with an expensive crowd. "Like I told Zac, I didn't see anything questionable a couple of nights ago. Then again, that was a special event and only in the bar. The gaming floor might be different."

"Did you see the gaming floor?"

"No. There was no opportunity." *Because you were too busy making Katya come.*

"What about South? Did you have any dealings with him?" The question was flat and direct, no implication whatsoever behind it.

Alex could feel himself tensing up again. "What? When I was at the Lucky Seven with Dad?"

"Yeah."

"No," he lied. "I didn't."

"You said once you never saw any of your dad's friends there."

Alex remembered. The day he punched his friend in the face when he'd found out Gabe was sleeping with Honor. What a fucking excellent day that had been. "Are you saying I lied?"

Gabriel let out a short breath. "No, Christ. Keep your fucking secrets if you want; I don't care. All I want to know is how deep this shit goes. Honor's life could be at stake and I will do anything, *anything,* to protect her, okay?"

Guilt shifted inside Alex at his sister's name. Gabriel was looking out for her now and nothing would get past him, but deliberately withholding information that might help was wrong.

A small hand in his, big blue eyes looking up at him as he'd taken her to school on her first day. He'd begged his parents to let him take her because she'd been scared and he'd wanted to show her there was nothing to be afraid of. He was her big brother. He'd protect her . . .

The alcohol sitting in his gut burned like acid.

"Okay," he said thickly. "I hear you. Look, what I know about South is that he's a prick. And he's ruthless. Loves power games. If he's swimming in cash and it's looking sketchy as fuck then your instincts are probably right." He put the empty glass back down on the table. "I'm going to get Katya to look around while I play." He paused. "I'm also in the process of getting South to participate in the game too."

"He doesn't play?"

"No, and he's famous for it. There are only ever seven players and he's never one of them."

There was a silence down the end of the line. Then Gabriel said, "Seven?"

"Yeah. Funny how that number keeps turning up, isn't it? Makes me wonder about Tremain and why he had a pair of Apocalypse dice when he wasn't a poker player." Another thought struck Alex. "The invites are always anonymous too. No one knows who sends them out; the dice just apparently turn up. It's assumed the invites come from South, but maybe they don't."

"Your father had six friends," Gabriel murmured. "That's too much of a coincidence."

"What? So the invites come from each of them? Could be, I guess, but why? What's the intention of the game? Especially when there isn't a prize pool. Is it entirely for fun or for other reasons?"

"Good point. You sent the names of the players to Zac? We need to figure out who these people are and why they were invited, see if there's any pattern."

"Yeah, I sent them on to him." Jesus, he really needed another vodka.

"What about the rest of your dad's friends? Not including South, Tremain, and your father, there were four others. Patrick Mantel, Will Elliot, Benjamin Jordan, and Evelyn Fitzgerald."

Alex knew the names. Knew the faces. All rich, privileged middle-aged men, just like his father. All of them powerful and arrogant as hell. He'd seen a couple of them at the Lucky Seven, but all they'd done was play a few idle games of poker, then retreat to his father's offices behind the bar. They'd always seemed much more comfortable sitting around in his family's lounge talking about their golfing games and their business successes.

"Elliot and Jordan are dead." Alex shifted on the couch, gesturing to the bartender to fill up his tumbler again. "They died some years ago if I remember. The others . . . They're just old men with God complexes and too much time on their hands if you ask me."

"So you never knew any of them?"

"No." And that wasn't a lie. He hadn't actually known them. "They were just Dad's friends as far as I was concerned."

"Right, well, Zac's already digging into their pasts. And we have the player names too. That's a start."

The bartender came over, poured Alex another tumbler of Grey Goose. He picked it up, stared at it. The words were there in his mouth and he wanted to say them. *How's Honor? Is she okay? Tell her I'm sorry. . . .* But he didn't say anything. Instead he raised his glass and took a sip.

At that moment, his phone chimed, indicating he had a text. He glanced at the screen, reading the notification. It was from Conrad and all it said was: *Your bet is on.*

How the guy had gotten his number Alex didn't know, but a bolt of triumph went through him. Fucking finally. A chance to get even. A chance for revenge.

He smiled, turning his attention back to the conversation with Gabriel. "If you've got anything else to ask do it now, because I've got shit to do."

After Gabriel had ended the call, Alex found he couldn't sit still, restlessness pumping through him. He wanted to get up and beat that fucker right now, but of course that was going to have to wait until the first game tomorrow night.

Perhaps he could work out instead. Let off some steam punching a bag or practicing a few forms.

Getting up from the couch and taking his vodka with him, he stalked through the bar, heading for the private gym in the basement of the building. The door was closed and locked when he got there, but he could hear the sound of feet moving on the sprung wooden floor.

He'd only given one other person the code to get in. Katya.

Heat swept through him, thick and hot. He'd kept away

from her the past couple of days, hadn't even let himself think about what had happened between them at Conrad's reception. Mainly because it wasn't the feel of her against him or even the sight of her coming under his hand that was seared into his head.

No, the thing that kept replaying over and over in his brain was the unthinking fear in her face as she'd stilled his hand. Then her obedience as he'd ordered her to let go. As he'd told her to close her eyes.

Her trust as he'd told her he'd keep her safe.

That, especially, he did *not* want to think about. Because there was no way he deserved her trust.

She may not have been an innocent, but she was a virgin nonetheless and he'd touched her up in a room full of people. Made her obey his commands, made her come in public just to satisfy his own selfish needs. It didn't matter that they had been sheltered by the screens shielding them. It didn't matter that she'd wanted it. It didn't matter that she'd argued him into it.

He should never have done it in the first place. He should never have crossed the line.

Sex was supposed to be physical only and he'd made damn sure over the years to dissociate it from emotions like shame. Like guilt. Any emotions at all in fact. There were too many bad memories tied up in it.

Yet somehow, those heated minutes in the chair with Katya had hit him in a place he wasn't expecting. A vulnerable place, bringing back feelings he hadn't experienced for years. And that wasn't supposed to happen. He wasn't supposed to feel.

It was sure as shit why it wouldn't happen again.

Alex punched in his code and pushed open the door, stepping into the gym, then kicking the door shut behind him.

Ahead of him was a large, open, brightly lit space. There

were mirrors along one wall and various different sets of fitness equipment. A treadmill. A stationary bike. Weight benches and cross-trainers. A punching bag.

Yet none of them were in use at the moment.

Katya was in the middle of the room, rising up from a low, sweeping kick. She wore a tight black tank top and black yoga pants, her bare arms and neck gleaming with sweat. Her hair was tied in a tight braid, the small blond wisps that had escaped sticking damply to her neck.

She didn't look at him as he entered, continuing on with her martial arts workout. He couldn't tell what it was, perhaps a mixture of styles, but it was fast, brutal, and absolutely beautiful to watch.

Or maybe that was just her. She was so graceful and yet at the same time incredibly powerful. Strong and sure. She moved fluidly, different stances morphing from one into another without a break. A stunning show of female strength, revealing the warrior beneath all the form-fitting gowns and high heels he'd forced her to wear.

Shit, he'd known those muscles he'd felt beneath her clothing weren't there for show. But what he hadn't realized until now was how extremely attractive it was to watch her move.

She was the most amazing thing he'd ever seen.

I wanted to be a dancer . . .

But her father had told her dancers were weak, or at least that's what she'd revealed at Conrad's reception. A strange thing to think when dancers were the very opposite.

She came to a stop down Alex's end of the room, her back to him. She was breathing fast and hard, the lights gleaming on her skin. "Good afternoon, sir." She turned around, passing a hand across her forehead. "I hope you don't mind me using your gym."

"Not at all."

"I was careful, I kept the door closed and locked."

"So people don't see my delicate lover delivering killing blows to imaginary opponents?"

"Yes." Her gaze was flat, which meant she was hiding something.

Automatically he wanted to know what it was, but the time for that kind of thing was over. He had to put distance between them, not close it.

"So is that a special form of martial arts then?" He knew he should let her go, get on with his own workout, but for some reason he just stood there, staring at her.

"It's a mixture of different styles, yes. Adapted for the special forces unit I was part of."

"It's beautiful," he said honestly.

She blinked a little at that, her expressionless mask wavering. "Thank you. I should let you get on with your own workout."

God help him, he didn't want her to go. "You could join me if you wanted. Show me a few moves."

Her forehead creased. "You know martial arts?"

"Kenpo. I learned from an old guy in a studio in New York years ago. I actually pay him to come and spar with me at least once a week when I'm there." He'd told himself it was because every man should know how to defend himself from attack. But of course, that wasn't the real reason. In the years after Conrad, after his father's death, he'd felt perpetually unsafe and learning how to kill someone with his bare hands had helped.

She eyed him and this time the look she gave him was very much that of a fighter measuring up an opponent. He found it almost unbearably sexy. "I don't know if that's a good idea."

"Why not?" The combination of restlessness and vodka was making feel wild and a little reckless, not the best of combinations. "Scared I'll beat you?"

"I don't think so." The look in her eyes was derisive and he liked that too.

Weren't you supposed to be keeping her at a distance?

Yeah, well, he had. Two days of distance. And this was only working out, nothing more, right? Besides, he just . . . couldn't let her go quite yet. He wanted to see her move again.

He stepped back, rolling up the sleeves of the business shirt he wore. "Come on. I promise I won't hurt you."

A familiar spark glowed briefly in her eyes. "With all due respect, I wouldn't let you. And in fact it's you who should be worried about getting hurt."

"Uh-huh." He bent to deal with his shoes, taking them off along with his socks. The wooden floor was cool beneath his feet. "I'm sure you'll pull back at the crucial moment."

She was frowning deeply. "Sir . . ."

He moved past her out into the middle of the room. "Indulge me, sweetheart. Conrad has accepted the stakes. He's going to play tomorrow night. Which means I need to let off a little steam."

The frown vanished, her eyes widening. "He did? But . . . your clubs—"

"I'm going to beat him; don't worry about that." Alex grinned at her. "I'm going to take him down and make him beg for mercy. Now, why don't you try the same with me? If you can."

The look on her face cleared, her expression becoming determined.

Ten seconds later he found himself on his back with her forearm over his throat, holding him down with surprising strength. Or maybe not so surprising. He'd felt that same strength in her grip when she'd held his wrist in the chair.

He panted, looking up into her face. She was flushed, the gold flecks in her eyes glittering. Beautiful.

You fucking idiot. What the hell are you doing?

He didn't know. All he knew was that not thinking about the moment she'd closed her eyes and handed her trust to him hadn't worked after all.

That the second she got close, it was all he could think about.

That he wanted her to do it again.

"Let's go again," he said.

Katya waited until he'd gotten to his feet. Many men got angry when they were taken to the floor by a woman, and yet it wasn't anger she saw in his eyes but something far more complicated. Desire was there, and with it the thrill of a challenge. The spark of competition she'd seen ignited in him time and time again.

It made her catch her breath.

He'd kept himself away from her since South's reception, citing too much work. The same old excuse he'd given her the time before that too.

And maybe it was true. Or maybe it was something else. Maybe it was her.

Some part of her hoped so, but the rest of her knew that to hope was a bad idea.

Since he'd given her that orgasm, it had been like he'd turned a key inside her. Switching something on. A flame that burned hot and strong, that was hungry for more.

Dangerous. Very, very dangerous.

Left to herself the past two days, she hadn't been able to think about anything else, which was reason enough to worry. Because it wasn't only the physical pleasure she kept remembering, but the moment in the chair, when she'd been overcome by the feeling of vulnerability, of being helpless and exposed in front of him. The soldier in her had been appalled.

She'd been scared. She'd been weak. And she could not be either again.

Since Alex had kept to the club, she'd had nothing to do, so that was why she'd spent most of the time down here in the basement, working herself into physical exhaustion.

Proving her strength over and over again.

And as Alex got back to his feet, sliding into a Kenpo stance, with his hands up and ready, she knew that here was another opportunity to prove that strength.

This time against him.

Are you mad? You know what happens when you get close to him.

No, that would not happen. She would be stronger this time.

Katya composed herself. Then came at him with a punch to the head, no warning. He slipped to the side, grabbed her wrist, and twisted around her, using his body as a pivot point, his other arm flashing out and around her throat, pulling tight. She went still, her chin up, the crook of his elbow holding her hard against the lean strength of his body.

"Not so confident now, are we?" He sounded smug and not even particularly short of breath.

Katya didn't waste time replying. She shot one hand up and back into his face, at the same time as she twisted in his hold, holding on to the arm around her neck, using momentum and her own body weight to turn it, then pull down, sweeping her foot around and taking his feet out from under him, bringing him facedown onto the floor in seconds.

"Fuck," Alex muttered as she pulled his arm into the small of his back, her knee against his spine. "You're good at this."

"Of course I'm good at it. My life and those of my clients depend on me being able to protect both myself and them." She released him and stepped back.

He rolled onto his side, then got up in a quick, fluid motion. "You really like this bodyguard stuff?"

"I like to protect people, yes."

"Why?"

She frowned at the question. "Executive protection was the most logical choice of a civilian career for someone with my skill set."

"I'm not talking logical, sweetheart. I'm talking about what makes you want to give your life for someone else's." He ran a hand through his hair, pushing it back. "Especially when you started out wanting to be a dancer."

The water in the bath was red. The tiles were red. Everything was red. Everything except her mother, who was so white she looked carved out of marble. Her eyes were closed and she was smiling, but when Katya said her name there was no response. She wouldn't wake up; she just wouldn't wake up . . .

Cold seeped through Katya's body, the ice of memory freezing her. "I was a child. Being a soldier was a more honorable ambition. And as for giving your life for someone, well, that's what a soldier does. That's what I was brought up to believe."

"Fun childhood you must have had." His voice was light, but the look in his eyes wasn't. Was he goading her? "What about this promise you made? To your Mikhail."

"He is not my Mikhail. And why are you asking me these questions?"

"Are you going to marry him? Is that what you're going to do when you get back to Moscow? Settle into married bliss? Go on romantic missions for two? Lovingly kill bad guys together?"

Oh yes, Alex definitely was goading her. Why, she had

no idea, but one thing was sure—he had to stop talking right now.

She came at him, aiming for his head with her fists, but he countered, weaving and knocking her hands away. He was fast and very powerful, and she could feel the energy in him as he caught one of her punches in his hand, his fingers closing around hers.

She jerked her hand back to her chest, pulling him in close, then shooting her other hand up to catch on his chin and pushing it up and back.

He cursed, stumbling away, and she let him go, waiting.

"Jesus," he muttered. "You're amazing."

An odd warmth settled inside her. Odd because it was almost as if she cared what he thought of her and she didn't.

Katya watched him as he moved a little way away, pulling open the buttons of his shirt and taking it off, discarding it onto the gym floor. The bright lights of the gym followed the cut muscles of his chest and abs, the sharp flex and release in time with his quickened breathing.

He was beautiful. Intellectually she'd always appreciated it, but before he'd touched her she'd been confused about the physical attraction she'd felt for him. Not now, though. There was nothing confusing about the deep pulse of hunger that sat low in her gut as she watched him move back into the middle of the room. Nothing strange about the way she wanted to touch him, run her fingers over his chest and stomach the way he'd done to her. Explore that hard, lean body.

He moved, exploding toward her in a blur of movement. And because she was too busy staring at him, he took her by surprise. A punch to the head made her dodge, only to run into a kick to her thigh that had her down on the floor on her knees, his hand gripping her arm and twisting it back.

She didn't give him time to get comfortable. Bending over suddenly, she put her free arm down on the floor, putting distance between them. Then she jerked her pinned arm out straight and rolled away from him, each movement strong and powerful.

It broke the hold and she was up on her feet again as he came toward her. And this time she didn't let herself get distracted by his bare chest.

This fight had to end right now. The atmosphere was too thick, too tense. It unnerved her. She would take him down, prove her strength, prove to him that she was immune once and for all.

But you're not and you know you're not.

Katya ignored the thought. As he came toward her she waited until the last moment, then sidestepped and swept her arm up, once again catching him beneath the chin, the momentum of his rush forcing his head up and back. Then, continuing with the movement, she pivoted behind him, brought her hands over his face, pulled, and jerked him down onto the floor, twisting him as he fell until he was flat on his face.

"Fucking hell," he gasped.

But Katya was done. She stepped over him and dropped to her knees, straddling his body, her hands hard against his shoulders, pinning him onto the floor.

"What do you want?" she asked quietly, holding him there. "Why are you goading me? If you're trying to prove you're stronger, you forget, I'm a soldier. I've been fighting men since I left military school. Men are always trying to prove themselves against me. They always fail."

He lay still and she realized abruptly that her hands were on his bare skin. He felt good. Strong, hot. There was power in the lean, rangy body beneath hers. Perhaps a power he didn't use to his best advantage.

Power you want used on you . . .

She blinked in shock at the thought, her breath catching.

And in that moment Alex moved. A powerful shift that took her utterly by surprise. One minute she was looking down at the back of his head; the next he'd flipped her onto her back and he was the one leaning over her, straddling her hips, his knees planted on both sides of her thighs, fingers pinning her wrists to the mat on either side of her head.

Her heartbeat thumped, the blood rushing in her veins as a deep unease wound through her. She wasn't supposed to be the one on her back. She was supposed to be the one proving herself against him.

It serves you right. You let him distract you. Again.

She shifted, trying to dislodge him, but he only held her harder, tighter. She tried again, a different move this time, but he anticipated it, his thighs clamping tight around hers, keeping her down. Another twist, a special one she'd learned from her commander, Konstantinov, but again, it had absolutely no effect on the man holding her pinned.

She was breathing faster now, her skin slick with sweat, that unease sitting like a sickness in her gut. She'd been held down before, been beaten before, but it had never mattered—she stored away the experience, using it to do better next time. Yet this . . . this was different. And it wasn't physical pain she was afraid of—he wouldn't hurt her; she knew that. It was a different kind of fear. A much more basic, primitive kind.

You are helpless against him.

"Doesn't feel so good, does it?" His blue eyes were sharp edged and glittering. "Being held down like this." There was a fierce, almost savage expression on his face and she knew that sharp thing glinting in his gaze. Fury.

"What do you want?" Her voice was hoarse. "Why are you so angry?"

He bent his head, staring down at her, rage flickering like a candle flame in his eyes. "I want your surrender. Give it to me. Now."

A shiver raced over her skin, her muscles locking as she tensed beneath him. Instinctively she wanted to resist, protect herself, but he was too strong to fight. And struggling would only end up tiring her.

"Why?" she asked, sucking in a ragged breath. "Did I do something wrong?"

"Give it to me, Katya."

"No. Not until you tell me why." She didn't want to give in, didn't want to be beaten. He might have the upper hand physically, but that didn't mean she didn't have other weapons.

The powerful muscles of his chest and arms flexed as he shifted his weight, and she was conscious of his heat. Of his skin slick with sweat. Of the press of him on top of her.

So good . . .

"Tell me you surrender to me, and I'll tell you why." His voice was little more than a growl.

She didn't have a choice, did she? Katya shivered. "Yes, okay." She had to force the words out. "I surrender to you. Now tell me why."

Something flared in his eyes. Triumph or satisfaction, she couldn't tell which. "Because right now, all I want is something I can control, Katya mine. Just one thing. And that thing is you."

God, he was hard. She could feel the length of his cock pressing between her thighs. Pressing against the ache there. A sweet, intolerable ache. She fought it. "Why me? Why can't you find someone else?"

"No one else is as strong as you are. And I need to test myself against strength."

Heat licked up inside her, a sensual wave moving over

her skin. Making her want to move her hips, shift them against that hard ridge between her legs, ease the ache.

No, she couldn't do that. She wouldn't give in. Struggling with the urge, Katya concentrated on the look on his face instead, trying to read it. "Why? Because of South? He accepted your bet and the game is tomorrow. Your clubs are at stake." She searched the deep midnight of his gaze, remembering the tension that had been there between himself and the other man. That strange, nearly sexual atmosphere that seemed so dangerous. "It's him you're testing yourself against, isn't it? This is personal."

A muscle leapt in his jaw, the tension in his body winding tight as a catapult about to be launched. "Of course it's fucking personal," Alex said suddenly, and there was nothing lazy or mocking about his voice now. Passion vibrated through the words. A ferocity that sounded like it had been years in the making. "I want to take everything from him. Strip away all his money and his power. And when he's left with nothing, I want that motherfucker on his knees begging me for mercy. Maybe I'll give it to him. Or maybe I'll just put a fucking bullet through his brain instead."

Katya remained motionless beneath him. The words echoed with the force of a vow. "What did he do to you?" she whispered, caught by the savagery on his face. "Why do you hate him so much?" But even as she'd finished asking the question, the answer was already there, stark and clear in her head.

It all added up. That weird tension between the two men. The open hatred on Alex's face. The promise of revenge . . . Conrad had hurt him and probably in a sexual way.

Alex blinked. As if he'd been somewhere else, looking at something else. "All you need to know is that he'll deserve everything that's coming to him," he said, his tone absolutely final, making it clear the conversation was over.

Questions lodged in her throat, but she couldn't ask

JACKIE ASHENDEN

them. *Did South hurt you? Did he assault you? Was it sexual, sir?* No, definitely not. Those were questions that were hard for dearest friends, let alone ones she could ask her employer.

He probably wouldn't answer anyway and it would only make things even more difficult between them. And, God knew, that didn't need to happen.

She tried a slight movement to indicate she was ready to get up, yet the weight of him on her and the strength pinning her to the mat didn't lessen.

"I . . . understand." She tried to make her voice sound normal. "So have we finished here?"

But Alex's focus shifted again and then narrowed. On her. "No," he murmured. "We are extremely fucking far from finished."

A shiver whispered through her, heat prickling her skin. She tried to swallow, her throat dry. "Please. Let me up."

Slowly, he shook his head. "I don't think you want that."

The unease she'd felt earlier returned in full force, twisting and knotting with the sensual heat generated by his touch, until she couldn't work out which was which or even what she felt.

Fear. You're scared.

No. Of course she wasn't. She just had to get up.

"Please. I . . . need you to let me go."

He frowned. The savagery had faded from his expression, but the edge in his gaze was sharp as a blade. "Don't be afraid, Katya. I won't hurt you; you know that."

"I'm not afraid." But her voice was faint, thready.

"Yes, you are. What's scaring you?"

How could she explain the feeling when she barely understood it herself? "Sir, please."

Alex moved again, a subtle shift of his hips, and another shiver chased through her as the pressure of his erection brushed the sensitive point between her legs. And he saw it, his fingers on her wrists tightening. "Is it this?" He shifted again, deliberately, sending yet more electric shocks of sensation racing up her spine.

Her brain felt cloudy, her limbs heavy. "No. No, it's not." It felt like she had to keep saying it in order to make it true.

"You're a liar, sweetheart." He leaned down, his mouth inches away from hers, his gaze infinite. "You're still fighting me. You were supposed to surrender."

She struggled for breath. Struggled against the bizarre temptation to close the gap and kiss him. He smelled of sweat and musk, and that subtle expensive aftershave she liked.

Delicious . . .

"I have," she said insistently.

"No, you haven't." His body moved and again that lightning strike of pleasure flashed through her. "You're so tense you're almost rigid."

"Sir—"

"Stop fighting, Katya." His mouth was so achingly close. "There's nothing to fight against."

Her breathing had become ragged. "You don't understand. I can't . . . I can't give in."

"Why not?"

"Because it's a weakness." *Red in the water. Blood on the tiles.* Her mouth felt like a desert. "And I . . . I can't be vulnerable. I can't be exposed. I have to be strong. I have to fight."

The darkness of his gaze held something she didn't understand and yet couldn't look away from. "Did you think you were weak the night you let me touch you?"

"I . . ." She stopped, her heart pounding in her chest. "I was afraid."

"You were, but you let me touch you anyway. You let me give you pleasure. You trusted me to keep you safe and

I did. And you will never know how strong you were in that moment. How powerful. Just like you're strong now."

She swallowed, her body aching with tension and hunger. With desperation. "Alex . . ."

"Let me prove it to you." He straightened, letting go of her wrists, his blue eyes never leaving hers. Then he laid one palm on her stomach. "Let me show you how strong you are."

Now her hands were free she could leave. She could twist and move, get rid of him. Get up and walk away. All her instincts were screaming at her to do just that, but . . . some lost part of her wanted to know what he meant. Wanted him to show her. And she was so tired of fighting. Sometimes she just wanted not to have to.

Alex didn't move and she knew he was waiting for her permission. So she gave it. "Yes," the word soft, almost a whisper. And then she lay still, her breath escaping in a long rush, her muscles relaxing.

Surrendering.

Finally he put one hand down beside her head, leaning over her. Looking down at her, his other hand motionless on her stomach. "Don't close your eyes this time," he said. "Keep them on me. And that's an order."

Wordlessly she nodded, trying not to tense up again as the palm resting on her abdomen slid down, pushing beneath the waistband of her yoga pants to the bare skin beneath. His fingers stroked over her skin, little caresses that made her tremble inside.

She wanted to look away, close her eyes like she had the time before, but he'd ordered her not to, so she didn't, making herself hold his gaze as his hand moved lower. Beneath the cotton of her panties, sliding through the curls between her thighs.

A sharp blade of pleasure cut through her, making her gasp aloud, the sound echoing in the room. Again her instinct was to fight against it, inexplicable fear wrapping cold fingers around her throat. But his fingers moved again, lightly brushing, then circling her clit, gentle and undemanding.

Yet that sword of pleasure wasn't gentle or undemanding. It was bright and vicious, making her groan, making her want to move her hips, relieve the desperate ache. She wanted to spread her legs, but he was still straddling her, preventing her, and the constriction made the pleasure somehow even more intense.

"You're wet, Katya," he said, stroking her, teasing her. "And hot. I know you like this. Do you have any idea what knowing that does to me? What giving me your surrender means?"

She didn't need him to tell her. She could see it all laid bare in his eyes, the blue gone smoky and dark with desire. His voice was rough, his expression tight with hunger. The evidence of her power. She could feel it uncoiling inside her, a deep sensuality she'd subconsciously been trying to repress for a very long time now.

His hand slid farther between her legs, one finger pushing gently against her entrance. And she gave in to the need to lift her hips, arching as she kept her gaze on his, feeling his finger slide deep inside her, tearing a moan from her.

"Yes," he whispered. "That's it. Let me know how good it feels." His hand began to move in a gentle, insistent rhythm, the slide of his finger inside her unbelievably intense.

She panted, unable to look away from the fierce beauty of his face, desire stamped along every line.

He was right. This wasn't weakness. This was power. This was strength.

And Katya gave herself over to it, gasping as he added another finger, stretching her, creating bright sparks of pleasure that ignited along her nerve endings, making her moan. His hand urged her faster, pressing harder. And this time as the climax approached, there was none of that reflexive fear. She kept looking at him, watching the desperate expression on his face flare and change as the orgasm caught her, making her cry out at the intensity of it, flames glittering behind her eyes.

Afterwards she lay there for what seemed a long time, the beat of her pulse loud in her head, shaking as he withdrew his hand from her body, his touch gentle as he adjusted her clothing. He didn't look at her.

"Please," she said thickly, sitting up, not even realizing she was going to speak until the words were out. "Let me give you something in return."

His gaze flickered back to hers. "I don't need anything."

Such a lie when she could see the rigid length of his erection pressing against the zipper of his pants. "You do. I can see that you do."

"Katya—"

"I want to give you something this time. I need to."

He began to shift away. "Now is not the time."

"So, you're afraid as well?" She hadn't meant it to sound so accusing, but she didn't take it back.

Alex stilled, half turned away from her. And for a long moment she thought he was going to carry on. Get up and leave.

But he didn't.

He turned back to her, still on his knees, the look on his face enigmatic. "You want to give me something?" His voice sounded rough. "Okay then. Give me your hand."

She did so, his fingers curling around her wrist. Then he undid a couple of buttons on his fly and held her palm to the hard plane of his stomach, pushing it down beneath the waistband of his pants and under the soft cotton of his boxers.

Her breath caught as she felt the heat of him, the rigid

length of his shaft against her fingers. She'd never touched a man like this before, had never realized how hard it would feel or how soft and smooth the skin was. The contrast was intoxicating.

His hand circled hers, closing her fingers around him. "Do exactly what I say, understand?"

She looked up, her heartbeat hammering in her chest as a sudden feeling of guilt assailed her. Oh God, what if his reluctance was due to what had possibly happened between him and South? What if this was a problem for him? Had she been wrong to insist? Then again, he clearly didn't have any problems with sex given what she'd seen of his sex life.

"You do want this, don't you?" she asked to be absolutely sure.

"Of course I fucking want it." There was an edge in his voice. "Why do you think my dick is hard?"

Okay, so that had been the wrong thing to ask. And no doubt more questions along those lines would only make him angrier.

"So what do you want me to do?"

A shadow moved in the deep blue depths. "Hold me firmly, like this." He squeezed his fingers around hers. "Then move your hand." He showed her, guiding the movement.

The breath hissed out of him as she tightened her grip, as she moved her hand the way he'd shown her. She couldn't stop looking at him, at the pleasure staining his cheekbones, at the fierce desire glittering in his eyes.

Now the power was with her. Even though she was doing what he'd ordered. It was fascinating. Addicting. How incredible to have this man literally in the palm of her hand, to be able to undo him in a way that wasn't about physical strength. Because she was undoing him, she was watching this jaded, cynical playboy come apart in front of her.

This was trust. Of a different kind than him trusting her with his life. This was him trusting her with his pleasure. Like she'd given him hers.

It made something gather tight in her chest. Made it ache in a way that didn't have anything to do with sex. Did it frighten him the way it had frightened her?

But she couldn't tell from his face. There was only a taut look there, like a man desperately searching for something and not finding it.

He whispered her name then, urging her movements even faster, and then she felt him suddenly go rigid, his eyes shutting tight. "Oh fuck," he murmured, his fingers around hers squeezing tight, his breathing harsh, his body shuddering.

She felt his cock pulse, her palm becoming slick as he groaned, his movements losing their rhythm. Then he bent his head, his body shaking.

But his hand remained clamped around hers and she didn't move.

People paid her to protect their lives, so that's what she did. Yet no one had ever trusted her with anything more. But there was more, wasn't there?

There was this. There was him.

CHAPTER ELEVEN

Alex picked his cuff links up off the black marble of the vanity and clipped them on, his movements sharp and precise. He didn't look at his reflection in the mirror, only running one hand through his hair. It was still damp from the shower, but fuck it. Conrad was always perfectly presented, but he could take Alex as he came.

Alex grinned at his own dark humor as he turned and strode out of the bathroom. Conrad wouldn't, of course, be taking him anywhere. This time he'd be the one doing the taking.

Over the past couple of days, he'd perfected his revenge plan. One that would take everything that mattered to Conrad and would, Alex hoped, leave him a sobbing, begging mess at the end of it.

First he was going to let Conrad believe he had all the power at the game, since that's what got the guy off and would lull him into a false sense of security. It would also give Alex and Katya some time to investigate things for Zac, Eva, and Gabriel, and Alex hoped they would get some important information that would be of use.

Then once that was achieved he would somehow get rid of the other players so it was just him and Conrad, a one-on-one game.

Then Alex would up the stakes. Make the other man

hungry. Make him want. Make him so desperate he'd do anything to win. Anything such as putting his own club up for grabs. All his money. His livelihood.

And only then, when he was sure of a win, would Alex beat Conrad, and he *would* beat him. Make him realize he'd lost everything.

And as the final pièce de résistance, Alex would get out a gun and put it to that fucker's head and make him beg for the last thing he had: his life. Perhaps he'd put a bullet through Conrad's brain, like Eva said. Or maybe he wouldn't. Maybe just the sight of Conrad crying in fear, the way Alex had sobbed when Conrad had bent him over the cold tiles of that bathroom, would be enough.

Whatever happened, one thing was certain. That motherfucker was going down.

Out in the lounge area, Katya sat on the couch, going through the purse on her lap. There was no sign that that was where she slept every night, folding up the blankets and putting them away so no one knew their real sleeping arrangements. He'd tried to get her to swap places so she had the bed, but she'd refused and hell, if she wanted to martyr herself on the couch then he was happy for her to do so.

She was wearing a cocktail dress that looked like a glittering green-gold spiderweb. It left one shoulder bare, the hem ending at mid-thigh, her long, toned legs on show. It was strapless too, her shoulders milky pale against the silk. He'd insisted she wear her hair down and she'd pulled the thick golden waterfall to one side. The colors gleamed in the light, gilt and caramel and deep guinea gold.

Jesus, she was beautiful.

But that didn't change how pissed off he was with her. *You're not pissed with her. It's yourself you're unhappy with.*

Yeah, well, that was true. He should have left the gym

after he'd brought her down on the mat and made her come. He should have left while he still had the control. But he hadn't. She'd made that comment about him being afraid and of course, like the fucking cliché he was, he'd had to prove that he wasn't.

It wasn't only that.

No, it wasn't. Their sparring match, the way he'd mastered her, beaten her, had made him so hard he'd been just about to explode. He'd always avoided strong women, preferring his sex easy to come by and easy to leave, with him having the upper hand. But he'd never realized how erotic it was to take a strong woman like Katya down like that. How intoxicating. And the sweet irony of it was that even lying under him, pinned by him, she hadn't been beaten. In a way, she'd been even stronger. Because he'd wanted her so damn badly.

Perhaps it had been stupid to point that out to her. To show her how powerful she was. But he'd hated seeing the fear in her eyes as he'd pinned her, knowing what it was like to feel helpless while someone stronger than you held you down. Yet what he'd hated even more was that she seemed to think sexual desire, one of the few things that brought him pleasure these days, that made him feel as if he'd truly left Conrad for dust, was a weakness she had to fight.

I can't be vulnerable. I have to be strong.

Why did she feel that way? Who had taught her that?

But no, he couldn't ask those things, couldn't get close. And certainly not now, just as they were about to leave for Conrad's game.

Christ, he wished he didn't want her so much. That everything about her didn't fascinate him in the way that it did.

She looked up as he stood there, her makeup perfect. Clearly she'd been practicing. Gold glimmered on her eyelids, making the green of her irises even more intense. "So, are we going into this game with you still angry with me?"

Goddammit. Did she even know how to be subtle?

Alex stuck his hands in the pockets of his tuxedo pants. There was no point in denying it, especially since he'd made it pretty obvious by going and hiding in his office again, making the excuse he was working on his game tactics. "Your timing is, as ever, impeccable, Katya mine."

She ignored him. "Being angry with me is a waste of energy. I'm not your enemy. Conrad South is. Or had you forgotten?"

He scowled at her. "You really think I'd fucking forgotten that, sweetheart?"

She rose to her feet, tall and straight, holding her purse at her side. Her gaze was very direct. "Should I not have touched you, is that what this is about? Are you punishing me for giving you pleasure?"

No. He was punishing her for the way she undermined his control. For the intensity of his desire for her. For her strength and her beauty. Her honesty.

For being a woman he couldn't let himself have, no matter how much he wanted her.

"Why would I do that?" he said flippantly. "Being angry about an excellent hand job is like getting pissed at your bank account for having a million dollars in it."

But she just looked at him and he knew she'd seen past his stupid response, just as she always did. "You are worried about this game." She didn't say it like it was a question. She said it like it was a fact, and shit, she was right, wasn't she?

He had his plan, it was true, but he wasn't relishing the shit Conrad would pull before the moment Alex would have the other man on his knees. And Conrad would pull some shit; of that Alex had no doubt.

Yet he didn't want to admit he was worried. Like her, he hated revealing weakness.

She had her hand on your cock. She made you come. What's more revealing than that?

Christ, yes. He knew how vulnerable sex could make you. How exposed you could be. It was why he chose the women he did. Why they never stayed for more than a night.

After Conrad had hurt him, it had taken him six months before he could even bear to touch himself. A whole year before he'd let anyone else touch him. On the night of his eighteenth birthday he'd gotten drunk at one of the Angels', Gabriel's motorcycle club's, parties and taken to bed one of the chicks who'd hung around the bikers. She'd been older, very experienced, knew her way around a man. And Alex was drunk enough that he hadn't had any flashbacks at all.

That was the night he'd *actually* lost his virginity–or at least, that's what he liked to tell himself. Not with Conrad, never that.

From then on, that's what Alex had wanted. Women who knew what they were doing. Who knew what they wanted from him. And didn't mind if he was drunk out of his head or high or doing any of the other things he used to help him forget. Until sex had become what it should be–a pleasurable, physical release, not something redolent with shame and guilt and a hundred other emotions that exhausted him.

But Katya . . . She was different. She wasn't experienced, at least not in this. She was the innocent and all this was new to her. These feelings would be new to her too. This was special to her. This mattered.

A strange feeling curled inside him. A sense of yearning. As if he wanted to be able to experience that newness too. Have it be special, have it matter. Not ripped from him along with his innocence.

Christ, even just to have her know him, because no one else did. Not even Gabriel, possibly the only person on the planet he was close to. And sometimes . . . God, sometimes it was so fucking tiring to be alone. To carry all these secrets around and not share them with anyone. To not share the pain with anyone. To know that the only person who could carry them, who could deal with them, was yourself.

Would it be so bad to let her know?

Well, but who the fuck was he anyway? The boy he'd been nineteen years ago was dead and he'd spent so long being Alex St. James, billionaire playboy, gambler, and club owner, he didn't even know if there *was* anyone else under all of that.

Perhaps there wasn't. Perhaps there was nothing there at all.

Alex made himself meet her steady gaze. "Yes," he said, speaking the truth. "You're right. I am worried about the game."

If she was surprised by the confession, she didn't show it. She only stared at him a long moment before taking a step toward him and holding out her hand. "If there's only one thing you take to the game, Alexei, then take this. You can trust me. With your life. With everything."

The sound of his name in Russian . . . It went all the way down into the darkness that was his soul. He didn't like the vulnerable feeling it left in him, yet the way she'd said it and the word "everything" resonated even more deeply. And he found himself reaching for her hand and holding on to it, the warmth of her skin against his.

There was no guile to Katya Ivanova. She didn't play games or try to manipulate. She was straight up, honest. Honorable. And he could see in the green depths of her eyes that she meant every word she said.

If there was one person on earth he could trust it was probably going to be the woman standing in front of him.

Tell her your plan.

No, he couldn't. Not yet. It would reveal too much, his anger and his hate. It would reveal how much this mattered, and he wasn't ready for that. Besides, he'd spent too long trusting no one but himself to give that trust away so easily.

Still, he wanted to give her something. So he raised her hand to his mouth and kissed the back of it. "You'll teach me those moves, won't you? The ones that had me on my back yesterday?"

She eyed him warily but didn't pull away. "Yes. Of course."

"Good." He lowered her hand and laced his fingers through hers. "Come, Katya mine. Let's go fuck a man up."

This time when they entered the Four Horsemen casino, the doorman in the foyer betrayed no surprise at all, merely inclining his head as Alex and Katya approached. The doorman didn't take them through into the bar either, guiding them instead to the elevators.

The doorman, Alex, and Katya went up a couple of floors, the doors opening directly into a large room hung with glittering chandeliers, the walls papered white, thick white carpet on the floor. There was a lavishly appointed bar down the other end, chairs and couches scattered about. And in the center of the room was a large black poker table circled by a rail.

Various people either stood or sat, talking among themselves and quietly sipping their drinks. Hangers-on of the players, Alex guessed. There were a number of others who weren't, though, women mainly, beautiful and expensively dressed. For decorative purposes only.

There were already a number of men and women sitting around the poker table. Alex had met several of them that night at Conrad's little reception, but he hadn't paid much attention to them. Which was unlike him, since studying his opponents was usually a good idea.

You were distracted.

Yeah, he had been. But ultimately those other players didn't matter anyway. He wasn't here to beat them. There was only one player who mattered as far as Alex was concerned.

Several of the people at the table looked up as he and Katya stepped out of the elevator onto the raised landing just outside the elevator doors. There were stairs sweeping down into the room, but Alex ignored them for a moment, surveying the room from his vantage point, partly to get a good look around but also partly as a show of confidence.

There were four people already at the table. A much older Chinese woman dressed immaculately in vintage Chanel, her night black hair now mostly silver. Her face still held the vestiges of what must have been a compelling beauty, but the look in her black eyes was completely cold. The woman had only been introduced to him as Mrs. Lau, a powerful businesswoman who'd taken the reins of her husband's manufacturing empire after his death.

Next to her, closest to Alex, was a powerfully built Arab man in an exquisitely made custom suit. A sheikh from some tiny Middle Eastern country Alex had never heard of. The guy had looked uncomfortable back at the reception and he still did now, leaning back in his chair, a ferocious scowl on his face.

The chair next to the sheikh, at the end of the table closest to Alex, was vacant, but the next one along had a woman sitting at it. A blond American heiress called Christine. She'd introduced herself at the reception, though he hadn't paid much attention to her, his head too full of Katya to notice. Christine looked like she was in her thirties but could have been any age, since he was sure she'd had some work done. She gave him a measuring look from beneath her way too long to be natural eyelashes, her full red mouth pouty.

Next to her was the scarred mercenary who had also been at the reception. The man's dark eyes were as cold as Mrs. Lau's, his expression completely impenetrable. There was something familiar about him that Alex hadn't noticed before but nagged at him now. Weird.

The seat next to the mercenary was empty, but Alex could see the fifth player standing near the bar, talking on his cell phone. Jason August, a Texan oil baron and walking cliché in his Stetson, his loud voice with its broad vowels ringing out over the room.

Conrad himself seemed to be absent.

"Mr. St. James, if you would take a seat," the doorman urged, making gestures toward the poker table.

Alex kept his fingers laced through Katya's as he descended the stairs and approached the table. It wouldn't hurt to give them a show with his adoring lover, though most of them had already seen him with his arm around her at the Apocalypse reception anyway.

He kissed the back of her hand again, seating himself down one end of the table, in between the sheikh and Christine, the heiress. Katya gave him a brilliant smile before moving down toward the bar. She'd been to enough of his games in her traditional bodyguard capacity to know that spectators were not permitted past the rail that circled the table protecting the players.

Her role for the evening was to see what she could scope out of the game and of the other people in the room. Perhaps talk to the other hangers-on and see what else she could find out. He'd asked her to leave the private gaming room to see what kind of information she could get from the main gaming floor, but she'd refused. Her place was near him, she'd said. To protect him.

That wasn't going to be a problem of course. Not with what he'd already put on the table in front of Conrad. His clubs. Himself. Conrad wasn't going to risk losing either of those with an ill-advised attempt on his life.

Alex sat down, nodding at the other players.

"Nice to see you again, Alex," Christine purred from his right. "Your first time playing in the Apocalypse?"

Tension gathered in his shoulders, but he ignored it, leaning his arms on the table and smiling at the woman as if he were sitting down to a relaxing dinner with friends. "Aren't we all Apocalypse virgins? I didn't think you got invited twice."

"Sure. Ordinarily." Christine's blue eyes flicked toward the Chinese woman. "Except if you're Mrs. Lau of course."

Mrs. Lau was talking in Mandarin to a man standing at her back, but obviously she heard her name, because she flashed both Alex and Christine an enigmatic look.

"In fact," Christine said, leaning in close, the plunging neckline of her blue gown giving him an excellent view of very round, fake breasts. "I heard that it's not really poker that goes on here."

Alex was careful not to let any reaction show. Instead he kept the smile on his face. "If it's not poker, then what?"

Christine flashed him a naughty look she must have practiced a hundred times in the mirror. "Could be anything. I know Conrad gets bored. He likes to mix it up a little."

Oh yeah. He certainly did.

A waiter paused beside Alex and put down a tray containing a crystal tumbler full of clear liquid on the small side table next to his chair. Grey Goose probably. Another of Conrad's power games. Showing that he knew you and your preferences without being asked.

Alex was tempted to wave away the drink, but that wouldn't convey the right message. That he didn't give a fuck.

Instead he leaned back in his chair and raised the tumbler in Christine's direction. "Here's to mixing it up then, darling."

At that moment a door near the bar opened and Conrad walked in.

He was immaculate as always, in a white tuxedo, the black bow of his tie perfectly centered, the red handkerchief he had folded in his breast pocket bright as a spot of blood against the white fabric.

The tension in the room suddenly hiked up, stretching thin and taut.

Alex didn't move, continued to take a sip from his glass, watching as the other man greeted a few people as he made his way over to the table.

The other players straightened in their chairs while Jason August finally made his way over too, sitting down with a grunt as Conrad stood at one end of the table. Conrad didn't focus on Alex in particular, his gaze meeting Alex's for a moment before passing on to the next person. As if Alex wasn't special in any way.

"Friends," Conrad said, smiling like he knew things other people didn't. "Welcome to the Apocalypse. You will find it less of a game and more an . . . experience." The smile on his face did not reach his eyes. "This year's tournament is going to be slightly different in that Mr. St. James down there has convinced me to join the players instead of sitting out like I normally do." He gave a chuckle, encouraging everyone to smile with him. "He knows I can never resist a bet."

The tension around the table loosened, the other players smiling along with Conrad and looking his way.

But Alex could feel the muscles in his shoulders and neck getting tight. He had to fight down the urge to launch himself across the table and strangle the other man with his perfect black bow tie.

Remember the plan.

Good fucking point.

Alex inclined his head as if acknowledging a joke, raising his glass in another token toast. Keeping his "I don't give a shit" smile pasted there.

Conrad gave a bit more speechifying, which Alex ignored, checking on Katya down near the bar before sweeping a glance over the rest of the players, noting their reactions. Mrs. Lau betrayed nothing, like the mercenary. Jason was handing his phone to an aide while Christine sipped at her champagne and fiddled with her poker chips. The sheikh stared at Conrad, his brow furrowed.

Alex dismissed him as a threat. The guy appeared inexperienced and Alex had never seen him at a poker table before, so what he was doing here was anyone's guess. As to the other players, Alex knew for a fact that Jason August liked to play fairly often and when he played he liked to win. Mrs. Lau was another unknown quantity and the fact that her poker face was pretty much perfect made her an opponent to be wary of. Christine seemed as inexperienced as the sheikh, but then she didn't have that unconscious discomfort that the sheikh radiated. Perhaps she was projecting inexperience as a cover.

The mercenary, though . . . Shit, there was that nagging familiarity Alex couldn't quite put his finger on. Yet he was sure he would have remembered a guy with a scar like that from other games. . . .

"Thank you for bearing with me, friends," Conrad was saying. "And that's enough of me talking. Now we get to

James here. You have a very lovely girlfriend over there by the bar. I nominate her to be your stand-in."

Fuck, no.

The response was instant and unequivocal. And it wasn't, despite what he'd told Christine, only because Katya was starting to become somewhat special to him. No one screwed around with his employees. No one.

With a lazy movement he swirled the vodka in his tumbler, managing to keep the slightly bored expression on his face and not let any of his fury out. "So let me get this straight," he said slowly. "You want to play strip poker, but the players don't strip, a nominated stand-in does instead?"

"In a nutshell, my dear boy." The prick was still smiling that smug smile, like he just made the best joke in the world. "That way we preserve our dignity and we all have something nice to look at. I'm sure I can find the ladies here something for their preference too."

"I have no problem with looking at girls," Christine said, her mouth curving suggestively. "Though I'm a little disappointed not to see Mr. St. James in the buff."

Alex laughed. "Oh, honey, don't give up hope yet. But you know, Conrad"—he didn't bother to keep the edge out of his voice—"I'm going to have to run that by Katya. I'm not sure she'd agree to taking her clothes off in front of a whole lot of strangers."

"Well, I guess that all depends on your poker skill, doesn't it?" Conrad's tone was slick as a pool of oil. "But I'm sure one of your lovers wouldn't mind. Aren't they all strippers and suchlike?"

Okay, so here was the shit he'd always known Conrad would pull, the little power games he liked to play. Probing for weaknesses, testing. And since Katya was here with Alex, it was natural for her to be Conrad's target.

There was a certain poetic justice to it in many ways.

Since if Conrad had been seeking to use one of Alex's usual lovers, it wouldn't have bothered him quite so much. Oh, he would have been pissed, but only in the same way as he would if anyone started screwing with him and his stuff without permission.

But Katya wasn't one of his normal lovers. And he didn't feel pissed. He felt furious.

Calm down. You have a plan. Remember it.

Yeah, the plan. And that meant putting up with Conrad's crap to lull the guy into a false sense of security. In which case, maybe a small, token protest would help. It would make Conrad think that Alex had revealed a weakness, that he'd been affected by Conrad's power plays. And that in turn would make Conrad even smugger. Possibly even complacent.

Excellent.

Alex let out a long-suffering sigh and sat back in his chair. "Cheap, Conrad. I didn't think we were at the 'make patronizing comments about my lovers' stage of the evening yet. Weren't you supposed to be cleverer than that?"

"You better pray she agrees, son."

"Oh?" Alex lifted a brow.

"Because if she doesn't, you're out of the game." Conrad's teeth flashed. "This game is mine and I make the rules. And if I want you out, you're out. Understood?"

Asshole. Alex lifted a shoulder. "Oh sure, but isn't strip poker a little juvenile?" He tilted his head slightly, unable to resist baiting Conrad. "I seem to recall someone talking about a game for men, not boys. But perhaps I'm mistaken."

The other man's expression didn't change, but Alex didn't miss the almost imperceptible tightening of his mouth. A hit. How satisfying.

"You have five minutes to get the lady to agree," Conrad said as if Alex hadn't spoken. "I'll organize stand-ins for the others."

Alex laughed. "Hell, Conrad, if you want my girlfriend that badly you know you only have to ask. No need to go through all of this strip poker nonsense. I'm always happy to share."

"I prefer my goods not to be shop-soiled." Conrad's hazel eyes glittered. "Are you in or out?"

Time to stop pushing. Alex put his tumbler down on the side table with a soft click. "Well, of course I'm in. But I'll probably need those five minutes."

Katya already knew Alex wouldn't need those five minutes. She'd heard what Conrad had said and had already made her decision.

The man was targeting Alex and using her to get at him; that much was obvious. Which meant she had to neutralize herself as a possible weapon. And the way to do that with a manipulative game player like Conrad South was to not give him any more ammunition. If she took the fun out of the game, he'd leave her alone.

She straightened from her position with the other spectators at the rail circling the table as Alex approached her. His mouth curved in his usual lazy smile, but there was a dangerous glitter in his eyes. He was furious.

"I presume you heard that?" he asked, sliding an arm around her waist and drawing her away from the other spectators where no one could overhear them, though that didn't stop every eye in the place from looking at them.

"Yes. And it's fine. I can do it."

He turned her so his back was to the room and she was sheltered by it; then he bent his head near her ear and she couldn't stop the shiver that went through her as his breath passed over her neck. "You don't have to."

It wasn't what she was expecting. She turned her head, meeting his gaze, reading the anger in it. "If you refuse, you're out of the game. And we haven't got what we came here for yet, remember?"

An expression she didn't understand crossed his face. "Getting your clothes off in front of a bunch of strangers was not part of your contract."

"I will do what I need to do for the success of the mission. Taking my clothes off is nothing."

"You really want to be naked in front of all these people?"

"Nakedness doesn't bother me."

"It did that night when I told you to get undressed."

Unfamiliar heat warmed her cheeks. "Yes, but that's because it was you."

"That shouldn't make any difference."

Katya swallowed. "Yes, well, it did. I don't know these people. I don't care what they think. They mean nothing to me." She let the implication rest there for a moment before continuing. "My body is only a tool, Alex. And if it's useful to you then why not?"

He looked at her for a long moment. "I'll do what I can to win so you won't have to be naked, at least."

"No, you can't do that either and you know it. South is a bully. If you show in any way that you care about the outcome, he'll use that against you."

His jaw tightened and for a second a hot spark of determination glowed in his eyes. A fury. "No, he won't. I'll make sure of that."

Katya opened her mouth to ask how he could be so sure, but then Conrad said, "Well? Time's up."

Alex didn't turn, keeping his gaze on hers. "I won't let him hurt you, Katya. Trust me." Again, that determined, certain look. As if he knew what he was doing. As if he had a plan.

A week ago that would have made her angry. That if he did, indeed, have a plan he hadn't seen fit to share it with her. Yet getting angry seemed pointless now and wouldn't help the situation. She had trusted him before; she would trust him now. And perhaps if she did, maybe he'd then trust her in return.

Responding to an impulse she'd never been conscious of before, Katya rose up on her toes and pressed her mouth to his. A swift, fleeting kiss that she hoped conveyed everything that couldn't be said now. Then she stepped past him and up to the poker table, met Conrad's hooded gaze. "I'd be happy to help out."

The man smiled at her, and it was greedy. "Excellent. A very good decision, my dear. Now, shall we play? Winner gets to determine which piece of clothing comes off which stand-in."

Some of the women she'd spotted around the room earlier had come forward to the table, taking their places behind the chairs of the various players. Clearly they were also stand-ins of Conrad's. There was only one man, lean and handsome, and he had come to stand behind Mrs. Lau's chair.

Had it been Conrad's intention to add this twist to the game all along? And had these people been invited to be spectators for that very reason?

Katya studied them as she took her place behind Alex's chair. They were all, without exception, very beautiful and expertly made up. But the look on their faces was blank. Strangely, they reminded her of the poker players seated at the table, as if they too were keeping their emotions in check, not letting anyone know what they were thinking.

The game began, the dealer dealing out the cards. Katya couldn't see Alex's face, only the rest of the table. The American woman was laughing while the tall Arab man, the sheikh, kept his gaze squarely on his cards, his lean, fiercely handsome face tight with some emotion Katya didn't recognize. The fat Texan was tapping away with a poker chip while Conrad sat there lazily holding his cards, his gaze on the rest of the players.

Alex won the first round. Decisively. He didn't even bother looking around the table, his gaze on Conrad as he said, "The necklace off your stand-in."

The woman behind Conrad, a stunningly beautiful brunette, nodded and undid the diamond choker she wore around her neck.

"A necklace?" Conrad raised an eyebrow. "When you could have had her dress? I'm disappointed, son. Very disappointed indeed."

"The necklace can be a bonus prize for the next winner," Alex said. "Unless it's something special of course."

"Not at all." Conrad held up his hand and the woman behind his chair put the necklace in it. He leaned forward and put the glittering diamond strand on the table. "We have to keep this fun, right?"

Several rounds passed, Alex winning all of them. The woman behind the Texan lost her shoes while—to keep things equal opportunities presumably—the man behind Mrs. Lau lost his shirt.

"Hmmm," Conrad said lightly as the cards were dealt out yet again. "Are you planning on winning all these rounds, St. James? Feeling a little protective of your girl maybe?"

Alex's gaze was on his cards. He lifted a negligent shoulder. "I just had some good hands. And this one's shit." He put it back down on the table. "I fold."

The Chinese woman won the round, and Katya saw Conrad's gaze flick to where she stood behind Alex's chair, could almost feel the silent urging the man was giving off. But Mrs. Lau clearly had no interest in Katya, because she gestured to the woman behind the sheikh's chair. "Take something off. I don't care what."

Conrad leaned his elbows on the table. "Oh, come now, Mrs. Lau. Take an interest. A good businessman or -woman should know their stock."

Stock? Interesting word to use.

Mrs Lau's cold, black eyes gave him a glance. She didn't say anything for a long moment, her face absolutely expressionless. "The dress," she said at last, turning to gesture at the woman. "Let us see."

The woman behind the sheikh's chair did as she was told without hesitation. She didn't even blush as she shrugged herself out of the cocktail gown she wore, placing it over the rail separating the table from the spectators.

"Very nice," Conrad said. "What do you think, August?"

The Texan's gaze was acquisitive because the woman was, it had to be said, very beautiful. "Pretty damn cute."

But there was something in Mrs. Lau's eyes as they ran over the young woman's figure that sent a shiver down Katya's spine. It wasn't in the least bit sexual, unlike the men's gazes. More as if she were studying a fine piece of horseflesh she wanted to buy.

Katya filed that away in her head for future reference as the game went on.

As the next couple of rounds proceeded, first the American woman won, undressing the single male stand-in down to his boxers. Then it was the scarred mercenary's turn to win. His gaze was dispassionate as he gestured for the woman standing behind Conrad to lose her gown.

The woman did so. She wasn't wearing a bra, but this didn't seem to worry her as she stepped out of her dress, straightening and standing there calmly.

"Beautiful," August said, whistling his appreciation. "I like good tits on a woman."

"I'm sure we'll be seeing plenty of those soon enough." Conrad smiled down the other end of the table straight at Alex as the dealer dealt another hand. "I think it's time to stop protecting your lady friend, son. I'm sure she can handle it." His smile widened, his gaze shifting to Katya. "Can't you, darling?"

Oh yes, he was playing with them. With both of them.

This was like the military school she'd gone to. Where the teachers would take the pupils outside in the middle of winter, make them stand naked in the snow, then throw buckets of cold water over them. Teaching them to suffer the pain and the cold. To bear it. Tough it out.

This was nothing compared to that.

She straightened her shoulders and made herself smile in return. "Of course I can."

Alex's lean figure, sprawling lazily in the chair in front of her, didn't move. "Well, shit, sweetheart," he said casually. "If you want to take your clothes off, far be it from me to stop you." Nothing in his posture or his voice gave him away, but she knew he was tense all the same. She could feel it radiating from him like heat from the sun.

And perhaps Conrad sensed it too, because his eyes had taken on a predatory glitter. It made Katya want to put her hands up, loosen her muscles, prepare to attack or defend. But she did neither, keeping her hands at her sides instead.

The round went on and she found herself gazing at Alex's hands. Long, with narrow fingers. The hands of a pianist. An artist. The hands that had touched her in the gym, given her such pleasure . . .

One was curled loosely around the tumbler of vodka that had stayed at the same level for most of the past hour. The other was spread on his thigh. No one else could see, but she could. And she knew the knuckles of that hand were white.

"Straight flush," Conrad said, laying his cards on the table. "My round, I believe."

There were only two others still in. The American woman pulled a face and threw her cards onto the table while Alex laughed and did the same. "It's yours. Buckle up, Katya mine. This shit is about to get real."

Conrad's smile widened. He wasn't looking at Katya

now; he was looking directly at Alex. "She can lose the dress."

Alex crossed one leg over the other, looking completely at ease. "Well, naturally she can lose the dress."

Katya began to reach behind her to grab at the zipper, but Conrad raised a finger.

"No. I don't want you to do it, sweetheart. I want him to take it off for you."

CHAPTER TWELVE

There was a second when Alex seriously debated the merits of saying to hell with his plan, flinging aside the poker table, striding over to Conrad, putting his hands around the motherfucker's neck, and strangling the life out of him.

But no, Alex couldn't do that. He was meant to be playing along, doling out small crumbs of his supposed pain to the bastard to keep him interested. Keep him feeling like he was the master puppeteer while in reality it was Alex who was the one making Conrad dance.

And using Katya to do it.

Jesus. Since when had she begun to matter? Yes, she'd become more than a mere employee since she and Alex had gotten to Monte Carlo, but a couple of shared orgasms didn't mean shit.

They didn't warrant the guilt settled down low in Alex's gut or the fury that ate away at him now. Guilt that he hadn't told her of his plan. That he was going to let her believe Conrad was getting to him. And fury that Conrad thought he could screw with her in the first place.

Alex didn't understand why it should matter to him that she be naked in front of these people. Why he should care so much about her modesty. Especially when she'd told him she didn't mind. Shit, this was war, wasn't it? And she was a damn soldier.

But whatever the reason, that didn't change the emotions that sat inside him. The fact that he cared.

He didn't want her to have to take her dress off in public for Conrad's personal gratification and the lecherous gaze of the other men around the table. He didn't want her to be a pawn in his private game of revenge.

Conrad was looking at him like he'd already won, as if this little power play had worked, which was all part of the plan. The guy was taking the bait like the power-hungry prick he was, picking up on Alex's barely concealed fury as Alex had hoped, pushing harder, further. Such as this latest ploy, getting him to take Katya's dress off. Another way to dig the knife in and wiggle it around, trying to hit a nerve.

Well, it might be all part of Alex's plan, but it didn't mean he had to like it. Though in a way, it made it easier that he didn't have to pretend to get angry. The only thing he had to do was conceal it badly and make Conrad believe he was trying to hide it.

He clenched his jaw so it looked like he was biting back angry words and shrugged a stiff shoulder. "Well sure, I can do that. Shall I get you a drink while I'm up? Fetch your dry cleaning too?"

Jason laughed and Christine giggled. The others only watched Alex as he got up from his seat and turned to face Katya.

She'd told him this didn't mean a thing to her and he could see it didn't. There was no fear in her eyes, only strength. She smiled at him and this time it was genuine, and obviously meant to allay his fury.

But it really didn't. Because he was still using her and he knew it.

He moved behind her, reaching for the zipper of her dress.

"Slowly," Conrad said. "We don't want to rush things."

Alex grinned, making sure it didn't reach his eyes. "Hey, it's me. You think I don't know how to put on a show?"

He had to use his guilt and his anger to put on a show. He had to keep thinking of his revenge. Of the information he would get for his friends. That was all that mattered. Certainly undressing Katya in public with a roomful of people watching didn't. She was a soldier after all. She was used to being used as a pawn, to following orders.

You're no better than Conrad. Using people. Playing with people.

Christ, he knew that. He'd always known that. The only difference was that he knew he was a prick and not worth the time of day.

Yet despite all of that, he put one hand on Katya's hip to reassure her as he began to draw down the zipper. She didn't shake or tremble as the green-gold silk began to loosen, her body rock solid. But his hand . . . it shook.

Fuck. Pull yourself together.

Carefully he pulled the zipper down and pushed the silk from her shoulders, easing it from her body and off.

She stepped from the green fabric, her chin held high.

Conrad's eyes had grown hooded as he looked her up and down. "Oh, nice, yes. Very lovely, my dear."

The others were looking at her too: Mrs. Lau as if sizing her up for something, August as though he wanted to devour her, Christine with a narrowed gaze, and the mercenary as if he were gazing at a rock rather than a woman, nothing at all in his eyes. The sheikh didn't look at her at all, his attention on the table instead.

Alex put his hands on her waist, her skin cool beneath his fingers. More reassurance but also to send a clear message to the rest of the table that she was his. "Naturally she's lovely," he said. "I have a reputation to uphold after all." He stepped around her, over to the table, and picked up the diamond choker he'd won in the first round. His

necklace now. "But I think she could use a little adorn-
ment." Turning back, he met Katya's eyes. She gave an
almost imperceptible nod. The color was high on her cheeks,
but there was nothing but staunch determination in her
expression. Gently he looped the choker around her neck,
a reminder to everyone else, should they forget, that she
was his. "There. Perfect." He stepped to the side and gestured to her. "Voila. Enjoy, *mes amis*."

Conrad's attention had shifted from Katya back to him
again, his eyes narrowed. Gauging Alex again. "She's still
wearing underwear."

Alex shrugged. "Yeah, I know. It's a pity. But you'll have
to win again if you want those off. One item of clothing,
remember? Rules are rules." He went back to his chair and
sat down. "Another round?"

Conrad sat back. "I was contemplating a short break.
So we could admire the view as it were."

No fucking way. It was another push, another test, but
Alex was sick of Conrad upping the ante all the time.

Alex took a leisurely sip of his vodka, only a taste, nothing more. "Well, sure. But that's not going to get her panties off, is it?" He made a show of looking around the table.
"Though, I mean, if everyone else wants a break—"

"I want the panties off," August said decisively. "Deal
again, South."

A glitter of irritation glowed in the older man's eyes.
"Very well. But let's up the stakes a little, hmmm?"

Excellent. Alex wasn't going to argue with that. Perhaps
he could use this as an opportunity to get some information. About the stand-ins behind each chair, for example.
Because there was something off about them too. He knew
the kinds of high-class hookers who hung out at these sorts
of places and they had nothing in common with the women
behind the chairs.

Hookers would hang off the arms of their clients, smiling

and laughing and making them feel important. They didn't
stand there with blank faces and empty eyes, looking like
they weren't there at all.

Like you did.

His throat tightened in sudden recognition. At the end
of his rape, when Conrad was finishing, Alex had pretended
he was at the St. James beach house in Cape Cod. Somewhere safe. Somewhere he'd been happy. Away from the
reality of what was happening to him . . .

Fuck. Those women were doing exactly the same thing;
he'd bet his life on it.

Something cold gathered tight in Alex's gut. What the
hell was going on here?

Christine leaned in toward Conrad, the expression on
her face avid. "Sounds good. What did you have in mind?"

"Well, we've viewed the . . . ah . . . merchandise so to
speak. Why don't we take the opportunity to test it out?"
Conrad's attention shifted to Alex. "A night with the girl
standing behind you, St. James."

The others were murmuring things, but he couldn't hear
them. His whole focus was on the man at the other end of
the table.

Earlier he'd used the word "stock' to Mrs. Lau when
suggesting clothing to remove. Now it was "merchandise."
The cold sank deeper. Something not right was going on
here, something more than just gambling; Alex could feel
it in his bones. And now he'd involved Katya.

Every part of him wanted to refuse, to tell the other man
to fuck himself, because he would never hand Katya over
to Conrad like she was a possession. But Alex needed to
know if his suspicions were correct. Which meant this had
to play out a little longer.

He toyed with his vodka tumbler. "A night? So delicate,
Conrad. Why don't you tell it like it is? You want to put
sex on the table."

Conrad only smiled. "Got a problem with that, son? It probably wasn't what you were expecting when you came in here, right? Well, the Apocalypse game is . . . unconventional and yes, surprising. But we've had no complaints in all the years we've been playing it. In fact, we've even made a few valuable friends over the years."

"Play, Conrad." The unfamiliar voice came from the mercenary, who hadn't spoken one word the entire game. It was harsh and cold as a beach in winter, the words sounding like an order.

Interesting. What was his deal?

Conrad merely shrugged. "Getting impatient, Elijah? I trust you have no problem with the stakes?"

"No," the man snapped.

"Excellent. Then of course, let us move on."

Alex put his vodka down. Another token protest was in order. "Here's a radical idea. Before we proceed, how about we ask the lady in question if she's happy with the stakes?"

Conrad gave a short laugh. "Oh, I think she's fine with it. Aren't you, darling? I mean, you don't really have another option. Not if you want to keep Mr. St. James in the game."

Christ, he was transparent. Wiggling the knife again, prodding for a reaction. Alex let a ripple of irritation cross his features, giving Conrad the response he was looking for as another sop to the man's ego.

Pity the irritation was actually real.

"I suppose Alex will just have to win then," Katya said from behind him, her accent even thicker than normal.

"And if he doesn't, you'll be quite safe with me, I assure you."

A hand rested briefly on Alex's shoulder. Katya's. She squeezed gently as if to remind him of her strength.

In the years after Conrad, Alex had always sworn to

himself that he would never feel shame or humiliation again. But he felt shame now.

You knew Conrad would use her.

Perhaps Alex had. And perhaps she would even have been okay with being used if she'd known the truth, because he suspected she was the kind of woman who would understand revenge.

But he hadn't trusted her with the truth. And here she was, trusting him despite it.

Look at you. Caring about someone . . .

Fuck. He didn't want to. He couldn't afford to. Emotion made you weak. Made you a victim, and he was no one's fucking victim. Not ever again. And hell, if he was thinking this kind of crap it meant that despite his best intentions, Conrad *had* gotten to him.

Which meant it was time to end the evening. And that wouldn't be a bad thing. He could win the information he came for, win Kaya, and get out. Spend the next day or so making sure he was in the right head space without all of this emotional bullshit clouding his mind, then issue Conrad his ultimatum. No other players. Just him and Alex.

Perfect.

He looked around the table. "Okay, but I think it's my turn to mix it up a little. Seven-card stud, anyone?" It was one of his preferred poker variants and he'd won several tournaments with it.

Maybe the others thought it was a good idea too, because they all looked at Conrad expectantly. Who only shrugged and nodded to the dealer. "Three rounds. Winner takes all."

Well, shit. First time in the evening Alex actually agreed with Conrad.

The dealer dealt out the cards and Alex picked his up, glancing at them. Two aces. And one on the table. This game was done already, unless one of the others had a straight flush with the remaining ace. Beside him Christine laughed.

The sheikh put his cards on the table immediately. "I'm out." He pushed his chair back. One of his aides said something sharply in Arabic, but the sheikh lifted a hand, silencing him.

Mrs. Lau shrugged and put her cards down. "I fold also."

Conrad pushed some chips onto the table. "I shall stand."

August tapped his poker chip against the table. "Fold with that kind of pussy on the table? I don't think so." He matched Conrad's bet with a couple more chips.

Alex looked to Elijah, the mercenary. Again, that flash of recognition, though the name meant nothing to Alex. The man looked back, his black eyes depthless. He didn't say anything, but he put his cards down and pushed them away with a sharp movement.

Another fold.

Christine smiled at Alex and pushed some chips into the center. Which meant her hand was shitty and she was bluffing it out. "You standing?" she asked.

Alex gave her a shark's grin back. "Oh, honey, definitely." He pushed some chips into the center.

The dealer put some more cards on the table. Not the elusive ace but a six. Not what Alex wanted, fuck it.

Down the other end of the table, Conrad narrowed his gaze. The other man betrayed nothing, just looked at him.

The dealer dealt Conrad out another couple of cards. Again, the ace wasn't in the upcards on the table, only a low club and a diamond.

Dammit. Okay, so, time to get some of that potential information on the table. Alex put his cards down and folded his arms. "Not sure I'm too happy with my girl being staked. I mean, if I don't win, I'll have to go back to a cold bed by myself." He gestured around to the stand-ins behind the chairs. "How about you share the love around, Conrad?"

Down the end of the table, Conrad frowned. "You want one of mine?"

"Yeah, I do. Fair's fair after all."

The other man didn't speak for a moment, his expression unreadable. Then he shrugged. "Sure, why not? You can have the sheikh's girl."

"Oh, come on," Alex murmured, goading. "Your brunette at least. Unless, of course, she's special . . ."

The brunette made no move, her eyes downcast. There were small marks on her neck that had been hidden by that diamond choker. Marks that looked like bruises.

Conrad's expression didn't change. "Fine. The brunette then. They're all the same to me." Abruptly he pushed a small tower of chips into the middle. "I'll even throw in another ten grand to match."

August made a snorting sound, his tapping poker chip speeding up. "Does this mean I can put in the girl behind me?"

"Of course." Conrad held out a hand. "Be my guest."

The Texan shunted some chips into the center. "And the lady behind me."

Alex studied him. The guy was as expressionless as Conrad, except that tapping chip was now slightly faster than it had been. Dammit. It meant the guy's hand was probably good.

Beside Alex, Christine gave another laugh. "Wow, the testosterone in here is killing me. Probably good I'm out." She put her cards down and shoved them away.

So, last round and only three still in.

Alex didn't need to see the cards already on the table; he'd memorized them. He tapped the green felt and the dealer dealt him the last card. Again, not an ace. A six.

Well, three aces weren't exactly the end of the world.

Unless Conrad and August had a straight, a flush, or a full house. Either one of them held the last ace or it was in the hands of one of the players who'd gone out if Alex's count was on. Which made a straight or a flush a definite possibility.

He shoved the rest of his chips onto the table, then sat back.

Conrad said nothing, but the force of his gaze was like a laser. Clearly he wanted to win and badly. He tapped the table and the dealer gave him a last card. A two of spades.

Thank fuck for lady luck. Because unless Conrad had a low straight, that was pretty damn bad for him. The man raised an eyebrow but shoved his last set of chips onto the table.

August grunted when he was dealt a king, frowning a little. But he got rid of the last of his chips all the same.

Alex looked at the other two men. Then he put his hand down. "Three aces."

Conrad's gaze flickered. Then he shrugged and put down his without comment. It was nothing. A queen and a couple of off suits.

August cursed and threw down his. A pair of queens.

Alex ignored the strange shot of intense relief that coursed through him. Which was just fucking insane, since relief was *never* an emotion he felt when winning a game. Sometimes there was pleasure at beating an opponent or satisfaction at a good bluff. But most of the time Alex didn't care much whether he won or lost, and that was part of the reason he was so good at it.

Not caring was the key.

Yet now he didn't want to pick up his tumbler or even touch his cards again because he was sure his hand was shaking. Jesus, he was a fucking wreck.

He allowed his smile to turn feral with satisfaction. "My game, I believe, gentlemen."

On his left, the sheikh rose abruptly from the table as if he'd been waiting for this moment for some time. "On that note, forgive me, Mr. South, but I have to withdraw for the evening. I have some other business I need to attend to."

Conrad too was smiling. As if he hadn't only lost a considerable amount of money but also the chance to dig his knife in as deep as it would go. "But of course, Your Highness. In fact, it is rather late. Perhaps we should end the evening on a high note and finish for the night now?" He glanced at Alex. "Congratulations, son. I presume you won't need the girl now, since you already have company tonight?"

"Why, Conrad? Welshing on a bet?" This time when Alex picked up his tumbler, it was rock steady. "Surely you should know that three in a bed is always more fun."

The older man's glaze flickered away as if he'd already lost interest. "Put your dress on," he said coldly to the woman behind him. "And meet Mr. St. James by the door. You're his for the evening."

The others were beginning to rise from the table as their various aides and entourages approached. The hum of conversation started up as people began the process of leaving. Conrad was talking to August, the two of them laughing at something.

A warm hand rested on Alex's shoulder again. Katya. "I was never in any danger," she murmured quietly from behind him. "I wouldn't have let anyone touch me."

He didn't want her to see his relief. Or his guilt. "Not here," he said, a terse reminder.

"Of course." Instantly her hand left his shoulder. "What are you going to do with the girl?"

As he pushed himself out of his chair, he could feel the weight of Conrad's gaze from the other end of the table. Assessing. Measuring. Looking for reaction. Alex bared his teeth at Conrad, his turn to wiggle the knife. "What do you think?" he said flippantly, making sure his voice carried. "We're all going to have a party together."

Silence behind him. Then she asked quietly, "Can you help me with this zipper?"

He turned to where she stood behind him, pleased to have the opportunity to give Conrad his back.

"I know you're not serious about the woman," Katya murmured. "You're trying to get information, aren't you?"

A narrow, pale strip of flesh showed between the two halves of Katya's dress, but he tried not to notice it as he carefully drew her zipper up. "That's the plan."

"Good. It was worth it then. And he didn't get anything from you."

She was wrong. Conrad had gotten something. Somehow he'd gotten Alex to care.

Ignoring her comment, he took her by the arm. "Time to go, sweetheart."

They started to move toward the exit, only to have Conrad catch them at the door, the brunette, now dressed, at his heels.

"Thank you for being so accommodating," he said to Katya, taking her hand and bowing over it in a pretentious, courtly kind of way. "Also for the view."

Katya's mouth twitched in a fake smile. "I'm a model. I'm used to taking my clothes off."

"And you can do that anytime, my dear." Conrad's hooded gaze switched to Alex, and despite his best intentions, he could feel anger blaze hot inside him like a fire. "Tomorrow night, son. And bring your lady friend with you again. It's always nice to have a bit of decoration about the place."

No. He wasn't going to bring Katya again. Of that he was certain. This was a private matter and it was better that she wasn't around, messing with his concentration. But he only gave a shrug, noncommittal. No point revealing his decision yet. "Perhaps."

"Oh, I think you should. You wouldn't want to find yourself cut out of the game now, would you?"

Alex let his smile become edged and sharp. "In that case, how can I refuse? I just hope you have something worth putting on the table next time round. Sexual favors are, after all, passé these days."

Conrad laughed. "As you say. But never fear, I think you'll be pleasantly surprised." He raised his hand, and before Alex could avoid it Conrad clapped him on the back. And when Conrad let his hand drop, Alex felt the man's fingers trail over him. A subtle reminder.

A long-forgotten nausea churned in his gut. He wanted to break those trailing fingers. Grab that arm and shove the man to the ground. Twist it until that broke too. Until the crawling feeling had disappeared from his skin.

But he didn't. He only smiled as if the touch meant nothing.

Maybe, when he had Conrad on his knees, he *would* pull that trigger after all.

Outside, the bite of winter was a welcome relief, chasing away the lingering sensation of Conrad's fingers. The brunette followed them to the car without a word, but Alex felt her muscles tighten as he put a hand on her back to help her in.

Oh, she definitely didn't want to be here; that much was certain.

He waited until they were all in the car and the doors closed, their privacy assured. Then he turned to the woman who was sitting next to him. "You don't want to be here, do you?"

She gave him one startled glance before the walls came down again, her expression impassive. "Of course I want to be here," she said mechanically. Her voice was thin, her accent American, from the South it sounded like.

"No, you don't. I know a willing woman when I see one and you're not it."

Her hands were tightly clasped in her lap, her fingers long and thin. She kept her gaze fastened on them. "I'm sorry. I really do want—"

"Where did you get those bruises?"

She seemed to shrink into the seat, not speaking, not moving, radiating terror.

"Answer him," Katya ordered crisply from the seat opposite them. "We will not hurt you."

Alex flicked a glance at her. That tone wasn't likely to help, surely?

"From him," the woman said unexpectedly, the words suddenly rushing out. "He likes to put his hands on my throat."

"Why do you let him?" Again, Katya's voice was firm, the question an order.

"Because I don't have a choice." Her head bowed, brown hair hiding her features. She was trembling.

Fucking hell. Alex didn't touch her, knowing that would be unwelcome. "What's your name?"

The woman shook her head. "I c-can't tell you."

"Why not?"

"They'll kill me. They said they would if I ever told anyone. And they'd make sure . . ." She took a ragged breath. "That no one would f-find my body."

He didn't think it was possible to get any angrier. He was wrong. "They will not hurt you," he said, letting the iron of his rage creep into the words. "No one will ever hurt you again."

Her head lifted, her gaze flicking to his for a second, then darting away again. But he could feel her shock.

"Here's what's going to happen," he said. "I need to

know the answer to a few questions. Then my driver is going to take you to the airport, where I have a jet that will take you wherever you want to go."

She began to shake her head, her body still trembling.

"You can trust him." Katya's tone was firm. Again, like an order. "You have my word."

The woman raised her head, and for the first time there was a spark of defiance in her eyes. "And who the hell are you?"

"My name is Katya Ivanova. I'm Mr. St. James's bodyguard. Ex–special forces of the Russian army."

The woman's hands twisted in her lap, clearly struggling with her fear. "I . . . Look, I have no money. I have no passport. I can't—"

"Leave that to me," Alex said. He'd call Zac and get him on to it. "I'll make sure you have everything you need."

Her face hardened. "What if they find me? They'll hunt me down once they know I've gone."

"Who?" he asked gently. "Conrad?"

She gave a jerky nod.

"Don't worry about him. I'll make sure he'll never bother you again. But first I need to know what happened to you."

Her head turned abruptly, her gaze on the narrow streets outside. "I'm from Georgia. I was . . . taken by some men after a shift at the restaurant I used to work at. I don't know how long ago that was, maybe a year. They tied me up, brought me to . . . I don't even know where. A city, I think. I was kept inside all the time and I only heard stuff like sirens and cop cars."

He glanced over at Katya, met her worried gaze. Jesus. This girl had been trafficked.

"There were other girls," she went on in the same thin, high voice, her attention firmly out of the window. "And we were brought into a room and there he was. Mr. South. He picked me and one other girl and then we were taken on an airplane here." Her mouth snapped shut all of a sudden, as if she'd said too much already.

But Alex had the information he needed. Conrad had trafficked women.

"Please don't tell the police," the woman said after a long moment. "I just want to go home."

Ah, shit, the police. The authorities had to be contacted at some point, it was true. But first Alex and Katya needed to find out more. The links between Conrad's casino and the Lucky Seven—if there were any links. The links between Conrad and his father's little group of friends, the Seven Devils. They *had* to find those things out first, before the authorities took it out of their hands.

Perhaps, when he got hold of Zac, he'd sic Eva onto them. She had a whole team dedicated to smashing trafficking rings and rescuing the people caught up in them. Because the thought of leaving those women there was . . . not good.

He was aware suddenly of a rising rage, like a black ocean. Filling him up. Rising and rising until he was almost choking on it.

The blank faces of those women. Katya naked. A slimy touch on his back.

He's got to you. He got you to care.

His fingers clenched into a fist on his thigh, completely without his volition. He didn't want this. He didn't want to fucking care.

Isn't that what this revenge is all about?

He could feel his nails biting into his palm. Because it was too late. It was too goddamn late.

Conrad had gotten to him. He did care.

* * *

Alex said nothing as they arrived back at the Fourth Circle, but Katya could feel the rage coming from him, filling the car with tension thick enough to cut.

It was obvious that was scaring the poor woman they'd rescued, but Katya didn't know how to help or give reassurance. So she only sat in silence as the car pulled up outside the Fourth Circle building, as Alex gave instructions to the driver to get the woman to the airport.

Katya didn't understand where the anger was coming from. Alex had clearly had a plan tonight, and whatever that plan had been, it had worked. He'd won the game and had gotten the information he'd been looking for. He should be feeling triumphant surely? Or satisfied at least. Yet he wasn't.

Was it something to do with her? The fact that Conrad had forced Alex to take the dress off her? She hadn't cared about that—it didn't matter. And in fact, she'd even preferred it. As exposing as it had been to stand in front of everybody only in her panties, the feel of his hands on her hips had been reassuring. As had the way he'd put the diamond necklace around her throat.

A mark of claim. His way of protecting her.

Not that she needed protection, but it had felt good all the same. As if he'd cared.

Why should that matter to you?

But she didn't want to answer that question right now. Just as she didn't want to try to figure out why it mattered so much to her that he was angry. She just wanted to know why that was.

Perhaps it was about something deeper. Perhaps it was about whatever had happened between him and Conrad. And the women in the room . . . God, did he see himself in those women? Did he see himself as another of Conrad's victims? Was that where all this was coming from?

Her fingers tightened on her clutch as they entered the

Fourth Circle foyer, music and laughter from the bar bouncing off the walls and the white-tiled floor. It was late, but the place was packed—pretty much normal for one of Alex's clubs.

"Why don't you go up to bed?" he said. "I'll be up in a bit."

Katya glanced at his shuttered face. So, he wasn't going to discuss it with her. Disappointment slid under her skin, sharp and cold as a knife. It was ridiculous. She had no right to feel it. She was a soldier, an employee. She did as she was told.

Yet none of that made the slightest bit of difference.

"Trust me," he'd said back in the casino. And she had. And now she wanted something in return from him. A sign that her trust was returned. But all she was getting was the usual. Blank walls and shut doors.

Of course what she should do now was what she was paid to do. Nod and go up to bed, do as she was told. Be the obedient soldier, follow her orders—

No.

For a second she stayed exactly where she was, the denial echoing inside her. And she knew in that moment that tonight she wasn't going to be the good soldier and follow orders. Be the obedient employee and do what the boss said.

Maybe last week she would have. But she wasn't the same person as she had been last week. Alex had touched her. Let her touch him. And that meant she deserved more than silence. Didn't she?

There were people around, so she slid an arm around his waist as if she was hoping to drag him off to bed. Rising on her toes, she murmured in his ear, "I would appreciate a debrief, sir."

He stopped, his posture tense, the expression on his face unreadable. "Not tonight, sweetheart. I'm not in the mood."

Katya dropped the girlfriend front. "I took my clothes off in front of a roomful of strangers for you. You owe me a debrief."

His jaw hardened, the anger in his gaze sparking. But he couldn't argue with her and she knew it. "Very well. Five minutes. And then I have to check on the club." He didn't wait for her to reply, just took her by the arm and walked swiftly over to the elevator.

She could feel the anger in his hold too, his fingers pressing hard against her skin. She could have gotten out of it easily enough, but this wasn't the time or the place, so she ignored it as they got into the elevator.

He didn't say anything as they rode up the couple of floors to their room, and she didn't press, keeping silent as they went down the hallway and Alex entered the code into the keypad lock on the door.

"Okay." He slammed shut the door behind them. "Let's fucking debrief."

Katya put her purse carefully down on the coffee table near the sofa. "I want to know why you're so angry."

"Because Conrad South is a prick who has apparently been trafficking women. Do I really need another reason?"

"It's more than that." She took a breath. "Is it what happened with me?"

His gaze flickered. "You didn't sign on for that kind of shit."

"It's part of the mission. There will always be some aspects of a mission that will be unpleasant. Taking my clothes off and being looked at is probably the least dangerous thing I've ever had to do."

Alex thrust his hands in his pockets. "And sleeping with Conrad if I'd lost the game? Would that have been an 'unpleasant' part of the mission too?"

"I wouldn't have let him touch me. I wouldn't let any

of them touch me." She studied Alex's fiercely beautiful face, noting the tight line of his jaw. "You had a plan, didn't you? Before we even went in."

That familiar hard, glittering look had entered his eyes, making them seem sharp as shards of blue glass. "No one fucks with my employees."

"That's not what I asked."

The atmosphere in the room became dense all of a sudden, heavy and full of pressure.

"What makes you think you deserve an answer?" His tone had turned silky, dangerous. "You're my bodyguard, Katya, not my fucking confessor."

She ignored that, studying him and the fury that poured off him. A restless kind of energy that had him pacing to the couch, then back to the door again. He needed a target, she realized. Something to take his anger out on. Or someone.

"I see," she said expressionlessly.

"What?" He stopped near the couch. "What do you fucking see? Did you expect something different? Were you hoping I'd tell you all my secrets like a fucking teenage girl?" There was an unbearably cynical note in his voice. "You're too sharp, Katya mine. You see too much. Because you're right. I did have a plan. And you were part of it." He began to stalk toward her, a slow, fluid movement, like a panther. "Don't forget I'm a game player, just like Conrad. You were my bait, my supposed weak point. A tool to hook Conrad. And, shit, did it work. He took you, hook, line, and sinker."

She stood her ground, watching him come. "I don't care what you use me for. If it's in the business of protecting your life then it's part of my job anyway." She lifted her chin. "But that's not the real question. The real question is what is making you so angry?"

Slowly, he came to a stop right in front of her. "No, it's

not. The real question is why the fuck should it matter to you?"

It was a good question, but she'd been avoiding the answer for days now. Perhaps it was time she stopped. "It matters because I care. I care about you."

"You shouldn't, darling. A couple of orgasms don't mean love." He smiled his shark's smile. "And if you're expecting me to reciprocate you're shit out of luck."

Katya stared into the hard glitter of his eyes, seeing the anger and the pain that lurked underneath the cynical edge. He was lying. Both to her and to himself. He *did* care. That's why he was angry. That's why he was saying these things. He wanted to distance her. Wanted to push her away. Because that's what he always did when he cared and he didn't want to.

"Stop pretending," she said. "I told you that you could trust me and you can. Tell me what's wrong. Tell me why you hate him so much."

He gave a harsh laugh. "You really think it's that simple? That all I need to do is tell you and it will go away? That everything will magically get better?"

"No, I don't—"

"You've got no fucking idea. Anyway, there's something else we could be doing other than talking." His gaze dropped down her body, openly suggestive, before rising to her face again. "Take off your dress, Katya. If you can do it for him, you can do it for me."

Oh yes, he was definitely trying to intimidate her. Push her away. But he was forgetting who he was dealing with here.

"Of course, sir," she said, placing a delicate emphasis on the "sir." "Anything you say." Reaching up behind her, she pulled down the zipper and stepped out of the bronze silk as it fell away.

And there was nothing weak in standing before him in

only her panties. It felt like a declaration of intent, making her strong, powerful. Especially when his gaze roamed over her, hot and hungry. Setting up that ache of desire inside her, a wave of heat sweeping over her skin. She hadn't cared in that room, in front of those people, because they didn't matter.

But Alex did.

She stared at him, looked into the searing blue of his eyes, and she could see what he wanted, could sense the desperate hunger building in him.

He was drowning again and he needed her to save him.

So Katya didn't wait. She carried on, sliding down her panties and stepping out of them. Standing there naked except for the diamond choker and her heels.

Then she straightened, keeping her hands by her sides.

"I didn't tell you to take your panties off," he said hoarsely.

"I know you didn't. But I wanted them off."

"Katya—"

"What are you going to do now?" She lifted her chin. "You won a night with me after all. Perhaps you should take it?"

He stepped closer, inches away from her, the heat from his lean body like a furnace against her bare skin. "You think I wouldn't? Conrad would have taken you."

"I don't care about Conrad. And you're nothing like him."

He sneered, sliding an arm around her waist, jerking her hard against him. "Don't be so fucking sure, sweetheart."

The material of his tuxedo pants against her skin was rough, the cotton of his shirt a smooth contrast. She put a hand on his chest, staring up into his hot blue eyes, feeling the beat of his heart fast and sure beneath her palm. "I know what you're doing. But you won't be able to push me away. I won't let you."

He lifted his free hand, shoved it into her hair, his fingers closing into a fist and pulling her head back. "Give me two seconds, Katya mine. I'll make you change your mind."

"Shocking me won't work. And you know I can have you facedown on the floor before you even have time to breathe if you try anything else. But you don't want that, do you? Not when it's me you really want."

Something moved in his eyes, a crack running through that hard, glittering façade. He took a breath, harsh and not at all steady. "Fuck, Katya. . . ."

She let her hand rest on the warm cotton of his shirt, moving a thumb back and forward over the fabric in a gentle caress. Feeling him shudder. "I want to give it to you, Alexei. You won me tonight. You can have me."

The fingers in her hair tightened. "Ah, darling. You really don't know what you're asking for."

"So why don't you show me?" She'd never seduced anyone in her life and she really had no idea what she was doing. But when he'd been angry and hurting like this before, her touch had helped. And she wanted to help now.

He needed her strength and so she would give it.

Katya rose up and pressed her mouth to his.

Heat flared between them like a tank of aviation gas before a match. An explosive flame that burned everything in its path.

Alex's mouth opened on hers instantly, kissing her like he was suffocating and she was air. And she let him, his tongue sweeping between her lips, exploring deep. And giving back the same in return, inexperienced and unsure but just as hungry, just as hot.

She wound her arms around his neck, arching against his body, the material of his clothes a delicious friction against her skin. Being naked while he was still fully clothed seemed the most erotic, the most powerful, thing in the whole world.

His hands gripped her all of a sudden, almost painfully tight. "You have to do what I say," he whispered hoarsely against her mouth. "Do you understand? I have to be the one in charge."

She did understand. This anger and this desire for control came from whatever Conrad had done to him; she was sure of it. But if that's what he needed then that's what she would give him. It would make it easier anyway, since she didn't know what she was doing. Besides, as she'd learned, there was a certain strength in surrender.

She nodded and his hands spread wide, coming around her, lifting her and carrying her over to the couch. He put her down onto it, covering her body with his, his mouth questing and hungry. Finding and seeking hers, devouring her.

Katya pushed her hands into the thick, black softness of his hair, giving him everything she could. She hadn't had much experience with kisses, but she didn't care. She only wanted the taste of him, the heat of him against her.

His hands moved over her, restless, seeking. Stroking her shoulders and down, finding her breasts, cupping them in his palms, his thumbs circling her nipples before pinching them, not hard but enough to send a sharp bolt of sensation straight to her sex. Making her gasp.

He pinched them again, his mouth moving down to her neck and throat, pressing hot, hungry kisses to her skin. Then his teeth biting, his tongue licking, soothing.

She couldn't get enough breath, each sensation taking the air straight from her lungs. The pleasure was so sharp, so intense. And yet it kept building. Layer after layer as his mouth moved down her body, his hands cupping her breasts, her nipples so tight they ached.

His mouth covered one nipple, sucking hard, tearing a groan from her as another electric shock of pleasure seared along her nerve endings. She had no time to feel awkward or shy, or any of the other things she'd thought she'd feel. He gave her no space to feel anything but what he was doing to her.

Alex's hands moved lower as he transferred his mouth to her other nipple, licking, nipping her sharply, making her cry out. His fingers stroked over her hips and thighs; then one hand slipped between them.

"Spread your legs," he demanded roughly. "Now."

She did without hesitation, letting them fall open, shivering and arching up as his fingers stroked the folds of her sex, tracing the shape of her in a light, tantalizing movement.

Katya moaned, her eyes closing as the pleasure began to wind tight as a clock spring, the world narrowing to this one aching point. "Alexei . . ." Her hands moved from his shoulders down his back, tracing the graceful shapes of his muscles beneath the cotton. Then her nails dug in as his fingers found her clitoris and began to circle, teasing her.

Her hips jerked, her breath coming fast and hard. "I can't . . . please . . . Oh God . . ." She didn't know whether she said it in Russian or English, but she didn't care. She wanted him to keep going, never stop, because she would die if he did.

"Wider." He came onto his knees, pushing her legs farther apart and looking down between them. Ferocity twisted his features, the skin drawn tight to the bones of his face. Like he'd been stripped of all those fascinating layers right down to the raw, elemental part of him. "Keep them like that."

She obeyed, her inner thighs beginning to tremble, her heart beating harder than it ever had even during the toughest training session. A week ago she would have pushed him away, horrified at feeling such weakness, at being so exposed. Now she couldn't take her eyes from his face, watching his reaction to her. Feeling the power of her sexuality.

"Watch," he ordered. Then he put his hand down between her thighs, spreading the folds of her sex. Katya trembled at the feeling of intense vulnerability that gripped her, but again she obeyed. Watching those long, clever fingers move on her slick flesh, feeling the stretch as he slid two fingers deep inside her.

She groaned, the eroticism of the sight making the grip of pleasure squeeze tighter.

His hand moved, his thumb seeking and finding her clitoris, circling it in time with the push of his fingers. The rhythm he set was at first hard and fast, then abruptly slowing, becoming leisurely before picking up speed again. He was playing with her. Teasing her. Proving his total command of her body.

Katya panted, struggling to keep her legs wide and her gaze on what he was doing to her. The pleasure was a vicious pressure, so tight, and release was so close. But he kept it just out of her reach. Like nearly reaching the top of a mountain, only to find the path to the summit barred and gated. So close and yet so far.

Increasingly desperate, her body shaking with frustration as he continued to toy with her, she reached for his hand so she could direct it to where she wanted it to go, to touch her to get her over that gate.

"Stop," Alex said harshly.

Katya moaned with frustration but did as she was told, her hand dropping away. "Please . . ."

He leaned over her, one hand beside her head, so she couldn't see anything else but him, the intensity in his face and the dark midnight of his eyes. "I'm the only one who gets to touch you. Understand? Only me. And when I say stop, you stop."

She struggled to take a breath. There was a note of something in his rough voice, something she knew was important. But she couldn't think through the fog of relentless pleasure, so she only nodded.

He sat back, reaching into his back pocket and taking out his wallet. His movements were precise, measured, and she didn't know why they drove her mad with frustration. He took out something, a silver packet.

Understanding burst in her fogged-up brain. A condom.

The air rushed into her lungs and she began to shake, which was strange. Because she'd always known this was going to happen. From the moment she'd taken off her dress, she'd known. Yet she'd never thought she'd be the one lying here, desperate and hungry. The one who would be begging. Who had her mouth full of pleading words.

She thought it would be him reduced to trembling and shaking and her the one giving him what he needed. She never dreamed she'd need this too. So much she felt tears prickling behind her eyes.

Katya bit her lip hard to stop it, a hot ball of inexplicable emotion catching in her chest. "Alexei . . ." His name escaped before she was ready and she had to bite her lip harder to stop any more begging from getting out.

He didn't look at her as he opened his pants. But his hands were shaking as they ripped open that packet. As they rolled the latex down over the length of his cock.

She wasn't the only desperate one.

The emotion in her chest began to spread out, moving through her, inexorable, unstoppable. Her vision blurred, a ragged, desperate breath filling her lungs. She didn't understand what was happening to her, where these feelings were coming from. As if somehow those earlier encounters with him had cracked the defenses she'd erected over the years and now they were falling, crumbling. As if they'd never been.

"Katya." He was leaning over her, the look in his eyes asking questions she didn't understand and didn't know the answers to. But she kept on looking anyway as she felt him push into her, a deep, hard thrust.

She cried out, a hoarse kind of sound she couldn't believe had come from her. There was no pain, at least not physical pain. And yet there was something. Unfamiliarity. Like she was too full, stretched. Both by him and by the emotion that she couldn't seem to control.

His hand slipped beneath her head, cupping the back of it, lifting her so her mouth met his, drowning her in the heat and the hunger of his kiss.

And then he began to move. Her fingers dug helplessly into his back as if they wanted to claw through the cotton into the skin beneath it. Because she was never going to survive this. The edge of pleasure was like a razor, cutting through everything that tethered her to earth. That protected her. So she could do nothing as she soared into the sky, going higher and higher.

His other hand beneath her hips, tilting her. The feel of him sliding deeper. So full. Stretched wide. Too much. And yet . . . not enough.

Alex moved harder, faster, and the hold she had on her emotions, on the pleasure that was slowly tearing her apart, began to slip. It was too hard to fight it, too hard to think her way through what was happening. All she could do was hold on to him and respond to the insistence of her body that had her moving with him in a rhythm she couldn't resist. A final letting go, a deeper surrender.

But it got too much. The edge of ecstasy too sharp.

It pierced her, transfixed her like a butterfly pinned to a board.

As the climax burst through her, Katya screamed, deaf and blind to anything but the pleasure as she fell from the sky and smashed to pieces on the ground.

* * *

Alex felt her convulse around him, her hoarse scream against his mouth, and let himself go, burying himself in the slick heat of her pussy, over and over until he couldn't feel the thick mess of emotions that had been drowning him, choking him. All tangled and conflicted and so fucking unwanted.

Until all he could feel was her around him, the smell of oranges overlaid with the musky scent of her arousal, the shaking of her lithe body under his. And the taste of her as he kept his mouth on hers, drowning himself in it so that there was nothing left but pleasure.

The orgasm, when it hit, was like pure heroin injected straight into his nervous system, laying waste to everything, leaving him gasping and shaking, unable to move or speak or do anything but lie there on top of her, trying pull together the jagged shards of himself.

There was a strange, metallic taste in his mouth, like blood. And when he at last raised his head and looked down at her, he realized, with sudden horror, that it *was* blood. Hers.

Katya lay beneath him, trembling like he was, eyes wide with shock. There was blood on her lip and the look on her face bore no resemblance to the reserved, icy Russian bodyguard she'd once been. It was more that of a woman who'd been broken apart, with no idea how to put herself back together again.

Familiar guilt began to break through the heavy sensual aftermath of the orgasm, a bitter, sharp feeling. Jesus Christ. Her lip . . . he'd bitten her.

Alex moved, withdrawing from her carefully before shoving himself away. Moving from the couch toward the bedroom and the bathroom.

He didn't look back, going into the en suite bathroom and

shutting the door hard behind him. He dealt with the condom, then leaned against the black marble of the vanity.

His arms were shaking, his heartbeat frantic. It was like he'd run a marathon flat out and was still running.

He'd tried to show her he didn't care. Prove to both himself and her that he didn't give a shit. That the emotions seething inside him weren't there. He'd used her hard, showing her how totally in command of her body he was. Showing her that he was the one in control. Making sure she was the one screaming for release.

It was how it had to be with all his lovers.

But Katya was not like all the rest. And the look on her face . . . The shock, the blood—

You said you wouldn't hurt her.

Alex took a shuddering breath, the guilt like a piece of broken glass inside him. He was under no illusions. Yes, he'd used her tonight, both in front of Conrad in aid of his plan and right now to escape the emotional fallout of the evening. But this wasn't about her, not really. It was about himself. About all the things he refused to deal with, all the things he'd spent his life escaping.

Excess was all about escape. The sex and drugs, the alcohol, were ways of putting distance between himself and his rape. His father's suicide. Ways to make sure he didn't feel, didn't hurt. And now he'd drawn Katya into it. Now he was using her the same way he used everything else– to distance himself from his emotions, to prove that he was still the one in control.

Which made him just as much of a selfish fuck as Conrad.

Loathing rose inside him, flooding the back of his throat.

Ah Christ, it wasn't her fault he was a coward.

There was a bottle of some kind of lotion sitting on the vanity near the sink. Before he could stop himself, he'd picked it up and hurled it at the mirror. It smashed beautifully, the mirror disintegrating into a shower of glittering shards.

What a fucking mess he was.

No matter what he did, he was still full of all these emotions that he didn't want. That he couldn't untangle. And she . . . Jesus, it was being around her that made it worse. She made him feel out of control. She made him feel, period. And that couldn't happen.

Which left him only one alternative: walking away.

Alex turned sharply and strode out of the bathroom, only to find Katya halfway across the bedroom, still naked. She stopped as soon as she saw him. Her face was white, the blood on her lip in stark contrast, but the shocked look had gone from her eyes. She was frowning.

"I heard something smash. Are you all right?"

So, the bodyguard was back, was she? Just as well. The bodyguard was better than the vulnerable woman who'd lain beneath him. Who'd given him everything.

Everything you don't deserve.

He didn't stop, walking past her without a word.

"Sir?"

He kept on going, through the lounge to the door.

"Sir, please."

He opened it, went through.

"Alexei?"

And slammed it behind him.

CHAPTER THIRTEEN

Katya stared at the shut door. She could feel reaction beginning to set in, both from what had happened between them and from the adrenaline that had surged through her in response to the sound of breaking glass.

She'd gone instantly into defense mode, shaking off the shock, confusion, and aching aftereffects of pleasure. Taking refuge in her bodyguard front. Rushing into the bedroom only to find Alex striding from the bathroom, apparently unharmed. And yet he wasn't okay; that much was clear from the look on his face.

His expression was a mask, his eyes opaque as glass. And he ignored her, walking past her as if she didn't even exist. Leaving, slamming the door on her.

Her throat tightened and she felt the prick of tears, a needle of hurt sliding beneath her skin. God, it didn't make any sense. None of this made any sense.

The way she hurt. Like he'd stripped a layer of skin from her, leaving all her nerve endings exposed and raw. Was this what happened when you made love with someone for the first time? Was it normal?

She hadn't expected blood or pain, since with all her physical training she'd probably lost her hymen a long time ago. And yet there had been both. Blood on her lip from where he'd bitten her and the emotional pain of his withdrawal. As if the sex hadn't mattered. As if now he'd taken what he wanted, she didn't matter.

You want to matter to him.

Did she? That hadn't been her intention and making love with him hadn't been that kind of transaction. She'd offered herself to him, given him what he'd needed; that should have been enough. She wasn't looking for more. And if he wanted to leave, then she wasn't going to run after him.

Crushing the hurt, Katya turned and went into the bedroom, pulling on a robe to cover herself before peering into the bathroom. There was glass everywhere, the mirror shattered. He must have thrown something at it.

Blood on the tiles. Pink hair floating around white shoulders. Pink because there had been blood in the water too . . .

Fear curled inside her heart, the jagged edges sharp, but she pushed it fiercely away. No, this had nothing to do with the afternoon she'd come home from school to find her mother's body in the bath, her wrists cut. Absolutely nothing.

Katya put the memory firmly from her head and went to the phone, making a call to one of the club's staff about the broken mirror and organizing someone to come and clean up the mess. Then she dressed and waited while a staff member came to clear the glass away, another replacing the broken mirror. They did it quietly and with such practiced efficiency that she suspected things like this happened quite a lot in the Fourth Circle club.

But as she waited, she still couldn't quite get rid of the fear that had solidified in her chest.

She took a breath, trying to calm it, but it wouldn't go away.

You weren't there in time to save her. What about him?

She was supposed to be his bodyguard, she was supposed to protect him, and yet she'd let him walk out. Because she'd felt hurt. How was that in any way professional? How was that doing her job?

It wasn't. It was letting her emotions compromise her mission. A mistake and one she had to remedy immediately.

Grabbing her Springfield from the green purse still on the coffee table, Katya strode out of the suite.

The bar of the Fourth Circle was still packed and it took her a while to search through the crowds, but Alex definitely wasn't there. Nor was he in the casino area. Which meant he'd left the club.

Katya tracked down Marc to the office behind the bar, trying to see if he knew where Alex might have gone. The man frowned. "I'm not sure. He usually either stays here or plays at the Casino de Monte-Carlo."

"Anywhere else?"

"I'm sorry, I don't know. Mr. St. James doesn't usually keep me up-to-date with where he is."

Of course he wouldn't. If he didn't keep in touch with his bodyguard, he was highly unlikely to tell the manager of his club.

Which left her with two choices: She either searched through every bar in Monte Carlo or contacted someone else who might know. Luckily, she had an idea who might.

Leaving the bar and the noise behind, Katya went through the foyer and out the double doors of the club, stepping into the frosty night air.

Her breath steamed as she took out her phone, walking down the steps of the club and away from the crowd of people trying to get in. She had the number saved in her contact list, and after a brief check on the time difference she pressed the button. It would be late evening in New York, and she hoped he'd answer.

And sure enough, within a few rings a deep voice on the end of the phone said tersely, "Woolf."

"Mr. Woolf? It's Katya Ivanova. Mr. St. James's body-guard. I need some information."

"Yeah, what do you want? Has Alex done something he shouldn't?"

"He left the Fourth Circle without me and I need to find him."

"Ran out on you, huh?" Gabriel Woolf's voice was expressionless. "You gotta keep better tabs on him, Ms. Ivanova."

Katya ignored the jab. "I was hoping you might have an idea where he may have gone. If you've been with him in Monte Carlo, that is."

"Well, he can't be far away because he called me half an hour ago."

"Oh?"

"He told me about the game and the woman you guys rescued. Pretty good timing, since Zac, Mr. Rutherford, finally got some information about the other players." A pause. "This is some serious shit, Ms. Ivanova. Alex needs to be careful. I hope you didn't let him leave without backup."

Guilt clawed at her, but she stiffened her spine. "I'm afraid I did. But I take full responsibility for it. That's why it's imperative that I find him now."

"You'd better. Alex can look after himself pretty well, but this is looking bigger than any of us thought."

"Then if you have any information as to his where-abouts, I'd appreciate it if you'd tell me now."

Another long pause. Then Gabriel said, "About five years ago, he and I were in Monte Carlo to find a good site for a Circles club. We went to this old place, a nightclub, not a casino. And we had a competition to see who could blow the most money in one night. I have no idea whether he'd go back there or not, but he won that competition. Blew the fun part of the evening." He brought his hands together in a sharp clap. "Let the end of the world begin."

The dealer approached the table and began to deal out the cards.

Alex sat back and sipped at his vodka, aware of the gazes of the other players on him, measuring him in the same way as he'd measured them. He gave them nothing.

But there was something odd about this game. The reputation of the Apocalypse was legendary, the rumors about only the best of the best being invited. The mysterious way the invitations turned up in the first place and the fact that no one was ever asked to participate twice.

Yet the people sitting around this table . . . They weren't the best of the best. They were rich and powerful certainly, but as poker players Alex was betting they were hardly the cream of the crop.

"I heard that it's not really poker that goes on here," Christine had told him.

So, if it wasn't poker, then what was it?

He settled back to observe the game as it progressed, going through a couple of early rounds with chips representing thousands of dollars being exchanged. Not that the money was important, or even the winning or losing at this stage. No, what was important was the chance to watch the other players, take note of their playing styles.

Christine tended to talk loudly and laugh when she had a crappy hand, sipping her champagne moodily when it was good. The sheikh drummed his fingers on the side of the table when his hand was bad, his fingers going still when it wasn't. Mrs. Lau and the mercenary were more difficult to read. Both kept their expressions completely blank, though the Chinese businesswoman's mouth went tight when her cards weren't what she wanted. August, on the other hand, was famous for taking a poker chip and tapping it on the side of the table regardless of his hand, usually in an effort to irritate other players. But after a couple of rounds, Alex found that the rhythm of the tapping changed slightly depending on August's cards. Faster indicated a good hand, slower not so much.

Conrad was a different story. His tells were almost impossible to discern. The guy had been playing too long and was too good at hiding to give himself away so easily. He seemed to shift in his seat a lot and would touch his hair every so often, but they were obvious and Alex was pretty certain he put them on for the benefit of the rest of the players.

Clearly Alex was going to have to pay more attention.

Another couple of rounds passed, the stakes getting slowly higher, the pile of poker chips collecting in front of Mrs. Lau getting larger.

Alex kept himself out of the majority of the rounds, losing a bit to keep everyone else feeling smug, then winning a couple of hands so he didn't look like an amateur.

Conrad seemed to be doing the same, letting the early glory go to Mrs. Lau more often than not. He was probably doing the same thing Alex was, saving himself for the later rounds.

About an hour later, Conrad announced a short break for refreshment purposes and Alex got up from the table to join Katya by the bar.

"Are you bored yet?" He leaned an elbow on the bar top.

She was sitting on a stool, elegant legs crossed, her purse in her lap. "I'm used to waiting. It doesn't bother me."

"What about intel then? Zac'll have my balls if I don't have information to pass on to him."

She frowned. "Something's wrong, isn't it?"

He wasn't surprised she'd picked up on his unease, and this time he didn't even try to hide it. "There's something off about this game. The players aren't pros–especially that sheikh—and the blonde is telling me that there's a rumor that poker isn't even the aim of it."

"That does seem strange. Do you need me to do anything?"

He thought about it a moment. "Get in touch with Zac. They've been trying to get some info about the players. Ask him if he's found anything on them yet."

"Okay, I can do that. You'll have to give me his number."

Alex left her to it while he collected another vodka for himself, mainly to hold rather than drink, since he never allowed himself too much while he was playing. Then he went back to the table, leaning on the rail that kept distance between the table and the spectators.

Christine approached him, leaning back against it. "You're quiet tonight, Mr. St. James. I thought you were supposed to be good. Or is that just to lull us into a false sense of security?"

Alex lifted a shoulder. He knew exactly what the point of this little interchange was, since she was telegraphing it loud and clear. Unluckily for her, he had no interest in her whatsoever. Which was weird, since he usually had some appreciation for a beautiful woman at least. "Perhaps my luck is off tonight."

"Oh, I don't think that's it. I think you're saving yourself."

"I don't save myself for anything, or haven't you guessed?"

Her blue eyes were guileless. "Aren't you? Not even for your blonde over there?"

He smiled. "That would imply she's special, darling. And no one's ever that special."

"Good to hear. Maybe she wouldn't mind me crashing the party then."

Fuck, he really couldn't be bothered with this kind of game, but he had to play it tonight regardless of whether he wanted to or not. "Party like that needs an invite."

"Are you giving me one?"

"Oh no, you don't get it that easily. You have to earn it."

She gave him an enigmatic look. "I think I can do that. The next round is the fun one."

He wanted to ask her what she meant by that, but at that moment Conrad ended the break, reminding the players to all return to their seats if they wanted to keep playing.

When everyone had seated themselves again, Conrad put his elbows on the table, lacing his hands together, a wicked gleam in his eye. "I think we've all got our heads in the game now, which means this round the gloves come off. It also means I get to make things a little more interesting." He gazed around and Alex found himself tensing as Conrad's gaze met his. "Money's off the table. But to keep it interesting, I thought we'd go old school and have a strip poker round."

Silence fell around the table.

Interesting. Alex flicked a glance at the others. The sheikh was clearly not happy, while Mrs. Lau was expressionless as ever. The mercenary was silent and motionless as a rock, but August laughed. "Holy fuck, South. You're not expecting me to take my damn clothes off, are you?"

Christine smiled. "Oh, come on, Jason. Where's your balls? I'm okay with it if you are."

The Texan leered at her. "Well, honey, if you're okay with it then—"

"I'm not envisaging the players getting undressed, August," Conrad cut in. "That would make it far too . . . easy, shall we say. I'm going to nominate stand-ins for you all instead." His gaze shifted to Alex's and the tension abruptly pulled tighter than a bowstring. "Starting with Mr. St.

a couple of hundred K in one sitting. It's a good place to start at least."

"That sounds good. What's it called?".

Gabriel gave her the name of the bar and directions. Then he added, "Let me know when you find him. He may be a selfish bastard most of the time, but he's also a friend and, with any luck, my future brother-in-law. If anything happens to him, there'll be hell to pay. The Nine Circles look after their own, Ms. Ivanova; never forget that."

She didn't miss the warning in his voice. "I understand, Mr. Woolf. Don't worry, I'll find him."

The nightclub ended up not being far, in the basement of one of the older buildings. There was a queue to get in, but she didn't have to wait long. The bouncer gave her a once-over but didn't search her. Luckily. She had a permit for her weapon, but she didn't think she'd be able to get in even if she presented it.

The interior was smoky and dim, the dance floor hot and dark and heaving with people. Music throbbed and, beneath it, the hum of people's shouted conversations.

Katya threaded her way through the crowds, trying to see. The tables were booths, which made it even harder, since she had to walk by each one to see who was sitting in them.

She almost missed him in the end, because he was sitting right in the back of a booth, in among a large group of people, playing cards. Small-stakes poker by the looks of the coins sitting on the table.

The air was sour with cigarette smoke, sweat, and spilled alcohol, the music a loud pressure in her ears. People brushed past her, the sheer weight of numbers meaning she had to withstand being pushed. But she didn't allow the external distractions to get to her.

Neither did she take any notice of the relief that flooded

through her as she saw him, his cards facedown in front of him. He had his usual tumbler of vodka at his elbow and a cigarette in one hand, his gaze on the table. As she watched, he pushed a few coins into the center and said something she couldn't catch.

The man to his left cursed while the rest of the table laughed.

Alex smiled and Katya's relief began to change, alchemizing into something else. That smile held a wild, dangerous edge. He had his eyes half-closed in a sleepy look, but she could see the sharp glitter of blue beneath his long, black lashes. There was purpose in that look. Determination.

He was here on a mission too, and whatever that mission was, she had a horrible feeling it wasn't anything good.

There was a crowd of people clustered at one end of the booth, watching the game. Katya shoved some people aside, ignoring the curses, getting close to the table. A couple of the players looked up to see what the stir was, their gazes settling on her, then looking away without interest.

And then Alex saw her, surprise flashing across his face so quickly that if she hadn't been looking directly at him she would have missed it. Then it was gone, his features wiped clean of all expression. He didn't say anything, only looked pointedly away from her, back down to the table and the game.

So he was going to play it this way, was he?

Well, she could wait. She was very good at doing that.

He knew she was there the moment she stepped up to the table. And once again, she surprised the hell out of him. He wasn't expecting her. Because when he walked away no one came after him. That was the beauty of being alone. You had no one to please but yourself.

But not tonight. Tonight Katya had come after him.

And she shouldn't have. It wasn't fair to be angry with her, not when all of this was his deal, but he was so angry already that he couldn't stop more from joining the bitter, seething mass eating a hole inside him.

How the hell was he supposed to put distance between them when she fucking followed him?

He sat back against the sticky vinyl of the booth seat, ostensibly looking at nothing in particular, a technique he'd perfected over the years. But in reality watching Katya.

She looked like she'd dressed in a hurry, yoga pants, a black top, and one of Scott's fancy suit jackets. Her hair was untidy, hanging over her shoulders in a golden mass. She looked tired, the dark circles under her eyes pronounced in the dim downlights of the bar.

And underneath all his anger and guilt, another kind of emotion gathered tightly in his chest.

He'd taken her virginity and then he'd left because he couldn't deal with the consequences. With the emotional fallout. This was all new to her and he'd acted like a complete prick.

But that's what he did, wasn't it? He walked away. He escaped. From the night in the Lucky Seven when he'd resolved never to come home, staying away when his father died, that's what Alex had been doing his whole life. It was selfish, but he'd always embraced that, accepted it. It was his armor, his protection. It kept him safe and he'd never felt bad about it.

Until now.

Alex sat there for a moment, looking at her. She had her bodyguard face on, the impassive one that showed nothing. But he could see past that now. He could see the woman behind that mask. And that woman was worried. And hurt. And confused.

She'd given him a gift tonight. She'd saved him from

the wave of emotion that had threatened to drown him, and instead of treasuring that gift, he'd flung it back in her face.

You petulant little boy. You're not sixteen anymore. You're a man. Start acting like one.

Alex threw down his cards and shoved the rest of his money into the middle of the table. "I fold."

The others looked at him in surprise, but he ignored them, extricating himself from the booth and coming to stand in front of Katya.

He didn't speak, reaching for her hand and beginning to lead her toward a quieter area near the back of the bar. She stiffened momentarily, then went with him, her hand motionless in his.

When they reached a relatively quiet space, he let go and turned. And before she could move, he stepped in, gripped her upper arms, and pushed her gently up against the wall.

Her eyes widened, but she made no effort to get away. In the dim light he could see the beat of the pulse at her throat–it was fast.

"What the hell are you doing here?" he demanded softly. "How did you find me?"

"I called Mr. Woolf to see if he could shed any light on where you'd gone." Her gaze was very direct. "And as to why I'm here . . . I'm your bodyguard, sir. And especially after tonight, I need to be wherever you—"

"Bull*shit*." His hands tightened on her upper arms. He didn't want to hear she was only doing her job. That he was only a client, only a mission. It shouldn't matter, he shouldn't care, but that didn't change the fact that he did. And for the first time in nineteen years he wasn't going to run from it. "You're here for me, aren't you?"

Her throat moved. Beneath the smell of cheap perfume, cigarette smoke, and the spilled alcohol, he caught the scent of oranges. Katya's scent. He bent his head, inhaling her.

"The truth, Katya. Give it to me."

"Of course I'm here for you." Her voice was hoarse, yet he could hear the strength in it. "What we're getting involved in with South is dangerous. I have to protect you."

The tightness in his chest constricted and suddenly he felt desperate. "You want me to say it first? Okay, I will. Fucking you on that couch was the most intense sexual experience I've ever had. And I would give anything at all to have it again."

Her jaw lifted, her eyes shadowed in the darkness. "Stop playing with me. Stop—"

"It was special," he interrupted roughly. "It mattered." He moved closer to her, their bodies almost touching. Saying the words out loud made him feel dizzy, as if he were drunk. "And I left because I'm a selfish, fucked-up prick and I have too many excuses. Because running away is what I do. Because the game with Conrad got to me and I was angry, and I used you so I didn't have to feel it." He paused and let the rest of it spill out. "But the real truth is that I left because being inside you laid me open and I had no fucking idea how to deal with it. I still don't."

Shock crossed her face. She stared at him, her mouth slightly open. Silent.

"Say something." Desperation gripped him tighter. "Tell me you came for me, Katya. Tell me you came because I matter to you and not just because I'm your fucking client."

He hated this feeling. Hated to be the one wanting something. Begging for it. It made him feel like he was back in that bathroom with Conrad touching him, helpless to stop it from happening. Helpless and vulnerable. Unable to escape. Unable to walk away.

Yet he had to give something to her after what she'd given him tonight, and the truth about himself was all he had.

Whether or not she'd want it was another story.

She was silent for a long time and it was with a strange, hollow sensation that he realized he had no idea at all what she was going to say. Or even what she was thinking.

"Katya." He tried to make it sound like a demand, but it came out sounding cracked instead. A plea or a prayer, he didn't know which.

Her brow furrowed. Then slowly she lifted a hand and touched his cheek. The brush of her fingers made his breath catch. Made the tight feeling in his chest gather even tighter. "Why is that so important to you?"

He couldn't lie. It was like he'd lost the ability. "Because no one's ever come after me before. No one's ever come for *me*."

The crease between her brows deepened, her fingers moving to his mouth, touching him. "Then yes," she said simply. "I came for you." And her stroking fingers slid into his hair, pulling his mouth down onto hers.

There was so much heat in her kiss. So much sweetness. The way her lips parted automatically, letting him in. The way her tongue touched his, tentatively exploring, then with more confidence. With more hunger.

His chest ached. He wanted to pull her close, devour her utterly, take what she was offering. But he didn't. He didn't want to take anything more from her. It was time for him to give instead.

So he only stood there, letting her explore, letting her deepen the kiss.

He'd never had a kiss like it. Soft. Gentle. Becoming more intense, until he felt her fingers close in his hair. Until she was leaning in to him, her other hand pressed to his chest.

Until they were both shaking.

Eventually he pulled away, staring into her flushed face and wide, dark eyes. "I think it's time to go home, don't you?"

She gave a wordless nod.

The journey back to the Fourth Circle didn't take long, but neither of them spoke during it. As if the weight of the truths that had been revealed hung heavy over them, the air too full of implications for speech. It wasn't the time for talking anyway, not yet. He felt too raw, and by the chill of her fingers in his he knew she felt the same way.

When they finally arrived back in the silence of the suite, the door shut behind them, she looked mutely at him and he saw the need in her eyes.

"We don't have to do anything," he said. "If you want to sleep, we can do that."

"I don't want to sleep."

"Then what?"

"I think you know."

He took a breath. "In that case perhaps it's your turn to show me."

He'd never given a woman control in the bedroom before, at least not when he wasn't drunk. When he was sober, he had to be the one who called the shots because how else could he make sure the sex stayed wholly physical? Keep the emotional distance between himself and his lover?

But he found he didn't want that distance now, not with her. She was special, *this* was special, and he wanted to mark that in some way.

She closed the distance between them, looking up into his eyes. "Show you how?"

Alex reached for one of her hands and put it to the buttons of his shirt. "You could start by undressing me."

She had no way of knowing the significance of what he'd asked her to do, that he'd never asked a woman to undress him before either. And perhaps that was for the best. Because he couldn't ignore the instinctive whisper of unease that went through him as she began to undo the buttons of his shirt. Nor could he hide the tension in his muscles as she pushed open the cotton.

But of course she saw it, her fingers touching his tight abs as she lifted her gaze to his, questions in her eyes. Yet perhaps she saw his reluctance too, because in the end she didn't speak. Instead she dropped her gaze to his chest, her hands sliding over his skin. Then she stepped in closer and pressed her mouth to the hollow of his throat and he felt himself begin to go up in flames.

Long years of reflexes had him pushing his hands into her hair, ready to pull her head away, control what was happening, and it was only sheer force of will that had his fingers stay slack and not pull. Letting her mouth trail over his collarbone, leaving a trail of sparks.

Trusting her.

Her hands glided down his chest, to his abdomen, stroking, caressing. Making his heart beat fast and his breathing fall out of rhythm. Her hands paused at his belt. "Shoes," she murmured.

He got them off, feeling stupidly clumsy, but then her fingers were undoing his belt buckle, pulling at the buttons of his pants, then drawing his zipper down. And his heartbeat began to rocket out of control and he had to curl his hands into fists at his sides to stop them from pushing her away.

I don't want this. I don't like this.

But no, this was Katya. And she wouldn't hurt him. She would stop if he asked her to, wouldn't she? The words crowded in his throat, but he didn't let them out. Turned out he had some pride after all. Besides, he didn't want to mar this experience for her with shit from the past.

So he locked his muscles, kept his gaze on her as she pushed his shirt off his shoulders, then eased his pants and boxers from his hips. She knelt in front of him, pulling the material down his thighs, her breath feathering over the exquisitely sensitive skin of his cock.

Please don't touch me there. It's wrong.

Fuck, why was he thinking this now? He needed to concentrate on Katya. Look only at her.

He stepped out of his clothing and she glanced up, and he knew what she wanted. But he couldn't let her, not now. It was one step too far. He bent and gripped her upper arms, drawing her back up again. Then he pulled her in close, sliding his hands around her waist and down over the curve of her butt, urging her up against him, the softness of her pressing against his cock a sweet ache.

Her palms lay hot on the bare skin of his chest, the gold flecks in her eyes glittering. "You don't want me to do that?"

"What? A blow job? No, not tonight, sweetheart." He pressed her harder against him, feeling desire rise and letting it burn. Letting it make ash of the memories in his head. "I want to be inside you again."

"I know I'm not experienced, but—"

"Another night, Katya mine, I promise." He'd had blow jobs before and they'd never made him have flashbacks like this. But then he'd always directed them, keeping them well within his control. And he didn't want that tonight, not with her. "Kiss me."

"Isn't it my turn to show you?"

"It is." He caught his breath, trying to let go. Trying to give this to her. "What do you want?"

There was a crease between her brows as she studied his face. "I think . . . In the bedroom this time. On the bed."

"Kinky. I like it."

"If you don't—"

He bent his head, kissed her once. Hard. "I do. And I want it." He released her and stepped back. "Come on then. Show me."

In the bedroom she made him lie on the bed and watch as she undressed. She didn't try to hide her impatience, her hands not quite so steady as she stripped, and he liked that.

Liked that so much. That she was as desperate for him as he was for her.

His unease had fallen away, old memories vanishing in the heat burning in her green eyes. As she came onto the bed next to him, naked, her hair a veil of gold across her shoulders, there was color in her cheeks. "Can I touch you?"

For an answer he took her hand, guiding it to his chest, then letting go, lying back as her fingers moved over him, stroking. Exploring. There was a fierce kind of concentration on her face, as if this was an important task that she meant to finish. That she meant to do her very best with, and fuck, the way she was touching him, it was certainly the very best he'd ever had. Not that he'd ever let another person touch him like this, at least not without instruction.

He had to battle with himself not to tear her hands away and make them go where he wanted them to, take charge of the process. When her mouth began a slow trail down his chest and abdomen, he fisted his hands in the sheets. "You can trust me. . . . With everything," she'd told him. And intellectually he knew he could. But emotionally he wasn't there yet, if he ever would be. So when her hand reached for his cock, her cool fingers closing around him, he found his own closing around her wrist, stopping her.

Her gaze flickered to his, uncertainty in her eyes. "What? Is this not enough for you?"

"Christ no," he said thickly. "Everything you're doing is perfect." Because it was, but he wasn't ready. "I just . . . I know I said this was your turn, but I can't wait. God, I want to taste you so badly." He didn't hide the raw note in his voice, letting it sit there.

"How do you mean?"

He moved, reaching between her thighs, his fingers brushing through damp curls to feel wetness and heat. "Here." He stroked her, making her gasp, watching the look in her eyes flare. "I want to put my mouth here. On your pussy. Taste you."

"But—" She stopped, inhaling sharply again as he brushed again over the soft blond curls between her thighs to emphasize his point. "You won't let me do that for you."

There were orders he could give, but he'd come this far without them; he didn't want to stop now. Besides, the truth could be a very effective deflection. "You think I lied back in the bar? That I didn't mean it? God, I'd give up every single one of my clubs. Every. Single. One." He held her gaze. "For a taste of you." And he meant it. Right now, with her naked at his side, he meant every word.

Her gaze was shadowed, smoky with desire. "In that case," she whispered, "I'm not going to argue with you."

And thank Christ. Because he was starting to get desperate. Again.

He reached for her, helping her adjust her position so she was the one lying back against the pillows. Then he shifted between her thighs, spreading them wide. "It'll be good, Katya mine," he murmured, holding her gaze. "I will make it so good for you."

"I know," she said, and he could see the trust in her eyes.

Everything in him drew tight. He'd given so many women pleasure in his life. But it had never been personal. Those women had been all the same and making them come had been easy because he'd only cared about it an abstract way. Because he didn't want any of his lovers to go away unsatisfied. It had been about him, in other words.

But this wasn't in any way abstract. This was personal. He wanted to make this good for *Katya*. Wanted to give her pleasure because she deserved it, not because he had a reputation to uphold or a point to prove.

Because whether he liked it or not, he cared.

Fuck, he was kind of nervous. Almost regretted the

breadth and depth of his experience. He had the weird
thought that this would be almost sweeter if they were dis-
covering this together for the first time. But they weren't,
and if he was going to make his experience count for something then perhaps he should be glad now that he could
use it to make this the best experience for her.

Wanting to build her anticipation, he didn't put his mouth
on her immediately, instead stroking her thighs with light
fingers, then her stomach. She shivered. He shifted, leaning forward a little, brushing his mouth over one inner
thigh, while he let his fingers trail down through soft, damp
curls. She was wet, the folds of her pussy slick under his
hand. Stroking her experimentally, he studied her face.
Watching how her pupils dilated. Her mouth opening. Her
breathing becoming faster. The pulse at her throat accelerating.

Fascinating to see the tells of pleasure. He'd always
known them of course, but he'd never watched them on a
partner's face, learning them like he learned the tells of
an opponent at the poker table. And not for himself so he
could exploit them. For her and her pleasure alone.

He eased a finger into her, hearing the sharp inhalation
of breath she took, feeling the slight lift of her hips and
tight clasp of her flesh around him. So hot and wet.

"Alexei . . ." His name was a whisper, the edge of desperation in it already.

"Watch me." He slid his finger deeper, brushed his
thumb over her clit, the lightest of touches. "Watch me,
Katya mine."

Her eyes were black, her cheeks flushed. She didn't look
away, keeping her gaze on his as he moved his hand in a
slow rhythm. Fuck, that desperate look in her eyes made
him so hard he could barely breathe. "Keep watching me,"
he murmured, and removed his hand.

She made a soft sound of protest, which he ignored. Instead he pushed her thighs wider and bent between them, nuzzling the smooth skin of her taut, flat abdomen, hearing the hiss of her sharply indrawn breath.

Christ, she was so responsive and she smelled so good. The scent of musk and salt, with the tart sweetness of oranges. He couldn't wait to taste her.

Gently he spread the wet folds of her pussy, opening her up like a flower, and her whole body stiffened. He glanced up, just to make sure she was with him, and met her gaze. There was only a thin rim of green around the black of her pupils, her breasts rising and falling fast.

"Are you ready?" he asked softly.

She didn't speak, only nodded.

It was all the permission he needed. He bent and licked her, running his tongue up the center of her sex like she was an ice-cream cone he wanted to keep from melting.

Katya groaned. "Oh . . . *bohze moy* . . ."

He slid his hands wide, gripping her hips to hold her down on the bed as he gave her another lick before beginning the delicate task of exploring her. Holy Christ, she tasted as good as she smelled, that sweet, tart orange flavor filling his senses.

She began to shake, her hips trembling beneath his hands. "Alexei . . . *pozhaluysta* . . ."

He slid his tongue deep inside her, dragging a short, ragged cry from her. Giving a woman pleasure had never felt so satisfying, never felt like such an achievement as making Katya cry out did. He kept watching her as he moved one hand from her hip, down over her stomach, pressing down with the heel of his palm at the same time as he licked her.

She said something in Russian, a stream of words he didn't understand, but he heard the frantic note in her voice nonetheless.

"Stay with me, Katya sweetheart," he murmured. "Hold on a little longer."

"Nyet . . . ah . . . ya ne mogu . . ."

He heard the word for "no," but he kept his gaze on hers, touching her gently, licking her, using the expressions of agonized pleasure that crossed her face as his guide to keep the orgasm she was desperate for just out of reach. He wanted to blow her mind, make her scream, have her come apart in total ecstasy. Because she deserved nothing less than that.

He kept her on the edge for as long as he could, until her ragged pleas were broken and hoarse. Then he pressed his thumb down on her clit, licked her hard and deep, holding her down on the bed as she flung her head back and screamed, her whole body lifting as the climax took her.

He couldn't take his eyes off her, watching as the ecstasy unfurled over her face. And he realized he'd never watched anyone come like this. He'd simply never been interested. But now . . . Christ, he'd never seen anything so erotic. She was flushed and shaking, achingly sensual and at the same time incredibly powerful.

He continued to lick and stroke her, bringing her down slowly until her screams had subsided into sobs. Until she was collapsed onto her back, one arm thrown over her face, still panting, her body sheened with sweat.

So fucking beautiful.

Alex moved, putting one hand by her head and leaning over her. She lifted her arm away from her face, staring up at him. Little tendrils of gold hair stuck to her damp forehead and her fair skin was pink, making the color of her eyes even deeper.

"It is always like this?" she asked in a cracked voice. "So intense, I mean?"

"No." He couldn't find it in himself to lie to her. "It's never like this."

"Oh." Clearly this wasn't the answer she'd expected. "Why not? You must do that to women all the time." It wasn't an accusation, merely a statement of fact.

"I've done it more than once, but . . ."—he paused, brushing a couple of golden curls off her sweat-damp forehead—"I've never wanted to watch."

"Really?" She frowned. "But you wanted to watch me?"

"I wanted to see you come."

"Why?"

"Because you're beautiful, Katya. You're sensual and passionate." He touched the curve of her cheek, feeling softness beneath his fingertip. "And I wanted to make sure it was good for you."

She stared up at him for a long moment, unspeaking. Then abruptly she pushed herself up and kissed him, another of her sweet, generous kisses that made him want to kiss her hungrily back, take everything he could from her.

But he held himself still, and when she pulled away he was breathing fast, his cock so hard for her it was almost painful.

"Now it really is your turn." She ran a fingertip across his mouth. "What do you want?"

"To be inside you."

"That can be arranged." Her forehead creased. "Protection?"

"Condoms are in the nightstand."

She shifted, reaching over to pull open the drawer and draw out a silver packet. He let her rip it open and showed her how to put it on him, watching as she rolled the latex down over the hard length of his cock. And Christ, the feel of her fingers on him—he wasn't going to last.

"Come here," he murmured when she'd finished. "I'll show you what I want."

She moved over him, straddling his hips, and he put one hand on her hip to guide her as she eased herself down on him, the wet heat of her pussy tight as a glove tailored especially for him.

"Oh . . . fuck . . . Katya . . ." he whispered, his knuckles white on her hip, the feel of her around him making his head spin. Holy hell. How was he going to survive this?

Alex tried to temper his own breathing, but he couldn't. He'd waited too long. Heat moved through him as she shifted her hips, and he sank deeper into her, a wildfire burning out of control.

She gasped, arching her body, the tips of her breasts brushing his chest.

His thoughts burned away in the heat, evaporating entirely. There was nothing but this. Nothing but fire and flame. Nothing but ecstasy.

Her fingers pushed into his hair, tilting his head so he was looking into her eyes. "Let it go," she whispered. "Let it go, Alexei."

And he was too far gone to understand what she meant or know whether she'd said it in English or Russian. At that moment he didn't even understand language at all.

Or at least only one kind. The feel of her pussy around his cock. Her skin against his. And the movement of her hips, driving him on, driving him deep.

In that moment it was all the language he needed.

Alex gripped her hips, thrusting hard, burying himself inside her, drowning himself, drowning them both, in pleasure.

He tried to hold on. He really did. But it was too much for him. And in the end, he moved his hand between them, stroking her clit as he pushed deeper. She screamed in his ear, her fingers curling tight in his hair, her body convulsing.

Then he lost himself. But before the end he found one word had come back to him, and as the climax annihilated him he said it.

"Katya."

CHAPTER FOURTEEN

Katya woke up the next morning feeling strange. First, when she looked at the clock on the nightstand it was 10:00 A.M., and she *never* slept later than seven. Second, she ached in odd places. Places that generally didn't ache even after a very strenuous workout. And third, it felt like something was missing.

She rolled over and sat up, frowning. And then realized what was missing.

Alex.

He wasn't lying beside her and he wasn't anywhere else in the room.

For a long moment she just sat there, a vague kind of disappointment settling in her gut. She'd expected . . . Well, she didn't quite know what she'd expected, but waking up alone wasn't quite it.

She cocked her head, catching a sound coming from the bathroom. Faintly she could hear the sound of running water. Oh, so he hadn't gone. He was only showering.

Relief filled her and she slipped off the bed, heading toward the bathroom.

Why are you going to him? What do you want? What do you think is going to happen?

She slowed to a stop in the middle of the room. Because those were all very good questions.

They hadn't discussed what would happen in the morning. Whether the previous night had been a one-off occurrence or they would continue as lovers. She hadn't even thought about it. But . . . they had to think about it, didn't they? Especially considering they were in the middle of an important mission.

You really can only think of the mission?

But what else was there? Sex didn't make all those other things go away. Alex still had a game tonight and his life was still at risk. Even more so now that they knew what they were getting into. Which made it doubly important that she remain focused on the end goal: protecting him.

What about what you want? He told you that you laid him open . . .

Katya ignored the stray thought. What she wanted was to do a good job, protect her client any way she could. And as for what she did to him, well, that was irrelevant, wasn't it?

She moved over to the bathroom door and pushed it open just as Alex stepped from the massive shower. Water sheened his body, highlighting all the intriguing dips and hollows of his muscular torso and running down his long, powerful legs. His hair was inky black and wet, dripping down his back as he reached for one of the thick, soft white towels that hung on the rail nearby. "You're up." He didn't smile. "I'm sorry, were you hoping to join me?"

"I'm too late anyway, I see."

"Yeah, sadly. I should have woken you, I know, but I thought you needed the sleep."

Katya watched him towel himself off, her mouth going dry. He hadn't let her touch him the way she'd wanted the night before, distracting attention away from himself with more pleasure. She'd spotted it easily enough but hadn't pushed him for the reasons as to why. She knew anyway, and besides, it had been a night of too many truths to keep pushing for more.

But now her fingers itched to run over his skin, trace the graceful interplay of muscles that flexed and hollowed as he moved.

An unfamiliar awkwardness gripped her. This whole situation was completely new and she was unsure of how to act. He was a client she'd just slept with and—

Alex casually slung the towel over the rail and stepped toward her, sliding one hand behind her head and drawing her in for a searing, possessive kiss. She responded automatically, reaching for him, her hands moving hungrily over the warm, damp skin of his chest. God, she could feel taut muscle beneath, the suggestion of leashed strength . . .

He released her, moving past her and through the door back into the bedroom.

Katya caught her breath. Her fingers tingled from the touch of his skin and there was a hollow feeling in her stomach. As if she'd been given a taste of something she hadn't realized she'd been starving for until now.

She turned, following him into the bedroom. He was standing by the closet, pulling out some clothes. A dark blue suit and white shirt, black boxers, all of which were laid on the bed.

"What now, sir?" she asked.

Alex raised a brow as he pulled on his boxers. "What did I tell you about the 'sir'?"

"Oh, I assumed that since—"

"Since I didn't pull you into the shower and fuck you up against the wall, we're back to being employer and bodyguard?"

She let out a breath, feeling exposed all of a sudden. "I . . . yes. I suppose I didn't think that."

"Well, we're not." The certainty in his tone was absolute.

"We didn't discuss this—"

"So, we're discussing it now. I expect to remain your lover for the remaining time here in Monte Carlo, understood?" He stepped into his pants, pulled them up, and fastened them, his impressive abs flexing as he did so. "Unless of course you don't want that, in which case we'll—"

"I want that." The words came out before she could stop them, and even though she was afraid of what they might mean, she didn't take them back.

What about the mission, Katya?

They could be lovers without it affecting the mission, surely? It wasn't the sex she needed to be careful about, after all, but letting her emotions cloud her judgment. If she was careful, it would be fine.

Alex reached for his white shirt and pulled it on. Then, ignoring the buttons, he came across the room to her and gently took her face between his hands. "I'm sorry, Katya," he said quietly. "I know this is new for you. I wanted to stay and talk to you about this, but it's late and I have a lot to do before the game tonight, okay?"

Yes, of course. The game.

She pulled herself together. "Of course. What can I do?"

He didn't linger, stepping away and doing up his shirt as he moved back over to the bed, reaching for his jacket. "I need you to follow up on the e-mail Zac sent me last night. About the rest of the Apocalypse players." He didn't look at her as he pulled on the jacket. "They're not primarily poker players, as I thought. In fact, apart from August, I don't think any of them are."

"So . . . what are they doing in that game then?"

"Good question." He ran a hand through his damp black hair. "I keep coming back to what Conrad said to Lau last night about 'a good businessman or -woman should know their stock.' Did you hear that?"

Katya thought back. It had been during the strip poker part of the evening. Mrs. Lau had been ambivalent about choosing a piece of clothing to take off the girl standing behind the sheikh. "Yes, I heard. Do you think it's related to what he's doing with those women?"

"I don't 'think,'" Alex said. "I'm pretty damn certain it's related. Because if he's referring to them as 'stock' then there's something pretty fucking dubious going on." He gave her a look. "They were businesspeople, Katya. All of them. Very rich businesspeople. And I'm thinking they weren't actually playing poker for the fun it. They were there for something else."

A cold feeling settled in her gut. "Those women?"

"It's looking like it. Perhaps the players are potential buyers or something."

She muttered a curse in Russian under her breath. "That's disgusting."

"It is." His voice was absolutely cold. "Which is why we're going to stop it."

Katya stared at him. He wasn't wearing a tie and his white shirt was unbuttoned at the throat, his hair damp and untidy, but that in no way detracted from his allure. He looked disheveled, but the glitter in his eyes was sharp, hard. Dangerous.

Desire twisted inside her and she was helpless to stop it.

You want to be more than just his lover.

No, she didn't. She couldn't. Being his bodyguard and his lover was one thing, but wanting more . . . Sex might not be a weakness, but getting emotional definitely was. And if that happened, she would have to leave him. For both their sakes.

"You look sad, Katya mine." He took a step toward her. "What's wrong?"

"Nothing," she said, ignoring the thought and the weird

sense of desolation that came with it. "I'm fine. So, will you forward me Mr. Rutherford's e-mail?"

"You're already CCed on it." He studied her a moment longer.

She was still naked, but his gaze didn't take in the rest of her body as hers had done with his. His gaze remained squarely on her face. And for some reason that made her feel even more exposed.

Katya glanced away, beginning to turn back toward the bathroom. "Good. I'll have a look over it this morning."

"Katya."

She paused but kept her back to him. "Yes?"

There was a long silence. Then he said, "I need a clear head for the game tonight. It's nothing personal."

Oh, wonderful. So he'd spotted her disappointment, which really shouldn't come as any great surprise, but still. She didn't want to appear desperate. She didn't want to be one of those lovers of his who clutched and hung on. Who didn't want to leave when it was time to go. Who always wanted more. Her mother had been like that and look how that had turned out.

But no, she wasn't her mother. She was stronger than that.

"I understand," she said levelly. "I'll see you later then."

He moved fast, so fast she wasn't prepared for his warm hand on her shoulder, pulling her around. Or for his arms sliding around her, pulling her up against him. Shocked, she could only stare as he pushed her back against the wall, pinning her there with his body. And then the shock slid away as he kissed her, another deep, hard kiss. She pushed her hands into his hair, the wet silk of it soft against her fingers, opening her mouth and kissing him back, desperate after all.

And when he pulled away, she couldn't help the words that came spilling out. "Do you have to go now?"

One corner of his mouth curved into a smile that took her breath away. Both rueful and wicked all at once. "You have no idea how much I want to stay. But I meant it about the game. I need my focus and touching you screws with it. I need to keep my distance until it's over, okay?"

Despite that smile, she could see the intensity in his eyes, a blue flame that made her want to tremble. He wasn't lying; he wasn't playing games again.

The small, hard knot of disappointment she'd been pretending wasn't there since she'd woken up that morning abruptly disappeared. She kissed him lightly, just once, to take the taste of him to last her through the day. And smiled back. "Then you'd better let me go, hadn't you?"

"I don't like this. I don't like this at all." Zac's expression was grim.

Alex kicked his feet up on the desk and stared at the computer screen in front of him. It showed the interior of the Nine's usual meeting room at the Second Circle, the fire burning in the grate, a food platter that was—as usual—untouched on the coffee table in front of it. Zac must have put his laptop on one of the side tables so Alex could see the couch in front of the fire and the armchair that was Eva's special seat. She wasn't sitting in it now, though, but standing in front of the fire with her hands out, obviously trying to get warm. The expression on her face was absolutely unreadable.

Zac stood opposite her, his arms folded, facing the camera, looking like an expensive and well-dressed undertaker in his perfect suit. If undertakers were usually built like a brick shithouse, that is.

"Okay, so we now know this isn't about poker," Alex said. "And the people playing aren't there for the game."

"So why the bloody hell were they invited in the first

place?" Zac's voice was terse. "Are they potential buyers? Business partners?"

Alex crushed the instinct that had him wanting to reach for a pen from the desk and toy with it. He couldn't afford to give in to any kind of revealing behavior, not even with his friends.

Yet he felt antsy and restless, like he couldn't keep still. Jesus, he had to concentrate. But the problem was all he could think of was Katya's green eyes staring into his. The feel of her bare skin against him. The taste of her in his mouth—

"Alex?" Zac was staring at him. "What the fuck are you doing? I need you to concentrate."

Ah Christ, this was ridiculous. He'd never been this distracted over a woman before. Over *anyone* before. With an effort, he tried to curb the restless feeling. "Yeah, well, get off my back and I might be able to."

Eva turned from the fire to face the camera, something intense flickering over her face. "They're potential buyers," she said with certainty. "And they want to buy women."

There was a cold, heavy silence.

He didn't want to ask why she was so certain. He had a feeling he already knew. "I'm not sure about the sheikh and Christine. But the others—"

"Are all businesspeople," Zac finished, unusually impatient for him. "But I couldn't find a single damn thing on any of them, which usually indicates something pretty dodgy. You don't get to be as rich as that without climbing over the back of someone. Usually several someones."

Alex frowned. "I know August is shady as fuck. And Lau has Triad links, or at least her husband used to."

"Yeah, they want to buy." Eva had turned fully to face the camera, her gaze sharp enough to cut. "Or maybe they want in on the action. Motherfuckers."

Alex wanted to say something else light and flippant, the way he normally did when he was uncomfortable, but he couldn't think of a single damn thing.

"Gabriel said you thought the invites came from the Seven Devils," Zac said.

"Yeah, it's an idea." And it was becoming less an idea and more of a certainty.

The expression on Zac's face sharpened. "Are there links between South's casino and the Lucky Seven? I mean, we know South was one of your father's seven and so was Tremain."

"Shit," Eva said viciously. "Didn't Gabe mention that the Lucky Seven had been a high-class escort joint as well?"

Unease slid through Alex. There had been women back when his father had first taken him to the casino, beautiful women in pretty dresses. He'd been such a fucking innocent, he'd thought they were the wives of the players. Or the girlfriends. He hadn't thought hookers.

On the screen in front of him, Eva took a few steps toward the camera. Her eyes had gone silver, sharp as an unsheathed blade. "Leave this to me, Alex," she said, a hoarse sound in her voice. "I'll deal with them."

It didn't take a genius to work out what that meant. "No. Not yet."

Her expression twisted. "Don't be a prick. This needs—"

"No, Eva," he cut her off coldly. "At least not yet."

"What the hell do you mean, not yet?" She'd taken another step toward the camera. "You have to—"

"Angel," Zac interrupted, his attention on her. "Let him speak."

Alex held Eva's gaze. "I have my own plans for Conrad, okay? You even gave me the idea, remember? So I need you to wait before we move on this. Just for a night."

Eva's mouth tightened. "Alex, I—" She stopped as the

sound of the door opening came through and the two on the screen glanced over in the direction of the room's entrance, off camera.

"Hey," someone said shortly, Gabriel from the sound of it.

Then another voice, a woman's. "Hi, guys, I hope you don't mind me interrupting." A figure appeared on the camera, small and slender, and very definitely female. Bobbed black hair. Beautifully dressed. "Oh," the woman said, "Am I—." She turned to face the camera.

And Alex met a pair of eyes as blue as his own.

Honor.

Her hand in his had been so small as he'd walked her onto the school grounds, her eyes wide and scared. And she'd held on to him as if she never wanted to let him go. As if he could protect her from the world . . .

Her mouth opened, but before she could speak Alex leaned forward and cut the connection leaving the image on the screen. His sister, with her mouth open, shock clear on her fine-boned face.

His hands were shaking. Everything was shaking.

He shoved the chair back and got to his feet, walking to the window and back again, struggling to get himself under control.

What are you so afraid of?

The truth. Everything. . . .

But no, he could not think of that. Of the fact that he was a fucking coward, that he'd been running for so many years he had no idea how to stop.

That wasn't the most important thing right now. Only Conrad mattered. Only the game. Only taking that prick for everything he had.

Alex ran a hand through his hair, took a breath. Then he turned back to his computer and closed the Skype window. Honor vanished.

If only making everything else disappear like that were as simple.

Katya sat at the roulette table on the Fourth Circle's empty gaming floor and gazed around the place. There was something sad about it in the middle of the day. Something vaguely tragic. Like an older woman disguising herself with makeup, hiding the cracks of age under a layer of paint. Clinging on to her youth.

One of the red velvet curtains over a nearby window had been pulled fractionally back, allowing the daylight to shine through. Dust motes hung in the air.

The cold light of day was never kind and revealed all kinds of things. The stains on the floor. The tear in one of the curtains around a group of chairs. A long scratch down one of the tables.

Without the music, the lights, and the people, without the night to hide all the flaws, it looked like what it was: a large, cold, empty room.

She let out a silent breath, Alex stealing into her thoughts once again. This room was like him in many ways. A man who was doing everything he could to hide, to distract.

The problem was the truth was still there underneath. And all the distracting in the world, all the pretty paint and lights and music, wouldn't change that.

She reached out and gave the roulette wheel a turn, watching as the red and black colors whirled. But no, she'd told herself after he'd left that morning that she wouldn't think of him in that way. Remembering the sex was okay, but thinking about the man was not.

Especially not with the game coming up tonight.

Which was part of the reason she was sitting out here, waiting for him to come out of his office behind the bar where he'd been ensconced for most of the afternoon doing God knows what.

She didn't want to interrupt whatever it was he was doing, but she wanted to talk to him about the game.

Ever since the morning, she'd been going over all the information she had about Conrad South and the other players Zac Rutherford had sent her. Digging up what she could about the white slave trade. Looking for anything that might link the names to any kind of trafficking rings.

But there was nothing and it disturbed her. This whole situation had suddenly gotten a lot more dangerous and she hated going into a dangerous situation with very little information. She wanted to be prepared and that meant they needed a plan. Or rather, it meant she had to get Alex to let her in on whatever his plan was, since he obviously had one. One he still hadn't told her about.

Again a little sliver of hurt caught at her, a flash of disappointment.

She ignored it. She'd let herself feel the night before, in the bar when he'd pinned her against the wall. When he'd told her the truth about why he'd left. Let the thrill of knowing she'd affected him settle down inside her, glorying in it.

But that's all she would allow. She couldn't let herself get closer to him. Like she'd told herself that morning, the physical aspect of their relationship was fine—they were already pretending to be lovers anyway, so a little reality wouldn't hurt—but anything more and things could get compromised.

"Katya?"

Pushing aside the thoughts, she looked up to see Alex shutting the door to his office and making his way over to where she sat.

"Were you waiting for me?"

"Yes." She stilled the roulette wheel as he approached the table. "I'm sorry, I don't want to interrupt anything."

"You're not." He was as impeccably dressed as he had been this morning except now his hair looked like he'd run his fingers through it one too many times. And there was a certain tension in his shoulders, a tightness around his mouth. "What's up?"

She frowned. "Perhaps I should be asking you that question?"

"It's nothing." He pulled out one of the chairs next to her and sat down in his typical lazy sprawl. "I was talking to Zac and the others earlier, getting their thoughts on the Conrad situation."

"Are they going to contact the authorities?"

His gaze flickered. He leaned forward and picked up the ball from the roulette wheel, rolling it through his fingers. "I'd prefer to wait until that girl we rescued is safe. She didn't want us calling the police, remember?"

She studied him silently a moment. "What is your plan, Alex?"

"My plan?" The silver ball flashed through his fingers.

"You told me you had one last night."

The ball stilled as he reached to give the roulette wheel a spin. "Oh, right. That plan." He dropped the ball into the wheel, where it made clicking sounds as it raced around the inside of it. "Why do you want to know?"

"Haven't we had this conversation? I need to know in order to protect you properly. This situation is even more dangerous now and we can't afford to take any chances. I don't want to go into this game—"

His hand shot out, stilling the wheel abruptly, the movement cutting her off. "You're not going anywhere."

She stared at him. "What? Of course I'm going to be there. That's what you hired me for. That's what—"

"No." Alex lifted his gaze from the roulette wheel, his eyes blazing blue. "You're not coming, Katya. You're staying here."

There was nothing but certainty in his face, and all the strength of his stubborn will.

"Why?" she demanded. "South said you couldn't play if I'm not there."

"Conrad South can go fuck himself," Alex snapped. "You're not going to be there and that's final."

She swallowed. "But you're going, aren't you?"

He didn't look away. "Yes."

"Why? You have the information you need; what's the point of playing now?"

Shadows moved in his eyes. The echoes of the past. Rage and pain, and something else she couldn't identify. And she realized he wasn't attempting to distract or conceal them; he was letting her see.

Her throat closed. "What?" she forced out. "What do you want from him?"

"What do I want?" Slowly, Alex picked up the ball and spun the wheel again, dropping the ball once more so it flashed around the inside rim. "Revenge, Katya mine. I want revenge."

She didn't need to know what for; she'd already guessed. But all of a sudden she wanted to hear his story, hear it in his own words.

Are you sure you want his secrets? Once you know one, you'll want them all.

But no, she needed to know this. It was background to the mission; it was vital.

Keep telling yourself that. . . .

Katya ignored the voice in her head. She focused on the man in front of her instead. The man who was looking right at her and not the wheel he'd set in motion. As if he wanted her to ask the question.

So she did. "What happened, Alex? What did he do to you?"

The wheel spun, the ball rolling around and around.

But Alex was completely still, like he'd been turned to stone. Only his eyes burned, sapphire blue turned dark as midnight. "He raped me," he said in a voice devoid of expression. "The fucking bastard raped me."

He didn't really want to tell her, and as soon as the words left his mouth he wished he hadn't. But he couldn't take them back. They were out there now.

Someone else knew. It was real.

He waited for the reaction, not knowing what to expect. Shock for certain. Perhaps disgust or revulsion to follow, then a side order of pity.

And he found he was sitting there in his seat, every muscle locked up like he was bracing himself for a blow.

Or readying yourself to run.

But no. He didn't want to do that. Not now. The time for running was over and had been the moment he'd realized Katya had come for him the night before. Because she was still here. Waiting for him in the seedy midday of the gaming room like a lily in a bouquet of wilting hibiscus. With her sharp, perceptive gaze and her strength.

And he didn't want to run from her. He wanted to give her the truth instead.

So he'd said it. He was tired of running anyway.

Her face didn't change and none of the things he expected crossed her face. She only looked at him, her gaze very direct, and said, "I know."

Oh fuck. Here was the shock, piercing him like a blade. "What?" he demanded, unable to help himself. "What do you mean, you know?"

She sat very straight in her chair, her hair in a simple ponytail down her back. "I guessed it was probably something like that. I could see how angry you were at him. You hated him, so I knew whatever he'd done was bad.

There was also a strange tension between you that felt . . . physical almost."

He didn't move, reflexive disgust shifting inside him. "Oh Christ, so it was obvious then?"

"No, of course not. I just knew because . . ." She hesitated. "You were *so* angry. And you were in pain. He hurt you and I knew it must have been bad to make you hate him so much. That it must have been deeply personal."

Every instinct he had was telling him to move, to get away from the look in her eyes. From the terrible understanding. But he made himself sit there and bear her gaze. And in that moment he realized that he wanted someone else to know. Because he was so fucking sick of carrying it by himself.

"It happened nineteen years ago," he heard himself say. "I was sixteen. Remember I told you about my father and the underground casino he owned? No one knew about it. It was a secret. But he drew me into it because he needed someone to spot card counters and I was good with numbers. I remember . . ."—his voice thickened strangely—". . . thinking how amazing it was to be part of it. Like I was in a special club that was only Dad's and mine. Christ, I would have done anything for him."

Katya said nothing, only watching him. *You can trust me with anything. . . .*

"Anyway," he said, and weirdly, he didn't have to force himself to go on, "Dad was losing money, running up debt. Conrad was one of his friends and was in on the casino. He paid Dad's debts for him for a while, but Dad had nothing to pay him back with. But . . . Conrad had decided that he wanted me and he cornered me one night, telling me that my dad was in serious debt. And that if he wasn't careful, he was going to get himself hurt. But that I could help him. All I had to do was—" He stopped abruptly, a bitter laugh forcing its way out of him. Why was this still so hard? "I think you can imagine what he wanted."

"I can," Katya said quietly. "You don't have to say it."

No, he didn't, did he? They both knew what he meant. A tenuous thread of relief curled through him and suddenly he didn't want the distance between them. He wanted her close, her body next to his the way they'd been sitting at the reception.

Alex didn't question the impulse; he only held out his hand to her. "Come here."

She didn't question, rising from her seat and moving over to where he sat as if she already knew what he wanted. And hell, she must have read his mind, because she seated herself in his lap with a graceful movement, leaning back with her head against his shoulder.

He slid his arms around her waist, holding her close. She was so warm, an intriguing mix of soft and firm, of curves and long, lean lines. He could feel her fingers on his arm, just resting there, her touch warming him like a ray of sunlight on a patch of frosty ground.

He turned his face into her hair, feeling the softness of it against his cheek. "I let him do it. I let him have me because I wanted to help my dad. But I made Conrad promise not to tell him what happened. I didn't want him to know. I didn't want anyone to know."

Katya's fingers moved on his arm, stroking him. Not saying a word, which was just perfect. Allowing him room to speak if he wanted to. And he did.

"He took me into the fucking men's bathrooms and he raped me, and afterwards I couldn't get out of there fast enough. All I wanted to do was run. Put as much distance between me and what happened as I could. I never saw my father again. He killed himself about a month later. After that my mother and my sister came to bring me home—I was living with Gabriel at the time. But I didn't want to do that either. I couldn't bear to go back. So I didn't."

Another moment of silence passed and he didn't break it, content to hold her in his arms, letting the scent of her take away the taint of the past.

Then she said softly, "But now you are going back. You're facing him again."

"I am." He found he was grinning savagely. "And this time he's going to be the one begging me to stop. I've been running from this for nineteen years, but no more. I will have revenge for what he did to me, Katya. I will have it."

Her fingers tightened fractionally on his arm. "I am coming with you, Alex." She said it like it was already a done deal, like there was no room for argument. "You need someone to have your back."

He'd never intended for her to be there; he'd never wanted anyone to see. It was supposed to be just him and Conrad, a private, very personal revenge. Like what had happened between them had been very private and very personal. And yet the thought of Katya being there, lending him her strength . . . Christ, it was so good. He'd carried this alone for so long and, hell, she knew all his secrets now anyway.

"Conrad will use you to get at me," he said, voicing the one concern he had left. "Like he used you last night."

"That doesn't worry me. You know I can protect myself if need be."

He looked down at her, found her gaze on his. "It's not physical harm you should be worried about. He gets off on power trips and he's a master at emotional manipulation. He will hurt you if he can."

But her gaze was steady. "Then we'll have to beat him at his own game, won't we?"

"We." He liked that. Fuck, no, he loved that. "That's all part of my plan, Katya mine. You see, he still wants me. He wants to own everything I have and me into the bargain. So that's what I put on the table. He'll have to put in a similar bet if he wants to stay in the game, which means his casino, all his money, all his power. And then I'll beat him; I'll wipe the table with him. And once I've done that, I'll get out my gun and I'll put it to his head and I'll make him beg for his life."

There was a spark in her eyes. A glowing emerald spark. "You don't need to bring a gun. You can use mine."

Alex's expression was fierce and she couldn't blame him. She wanted to get her gun and go and shoot South herself after what Alex had told her.

He'd been sixteen. A boy . . .

The tight feeling in her chest wouldn't go away, a complicated mixture of anger and sadness. And something else, a lurching, frightening emotion she didn't quite understand. One that made her want to touch him, hold him. Give him comfort. Take away all the pain and fear he must have experienced.

She felt his fingers close around her ponytail, gripping her. "Does it change things?" he demanded suddenly. "Knowing what he did to me? Does it change the way you see me?"

"No," she replied with absolute truth. "I guessed anyway days ago."

His gaze roamed over her face, as if he was searching for something, that fierce expression still burning in his eyes. He had his fingers tight in her hair, his arm around her waist like an iron band. Holding on to her tightly. "Are you sure? Because you're the only one who knows, Katya. I've never told anyone else."

Another lurch inside her chest. One that made her breath catch and her heartbeat accelerate. And she knew it was about more than desire. More than lust. That it ran deeper, wider, than either of those.

She thought she could keep this separate, that she didn't have to feel anything emotionally for him. But that was only a lie she told herself to make herself feel better.

She was the only one who knew this truth about him. The only one who knew his secrets. How could she keep herself separate after that? Because the answer to give him, to keep the emotional distance between them, was, *No. I'm not sure.*

But that was a lie too far. And she couldn't do it. The things he'd told her deserved more. He deserved more.

So instead she said, "Yes. I am sure." And then she shifted, sliding a hand between them, her palm covering the front of his suit trousers. "Would you like me to prove it to you?"

She heard the catch in his breath, saw the flame ignite in his eyes. He was already hard beneath her hand, the heat of him burning through the fabric of his pants. "I seem to recall something about not screwing you today. That I needed to get my head in the game for tonight."

"Actually, I think this is exactly what you need." She traced the long, hard shape of him through the material, holding his gaze as she did so. "I think you need me before you go face him tonight. Because I'm the only one who knows. Which makes you mine." She squeezed him. "He can't touch you, Alexei. He can't ever touch you again."

He stared at her a long moment, his expression opaque. Then he let go of her ponytail and reached instead for the buttons of the white blouse she was wearing, gently beginning to undo them. "I've never been anyone's before," he said softly. "I think I like it. But as a sop to my masculinity, I think you're going to have to prove to me that you're mine too."

She swallowed, trying to read the look on his fiercely handsome face. He was looking down at what his fingers were doing, methodically undoing each button of her blouse. "Am I yours?" The question came out before she quite knew she was going to ask it, a pleading note in her voice that made her want to cringe.

His hand slid into her blouse and beneath the delicate white lace of her bra, cupping her breast, the heat of his palm like a brand against her skin. He shifted his gaze to meet hers. "Do you want to be?"

Yes. Yes. Yes.

"Da." It took her a moment to realize she'd answered in Russian.

His mouth curved, his thumb circling her nipple, making her shiver. "Show me how much."

There was no one here; the room was empty. Nevertheless, it was a public place. And yet she found she didn't care. She squeezed him again, his cock getting harder and harder, running her thumb down the length of his shaft and back again.

He murmured something, a curse under his breath; then he lowered his head and she thought he was going to kiss her. But he didn't.

As he pulled aside the lacy cup of her bra, his mouth covered her nipple instead.

She closed her eyes, a soft gasp escaping her, a lightning strike of sensation arrowing straight down to her sex. Her fingers pushed into his black hair, and she shuddered as he nipped her, a sharp shot of pain, drowned almost instantly by the soothing lick of his tongue.

Of course she was his. How could she be anyone else's? After this?

"Since you're mine, I'm going to fuck you, Katya," he murmured against her skin. "Right here, on the roulette table." A hand slid up her thigh, beneath the skirt she wore, another of Scott's little minis designed to show off her legs. And she shuddered again as his fingers found her sex, stroking her through the fabric of her panties. "So if you don't want that, you'd better let me know right now."

She couldn't speak, her voice completely gone. All she could do was reach for the zipper of his pants, tugging it down so she could touch him the way he was touching her, the length of him hot and hard in her hand.

"I'll take that as a yes," he whispered, nipping her again.

Then he moved, lifting her in his arms and setting her on the green baize of the roulette table, pushing her legs apart so he could stand between them. Then he pulled his wallet from his pants and took out a condom. "I want you to do it for me," he said, handing it to her. Then he undid his pants.

Touching him. He wanted her touching him, unlike last night. Her throat felt full, that strange, frightening feeling turning and shifting in her chest. But she swallowed it back, her hands shaking as she ripped open the packet and took out the latex. She'd done this last night for him and it had been far easier than expected, at least easier than stripping an Uzi. Yet right now she wasn't sure she could do it.

And he obviously sensed her worry, because then his hands covered hers, guiding her, both of them rolling the latex down, protecting them.

Then he said, "Put your arms around my neck."

She did, shivering as his hands slid her skirt up, as he pulled her to the edge of the table. His blue eyes stared straight into hers and this time she was the one who was drowning.

"Alexei," she whispered helplessly as she felt him pull aside the lace of her panties, baring her. As the blunt head of his cock pushed into her, the exquisite stretch of him made her gasp.

His arm came around her, holding her tight against him while his other hand gripped her ponytail again, tugging her head back. "No more distance, Katya," he said raggedly, the rough note in his voice like a caress. "No more secrets. Not while you're here. Not while you're mine. Understand?"

The feeling rose up inside her, tangling with the pleasure, turning intense. Vast. Inescapable. She was going to drown; she was sure of it.

It wouldn't be so bad to drown in his arms. . . .

But he must have known, must have seen her distress, because the grip in her hair turned gentle, so he was cupping the back of her head, holding her steady for a kiss that just about killed her with its gentleness. With its soft heat.

That made a sob catch in her throat as he began to move inside her in a slow, intense rhythm.

It was his turn to save her. His turn to help her breathe.

Her arms curled tight around his neck, her mouth opening to his. Her body shifting and moving with the rhythm he set.

The clutch of pleasure intensified and the gentleness began to change. His mouth was harder, hotter. A savage kiss that demanded nothing less than complete surrender. She gave it to him unhesitatingly, let him take control because she sensed that's what he needed right now.

He tugged her hair out of its ponytail and pushed her back down onto the table, spreading her hair out around her on the green baize. "Let me see it," he ordered, his voice rough. "I want to see what I do to you. I want to hear you scream."

That fierce, hungry glint was back in his eyes and he was looking at her like she was the only woman in the world. And in that moment there was nothing she wouldn't give him.

She put her hands above her head, arching her back, opening her mouth, and gasping as he drove into her. Letting him hear the pleasure he gave her.

Faster. Harder. His hand moving between her legs,

stroking her clit as he thrust, ratcheting up the pleasure so it became nearly agonizing in its intensity.

"Alex . . ." she said hoarsely. "Oh, Alexei, please . . ."

He leaned over her and slid one hand behind her head, his blazing blue eyes the only things she could see. "Come for me, Katya mine. Come just for me."

Then he moved his hand, gave one last, deep thrust.

And Katya let herself drown.

He felt her come, her pussy convulsing around him, her legs wrapped tightly around his waist, and his own climax rushed over him like an incoming tide. And it was all he could do just to hold her as it swamped him, leaving him shaking like an old man.

But that was okay. She was shaking too.

Afterwards he became aware of where they were, and like it had at Conrad's reception, it felt wrong. To have her here where anyone could walk in and interrupt.

Pulling away from her, he first dealt with the condom, then gathered her into his arms. She didn't protest, only putting her head against his shoulder. "Where are we going?"

"Upstairs. I don't know about you, but I could do with a shower."

"But you just had one this morning."

"Yes, but you weren't in it."

She smiled at him and for some reason he felt it like a touch.

No, there would be no more distance between them. No more secrets. And having her know almost all of his was freeing in a way he'd never imagined.

Upstairs, he turned on the shower, then slowly and carefully stripped her bare. Then he got himself naked and pulled both of them into the shower, pushing her against the shower wall and letting the hot water wash everything away.

Her body was as sleek as a seal's and her mouth was hungry beneath his as he kissed her. And he was about to lift her against the wall and take her again when her hands pushed against his chest.

He lifted his head, looking down at her. Her face was flushed, water droplets catching in her eyelashes. "What?" he demanded.

"I want to give you something, Alex."

"What are you talking about?"

She didn't speak, only slipped away, coming around behind him. He turned and caught her brilliant green gaze.

Then she sank to her knees in front of him, water streaming over her hair and pale skin. "You've tasted me. Can't I taste you?"

His breath caught, unease twisting inside him.

But she didn't touch him, her gaze searching his face. "He's still in your head, isn't he?"

Alex wanted to say no, but of course that wasn't true. If it were, he wouldn't be hesitating. "He sucked me off." He forced the words out because he'd told her he didn't want any more secrets. And Jesus, she knew just about everything else. "And I didn't want him to."

She paled, yet her gaze didn't leave his. "But he's not here now."

He reached out, cupped her cheek. "Katya, I—"

"He can't touch you, Alex. Remember that. Not while I'm here."

Almost of its own accord, his thumb stroked her lovely mouth, tracing the outline of her full lower lip. Christ, he could do this, couldn't he? After all, it was pretty ironic, a playboy afraid of a blow job. . . .

When he sucked you off, you cried as you came. And he laughed.

No, fuck that.

His hand dropped and he leaned back against the shower wall. "Do it."

Katya gave a single sharp nod. Then she knelt upright and put a hand on his thigh. "Watch me. Keep your eyes on me."

He wanted to laugh at the irony of the reversal, but he suddenly felt too desperate, too raw, for laughter. "Of course," he said roughly. "Where else would I look?"

Her cheeks had lost that pale look, her eyes glittering. She reached for his cock and instantly he was hard at the slick feel of her fingers around him. At the sight of her pale skin circling his dick. Then he noticed that her hand was shaking.

This is different. She makes it different.

He put his hand around hers, the way he had when she'd put the condom on him. "Don't be afraid."

"I've never done this before." She took a little breath. "I want this to be good for you."

Who'd ever told him that? Who'd ever said, *I want this to be good for you*? No one. He'd said it to lots of other women, but no one had ever said it back. No one had ever wanted it to be good for him.

The unease, the strange cold, began to fade.

"It will be," he said. "Feel me, Katya. This is what you do to me. Nothing you do could ever be anything less than spectacular."

She flushed, pink staining her cheeks, holding his gaze. "Let go."

He released his hold, his hand dropping away. And a shudder coiled at the base of his spine as her fingers gently squeezed him.

"Look at me, Alex."

And he did, looking down into her eyes. Green and gold. So beautiful. Familiar.

"Tell me what to do."

"Lick me. Use your tongue."

She leaned forward, and he took a sharp breath as he watched her lick the head of his cock, the heat of her tongue sending a pulse of electricity all the way down his spine. She blinked at the sound, but when he pushed his fingers into the wet silk of her hair, gripping her again, she gave him another lick, watching his face.

Desire climbed, an exquisite pressure, and there was no unease. No fear.

Because this *was* different. This was Katya kneeling at his feet. Katya with her mouth on him. Katya who was making sure Conrad never touched him again.

He had a fistful of golden hair and he closed his fingers even tighter on it, using the softness to remind him where he was and who he was with. A lifeline.

"Open your mouth," he ordered, unable to help himself, his voice fraying as her tongue circled the head of his cock. "Suck me. Do it now."

Her pink mouth opened and took him in, searing heat engulfing him.

"Oh . . . fuck. . . ." He kept watching her, unable to look away as her mouth moved on him. She'd put her free hand on his hip, clutching him to steady herself as she began to suck him. She was tentative, unpracticed, but he didn't care. Because for the first time in his life the fear seemed to have melted away, leaving only a pleasure so deep he couldn't think.

He kept watching, guiding the movements of her head with his grip in her hair, feeling the sheer weight of that pleasure begin to crush him.

"I'm going to come, Katya," he whispered. "And I don't want you to stop. I want your mouth on me when I do. Do you want that?"

Her fingers spread on his hip, pressing him against the wall of the shower, giving a short, sharp nod of her head.

And then she kept going, drawing him in deeper, increasing the suction until he felt himself begin to spin out of control. Until every single fucking thing began to spin out of control.

And it was beautiful and it was right and he joined the chaos, throwing back his head as the orgasm exploded in his head, a bright flare of color and light in the darkness. Blinding him, annihilating him.

It took him hours to come down from the high, or at least it felt like hours. And when he did, Katya was still kneeling at his feet, the water streaming over both of them, her hair clutched tight between his fingers.

His lifeline.

Slowly, he released her, then reached for her upper arms, drawing her slowly to her feet. A flush had crept down her neck and shoulders. "Was that—"

"Perfect. It was absolutely fucking perfect."

Her mouth curved and it stole his breath completely. "Is there anything else I can do for you?"

He leaned forward and kissed her, tasting himself on her lips. And it was so fucking erotic he was hard all over again.

"Yes," he murmured against her lips. "You can do that again."

CHAPTER FIFTEEN

Alex got out of the car and held the door open as Katya got out. She was in one of Scott's gowns tonight. Black silk and relatively modest, the neckline wide across the shoulders to reveal their lovely shape and the ivory skin of Katya's throat and neck. The rest of the gown was saved from complete austerity by the cut, following every inch of her lithe, athletic figure, the hem brushing the floor.

A wave of possessiveness gripped him as he watched her, which was unusual for him, since he didn't get possessive of his lovers. But . . . the way she'd touched him in the shower earlier that day, like she was claiming him for herself, claiming him back from Conrad, had been so fucking good. Made him feel so fucking powerful. More like himself, the way he was always meant to be, not someone frantically papering over the cracks and hoping no one would see.

She'd been right. He had needed her. Had needed to be inside her, have her hands on him, her mouth, covering himself with her warmth and her scent, canceling out those bitter memories. So Conrad couldn't touch him.

No one can, not while you're hers.

And that wasn't an unpleasant thought. In fact, the thought of being anyone else's seemed strange right now. Wrong on some deep level. He knew he shouldn't be thinking that, though, so he didn't examine the feeling too closely, watching Katya come toward him instead.

The gown had been her choice for the evening and he'd approved. It made her look sexual yet powerful, a woman in control. Definitely not the plaything she'd given the impression of being at the past two visits to the Four Horsemen. Perhaps it gave away her true nature more than was advisable, but shit, he didn't much care anymore. Now she was both his bodyguard and his lover, and regardless of her role tonight, she would be a strength, not a weakness.

And she would be beside him when he crushed that motherfucker into the ground.

Intense satisfaction moved through him and he smiled at her as she put her hand on his arm. She smiled back and his breath caught. Ah, so that's what she looked like when she smiled. Goddamn, fucking beautiful.

He put his hand over hers on his arm, touching her skin as they walked up the steps to the casino and into the foyer. The doorman inclined his head, showing them to the elevators.

But when they got to the gaming room floor and the doors opened, they found the room empty but for Conrad sitting down one end of the poker table. He rose as Alex and Katya stepped out of the elevator and into the room, a smile on his face. "Welcome. I was wondering when you'd arrive."

Alex didn't move, didn't allow a trace of his surprise to show on his face. "Oh, are we late? Or perhaps the others are even later?"

Conrad's smile widened. "Ah well, I'm afraid the others won't be joining us this evening. Their game is over. It's just going to be you and I tonight. And of course your lovely bodyguard."

This was all excellent. Conrad had gotten rid of the other players and Alex hadn't even needed to do a thing. And if the prick was hoping he'd be shocked that Katya had been unmasked, he was sadly mistaken.

Alex laughed. "Took you long enough to figure that one out. I thought you'd guess the first night."

"Well, she was moderately convincing," Conrad admitted, seating himself once again. "Especially during the reception when you gave her an orgasm in that chair. Which was quite . . . arousing, I have to admit. You've got quite the way with women, son."

Of course he had seen. Had watched them. Had watched her . . .

Despite himself, a small bubble of rage burst in his head, a bright explosion of color, while at the same time it felt like he'd taken a bath in raw sewage. Her first orgasm, that private moment, taken from her. Watched by this man with his prurient interest.

The pressure of Katya's hand on Alex's arm increased as she gave him a small squeeze. A reminder of her presence and her strength. Conrad couldn't touch him anymore. Couldn't touch either of them . . .

Conrad's gaze was cold, watching Alex with the same detached interest as a snake watches a mouse in preparation for devouring it.

He let his mouth turn up in a satisfied shit-eating grin. "Glad we could provide some entertainment."

"I thought you'd be pleased." Conrad's hooded gaze flicked to Katya. "She's even blushing, bless her. But tell me, what was the point of the deception?"

Alex made a careless gesture. "A bit of fun. You know how it is." He allowed his smile to fade a little. "So what happened to the rest of them? Don't tell me their playing put the fear of God into you?"

Conrad laughed. "Shit, no. If you hadn't noticed, they couldn't play their way out of a wet paper bag. No, I thought if I was going to play, then I wanted a real challenge. After all, I don't get many of them these days." Idly, he picked up one of the packs of cards on the table, sliding them out of their box. It was a new pack, his fingers delicately pulling off the plastic wrap with small, precise movements. "I confess, son, that your little wager piqued my curiosity. Those Circles clubs of yours are very successful. Plus there was also that . . . other matter you promised. I don't want any outside interference and I don't want any other challengers. Tonight, it's just you and me." He raised a brow. "I hope you don't mind."

As if. "Why would I mind? Apocalypse was never about the poker anyway."

Something flickered in the other man's gaze. Fucking finally. Had he surprised him?

Conrad had begun shuffling the cards, snapping them from one hand to the other in an idle display of dexterity. "Of course it wasn't about the poker. Which begs the question as to why you're here?"

"I was invited." Alex turned and began to descend the stairs into the room, Katya silent beside him. "You know that."

"Revenge?" Conrad's voice was casual. "Is that what you're after?"

Alex pulled out the chair next to him for Katya, gesturing for her to sit. Using the moment to think. Did he want it all out on the table right now? Or did he want to deny it? Make Conrad push?

"Revenge?" Alex gave a short laugh, deciding he wanted to see how far the other man would go. "After nineteen years? Hardly. Why would I bother?"

Conrad's hands paused mid-shuffle, his flat hazel stare sharp as a needle. Then he smiled. "I took your virginity in a casino bathroom, boy. I used you hard. I would have thought you'd have something to say about that? Or is it only that you're coming back for more?"

The silence that fell was complete, redolent with the other man's satisfaction. He thought he'd delivered Alex a mortal blow, or at least one that would gut him. That would humiliate him. And maybe if Alex hadn't already told Katya what had happened, it would have done both. But he had told her. He'd said it out loud. And somehow doing that had drained both the pain and the humiliation from the truth.

Yet it was a truth that should have been Alex's to give, and in bringing it up now in front of Katya it felt like once again Conrad was seeking to take his choice from him.

The rage already simmering inside him threatened to break through. It would be so easy to launch himself across the table and choke the life out of that motherfucker. So easy . . .

But no. He had a plan and he was going to stick to it. The son of a bitch had to suffer.

Alex pushed away the anger. Made himself diamond hard. He turned to his own seat and dropped into it, leaning back as if he were completely at his ease. "Christ, was that what happened?" he said casually. "I can't remember. It was so long ago."

"Really?" Conrad's voice dropped into a purr. "I remember it. How you came in my mouth when I sucked you off. And how you cried afterwards. It was quite endearing."

Alex laughed, because again, Conrad was trying to hurt him. And again, he failed. Katya had already taken that particular pain away. "Jesus. Well, I was sixteen after all. Anyway, I've had my dick sucked by a lot of different people over the years. The faces tend to blur, if you get my drift." He paused and lifted an eyebrow. "What? Did you want to be special, Conrad? Were you hoping I treasured those memories? That I was desperate to relive them again?"

The other man's gaze flickered and he gave a short laugh,

but this time it sounded a little forced. "Of course not. How much fun would that be?" Abruptly he put the cards back down on the table. "And as much fun as all this small talk is, perhaps we should get to the game?"

Clearly Conrad had been expecting Alex to get angry or lose his cool, or fall to pieces or something. Well, he could wait all night for that to happen. Alex wasn't sixteen anymore.

A staff member came over to the table, placing a vodka on the side table next to Alex and a glass of champagne next to Katya.

Conrad shifted and pulled something from the chair next to him, a slim, black laptop. He placed it in the middle of the table. "I promised you I'd have something worth staking at the next game. Here it is."

Alex said nothing, merely waited. Of course the stake wouldn't be the laptop; he wasn't that stupid.

After a moment, Conrad opened the laptop and pushed a button; then he turned the screen so it faced both Alex and Katya. "I think you'll find this interesting."

A video started to play, the picture grainy and dimly lit. The interior of what looked to be a bar of some kind. It was vaguely familiar.

It's not a bar and you know it.

Alex stilled, staring at the screen. The camera must have been up high, in the corner of a ceiling or something, because it gave an excellent view of a dark-haired teenage boy walking toward the doors of a men's bathroom, another, taller man walking behind him.

There was no sound, but Alex knew exactly what was happening. The precise words the boy said as he stopped abruptly, turning to the man behind him to ask something. And the man's response before the guy turned the boy round roughly and shoved him through the doors into the bathroom.

The video kept playing as another man placed himself casually in front of the doors—a guard.

You're mine. He can't touch you.

He tried to keep breathing, tried to keep his muscles from tensing. And he might have succeeded if another man hadn't suddenly come into view, standing in front of the guard, talking to him. A familiar man. Black haired and tall. He began to gesture at the guard as if he was having an argument with him, wild, angry movements.

A weight like the foot of a skyscraper pressed down on Alex's chest, forcing all the air from his lungs. Suffocating him.

The man tried to shove the guard out of the way, but the guard came back with a right hook catching the dark-haired man in the face, knocking him completely to the floor. He lay there for a long moment, and as he slowly got back to his feet the guard pulled a gun from his jacket and pointed it him.

For a long moment the man stared at the guard. Then he turned away, his face at last fully turned toward the camera. The picture quality was terrible, his features unclear, but Alex knew who he was all the same.

It was his father.

Katya's mind raced as she tried to make sense of what was happening in the video on the laptop. As she tried to make sense of the whole of the last ten minutes.

Alex was sitting beside her, rigid. As if he were watching his own death playing out on the screen in front of them.

"I assume you spotted your father?" Conrad asked. "He tried to stop it, as you can see. With no success alas. But then Daniel was always something of a coward."

Alex said nothing and the video abruptly switched to another view, this time a white-tiled bathroom.

A deep foreboding began to uncoil inside her.

There was a man in the shot, roughly turning a teenage boy around to face the mirrors. Then pushing him down and pressing his face against the white china of the sink.

Oh God . . .

Alex leaned forward and closed the laptop with a calm, measured movement.

"Oh," Conrad said, sounding smug. "Are you sure you don't want to see any more? Might help you refresh your memory."

I took your virginity in a casino bathroom . . .

How you came in my mouth when I sucked you off. . . .

Katya found herself gripping the arms of her chair tightly.

"Or even," Conrad went on in the same tone, "Miss Ivanova might like to see? I understand some ladies appreciate men together as men appreciate women together."

Katya had always believed no one actually ever deserved to die. Yes, she'd taken lives, had killed three men in the course of a mission. Men who were only soldiers doing their duty just as she was doing hers in killing them. She had felt remorse for what she'd done and yet she'd accepted it as part of a soldier's lot. Her father had no patience for conscience anyway.

But staring into Conrad South's cold hazel eyes she changed her mind. Some people *did* deserve to die and die painfully. And if Alex didn't want her gun, she'd shoot South herself.

South wasn't even looking at her now, his gaze focused entirely on Alex.

Who was still sitting back in his chair, one foot resting on his opposite knee. He had one elbow on the chair arm, his chin in his hand, while his other hand was resting on his thigh. His posture was relaxed like he was sitting in a bar, having a drink with friends.

But the expression on his face, the skin was pulled tight to the immaculate bone structure beneath it, made pain start in her chest. His eyes glittered in the light, sharp and brittle as glass.

"I'm sure Miss Ivanova doesn't need to see it," Alex said, his voice deceptively mild. "It's ancient history anyway. Call it a moment of youthful insanity." He didn't look at her, watching Conrad instead. "You promised me he wouldn't ever know."

Down the other end of the table, Conrad smiled. "I'm sorry, son, but he already knew. He knew even before I took you."

Alex said nothing, motionless in his chair.

"He had nothing to pay his debts with. And then I told him I wanted you." Conrad toyed with the cards. "He agreed. Clearly he felt bad about it, though. Maybe that's why he shot himself? At any rate, I'm sure he appreciated your sacrifice, as that security tape proved."

Katya went cold all over. Alex had mentioned his father's suicide but not that he'd shot himself.

Blood all over the bathroom and she wouldn't wake up, no matter how loud Katya screamed.

"So that's all you have?" Alex's voice had sharpened. "A security tape?"

Katya ignored the cold grip of memory, focusing on Conrad.

"A security tape with the whole incident on it," the other man amended gently.

"Aw, you kept it. How touching."

"Insurance, son. When I have something on someone, I like to keep it in case of a rainy day."

"Yet you're willing to put this on the table?"

Conrad sat back in his chair. There was a brandy glass beside him and he picked it up, swirling the amber liquid around inside it. "Your Circle clubs are a big draw. And I confess to liking the idea of remodeling them into something more suitable. Or maybe even demolishing them, I haven't quite decided yet. Anyway, I had to find something decent to match it."

"The tape is not enough," Alex said coldly.

"Son, I think this tape is more than enough. Because you're desperate for this tape. I think you'd sell your soul for this tape. This is the only hard copy and the only digital copy is the one on that computer. If you win, both are yours. And you can get rid of them once and for all." He took a sip of the brandy. "Or maybe not. Maybe you'd like to keep them to view for your own pleasure."

Alex was silent for a moment, his expression so impenetrable that even Katya had no idea what he was thinking, and she was getting good at reading him. "I want more, Conrad. I put my livelihood and my body on the table, and all you're giving me in return is a fucking tape?"

"It doesn't have to be the only copy." The other man's voice was calm. "I could make sure there are copies everywhere."

Alex laughed, the sound brittle as the blue of his eyes. "Go ahead. It wouldn't be the only sex tape of mine that's been uploaded onto the Internet. I'm sure most people wouldn't give a shit."

"Oh, most people wouldn't. . . ." Conrad paused. "But your sister might. And so might your mother."

Cold fingers closed around Katya's heart. She'd never hated anyone as much as she hated the man sitting opposite Alex right now. The man slowly peeling apart Alex's past and exposing it to the light of day.

Alex made no move, betrayed absolutely nothing of what he was feeling. But Katya could sense the rage seeping from him.

I took your virginity in a casino bathroom . . .

What had happened to him had hurt. And no matter what he told her, it was hurting him still. Why else hadn't he wanted her to go down on him last night? Why had his muscles felt so tense? Why he hadn't wanted to let go?

The heavy, suffocating feeling in her chest grew into a deep, nagging ache. She wanted to help him. Grab her gun and protect him, kill the man hurting him. Anything to stop the pain, take it away. But what could she do? This was Alex's fight, not hers.

She swallowed, her hands closing on the little black velvet clutch, feeling the reassuring outline of her Springfield. They'd both agreed before they arrived that she would hand him the gun at the right moment. But it wouldn't take much to get it out now. A couple of seconds and then it would all be over. She'd make sure she wouldn't miss.

Alex sighed, a long-suffering sound. "Fucking families. Maybe you're right. Maybe just to be on the safe side, I should have the tape."

Conrad smiled. "I thought you'd see it my way." He reached for the pack of cards again.

"But you're not getting either me or my clubs if you don't put the Horsemen on the table too," Alex said clearly.

The other man froze, looking down the table at Alex. "You didn't hear me when I said I'd show your mother and sister?"

"I heard." Alex's voice was like ice. "And you'll know that I haven't seen either of them for nineteen years. So you tell me, why would I give a shit what you showed them?"

"But you want the tape. You just said—"

"The Horsemen, Conrad. Stake it. Or I'm taking the Circles clubs off the table."

A heavy silence fell, the two men staring at each other.

There was something deadly between them, a game full of spikes and barbs and sharp, cutting edges. A game where any wrong move could eviscerate an opponent or you might end up cutting yourself open instead.

Or an observer like her.

Helplessness welled up inside her. Like that moment when she'd stood beside a bath full of red water and shaken the woman lying in it. Then tried to bind the gashes in her wrists with towels. But nothing had worked. She was already dead.

Slowly, Alex leaned back in his chair, not taking his gaze from Conrad's. "Of course it's up to you," Alex said into the silence. "But if you want me, you're going to have to work for me. I'm not giving it up for free anymore, old man."

The tension in the room, already taut, kicked up another notch.

Conrad's cold hazel eyes glittered. Abruptly he lifted a shoulder. "Fine. I'll throw in the Horsemen. Now, I assume you don't mind if I deal?"

This time Alex didn't smile. "Not at all. Deal, you fucker." He shifted in his seat, and as he did so he very casually leaned over and put his hand over hers where it rested on her clutch. He didn't look at her, but he must have picked up on her own tension and was trying to reassure her.

The warmth of his hand felt good, the tension in her arm slipping away. No, of course she couldn't shoot Conrad right now, not when Alex wasn't finished with him.

Alex removed his hand, picked up his tumbler, and sipped from it. Katya couldn't bring herself to touch her own wine, a dull nausea collecting in her stomach at South's gall.

The things South had said, seeking to undermine, to

shock. To hurt. That tape. Alex's father, who'd known all along what was happening to his son . . .

Bastard. South was a bastard. And yes, he deserved to die.

Yet still her hands tightened on her Springfield as he dealt out the cards. She didn't know what poker variant they were playing, but it seemed to involve discards and more cards being dealt.

Alex glanced down at his cards. His expression didn't change as he discarded something from his hand, then put the rest down. He looked at Conrad, pinning him with his gaze like he was trying to burn the man to ash.

Katya knew the feeling.

Conrad glanced at his cards too and chuckled. "Oh, son, you better prepare yourself. I'm thinking this table might be a fine place to start the evening. What do you think?"

More outright psychological warfare.

Alex raised a brow. "Does this mean you're folding?"

"Not at all." Conrad dealt himself another card, then discarded. "I'm just pointing out that you may want to fold yourself. To prevent any more humiliation."

"Oh, I don't think so." Alex tapped the table for another card.

"Are you sure you want to do that? The odds are lousy."

"The odds are always lousy. That's why it's balls that count."

The older man gave a short laugh that almost sounded genuine. "Fuck, boy. Looks like you've learned a thing or two."

"A lot can happen in nineteen years. Now deal me the fucking card."

Conrad did so, and as Alex looked at it Katya felt the tension draw tighter.

He's going to lose.

She didn't know where the thought had come from, since

he gave absolutely nothing away, but nevertheless, she could sense it.

Surreptitiously she glanced down at her lap and moved one hand, reaching into the special compartment built into her purse where her gun was. Her fingers closed around the grip, the metal cool against her skin. A reassurance.

This game would be over one way or another, but she would make damn sure that Alex didn't go down with it.

Alex discarded.

Conrad was smiling, openly triumphant. "I was hoping this might go on for longer, but hell, all good things must come to an end. And maybe it's for the best. You and I need to get an early start, since I have plans for you, son. Big plans." He leaned back in his chair. "I'm calling."

Alex had gone very still, his expression tight.

Oh God, he *had* lost.

Her heart climbed into her throat. She tried to breathe and relax because otherwise her hand was going to shake and when she pulled the gun she might miss.

Alex laid his cards down.

The smile disappeared from Conrad's face.

A full house lay spread on the table.

Conrad had been right. The odds *were* lousy. But Alex'd had a shit hand right from the start and only playing those odds were going to win him the game. If it had been just any game, he would have folded. But this wasn't just any game, and although he had Katya's gun he wanted to win. He wanted to win *everything*.

Because what he'd done for his father had, apparently, been for nothing.

Alex still couldn't get his head around it. That his father had known all along. That he had agreed to it *beforehand*. And it didn't matter that he'd perhaps changed his mind and tried to stop it from happening.

He'd known. He'd let it happen.

He'd let his son be raped by one of his friends.

"What I'm going to show you is going to be our secret, okay?" Alex's father had told him that first night as they'd sat in the car in the alley near the Lucky Seven. *"You can't tell anyone, not a soul. You can do that, can't you, Alex? You can keep a secret?"*

And he'd said yes. He'd do whatever his father wanted because he loved him. But in the end, that secret had cost Alex dearly. It had cost him everything. The only thing he'd had after his father had died had been the knowledge that at least Daniel St. James had never known what his son had had to do to clear his debts.

Now Alex didn't even have that.

No. You have revenge.

A feral smile pulled at his mouth. Oh yeah, that's right; he did.

A full house was good, but there were other hands that could beat it. And unless Conrad had been bluffing, those lousy odds were on him having something better.

But it didn't matter. Whatever Conrad had, Alex had an insurance policy sitting in Katya's purse.

The other man's eyes were glittering and a savage kind of smile began to turn his mouth. "That's a good hand, son. But I've got—"

Then all hell broke loose.

The elevator doors at the raised entrance of the room opened suddenly and one of Conrad's staff rushed forward. "I'm sorry, Mr. South. I tried to stop them, but they were most insistent."

Alex turned in time to see the doorman pushed roughly aside by a massively built guy in black. The dead-eyed, strangely familiar mercenary. He was flanked by two other men, both in black and both looking like they were ready to crush something with their bare hands.

Conrad shoved his chair back and rose. "What the hell is going on?"

"This game is over," the mercenary said, his voice flat and cold. He came down the steps that led from the elevator doors down into the room and came straight over to the poker table, reaching into his jacket as he did so.

There was a rustle of movement at his side. Alex whipped his head around to see Katya had also shoved her chair back, her Springfield in her hand, the barrel pointed directly at the mercenary's head.

But the guy didn't even glance in her direction. He simply took his hand from his jacket, revealing a pistol with a silencer on it. Then he pointed it at the laptop sitting in the center of the table and fired.

"What the fuck, Elijah?" Conrad demanded, his previous cool completely gone. "This is none of your concern. That was—"

"That wasn't your property to give away," Elijah said. "Still less at a poker game." Calmly, he lifted the gun and pointed it at Conrad's head. "Which is now over, Mr. South. You need to leave. I will deal with Mr. St. James here."

Conrad ignored the gun, staring at the man. "I won. And I want my fucking winnings." With a flick of his hand, he turned over his cards.

Four of a kind. Aces.

Alex had lost.

"Your winnings are of no interest to me." Elijah put his finger on the trigger. "You've made a few mistakes. And you know how he hates mistakes."

"You wouldn't dare."

"I'm not a poker player, Mr. South. I never bluff."

Conrad stared back at him, a muscle flicking in his jaw. Then he cursed, low and vicious. "This isn't over." His furious gaze met Alex's. "You owe me."

Alex stared back, his fury beginning to rise. "You're right, prick. It's not. And I do owe you. I owe you a bit of revenge." Because whatever Elijah was doing here, it looked like Alex's revenge plans were going to have to wait. There was no way he and Katya could fight three heavily armed men with one handgun.

"Revenge? You think that's the only—"

"Shut the fuck up, South," Elijah interrupted flatly. He made a gesture with his gun to the two men flanking him. "Please escort this piece of shit into his office. He needs a little reminder about the dangers of hubris."

Still cursing, Conrad was taken out of the back of the room by the two guards, the door closing behind him.

Elijah put his gun away, then went over to the bar at one end of the room, reaching up to get something behind one of the bottles. Then he began to move around the rest of the space, doing something to a picture on the wall, then a vase on a pedestal near the elevator door entrance.

Alex stayed where he was. Reaction had begun to set in, adrenaline pumping through him in a burst of thwarted rage. He wanted to punch the guy in the head, grab his gun, and tell him to fuck off. Leave Conrad to him.

But he couldn't win this round, not against this guy. The only consolation was that if he let it play out, he might get something that could be useful for Zac, Eva, and Gabriel.

Beside him, Katya stood with her own weapon trained on Elijah. Tall and strong and deadly. Stubborn. Beautiful.

Christ, he wished she hadn't had to see that tape. Telling her was one thing, but having her see it was quite another. Having her know that his father had sold him, pimped him to a friend . . .

A wave of humiliation washed through him, his hands clenching into fists at his sides.

At that point, Elijah finished what he was doing and

came back to the poker table, his scarred face expression-less. "You need to leave, Mr. St. James."

He had to force himself to speak. "Excellent timing. I was just about to."

"A word of advice first."

Alex pushed the chair back and stood up. "And what would that be?"

A flicker gleamed in the other man's black eyes. "Leave Monte Carlo. Go back to New York. There's nothing for you here."

And what the hell did that mean? Alex studied him. "What makes you think I'm here for anything other than a poker game?"

"Do you really think Mr. Rutherford's attempts at be-ing Sherlock Holmes have gone unnoticed?" Elijah's voice was cold. "Or that setting free Mr. South's little gift to you, the one who arrived back in the States not too long ago, wouldn't be spotted? You and your friends are making nui-sances of themselves and have attracted the wrong kind of attention. I would advise that when you get back to New York, you tell them to go and find something else to do."

Shock coursed down Alex's spine. "What the fuck do you mean by that? And who the fuck are you anyway?"

"Someone who's looking to minimize civilian casual-ties."

"Casualties? Since when do mercenaries give a shit about casualties? 'Kill 'em all; let God sort 'em out.' Isn't that the code?"

But the man was already turning away. "Take my ad-vice, Mr. St. James. At least if you don't want the people you care about to get hurt. Because they will get hurt, believe me."

Alex took a step toward him. "Who are you? I know you, don't I?"

Elijah stopped halfway up the steps to the elevator doors and looked at him for a long moment. "No," he said flatly. "You don't." Then without waiting for a response, he continued up the stairs to the elevator. The doors swept open and he was gone.

A hand touched Alex's arm.

He turned to find Katya standing next to him, frowning in the direction of the elevator. "What's going on? What was that about?"

"I don't know. But he's familiar in some way—" He stopped. There was no point thinking about that now. Not when there were more important things to worry about. Like alerting Zac and Eva to the fact that their investigations and the release of the woman had been discovered. Like telling Gabriel to make sure Honor was okay.

Jesus . . . Who was Elijah? And how the hell could he just walk into Conrad's casino and put a gun to his head like he owned the place? Holy shit, did *he* own the place? Perhaps Conrad wasn't acting on his own after all? There was a connection here. A connection they were all missing—

"Alex?" Katya's hand on his arm again.

A shiver went through him, and through it all hunger beginning to gather. Even now, even with his revenge plans in ruins, all he could think about was having her.

No more distance.

He'd told her that earlier and he'd meant it. But now everything had changed.

What would she think, this general's daughter, of a man whose own father hadn't valued him enough to protect him? Actually, he didn't want to know. Handling it himself was enough to bear without wondering what Katya was thinking too.

And anyway, he had to think about what he was going to do now, where he was going to go. Because he couldn't follow up on his revenge plans for Conrad if he had to leave town like Elijah had said. Which left him back at square one.

Her hand on his arm was suddenly too much. He shook it off, ignoring her sharp look. "Come on. We have to get back. I have people to talk to."

CHAPTER SIXTEEN

Katya didn't expect him to vanish when they returned to the Fourth Circle, but the moment they stepped into the foyer he strode off toward the bar without a word, leaving her standing there alone.

She stared after him, not knowing what to do, a dull hurt settling down inside her. He'd said no more distance. No more secrets. And yet he was escaping again, running again. Protecting himself.

Her throat closed, the hurt moving through her, unexpectedly sharp.

She hadn't realized until now how much it had meant to her to be the one he told his secrets to. To be the one he let close. And now he'd changed his mind.

Are you surprised? After what happened in that casino?

Alex had thought his father hadn't known what Conrad had done to him. Yet his father had known about it from the start. Had even agreed to let his son be payment for his own debts. That knowledge must have been like a knife slashing an old wound, leaving a ragged, bleeding hole.

Katya looked toward the doorway that went through to the bar, where Alex had disappeared off to.

She couldn't let him do this, not again. Yes, he was a selfish, debauched playboy with no God and no soul. But he was also a man. A flawed man. A man with demons. Who was fighting them as best he was able.

And he was losing.

Katya headed through the doors and toward the bar. The place was once again packed full of people and it appeared some kind of masquerade party was going on, because most of them were in some kind of costume, wearing glittering masks.

People called to her as she strode through the crowd, and some of them reached out as if to draw her in, absorb her into the revelry. But she ignored the calls, shook off the touches, not caring whether she seemed rude or not. Those people didn't matter. The only thing that mattered was the man she had to get to.

He would see her approach through the privacy glass, of course. And maybe he'd keep the door locked so she couldn't get in. Then again, a locked door wouldn't keep her out, not when she had a gun in her purse and a silencer. That keypad wouldn't last two seconds once it had a bullet through it.

Threading through a knot of people, Katya came to a stop in front of the office door. The heavy red velvet curtain had been pulled back from the glass, no doubt giving him a clear view of her standing there. She knocked anyway.

Nothing happened for a long time and she began to reach for her Springfield, ready to shoot the lock. Then the door was abruptly pulled open and Alex was standing there, his mobile pressed to his ear. "Just a minute," he said to the person on the other end of the call. "What do you want, Katya? I'm busy."

"I want to talk to you."

"Can't it wait? I'm on the phone."

"No," she said. "It can't." And she pushed past him, striding into his office before he could stop her.

Behind her, Alex muttered a curse. "Shit. Sorry, Zac. I'm going to have to call you back."

The door closed, the sound of the party going on outside fading into a low hum of background noise.

Katya turned around.

Alex was still standing by the door, his blue eyes gone diamond hard. "What the fuck do you want?" He chucked his phone onto the red velvet sofa positioned in the middle of the office, at right angles to his desk. On the low table in front of it was a tumbler full of clear liquid. So he was hitting the vodka already, was he?

"You said no more distance," Katya said, ignoring the fury glittering in his gaze. "You said no more secrets."

He pushed his hands into the pockets of his pants. "And?"

"So why are you walking away from me? Why are you shutting me out? Did you not mean it?"

"I don't have to tell you everything, Katya."

"No, I know you don't. But what happened in that casino hurt you. And I . . . I don't like it. I want to help. I want to make it better."

His mouth twisted. "Well, Mommy's kisses always make it better. You could try that."

"No," she said fiercely, closing the gap between them. "Don't do that. Don't play it down. Don't make it mean nothing. You told me what happened to you, Alex. You said you were mine. You can't do that and then push me away."

He'd gone still, watching her, motionless apart from the sharp rise and fall of his chest. "And what if I don't want that? Are you going to respect my right to tell you to fuck off? Or are you going to force me like Conrad?"

The words were hard, like stones. And she felt them hit home. Every one.

She swallowed, staring into his shadowed face. He'd had

everything taken from him and it must feel to him like she was trying to take from him too.

So no wonder he was hurt. No wonder he was protecting himself.

"My mother died when I was ten," she said hoarsely, wanting to give him something, a secret in exchange for his. "She was a ballerina with the Bolshoi. She was . . . so beautiful. But emotionally very fragile. I came home from school one day to find her floating in the bath. She'd cut her wrists and there was blood everywhere, in the water, in her hair. I couldn't save her." She stopped all of a sudden, her throat constricting.

Alex was silent, his jaw tight, every part of him rigid. His eyes had gone dark, the expression in them opaque as the privacy glass shielding them from the bar outside. "I'm sorry for your loss, Katya," he said, his voice cold, hard. "But I'm not your mother and it's not your job to save me."

"But it *is* my job. Who else is going to do it? Especially when you don't seem to want to save yourself."

"You only want to save me because you couldn't save your damn mother."

He's right. That's exactly what you're doing.

"No," she whispered, forcing herself to speak. "That's not it at all."

Alex moved suddenly, his fingers catching her chin, tipping her head back, holding her in place. "Isn't it?" he demanded. "Isn't that why you're in here now, trying to get me to talk? Trying to get me to trust you? Trying to get close? It's not for me, sweetheart." The burning fury in his eyes focused on her like a beam of sunlight refracted through a magnifying glass. "What didn't you do for her, Katya? How did you let her die?"

A burst of bright anger flared inside her. "I tried!" She jerked her chin out of his grip. "But she'd lost too much blood and—"

"It's more than that. I can see it in your face."

There were tears in her eyes. God, she hadn't cried for years. Not since her mother had died.

"She was weak, Katya," her father said. "She should have been stronger. Like you."

"I wasn't strong," she whispered, to her father. To herself. "I tried to be, for her. I tried not to make demands, to be a good girl. Tried not to get angry or upset. But it was hard having to take care of her all the time. I was the child and I wanted my mother to take care of me. But she couldn't. And in the end, she broke." Katya looked down at the floor, her chest hurting, her throat tight, unable to meet his gaze. It was difficult to be vulnerable, like giving someone a knife and then baring your throat. "After she died, my father told me I shouldn't grieve. That she was weak. And that from now on he was going to make sure I wouldn't be." She paused. "And I wasn't. That's what I am, Alex. I am strong. So I can make sure no one else breaks."

A silence fell over the office like a thick blanket. Heavy and suffocating.

"No, you're still trying to be strong for her," Alex said at last, a bitter note in his voice. "When she should have been the one to be strong for you. She should have been the one protecting you. Just like my father should have protected me."

Slowly, she lifted her head. His gaze was black, dark holes into nothingness.

"I always thought Dad broke because of the secrets he kept from my mother. The lies he must have told. But it wasn't, was it? He didn't save me. And maybe that was what got to him in the end."

She took a slow, silent breath, staring at Alex's set face, everything drawn tight and close to his skull. He looked like he was in agony. "That was the only thing I had. That I saved him, protected him. That was the only thing that kept me going. And then he died. But at least he didn't know; that's what I told myself. At least Dad didn't know what I had to do for him." His gaze moved past her, to the window looking out onto the club. "But he did know. He was the one who fed me to the fucking dogs. He didn't save me. He didn't protect me. I was nothing to him in the end."

Pain spread out inside her. A raw, angry hurt for the boy he'd once been and the man he was now. For the betrayal that she knew cut like a razor. A dull, blunt razor. Leaving scars in its wake, bloody wounds that never healed.

"I'm sorry," she said thickly. "I'm so sorry for what happened to you. I didn't mean to force you to share things you didn't want." She took a step toward him, her heart aching. "But you should know that you matter, Alex. And *I* would have saved you. *I* would have protected you."

"How do you know?" His gaze shifted back to hers, glittering in the darkness. "How do you know if I'm even worth saving?"

Her heart broke for him then, a crack running straight down the center. "Of course you're worth saving."

"Why? What have I done for anyone? I've been a selfish prick all my damn life. The only thing that was worth a damn didn't even end up counting."

She couldn't keep that distance between them any longer. Moving before she was even aware of doing so, Katya closed the remaining gap, coming right up close, standing in front of him. She didn't touch him even though her fingers desperately wanted to trace the line of his jaw, ease the tension from his mouth. She got the sense that a touch would be a step too far right now.

"Alex, no." Her voice sounded like she had a throat full of cotton wool. "It counted. Just because he knew all along doesn't lessen what you did for him. Because you did it out of love. You loved him. You wanted to protect him."

Alex looked away. "I've done nothing but hurt people,

Katya. My mother. Honor." A long pause. Then his attention shifting back to her. "You."

He shouldn't have walked away from her in the foyer, but he couldn't face talking about it. Having her sharp, perceptive stare on him. He couldn't bear the thought of her realizing what he already knew deep in his heart. That there was no one behind the mask of Alex St. James, playboy gambler. Or if there was, it was a man who had no value. Who wasn't worth saving.

Her face was pale in the dim light of the office, the brilliant green of her eyes shadowed. And he hated the look in those eyes because she was looking at him like he *was* someone worth saving after all.

And it was a lie. His whole fucking life was a lie. One big pretense. Cards and booze and women and money, all distractions so people wouldn't see the truth. That there was nothing and no one there.

"You have not hurt me," Katya said, her voice thickening.

"Haven't I? I made you come here. I drew you into this shit with Conrad knowingly. I used you. I seduced you. I played with you like some—" He broke off abruptly as her hand pressed to his chest, the heat of her palm stopping the words in his throat. The expression on her face was fierce, like she was angry.

"I'm not some weak little girl, Alex. You know this. Yes, you drew me into this and yes, you played with me. But you also challenged me. You woke something in me I didn't even realize was there, something I lost when my mother died." Her hand pressed harder. "Pleasure. Sensuality. And at the same time you had nothing but respect for my skills. You never ran them down or mocked them. You didn't even care when I beat you on the mat." Her thumb was moving on his chest, stroking. "You let me protect you and you used my strength the way I asked you to. What more could a bodyguard ask for? What more could a woman ask for?"

Her touch was painful. Her words hurt even more. "Katya, you can't—"

"Your father made a choice, Alex. Just like my mother. And though we can hate the choice they made, the responsibility for that choice lies with them. Not us." She stepped even closer, her body millimeters from his. "We can't blame ourselves for their choices. We can't let them break us."

"Stop," he said quietly, because it hurt, it just fucking hurt. "Stop trying to save me."

"I'm not. I'm trying to help you save yourself."

The words struck home, catching on something inside him. And he suddenly felt swamped by the scent of oranges and musk. By seductive warmth and softness. Strength and sensuality. Everything that had been missing in that bathroom in that casino. In his whole goddamn life.

He met her eyes, looking into the green heart of her, the gold flecks glittering like buried treasure, burning with her fierce, indomitable will. "Don't let him win, Alexei," she whispered. "Don't give Conrad this victory too."

And he knew exactly what she meant, because it was true. Conrad had told Alex about his father to hurt him. To exert his power over him. To make him feel like he was worthless. Even now, nineteen years later, that prick was still making him bleed.

"I don't want to," he said hoarsely. "I was supposed to be the one taking the victory. Taking everything he had and putting a gun to his fucking head. Finally getting over what he did to me. Putting it behind me once and for all. But now, shit . . . Even that's been taken from me."

Her other hand joined the one already on his chest. "But you don't need that to put it behind you." Her fingers spread out on the cotton of his shirt. "Because that won't change anything, Alex. The change has to come from you, don't you see? Conrad is a liar. To win you have to believe you're actually worth saving."

He didn't even realize he'd raised his hand until he felt his fingers close in the golden softness of hair, gripping it tight in his fist. His lifeline. "How do I do that, Katya?" he said hoarsely, desperately. "What if there's nothing left to save?"

She looked up at him, her body pressing gently against his, warm and pliable as candle wax. Something glittered in her eyes. "There is," she whispered. "There is *so* much." Slowly, her fingers undid the top button of his shirt, then another and another. Then she slipped her hand beneath the cotton, the heat of her palm against the bare skin of his chest, settling over his heart. "There is you." Her thumb moved over his skin, back and forth, stroking. And it wasn't sexual, only reassuring. Affirming.

He'd never had that kind of touch before. Or if he had, it was before he'd left home, when he'd still had a family who cared about him. Before everything had blown apart.

After that the only people who'd touched him were his lovers, and from them he only wanted sex, not comfort. Escape, not reassurance. But now . . . Now he craved Katya's touch in a way that had nothing to do with love-making. It went deeper than that. It went all the way down to his soul, a bone-deep yearning that he was powerless to stop.

So he didn't.

Alex pulled away, then took her hand. Her forehead creased as he led her to the couch in the middle of his office and sat on the edge of it.

"What do you want to do?" she asked, looking down at him, still frowning.

"I want you to hold me."

Her mouth opened, then shut; a small, strangely tender smile curved her mouth. It made his heart ache. She didn't say anything, only sitting down beside him and putting her arms around him. He turned his head, his cheek against her hair, gathering her as close in turn.

"Lie down with me," he murmured.

And she did, shifting with him as he stretched out on the couch with her beside him, her long, lithe body pressed against his, her arms around him. Holding him.

He turned his face into her neck, inhaling the unique, sweet scent that was all her, and felt her fingers in his hair, gently stroking, over and over.

They didn't move for a long time. And they didn't speak. There was no need. The warmth of her body next to his, the feeling of her fingers in his hair, was all the communication he needed.

Outside the office, the music thumped and the noise of the crowd battered against the walls.

They probably all thought he was doing her on the desk. Or on the floor, or wherever.

They'd never dream he was actually lying on the couch with her, fully clothed, letting her hold him. And it was strange to think that right now, in this moment, that was even better than being inside her. That even though they were dressed, they were closer to each other than if they'd been naked.

He didn't know how that worked, and quite frankly, he didn't much care. Because he'd never felt like this before. As if, for the first time in nineteen years, he was at peace.

As if he didn't have to run.

Alex closed his eyes, his arms tightening around her.

Maybe she was right.

Maybe there was something left of him after all.

CHAPTER SEVENTEEN

As the plane touched down at JFK, Katya shifted in her seat. It felt odd to be back in her bodyguard pants and shirt. To not be restricted by a too-tight skirt or ridiculously tall high heels. It even felt strange to have her Springfield back where it belonged, in the shoulder holster she wore under her jacket.

Seated opposite her, Alex seemed to be having no such issues, his attention totally focused on the laptop he had open on his knees.

They'd left Monaco that morning and she'd spent most of the flight--to her own surprise–asleep. Unsurprising considering the night they'd spent together. They'd both fallen asleep on the couch in his office and then woken sometime in the night, starving for each other.

He'd taken her upstairs to their suite, where they'd dealt with that hunger, not falling asleep until dawn. Nothing was said about what would happen when they got back to New York. The time hadn't been right and there were better things for them to be doing.

But they really needed to talk about it now. For a start, her contract with him would be fulfilled, which meant she could leave. And she also needed to make sure he'd be true to his promise to help her with Mikhail.

There's another thing you're ignoring. Your feelings about him.

Her feelings were . . . irrelevant. A variable she hadn't counted on and one that wouldn't affect anything. She still had a promise to Mikhail to keep, a loyalty to fulfill, and she couldn't go back on that regardless of how she felt about Alex.

"Fucking New York," Alex murmured as the plane began to decelerate. "Another beautiful day, as usual."

It wasn't a beautiful day. The sky outside was gray, the clouds heavy with more snow to add to the piles already on the ground.

"Alex," Katya began. "I need to—"

"Talk to me?" he finished. "Don't worry. It's been taken care of."

She frowned. "What's been taken care of?"

Alex closed the laptop abruptly. "I should have told you last night."

"Told me what?"

"I called Zac. I gave him the go-ahead for the operation to get Vasin out."

Katya blinked, the news taking a couple of moments to sink in. "Mr. Rutherford is rescuing Mikhail . . . ? But . . . when did this happen?"

"I called him last night. Before you came into the office." He glanced down at his watch. "Zac had a contact where Vasin is being held and the operation was carried out a couple of hours ago."

She straightened in her seat, shock coursing through her. "You should have told me. I wanted to know—"

"I'm sorry, Katya. I really am. But . . ." He hesitated. "I forgot last night, and this morning, well, you know me; I'm a selfish bastard. I didn't want you thinking of him. I wanted you all to myself."

Her throat felt dry, the strange ache in her chest painful. Perhaps she should have been angry that he'd kept it from her, but she wasn't. No, she was pleased. Pleased he'd wanted her that badly, that he'd been selfish about it.

She folded her hands in her lap. "You know what this means?"

"Yes." Slowly, Alex leaned back in his chair and folded his arms. "It means you'll be leaving my employ and going back to Russia."

His tone was so cool and matter-of-fact, and a tiny hot spark of anger flared inside her. Which didn't make any sense, since she'd made the decision to leave herself. She found her hands clasped together tighter than they should have been. "I won't be returning. You understand that, don't you?"

"I realize that."

She searched his face, though she couldn't have said what she was searching for. Whatever it was, she didn't see it. There was regret in his expression but nothing else.

Katya ignored the inexplicable twist of anguish in her heart. "I'll be sorry to leave," she said levelly. "I've enjoyed my time with you."

There was a long, tense silence.

"Fuck this," Alex said suddenly, and leaned forward, reaching out to take her hands in his. The look of polite regret on his face had vanished as if it had never been, his eyes blazing blue. "Don't go, Katya." His voice was fierce. "Stay with me."

Shock pulsed through her. For a second she couldn't move, a burst of something bright racing through her veins. His hands were warm around hers and all she could think about was the feeling of him in her arms on the couch the night before.

His long, lean body had been still and relaxed, and he'd let her touch him. Let her give him comfort and reassurance. With nothing sexual getting in the way, there had been only trust and a deep, wordless understanding between them that even now she couldn't stop thinking about.

And that terrified her. Her emotions were already far too involved as it was; she couldn't afford to get in any deeper. The things she felt for him made her feel exposed, weak. And she couldn't be weak. She had to stay strong. For him. For Mikhail.

For yourself.

"I'm sorry. I can't." Her voice sounded strangely flat. "I made a promise. I'm sure you understand."

A silence fell, the blue flame in his eyes burning hot. And for a moment she thought he was going to argue, was going to try to convince her otherwise. Then the flame flickered and went out. Alex let go of her hands and sat back in his seat, looking away, out through the window at the gray sky welcoming them back to New York. "Sure. I understand. It's a pity. I've enjoyed having you around." Like hers, his voice was flat.

Her fingers felt cold, as if he'd sucked all the heat right out of her when he'd let her go. And her chest ached even worse, anguish twisting tighter.

She ignored it. She'd allowed her armor to crack with this man, had let him in a little way. And it had been glorious while it lasted. But she couldn't open herself more, not when she had another man to save.

Use Mikhail as an excuse if it makes you feel better. You're just afraid.

Katya ignored the snide voice inside her head.

She wasn't afraid and she didn't hurt. Pain was nothing anyway.

She was a soldier and she continued on despite it.

They were all there waiting for him in their usual meeting room in the Second Circle.

The fire was lit, food waiting on the low table in front of

it–food none of them ate but he liked to have served all the same, just in case. He'd made sure the scotch decanter was full for Gabriel and there was wine for Zac, who preferred it. And that the room was warm, because Eva got cold.

He liked to have it prepared for his friends, even though they had no idea he'd always personally made sure all of them were catered to.

Which made it hard to come in and find them all standing there, looking at him like he'd done something wrong.

"Aren't you going to ask me whether I had a nice vacation?" Alex asked flippantly, shutting the door behind him.

Gabriel was standing by the fire, his arms folded over his chest. "It wasn't a fucking vacation, Alex. You weren't there just to spend some money and screw some women."

There were so many emotions tangled together inside him. Regret. Yearning. Loss. And pain . . . Ah, but he couldn't think of any of that now.

Alex met his friend's dark eyes. "Is that how little you think of me? That all I went there for was money and sex?"

The other man at least had the decency to look away. "Shit, you know I didn't mean that."

"Yeah, you did."

"More information, Alex," Zac said from his position on the couch, not even turning to look at him. "That's what we wanted. Yet all I got from you yesterday was an order to make sure your bodyguard's lover was released from—"

"He's not her lover," Alex growled, unable to help himself. "And I owed her a debt."

Eva, perched in her usual chair, glowered at him. "What kind of debt?"

Well shit, he'd let it get to this point, hadn't he? Where they were all pissed off with him and they had a right to be. He hadn't exactly been open about anything, hoping to keep all his secrets, his shame, from them.

Don't ask, don't tell. That had been one of the first rules of the Nine Circles club and they'd all kept to it religiously. Guarding their secrets from one another, keeping them hidden. But that came with a price. Isolation. And he was starting to realize that he didn't want to be isolated anymore, not now he knew what it was like to have someone.

Katya . . .

He wished suddenly, intensely, that she were here. But since they'd gotten back to New York the day before, she hadn't been around, organizing her trip back to Moscow. That and waiting to hear whether Zac's little operation with Vasin was successful.

Alex had left her alone, making sure they returned to their previous boss/employee relationship. It was easier that way. At least, he imagined it was easier. But it didn't feel like that, not when she was near. Not when all he wanted was to keep her with him and make sure she never left.

He couldn't do that, though. He'd given her a choice and she'd chosen to leave. He had to respect that. Choice was, after all, extremely important. Even if he hated the choice she'd made and wished he could change it.

Alex walked forward, coming over to the fireplace where Gabriel stood. The other man shifted, allowing him some room next to the fire. "The debt I owe to Katya isn't any of your business," he said shortly to Eva. "In fact, Katya as a whole is nobody's business but mine."

Eva's gaze narrowed. "What have you done? You sound like you—"

"What?" Alex stared back, meeting her gray eyes head-on. Daring her to make her usual insinuations. "I sound like I what?"

"Alex." Zac hadn't moved from his position on the couch, but his voice held steel. "You will not talk to Eva like that."

Alex glanced at the other man, hot anger surging up inside him.

The tension in the room pulled so tight it felt like it was going to snap and that if it did something would break. Maybe irrevocably.

And he understood then, with sudden, blinding clarity, that he didn't want that, not with these people.

He'd created this club, this group of misfits. It had happened at a party, his thirtieth birthday. There had once been nine of them, all of them drunk on tequila, playing poker and talking shit. Misfits in the world of the superrich, people hurt and betrayed by money and power. And it had come to him that he could give them a place to go. A place to be safe. The kind of place he'd never had himself.

You wanted a family.

Well, fuck, that was true, wasn't it? His real family had imploded, so he'd created one of his own. And just like family, they didn't get on all the time. They kept secrets from one another. They argued. But they all knew the deal just the same; they were here as allies because they all wanted the same thing.

To not be alone.

The people in this room had no one else, only one another. And with whatever they were facing now, they needed one another more than ever.

The breath went out of him and with it all the anger.

"I'm sorry," he said. "You're right to be suspicious of me. To doubt me. I haven't exactly been honest with any of you. But I've learned a bit about honesty in the past few days and I think it's time I told you some things about myself."

The room was absolutely silent. And then Eva, perhaps guessing at what was to come, said, "You don't need to—"

"Yeah," he interrupted gently. "I do need to. I don't expect it from anyone else, get that straight right now, but this . . . It affects us." He glanced at Gabriel, standing beside him. "I should have told you this a long time ago, brother. But I didn't."

Gabriel just stared at him, and there was an expression in his eyes that Alex hadn't seen before. Understanding.

Honor. That's Honor's doing.

"Nineteen years," Gabriel said. "Am I right?"

It didn't surprise him that his friend knew exactly what he was talking about, since he was the one who'd taken Alex home. Who'd patched up the bruises on his face that Conrad had put there. And who hadn't asked any questions. Not a single one.

Alex nodded.

The other two were silent, watching him. This was going to be harder than he thought, fuck it.

He turned around, so his back was to them, staring down into the fire. One day maybe he'd be able to look someone in the eye when he told this story, but not now. Not today.

God, he needed a drink . . .

No, you don't. You need Katya.

He closed his eyes, the dry heat of the fire against his skin. But Katya wasn't here and so he'd have to do this by himself.

"I had a personal reason to go to Monaco," he said, trying to keep his voice level. "To play in Conrad's game. And I know more about the Apocalypse, about Conrad, and about Dad's Seven Devils than I've told you."

There was only silence behind him.

"You know Conrad was one of them," he went on. "He used to play at the Lucky Seven. Dad used to bring me there to watch for card counters, make sure everyone was playing properly. He used to tell me . . . that it was our secret. Something we were in on together, so I wasn't to tell anyone. I knew that it wasn't right, that the gambling wasn't legal, but I didn't know all the other shit, the drugs and the prostitution, was part of it. Anyway, I kept his secret because my dad was my hero. And I loved him."

The room utterly quiet except for the crackle of the flames in the grate, no one said anything. Waiting for him to continue.

"I wanted to do him proud, so I kept his secret. But what I didn't realize was that the casino was losing money and Dad was getting into a lot of debt. I knew one of his friends had been . . . watching me." He opened his eyes, stared into the yellow-orange flames. "I'm sure I don't need to explain what I mean by that."

"Conrad," Gabriel said, his voice a low growl.

"Yeah, Conrad. One night, when the Devils were visiting the casino, he bought me a beer at the bar. I wasn't allowed to drink, but shit, an adult buys you a drink, you don't say no. And I liked beer, so I drank it. And while we were drinking, Conrad told me that Dad had gotten into debt and that he'd paid Dad's debts himself. But he needed to be paid back and Dad had nothing to pay him back with. Then he told me how I could help."

"Oh fuck." Eva's voice was soft. "Please don't—" She stopped suddenly.

Alex kept his gaze on the fire. "I'd like to tell you that you were wrong, Eva. I really would. But you're not. He said he'd wipe Dad's debts if I gave him myself."

"Son of a bitch," Zac murmured, the steel in his voice becoming harder, pure titanium. "You were a boy."

"I think that only added to the appeal." Alex put his hands on the mantelpiece, leaning against it. "Conrad gave me a day to think about it, but I really didn't need a day. I was worried for my father and I didn't want anyone to hurt him. So I told Conrad he could have what he wanted. Just as long as Dad didn't know about it. He agreed."

"That fucking prick," Gabriel said roughly. "I'll kill—"

He stopped suddenly. "What the hell? What are you doing in here?"

Alex turned.

Katya was standing in the middle of the room, her hands behind her back, her color high. "I'm sorry," she said. "I didn't mean to interrupt."

"Yeah, well, you did." Gabriel scowled at her. "You know the rules, Ms. Ivanova. No one is allowed in here when a Nine Circles meeting is in session. Especially when you come in unannounced."

"I'm sorry," Katya repeated. "I knocked, but no one answered."

"There was a reason for that," Zac said, his tone absolute. "If you would be so good as to wait outside, we would—"

"She stays," Alex interrupted him, unable to take his eyes from her face. "I want her to hear this too."

Another silence fell, and he knew they were all looking at him. And looking at Katya. And making assumptions.

Let them. He didn't give a fuck what they thought.

Katya stared back at him as if the others didn't exist. "If you need me," she said softly, "then I'll stay."

"You heard what I said just now?"

"Yes."

He didn't turn back to the fire. Instead he looked at her. "I didn't want to go, but I went. I went into that bathroom at the Lucky Seven. And I let Conrad do what he wanted with me. But he didn't honor his promise. He told me in Monte Carlo that my father had known all along. He told me that Dad was the one to offer me in the first place. And that that was why Dad killed himself." There was so much strength in Katya's eyes. So much understanding. He would not break. He wouldn't. "I pretended what happened to me didn't mean anything. I pretended it didn't matter. I left my family and I didn't speak to my mother or my sister for nineteen years because I was too angry. Too ashamed. And then Conrad turned up again." He took a breath. "And I realized it did matter after all. I went to Monaco to put Conrad fucking South in the ground. To obliterate him. But then we were warned off."

Zac's attention's sharpened. "Warned off? What do you mean? By whom?"

It was Kaya who answered, her voice calm, cool. "One of the Apocalypse players was a mercenary. Name of Elijah. The second night involved a personal game between Mr. South and Mr. St. James, which was interrupted by this Elijah. He seemed to be the one calling the shots and he accused Mr. South of . . . hubris, I believe."

"Why?" Gabriel was scowling at Katya; then he switched his attention to Alex. "And what the fuck is this about a personal game?"

Alex met his friend's gaze. "Like I said, I wanted to obliterate Conrad. I wanted to take everything of his and leave him with nothing. And he . . . wanted me."

"What?" Eva's voice was stricken. "Alex, you didn't . . ."

He looked at her, and for the first time since he could remember he saw pain in her guarded gray eyes. *She knows what this means. This is personal for her.* "I did," he said steadily. "I wanted him to stake everything. Then I wanted to take it. Then I wanted to hold a gun to his head and make him beg for his fucking life."

The pain changed to a spark of pure silver. Oh yeah, she knew all right.

"But clearly that didn't happen," Zac murmured. "You said this Elijah interrupted the game?"

"I didn't," Alex answered. "Katya did. But yes, he burst in with a couple of guys, started waving guns around. He told us 'they' didn't appreciate your Sherlock Holmes impression."

Zac frowned. "What?"

"He mentioned you and Eva, and then he mentioned the woman I sent back on my jet. Someone knows we're digging around, Zac. That we have more information. And someone doesn't like it. I don't know how Elijah is connected with all of this, but he is in some way. And so is Conrad."

"Shit," Gabriel muttered. "And we're still no closer to finding out who shot Tremain. Which means Honor is still in danger."

Zac pushed himself up from the couch, began pacing. "No one should have been able to spot us online, and I was careful organizing documents and protection for that girl." He came to a halt in front of Eva's chair, looking down at her. "You were careful too, weren't you, angel? You covered your tracks."

An offended look crossed over her face. "I can hack anything and get away with it. No one has ever caught me, so don't make this my fault."

But his frown didn't lift. "I did once, if you remember."

Oddly enough, a faint blush rose to Eva's pale skin. "I'm better than that now. Jesus, if I can get into the CIA's database and out without getting caught—" She stopped. "Unless we *are* talking about the CIA here."

"It could be." Katya's voice was unexpected. "Just before he talked to us, Elijah went around the room looking at various things. I believe he was doing a sweep. I think there were cameras in the room."

Alex frowned, remembering Elijah's odd movements. "And he interrupted just before Conrad put his cards down." He looked around at everyone else. "Conrad was going to win, and given how fucked off he was at the interruption, I'm betting he didn't know Elijah was going to come in, guns blazing."

Zac's head turned, his golden eyes focusing on Alex. "So

you know all this and you waited to tell us until now? You didn't think I needed to know when you spoke to me about Vasin's rescue?"

"Mr. St. James would have," Katya said before Alex could respond, taking a couple of steps forward, as if she wanted to put herself between him and Zac. "Except he was distracted by me."

Zac's head snapped round. "Distracted how?"

Color stained Katya's cheeks. Her mouth opened, but Alex wasn't going to let her be interrogated by Zac in a-hole mode. "Like I said. Katya is no one's business but mine."

Zac turned back to look at him. And for a moment Alex felt the sheer force of the man's will like a battering ram. But he'd never let Zac walk all over him before and he wasn't about to start now. He had his own will and it was just as strong. He met the other man's gaze like Katya did. Calmly. "Are we clear?" He raised an eyebrow.

Zac didn't look away, but he gave a slight nod in acknowledgment. "This personal game, then. How did that occur? And why?"

"I wanted revenge," Alex said simply. "Like I said, I wanted to take everything from him. But in order to do that I had to stake something he wanted."

"What was that?" Gabriel demanded.

"Myself. And the clubs."

"Holy shit," Eva murmured. "Please tell me you seriously didn't do that."

"And what about him?" Zac asked. "What was his stake?"

The video began replaying in Alex's head, his father shoved aside by the guard, then a gun put at his head. An aching kind of sadness filled him and he wanted to turn away, but instead he found himself looking back at Katya. "His stake was a security tape," he said in a low voice.

"Footage from the night Conrad raped me." Because it was rape; he'd always known that. He'd just never said it aloud with people who knew the truth before. "Conrad had put a security guard on the bathroom door so we wouldn't be interrupted. But the tape shows Dad . . . arguing with the guard. He was trying to stop it."

"Christ," Gabriel said. "That motherfucker."

"That's not all." Alex made himself go on. "The tape also contains footage from the bathroom."

Katya's face was full of something he didn't quite recognize. She'd come forward to stand near the couch, her hands resting on the back of it. And he wanted everyone out of the room suddenly. Wanted to go to her and hold her.

But he couldn't. He had a feeling that if he touched her again he wouldn't let her go. And Mikhail Vasin could go get fucked.

"Oh, Alex," Eva said quietly. "Was he blackmailing you?"

Alex kept his gaze on Katya. "He threatened to put the tape online. I told him I didn't give a shit, that I had plenty of sex tapes out there." He stopped suddenly. It didn't seem right to explain that Conrad had then threatened to send it to Honor and his mother. And that he hadn't cared. That his revenge was more important to him than his mother and sister.

"Mr. South then threatened Mr. St. James by saying his mother and sister wouldn't like to see it," Katya said instead, taking up the thread of the story, her calm, cool voice stripping Conrad's blackmail of its emotional power. Taking away his own guilt. Making it just a series of facts strung together. "Mr. St. James didn't want that to happen."

"He threatened to send it to Honor?" Gabriel's voice was a low growl. "Jesus, he's fucking dead."

"As Mr. St. James said," Katya went on smoothly," Mr.

South was on the point of winning when Elijah interrupted the game. He put a bullet through the laptop which contained the video."

Zac went still. Then he glanced at Alex. "He didn't want anyone to see?"

Alex took a long, silent breath. He'd almost forgotten about that in the middle of everything that had happened. "No, he didn't." He paused as realization broke over him. "There was no way he could have known about that footage. Unless he'd been watching us." He stared at Katya. "You were right about the cameras. That's the only way he could have known."

Katya nodded. "In which case, the real question is why was he watching?"

"And who was he watching for?" Eva echoed.

Gabriel shifted beside the fire, his leather jacket creaking. "You told me you suspected the invites to the game came from your father's friends? The Seven Devils?"

"Yeah. I'm pretty certain of it."

"So who invited Elijah?"

And that was probably the most important question of all. Alex glanced at his friend. "We need more investigation. We can't let this go."

"Damn fucking straight."

"We need to proceed carefully." Zac's voice was full of absolute authority. "If they've spotted the investigations Eva and I have been carrying out, if they know about the girl, then they know that we've uncovered the possibility of a trafficking ring. They won't let that go. And it will put Eva at risk."

"Oh, for fuck's sake." Eva got up in a sudden quick movement. "And if anyone puts Zac in harm's way then they'll have to answer to me."

Since she only just came up to Zac's shoulder, her statement seemed slightly ridiculous. She glowered at everyone.

"Yeah, I know, right? It *is* ridiculous. I am not someone to be protected. I am the CEO of one of America's most successful software companies and I can look after my own fucking self." She flicked a glance in Zac's direction. "So back off, asshole. When I want your help, I'll ask for it."

Zac said nothing, but there was something in his amber eyes as he looked at Eva that went beyond mere irritation. Alex couldn't decipher it, but wherever the hell Zac's over-protective tendencies were coming from, they were going to interfere.

"Eva's right," Alex said. "She can take care of herself. And besides, we need her, Zac."

A muscle twitched in Zac's jaw. It was clear he was not happy with this development. "Very well," he said with obvious reluctance. "But as I said, we're going to have to proceed carefully if we don't want to draw their attention again."

Gabriel prowled over to the table and lifted the stopper on the decanter, splashing some scotch into a glass. "How many copies of that video are there?"

"Conrad said only one digital copy on the laptop and a hard copy," Alex answered. There was vodka on the table too, but he didn't feel the need of any. No, he wanted something else entirely. Pity he wasn't going to let himself have it. "But don't worry. I didn't take his word for it."

Gabriel knocked back the scotch, then put the tumbler back on the table with a click. "Seems this Elijah guy was pretty intent on destroying it. Which means we need to get our hands on it somehow."

"I would think that Elijah would have made Mr. South destroy any copies he had," Katya said, her unfamiliar voice once again making everyone look at her, clearly having forgotten she was there.

But Alex hadn't forgotten. "Good point." He shoved his hands in his pockets. "But I'm betting he wouldn't have destroyed all of them. He's bound to have kept some for . . . insurance purposes."

"We need to see what's on that tape that Elijah, or who-ever the hell is employing him, wants kept secret." Zac didn't touch any of the liquor on the table. Or the food. He began to pace again. "Especially since we've reached a dead end on virtually everything else."

Frustration slid through Alex. "Nothing on Dad's Seven Devils? Nothing at all?"

"No. My contacts didn't find anything on the rest of them. And Eva didn't find anything digitally either. Or at least they've hidden it well, if there is."

"What about the other players?" Surely Zac would have discovered something on them?

"There are some dodgy links. None of those people you were at the table with were clean. But there's nothing we can trace back to Conrad or any of the other Devils. Or the Lucky Seven. If there are tracks there, they've covered them completely."

"Fuck it," Gabriel said, and poured himself another scotch. "Then we definitely need that video."

"I can hack into South's computer," Eva offered. "In fact, he's got quite a network from what I saw. I didn't find any-thing the first time I looked, but then I wasn't looking for anything particular." The look on her delicate face sharp-ened. "If a copy of that video is there, I'll find it."

"Be careful, angel," Zac cautioned as if he couldn't help himself.

Eva rolled her eyes. "I'm always careful."

Alex stared at the two of them. They didn't have to do this. Neither Eva nor Zac was personally invested in his family's secrets and if this proved as dangerous as he sus-pected it was going to be—"You can walk away," he said suddenly. "Zac. Eva. This is my family's business. You guys don't have to involve yourselves." He didn't need to include Gabriel. He was already involved. And besides, Alex knew what Gabriel would have told him to do with his caution.

"Are you kidding me?" Eva shot back. "Sure, it's your family, Alex. But that makes it our family too. I thought the whole point of the Nine Circles was that we stuck together because we had no one else." She gave him a sharp look. "Or am I wrong?"

These people were his friends and friends supported one another. Why did he keep forgetting that? "You're not wrong. But I came back to protect you all. I don't want to drag you back into something you don't want."

Eva shrugged. "Too bad. You've already dragged us. And hey, it's not like we're without resources, right?"

"I guess."

"Good. So. What information have we got so far?"

The discussion moved on and the atmosphere of tension that had been in the room at the start of the meeting dissipated.

As the other three fell into a discussion about the other players, Alex went over to where Katya still stood, waiting silently. "Why are you here?" he asked. "Did you need something?"

She stepped back from the couch, her hands once more behind her back. "Yes. I wanted to inform you that the operation to rescue Mikhail was successful. I just got the word. They're organizing a video call because he wanted to speak to me ASAP."

The disappointment was bitter, but Alex ignored the feeling. It was good Vasin had gotten out. Good that the first thing he wanted to do was speak to the woman who'd made him such important promises. "That's great news," Alex said, trying to make it sound like he was actually pleased and not wanting to hit something. "So I guess you'll be heading back to Moscow soon."

Her gaze flickered away from his. "I managed to get a flight tomorrow morning. I . . . hope that's okay. I know it's not enough notice but . . ."

"It'll be fine. I'm going to need to rethink my security anyway if we continue investigating Conrad."

Katya kept her attention on the couch in front of her. "Will you . . . keep me informed? Having gone with you to Monte Carlo, I'm quite interested to know where your investigations lead. And if you need any help . . ." Only then did she look at him. "Any help at all, please don't hesitate to ask."

If there was something more there, an underlying meaning to her words, he didn't see it. And for a second he couldn't speak because he wanted so much for there to be something. Anything. Instead he put his gambler's mask on, betraying nothing of the need clawing up inside him. "Of course. I'll let you know." He gave her an empty smile. "Now, if you don't mind, it's probably better that you leave. Nine Circles business, Katya mine."

Except she wasn't his. And she never would be.

CHAPTER EIGHTEEN

Katya sat down in the lounge of Alex's apartment and adjusted the laptop once again, making sure the camera was pointed at herself and the microphone was working. The call from the people who'd gotten Mikhail out would be happening at any moment.

Alex was still in the special room downstairs in the Second Circle with the rest of his friends. They'd been in there hours now. It had been stupid to walk in on them earlier, but when she'd gotten the call that Mikhail was safe she hadn't been able to stop herself from wanting to go and at least offer her personal thanks to Alex and to Mr. Rutherford.

She hadn't expected to stumble in on Alex giving a full-blown confession. She'd been all set to leave the moment Mr. Rutherford had challenged her. Except then Alex had told her to stay. And he'd looked at her the whole time as he told her his story.

He hadn't looked away from her, his blue eyes pinning her to the spot, holding her completely still. And she knew how hard it was for him. Knew what he'd had to go through to get to this point—

There was a chiming sound from the computer.

Katya swallowed. God, here she was, waiting to speak to the man she'd promised herself to, whom she hadn't seen for two years, and all she could think about was Alex St. James.

She leaned forward, hitting a button on the keyboard, and the video call window popped up. The video was choppy and grainy, but she could quite clearly see the man in the middle of it anyway. He was sitting on a chair with a table in front of him where the camera must be situated. The room behind him was bare, the walls concrete blocks.

"Misha?" Katya leaned forward, her throat constricting.

The man at the table was very different. The Mikhail she remembered was blond and good-looking. Always smiling. But the man on the screen was not him. This man was gaunt, his cheeks hollow, his eyes empty. The blond hair she remembered had been shaved close to his skull and he was covered in bruises. He looked like he'd been through hell.

No, he looked like he was still there.

"Katya," he said, and she barely recognized his voice. He sounded like he had a mouthful of gravel.

Her eyes filled with unexpected tears. "Oh my God. It *is* you. You're alive," she said, falling into Russian easily. "We thought you were dead. When you disappeared, the government wanted to—"

"I don't want you coming back for me."

The words were flat, expressionless. Just like the look on his face.

She blinked. "But, I—"

"Thank you for organizing this rescue and you can pass my thanks on to Mr. Rutherford too. Don't think I'm not grateful, but . . ." He stopped and something like pain crossed his face. "I've been gone a long time. Things have happened. And I'm . . . different now." He looked away from the camera for a moment; then he glanced back, looking directly at her. "You made me some promises, Katya.

And I haven't forgotten them. But I can't accept what you promised anymore. I'm sorry."

Shock moved like an icy wind over her skin. "But I . . . I swore I wouldn't leave you there and I didn't. I waited for you, Misha. And I want to come back and see you. I want—"

"Katya," he interrupted softly, leaning forward so his face was near the camera. And she could see more bruises marring the handsome lines of his face. Scar tissue pulling at his mouth. And his eyes . . . God, they were full of darkness. *Like Elijah's.* "You shouldn't have waited for me. And I don't want you to now. Things are different."

"If you're worried about my father, I can talk to him. It'll be okay."

"No. It won't be okay. Nothing will ever be okay." He turned his head away again, looking at something or someone off camera. "Don't come back for me. Please."

"Misha . . . I can't just leave you—" She stopped abruptly as Mikhail leaned forward and the video screen went black.

He'd cut her off.

Katya stood up, grief catching in her throat, aching in her chest. What had they done to him? God, they must have hurt him so badly. She wanted to call back straightaway, but she knew that wasn't a good idea. Mikhail had only just been rescued and he'd been traumatized obviously. He needed some time to rest and gather his strength. Some time to recover from his ordeal.

He couldn't seriously mean for her not to come back for him, could he?

She skirted the coffee table, paced to the windows and their view over the New York skyscrapers. It was snowing again, soft, fat white flakes drifting noiselessly against the glass.

Two years she'd waited for him. Two years she'd been

loyal. She'd left her father and her country, losing her faith in both because of him. And she knew it was unfair, knew it was selfish, but it hurt that the first thing he'd said to her after being rescued—a rescue that she'd organized—was not to come back.

Another person who doesn't want to be saved . . .

The thought came as softly as the snow, an icy blanket settling over her mind.

Katya closed her eyes. But it wasn't the broken shell of the man she'd promised herself to that she saw. It was Alex's blue eyes as he'd talked about his father on that videotape. And the empty smile as he'd told her to leave the room.

But what was the point thinking about him? He didn't need her. And Mikhail did, regardless of whether he'd told her to stay away or not. She'd waited for two years for him and she couldn't abandon him now, no matter what he said.

Coward.

But she didn't take any notice of that whisper. She had to be strong for Mikhail because he still needed saving and that was all that mattered.

It was the only thing that did.

Alex sat on the couch in the Nine Circles room and looked at the vodka bottle. It was tempting to take it, pour himself a large tumblerful. But as he'd already decided, it wasn't vodka he wanted.

He sighed and leaned against the back of the couch.

The others had all gone now, the fire burned down. The meeting had gone on far longer than they'd planned, talking about what their next move would be, where they went from here.

Eva was going to try hacking into Conrad's network, while Zac continued his investigations—albeit much more carefully—of the Apocalypse players. Gabriel had taken on the task of looking into the businesses of the remaining Seven Devils–all except Conrad. Alex had demanded that Conrad be left to him and Gabriel hadn't argued. No one had. They all knew that Conrad was Alex's to deal with.

Zac had made it clear he had contacts who could come in handy if Alex wanted to use them. Special contacts for "special" jobs. He knew what that meant. Assassins. Thing was, he wasn't sure he wanted someone else to take Conrad out. In fact, he wasn't sure he wanted Conrad taken out at all.

After Katya had held him, it seemed pointless now.

Nineteen years of pretending the man didn't matter, and it was only now, after Katya, that Alex realized he *truly* didn't. That the only power the man had was the power Alex chose to give him. And by choosing not to exact revenge, he was denying Conrad that power.

It felt right. It felt true. And perhaps he'd always known it. But this was the first time he'd actually *felt* it.

A soft sound came from outside the door, and despite himself, his heart clenched tight. Was it Katya? Jesus, it had better not be. He didn't think he could pretend not to give a shit while she walked away again. In fact, it would be better to ignore her completely until she was gone. He didn't want to have to tell her to go, that it was club business, not hers, again. A deliberate move and a necessary one. To protect himself . . .

"Katya?" He didn't turn. "I thought I told you—"

"I'm not Katya." A familiar voice. A hated one.

A cold bolt of shock went through Alex. He rose sharply to his feet and whirled around.

And saw Conrad closing the door with a quiet click and locking it.

"What the fuck are you doing here?" Alex demanded hoarsely. "How the hell did you get in?"

"Your security is a trifle lax, son." The other man came

slowly toward him, the couch standing between them. "And as for why I'm here, well . . ." His hazel eyes glittered in the dying firelight. "I've come to claim my fucking winnings."

Christ, the man must have left Monaco right after Alex had. And as for the club . . . He was going to have to have words with the Second Circle security team if this prick could walk right into the Nine's clubroom.

Alex took a silent breath, relaxing his muscles. However Conrad had gotten in was irrelevant at the moment anyway. What mattered was that he was here.

As the shock ebbed, it wasn't anger Alex felt. Or even fear. It was . . . pity. That this was all the guy had. Chasing after the boy he'd raped all those years ago.

Alex allowed himself a smile. "Why, Conrad, you came all this way. I'm flattered; honestly, you've got no idea."

The older man's expression was cold, and with a start Alex realized Conrad was furious. "I thought better of you, son; I really did. What kind of gambler are you who leaves without paying his debts?"

"Perhaps your pit bull frightened me away?"

Conrad gave a short laugh. "My pit bull? Oh, Elijah? He's not mine. He's nothing. An irritation. I've dealt with him."

"Really? Just like that? He looked like he meant business to me."

"He's got nothing to do with this. With us. He interfered in a personal matter and that's not acceptable." Conrad reached into his jacket, pulled out something. A memory stick. "Look. I even bought an incentive for you."

Alex tensed. "And that is?"

"A certain video. Elijah made me destroy the hard copy of course, but I confess I lied a little when I told him I didn't have any digital copies." His mouth curved. "I never go anywhere without an insurance policy."

Shit. There it was. Exactly what they needed. "I take it Elijah knows nothing about that?"

"Of course not."

"What's on it that he took offense to anyway? Apart from the rape of a sixteen-year-old boy?"

Conrad laughed again. "Very clever. But what Elijah is after is none of your business. The only thing you need to concern yourself with is paying me what you owe me."

"Give me one reason why I should give you anything."

Conrad moved, coming around the side of the couch, slow and predatory, the firelight casting shadows over his face.

And Alex felt . . . only surprise. Because Conrad didn't seem so sinister now. He obviously looked after himself, but there were wrinkles at the corners of his eyes, sagging along his jaw and his neck, his waist thickening.

Conrad wasn't a young man anymore.

"You came all this way just for me?" Alex asked, vaguely curious. "Why?"

The other man stopped and was silent a long time. Then he said, "Because you were so fucking afraid of me. And fear has always been the most potent aphrodisiac I know." He smiled and for the first time, Alex saw past that smile. Saw the desperation underneath it. And the fear. Jesus. This sad, desperate old man was afraid.

"Is it?" Alex said quietly. "So why are you scared then?"

Conrad moved suddenly, closing the gap between them, anger burning bright in his eyes. "You think you rule the world, don't you?" he hissed. "You think you know everything, you arrogant little shit. But you're young. You barely even know you're alive. Wait until your life is slipping away from you, the years getting shorter and shorter. You'll grab at anything you can to stop it. Anything." He reached into his jacket again and Alex knew this time what he was going to pull out. And that it was too late to do anything about it.

The gun was small, but size didn't matter when the barrel was pointed at your head.

"Can you feel it now, *son*?" Conrad murmured. "Can you feel your life slipping away from you? Can you feel the minutes growing shorter? The seconds ticking down? It'll come for you, like it's coming for me. But you know, perhaps you'll go first. After I relive a few old memories of course."

Perhaps he should have been afraid. Yet he wasn't. He felt calm. Sure of things. More certain than he'd ever felt in his life.

He didn't look at the gun; he looked at Conrad instead. Into the old man's cold eyes. "Pull that trigger then," he said. "Maybe I was once afraid of you. But I'm not anymore."

"You think I wouldn't do it? I could bend you over the arm of that chair, fuck you right now. Make you like it. Then I could put a bullet through your brain. Easily."

Alex only stared at him and all he could feel was pity. "You won't do that. You're too much of a fucking coward."

"That's what your father said." Conrad smiled. "Before I shot him."

It didn't penetrate for a second because the words, at first, didn't mean anything. How could Conrad have shot his father? Daniel St. James had killed himself. Everyone knew that.

"Bullshit," Alex said.

The old man laughed. "He was going to go public. He was going to take everything to the police. I told him it would be a mistake, but he wouldn't listen. He wanted justice for you, can you imagine that? He wasn't happy when I told him you'd agreed to it, that I'd had your consent. In fact, that only seemed to make him more determined."

Shock froze Alex to the spot.

"You see my dilemma," Conrad went on. "He was going

to expose us all. So I had to do something. Making it look like suicide was easy. And in a way he *did* kill himself. If he hadn't been so fucking stubborn—"

There was a sound at the door and abruptly it opened.

Conrad turned sharply, the gun aiming at whoever was coming through the door.

Katya.

Everything slowed down, like a movie moving frame by frame. Conrad's hand lifting, his finger moving to the trigger, Katya going for her weapon. Too late. Too fucking late.

A knife edge of raw anguish tore through Alex's shock, shattering his paralysis. That bullet would hit her and there would be no way to avoid it. No way to stop Conrad from pulling that trigger. No way to stop the death that was coming for her.

Except there was one way.

She thought he was a man worth saving. But she was a woman worth dying for.

Alex reached out and grabbed Conrad's arm, pulling it down at the same time as he stepped in front of the gun. It fired. There was a concussion and he felt something explode through him, like being hit by a car at high speed. It took him a moment to realize he was on his back and he couldn't move, though oddly enough there was no pain.

Someone screamed his name.

Katya's face appeared in his slowly clouding vision, tears streaming down her face. "Alexei . . . Oh, my Alexei . . . You stupid, stupid man. *Nyet . . . nyet . . . .*"

He tried to smile. Tried to speak. But his voice wouldn't work. With supreme effort of will, he managed to get his hand over hers where it rested on his chest. It felt wet, but he didn't want to think about that. He only wanted her to stay. Only wanted her to stay and never leave him.

"Don't go," he whispered, or at least he hoped he managed to get it out. And he hoped she heard.

I think I love you. Please don't leave me.

But he had to say the last in his head. Before the blackness came.

CHAPTER NINETEEN

Katya sat in the plain, white hospital waiting room, her hands clasped together in her lap. There were magazines on a table nearby, but she couldn't concentrate enough to read. Across from her, sitting on another chair, Eva King was biting her nails and jogging her foot as if she couldn't keep still. Beside Eva, his arms folded, his gaze on the door to the waiting room, was Zac Rutherford.

Gabriel Woolf sat on another chair, a slender, black-haired, beautiful woman at his side. Honor St. James. Alex's sister. Gabriel was holding her hand, but she was as white as a sheet all the same.

Katya knew how she felt. As if her insides had been ripped out.

They'd already had a doctor come in to say Alex had pulled through the operation to repair the mess of his shoulder that had taken the brunt of Conrad's bullet. Now they were waiting for him to wake up.

None of them had spoken to Katya since she'd given them the details of what had happened. Conrad's unexpected arrival. How she'd gone down to the Nine Circles room to give Alex the time her flight would be leaving, only to find him standing there with Conrad holding a gun to his head.

A gun that had soon been turned on her.

Except Alex had stepped in front of it.

The stupid man had taken a bullet for her. Which wasn't how it was supposed to go. No, she couldn't possibly have put herself between him and Conrad's gun. There had been a couple of meters to cross, plus a massive couch in the way. And his finger was already pulling the trigger as she'd reached for her own weapon.

But that wasn't the point. The point was that she'd failed her most important directive: to protect the life of her client. In the end her client had been the one protecting her.

She hadn't saved him. She hadn't been strong enough.

And now, you're the one breaking.

Her fingers gripped one another tighter, her vision full of the blood staining his white shirt. The deep blackness of his eyes as they'd looked up at her. His hand squeezing hers as she'd tried to stop the blood. "Don't go," he'd whispered. And she'd told him she wouldn't. She'd stay; she'd never leave. Over and over until the paramedics had arrived and he'd been taken away. Touch-and-go, they'd said. But not to her. The police had arrived by then to examine the crime scene. And the body of Conrad South

Whom she'd shot the moment Alex had fallen.

She'd regretted every life she'd taken, but she didn't regret that one. Not one bit.

That's not enough to make up for your failure.

Katya swallowed, her throat dry and tight. She couldn't have reached him. She couldn't.

Why had he stepped in front of that gun? Why had he taken that bullet?

It was her mother all over again. It always ended in blood. Blood all over her hands . . .

She shut her eyes suddenly as tears prickled. No, she wouldn't cry. She had to be strong. She had to be—

"Miss Ivanova?" The voice was soft and female.

Katya opened her eyes to find that Honor St. James had

left her seat beside Gabriel and had come to sit next to her instead.

"Hello," Honor said, and held out one slim hand. "I don't believe we've met. I'm Honor. Alex's sister."

With an effort, Katya unclasped her hands and took Honor's. The other woman's fingers were icy. Or maybe hers were; she couldn't tell. "Katya Ivanova. I'm Mr. St. James's bodyguard."

"Yes. I gathered that." Honor's blue gaze was very direct in the same way her brother's could be. "In which case I find it very interesting that he took a bullet in order to protect you."

There was no condemnation in her voice, but Katya felt it all the same. "He protected me because he would have done that for anyone, Miss St. James."

There was a small silence. Then Honor said softly, "No, Miss Ivanova, I don't believe he would have. My brother hasn't spoken to me for nineteen years. He refuses my calls. He ignores my texts and my e-mails. I know how he lives, I read the gossip columns. He lives the life of a selfish man. He's famous for not caring about anything or anyone." She paused. "And yet he takes a bullet for his bodyguard. Why would he do that? What makes you special?"

Katya's jaw tightened. She needed to admit the truth. She needed to take responsibility for her failure. "Your brother and I had an affair in Monte Carlo," she said thickly. "It wasn't planned and I'm not . . . special. It wasn't serious on his part. But it happened. And maybe . . . he felt a sense of obligation that caused him to take a risk for me."

Liar. You know why he took that bullet for you. For the same reason he asked you to stay . . .

Honor's gaze was piercing. "Obligation? Alex risked death for you, Miss Ivanova. You don't step in front of a loaded gun because you feel obligation for someone. You do it because you love them."

She'd known and yet still she felt the words like an electric shock. "No, Miss St. James. Loving someone is not the only reason to take a bullet for them. Believe me, I know. I'm a bodyguard. I don't love my clients."

"Alex was the one paying you. And he's never done a selfless thing in his life."

"People are wrong about him. He's a good man."

"I never said he wasn't." She paused, her gaze searching. "You're in love with him, aren't you?"

Katya couldn't bear the look in the other woman's eyes and finally glanced down at her hands.

You are. You know you are.

No. She wasn't in love. She couldn't afford love. Love made you vulnerable. Love made you weak. And when love vanished, it nearly killed you.

Honor let out a soft breath. "He'll break your heart; you know that, don't you?"

It didn't matter. Her heart had broken long ago. "My heart is irrelevant," Katya said hoarsely. "I don't want anything from him."

Honor sat back. "Really? You'd be the first woman in the world who didn't."

"Nevertheless. I will be returning to Moscow as soon as I've finished speaking to the police concerning Mr. South."

There was another silence; then Honor said, "Mr. South . . . he was threatening Alex, or so they tell me. Did he . . . did he have anything to do with why Alex won't talk to me?"

"That's not my story to tell. But I can say that Mr. South deserved the death I dealt to him."

Honor gave a short nod. "If he was going to kill Alex, I'm quite sure he did."

At that moment, the door opened and a doctor put her head around it. "Mr. St. James is waking up now. I don't advise you all go in at once, though."

The rest of them had started toward the door already, but Honor's clear voice cut through the room. "No. I think Katya needs to see him first."

Katya looked at her in surprise. "I can't possibly—"

"You can," Honor said. "He was prepared to die for you. I think he'd want to see you first of all."

She wanted to protest, but the doctor was waiting for her and everyone else was staring. And she felt a sudden clutch of fear. As if walking through those doors with the doctor, to Alex's room, would decide something. Choose something.

But she couldn't refuse, not with all his friends—his sister for God's sake—waiting for her. She had to be strong, remember?

So she fought down the fear, got to her feet, and followed the doctor along the white, echoing corridors of the hospital.

Eventually they came to a room and the doctor showed her in, closing the door behind her.

There was a bed in the middle of it, with lots of tubes and the beeping of a heart monitor, and a man lying in the middle of it. Pale, his black hair on the white pillow like spilled ink.

Alex.

The pain in her chest crept outward, coiling around all her limbs and squeezing tight. She didn't want to breathe, he was so still, only the sound of the heart monitor letting her know he was even alive.

Quite suddenly his eyes opened, a narrow strip of sapphire gleaming between long, black lashes. And the pain in her chest felt like it was going to claw its way out.

"Why?" The word burst from her before she could stop it. "Why did you do that?"

He smiled. The bastard actually smiled. "Come here, Katya mine," he murmured, his voice a mere whisper of sound.

But she couldn't move, her breathing coming short and fast. "No. Tell me why. I need to know. I need to know why you took that bullet."

"And I need you to come closer. I'm in no condition to shout."

Her feet were like lead, but she made herself move over to the bed, coming to stand beside it and looking down at him.

His mouth still had that curve to it and she didn't know why. "Take my hand."

"Why?"

"Just do it."

She didn't want to touch him, fear nestling like an ice cube in her chest. But she didn't know what she was so afraid of, so she ignored the sensation, lifting her hand to put it over his where it rested on the blanket. He felt cold, like his sister had. Slowly, painfully, he turned his hand over and laced his fingers through hers.

Inexplicable tears filled her eyes. "Alex. Please . . ."

His fingers tightened. "Before Conrad appeared, I told myself that I was going to avoid you. Because if I touched you again, I didn't think I'd be able to let you go." His voice was cracked and broken, but she heard every word. "So here I am, touching you, Katya. And that makes you mine. You always were, remember?"

A tear ran down her cheek and hit the sheet. "Don't . . ." she whispered, her voice as thready as his.

"You know why I took that bullet for you," he said, relentless. "You know."

Another tear rolled down her cheek. "You would do that for anyone. You would—"

"No, I wouldn't." And there was no denying the certainty in his voice. No escaping it. "I mean, I wish I was that altruistic. But I'm not. You're the only person I've ever wanted to die for, Katya Ivanova."

She bent her head, the tears rolling down her cheeks without stopping. She couldn't understand why she was crying. Why every word felt like a needle point of glass sliding under her skin. Why she felt like she was breaking apart. "Please . . ." she murmured thickly, "don't say it."

"Don't say what? That I'm in love with you?"

She shook her head. "You can't."

Alex's fingers closed around hers. "Look at me."

The command in his voice was undeniable and she couldn't disobey. Lifting her head, she met his eyes, the impact of his gaze hitting her harder than any bullet. There was something powerful in the blue depths, something that hadn't been there before. Certainty.

He released her hand and touched her face, his fingers gently brushing away the tears. "Why are you crying?"

Her throat was tight, her breathing harsh. "This is my fault. If I hadn't crossed the line, if I'd never have slept with you, none of this would have happened. If I'd been stronger, you wouldn't nearly have died."

"Come on, what did you tell me about taking the blame? That we can't take responsibility for other people's choices? Sweetheart, without you I would still be hiding from what Conrad did to me. Still pretending it didn't matter." His fingers brushed her mouth. "You made me face it, Katya. And you made me deal with it. You made it better. You gave me strength when I had none. The question isn't why did I take a bullet for you? The question is why *wouldn't* I take a bullet for you?"

She tried to blink away the tears in her eyes, but it wasn't working. "You shouldn't have had to, though. It was *my* job to protect you and I failed. If I'd done my job properly, you wouldn't have been in that position."

But he only smiled and it wasn't the lazy, mocking smile she was familiar with. This smile was warm and genuine. It made her heart stop. "I'm not a mission, sweetheart. And my choices are my own. And stopping Conrad's bullet was the best decision I ever made."

Her throat closed up. "You don't understand. I can't be with you, Alexei. There is another man who needs me more."

His blue eyes glittered. "Mikhail?"

"Yes."

"What about what you need, Katya? Have you ever thought about that?"

"I—" She stopped, staring down at the white sheet and their linked hands resting on top of it.

His fingers tightened with the ghost of his old strength. "Stop trying to save your mother, sweetheart. She doesn't need you anymore. But I do. And I think you need me too."

The words were loud in her head, echoing down the years of her life. All the way back to a little girl standing beside a bathtub, looking at the woman in it. The dead woman with a smile on her face. The woman who'd left her without even a good-bye.

More tears filled her eyes, so she closed them, the tears falling onto their linked hands. "I can't. I can't need anyone." Her voice sounded scraped raw. "I have to be strong. I have to."

"Why, sweetheart?" There was so much gentleness in the words, a tender note she'd never heard him utter before. "Who do you have to be strong for?"

And she felt something break loose inside her. "For myself. Because it hurts. Because she left without even a good-bye. Because one day she was there, kissing me good night; the next she wasn't. And I miss her, I miss her so much." The words came out of her in a flood. "But if I'm strong, the pain goes away. And I'm tired of hurting, Alexei. I'm just so tired of it."

"I know," he said quietly. "But you can't be strong all the time. And it doesn't get rid of the pain. That's why you need someone to be strong for you. To help you through the times when you can't bear it. When it gets too much." His fingers tightened through hers. "You were strong for me. Now it's time for me to be strong for you. Give me your grief, Katya mine. You don't have to be strong now."

She didn't think it would be so simple to do that. To stop being strong, to allow herself to grieve for Anna Ivanova. But with her hand in his, the warmth and subtle strength in his around hers, it was. And it was painful. Then again, when you loved someone, when you cared, pain was always going to be part of it.

And afterwards, when she was quiet, when the tears had dried up, it was like her heart shuddered. Like it had stopped and he'd restarted it.

She finally raised her head and looked into the vivid blue of his eyes. "You really want me to stay?"

"Yes. I told you. I'm touching you. And that means you're mine."

"For how long?"

"How about forever?" He smiled. "I'm a selfish man, sweetheart. I want you to stay with me because I love you. Because if you don't I will follow you to the ends of the earth to bring you back. And I will never, ever let you go."

This was happiness, she realized then, with sudden, blinding insight. Right here. Right now. Clasped in her hands. And that the key to it wasn't strength but vulnerability. Opening yourself to another person, admitting to yourself that they were important.

That what you wanted was important.

You can't lose it. You can't lose him.

No, she couldn't. No one had ever wanted her like this. No one had ever warned her he'd come after her. And certainly no one had ever wanted to die for her.

No one except Alex.

He needed her, certainly more than Mikhail did. And perhaps he was right. Perhaps she needed him too.

Perhaps her heart wasn't so irrelevant after all.

All he wanted to do was get out of this fucking hospital bed and take her in his arms. But of course he couldn't do that.

"Katya," he croaked, ignoring the dizzy, floaty feeling of the anesthetic. There were tears rolling down her face and her fingers in his were loose.

Abruptly she looked at him, the color of her eyes like the grass after rain. She lifted her free hand, wiped the tears away. "You really love me?"

"I do. But I've never loved anyone before. You'll have to show me how it's done."

"Seems I'm always showing you how to do things." She bent her head, lifted his hand, kissed the back of it. She said something in what sounded like Russian. Then she murmured in English, "I love you, Alexei."

He closed his eyes a moment against the fierce rush of pleasure that gave him. Wishing he weren't here. Wishing he were with her in bed. Nothing between them. "And you'll stay, won't you? You're not going to leave?"

"No, I'm not going to leave. But . . . there may be a difficulty." Her voice sounded hoarse. "I shot Conrad. He's dead."

He should be appalled. He wasn't. Conrad didn't matter. He'd never mattered. Of course there was the issue of the bombshell he'd dropped right before he'd aimed the gun at Katya, but Alex didn't want to think about that right now. That could wait until he felt ready to deal with it.

"Good," was all he said.

"I'm sorry," Katya murmured. "You should have had the honor."

"So bloodthirsty, Katya mine. No, I'm glad you did." He opened his eyes, met hers. "You shot the gun, I took the bullet. Seems fair."

It was faint, but her mouth curved, so he counted that as a victory. Then she bent over him and his victory became something even more special as she brushed her mouth over his.

"Your friends are out there," she murmured against his lips. "They want to see you. And . . ." A slight hesitation. "Someone else."

He knew who she meant. But the weight that had been hanging over him for so long was gone. He didn't need it anymore. "Can you get her for me?"

Katya straightened and she smiled properly this time. Then without a word, she went out of the room.

A minute later, a figure appeared in the door. Slender. Black haired. Blue-eyed.

Alex swallowed. "Hello, Honor."

EPILOGUE

Zac stopped the video, peering at it. He'd been looking at it frame by frame, searching for clues. But for the life of him, he couldn't work out what was in it that the mysterious mercenary Elijah had been desperate enough to destroy.

Eventually, frustrated, Zac sat back in the seat of his office, staring at the screen.

At that moment, the door opened and Eva wandered in. Late for their lunch date as usual.

Irritated, Zac reached for the screen and spun it around to her. "Do you see anything there? I've been studying this damn thing for days now and I'm buggered if I know what's so important about it."

Eva scowled, then narrowed her gaze. "Why are you asking me? I haven't seen . . ." Her voice trailed off. Slowly, the color leached from her face.

Instantly Zac stiffened, dread tightening in his chest. "Eva?"

She stared at the screen a long time.

"Eva," Zac demanded. "What the hell is it?"

Slowly, she met his gaze. "Nothing," she said. "Nothing at all."

Read on for an excerpt from

YOU ARE MINE

the next sensational romance from Jackie Ashenden.

COMING SOON FROM
ST. MARTIN'S PAPERBACKS

Slowly, Zac stretched out his legs and crossed them at the ankles, studying her over his steepled fingers. "Sit down," he said, allowing the hard edge of authority to creep into his voice.

She ignored him, her palms pale and spread out like starfish on the window, her long, straight silver hair falling over her shoulders. Her gray eyes were wide, fear and anger glittering in the depths. "How the fuck did you get in here?"

"I have a key."

Her eyes widened ever further. "You have a key? To my freaking apartment? How dare you—"

"A key that I've had since I leased this apartment for you five years ago," he interrupted in the same calm tone. "A key that I have never used until tonight."

Her mouth closed in a hard line. Her finely carved face was pale, yet there was an obstinate jut to her chin. And beneath her silvery bangs, her eyes—almost the same color as her hair—were full of sparks.

Christ, the woman was a bloody turn-on. She was a delicious combination of delicate fragility and iron strength. Possessing such deep passions yet armoring herself with a tough shell that dared the world to crack it.

No wonder she'd always fascinated him. Why he'd found

all other women boring in comparison. No one else had her will or her strength. Or her secrets. She was a challenge he'd been resisting for too long—to both their detriment probably.

"This is my private apartment, Zac," she said in a shaky voice. "You've got no right to waltz right in here unannounced and just—"

"I don't care about your fucking apartment. What I care about is the information you've been withholding."

"I don't know what you're talking about."

"Oh yes, you do. It's time for that discussion now, Eva."

She said nothing, staring at him.

"Answer me." This time he didn't bother hiding the order, injecting all his will into it.

"No." The word burst from her as if she'd forced it out. Her chest heaved, the curve of her small, beautifully shaped breasts outlined against the tight cotton of her black t-shirt. As usual, she was in jeans and heavy boots in addition to the t-shirt.

All part of her armor. Nothing pretty or feminine was allowed.

Yet she didn't need pretty or feminine. There was a reason he called her angel and it wasn't only because that had been her hacker handle.

She reminded him of an angel. Beautiful and fragile. Ethereal and otherworldly. Untouchable. A fallen angel in her black boots and skinny jeans.

"Do you think I will hurt you? Is that what you think?"

She didn't move. "Get the hell out of my place, Zac."

"Not happening. Like I told you, I have some things I want to discuss."

"Oh, fuck, you can't expect to come in here and—"

"Seven years, Eva. Seven years I've done everything you wanted. I've kept my distance. Respected your boundaries.

Been your friend and asked for nothing in return." He met her gaze. "But now I've come to collect."

Her jaw was tight and it was obvious she was struggling to contain her breathing. "Collect what? Jesus, since when did our friendship become a damn transaction to you?"

"Since the lives of our friends were put in danger."

Color crept into her cheeks. "Look, I can find the identity of that guy no sweat. It won't take long." Her throat moved as she swallowed. "In fact, why don't you take me out to the island? You can protect me while I investigate."

Of course she'd go for that option. Of course she'd expect him to fall in line, like he always did. "What do you think I am? Your tame housecat? Do you think you can order me around to suit yourself?" He held her gaze, letting the mask of the gentleman slip just a little. Letting her see the beast he was inside. "I'm not your fucking pet. And the sooner you understand that the better."

Anger flared in her eyes. "I'm not stupid, Zac," she said. "I know what you are."

He watched her, studying the delicate architecture of her face. He'd been learning Eva King for seven years and he knew all her expressions, all her moods, all her little gestures. "I'm not sure you do. You only see what I let you see. And I've been protecting you for a very long time." He leaned forward, noting the almost imperceptible flinch she gave at the movement. "And I know you're not stupid. What you are is scared."

"Bullshit." That anger burned bright, as if he'd personally insulted her. Her fingers flexed on the glass as she pushed herself away from the windows. "I'm not scared."

It was a low move because he knew she hated being told she was afraid. That she'd react to it. Nevertheless, it was true.

He put his elbows of his knees, linking his finger loosely.

"Then if you're not scared, tell me what happened. Tell me how you know the man in that video. And why you'd get a personal email warning you off. We need the background, angel. We need to know those connections." He paused, holding her silver gaze. "Or are your friends' lives less important to you than your fear?" Another low blow, but he wanted to push her, stoke her anger. That was preferable to her being afraid.

The color in her cheeks deepened. "No, of course not."

"So tell me." He paused. "I won't ask again."

"Oh Christ. You're not my damn father, Zac, so quit telling me what to do."

She was stalling, that much was obvious. Which meant he was going to have to push her again and this time go further.

The time had come for him to stop protecting her from himself.

Slowly, he got up from the chair and rose to his full height.

Her head tipped back as she tracked the movement and he caught a fleeting apprehension cross her face. Then as quickly as it had appeared, the expression vanished, her usual sarcastic, prickly mask firmly back in place.

"I think," he said gently. "That it's time someone told you what to do more often. And that you should listen."

"Or what?" She was operating on sheer bravado now, he could see it. "Are you trying to intimidate me? Is that what you're trying to do?" She took a step towards him, then another, coming closer. "Nice way to treat your friends, asshole."

All the color had leached away from her face, her cheeks pale as ashes. Her eyes glittered, fear bright in them despite her tough words.

That was the problem with his angel. She was a fighter and it was her greatest strength. Yet it was also her greatest flaw. Because she didn't know when to stop. That sometimes there was more strength in surrendering than in fighting.

You can teach her how to do that.

Oh, yes. He could. There were so many things he could teach her if she'd only let him.

Zac took the last step, closing the distance between them, getting right into her personal space. He wasn't touching her but they were only inches apart. It was a tactic he used to intimidate and overwhelm. To assert his authority, his dominance.

Because if there was one thing Eva King had to learn it was that he was the one in charge here and always had been. Yes, her anger was preferable but her fear was a useful tool too and he would use it. Especially when it came to protecting her life and the lives of their friends.

Her eyes widened at his nearness, but she held her ground. She was nothing if not brave.

He'd never been this close to her before since she didn't like to be touched. So close he could feel the warmth of her slight body, see the quickened beat of her pulse at her throat. Smell the sweet, subtle scent of the jasmine and vanilla body lotion he knew she favored. Christ, it was delicious. It woke urges that had lain dormant for a long time. Urges that hadn't even flickered for the sub in Limbo days ago.

Not a good sign. Because as much has he wanted to do it, he wasn't here to dominate her. She wasn't ready even if she'd shown an interest in him. And she'd never shown an interest. Not once.

No, he couldn't satisfy those urges. He was here to get information out of her and that was it.

"Are you challenging me?" Zac murmured softly, looking down into Eva's white face. "Because if you are, you're making a mistake. I'm not a man you want to challenge."

Her chin came up, courageous to the last. "Yeah and why is that? What are you going to do? You can't force me, Zac."

He smiled and let the mask of the gentleman drop entirely. "Oh I won't have to force you, angel. There are ways and means, and believe me, I know all the ways. I can make you want to give it to me." He let his smile turn savage. "I can make you want to give me everything."

Eva couldn't move. She could barely breathe. Her fear battered against the walls of her control, demanding she run, screaming at her to back away, throw herself out of the windows, something. Anything to get away from the man standing right in front of her.

Towering over her. So tall and dark and intimidating it was all she could do not to whimper.

But she wouldn't give in to the terror. She never had, not while she was on the streets, not while she was in the House, not when He had had her over and over again, and certainly not now.

Even so, she couldn't quite process the fact that the man she'd always thought of as being safe wasn't quite so safe any longer.

On the surface he was still the same Zac she knew, wearing a beautifully cut suit even in the middle of the night, every button done up, the lapels of his black shirt perfectly pressed, tie of dull gold silk knotted just so.

But something had changed. Like a blade drawn from the scabbard, he was all razor sharp edges and bright, glittering danger. A danger she'd never really understood.

I'm not your fucking pet . . .

The smile on his face held no amusement, only a savage intent that made her heart race even faster, panic burning in her blood bright as magnesium. It was the smile of a predator, pure and simple. And the look in his amber eyes . . . wolf's eyes.

She'd always thought the heat in them was anger. But this wasn't anger. This was something else, something far more intense and far more complicated.

The world spun as she became aware of other things, other aspects of him she'd never noticed.

Because you've never let yourself notice.

His height in comparison to hers had always added to that feeling of safety but now . . . she didn't feel safe. She felt something else she couldn't quite pinpoint. It was fear yet there was another element in there like . . . excitement. The breadth of his shoulders too and the hard strength she knew went right down through muscle and bone to the core of him. The kind of strength you could dash yourself against and never make a mark. The kind of strength you could rest on, that could hold you up . . .

Her breath caught, a tight sensation in her chest, a pulse somewhere down low inside her.

Jesus Christ. What the hell was happening to her?

These weren't feelings she'd ever associated with Zac, at least not the Zac Rutherford she knew. But then this man *wasn't* the Zac Rutherford she knew. He was someone different. And he . . .

Terrifies you?

No, of course *he* didn't terrify her. What a ridiculous thought. Okay, so he wasn't acting like the friend she'd come to know and rely on for the past seven years, but he was still the same guy underneath that. Wasn't he?

"Give you everything, huh?" Ignoring the tremble inside her, the dread that dried her mouth and made her breath catch, Eva forced herself to lift her hands and touch him, smoothing the lapels of his suit in a casual movement. "That sounds ominous."

She only wanted to prove to herself that these feelings didn't matter. That she wasn't afraid and that he didn't intimidate her.

She'd never touched him before, not once in all the years she'd known him. Yet as soon as her fingertips met the fine wool of his suit, she understood that she'd made a mistake.

Even through the fabric she could feel the heat of his body and the hard, tensile strength that was part of him. Like a wall between herself and a raging fire. And if that wall were to collapse, she would be consumed . . .

She looked up, unable to stop herself and as she met his intent, golden gaze, realized she'd only compounded her mistake by looking at him. Because there was the fire she'd sensed, burning in his gaze. Burning her to ashes.